LAWS

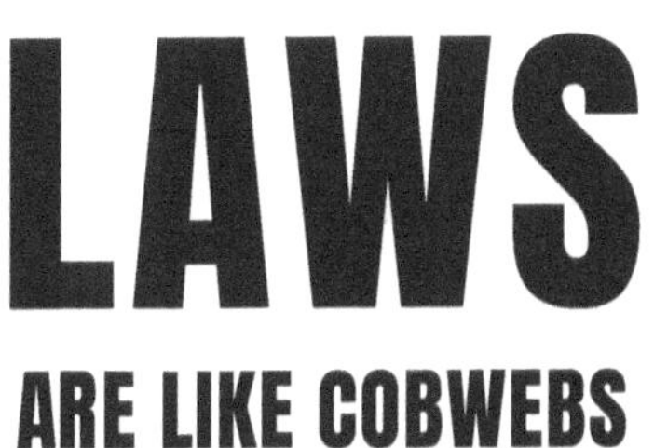

ARE LIKE COBWEBS

Also by John Tully

Novels

The Peregrinations of Geordie Stubbs, Rogue
On Shipstern Bluff
On an Alien Shore
Robbed of Every Blessing
Dark Clouds on the Mountain
Death is the Cool Night

Non-fiction

Labor in Akron, Ohio, 1825-1945
Crooked Deals and Broken Treaties: How White Settlers Displaced American Indians in the Cuyahoga Valley
Silvertown: The Lost Story of a Strike that Shook London and Helped Launch the Modern Labor Movement
The Devil's Milk: A Social History of Rubber
A Short History of Cambodia: From Empire to Survival
France on the Mekong: A History of the Protectorate in Cambodia, 1863-1953
Cambodia Under the Tricolour: King Sisowath and the "Mission Civilisatrice" 1904-1927

LAWS

ARE LIKE COBWEBS

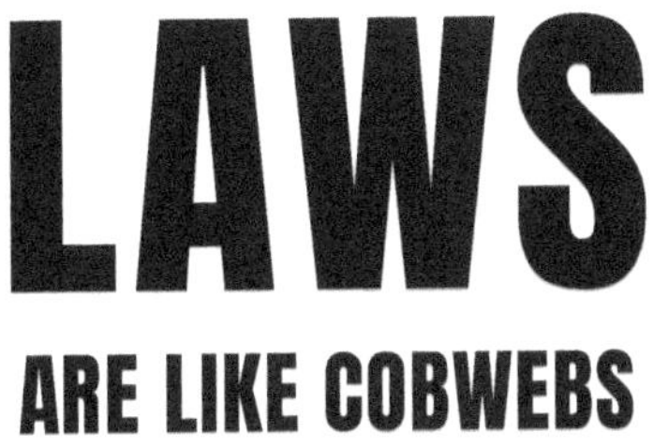

John Tully

ASHWOOD
PUBLISHING

ISBN-paperback: 978-1-7636921-3-8
ISBN-epub: 978-1-7636921-4-5

Published by Ashwood Publishing, Cradoc, Tasmania.
ashwoodpublishing.com.au
info@ashwoodpublishing.com.au

This is a work of fiction, and the persons, events, and places depicted herein are fictitious or, in the case of real locations or public figures, are used fictitiously.

Cover images Valadimir Mulder/Shutterstock, rodonar/Shutterstock.

The work of Ashwood Publishing is nurtured by the beautiful country of the Melukerdee people in the Huon Valley in southern Lutruwita/ Tasmania. We acknowledge and pay respect to the traditional owners and their continuing custodianship of this place.

 A catalogue record for this work is available from the National Library of Australia

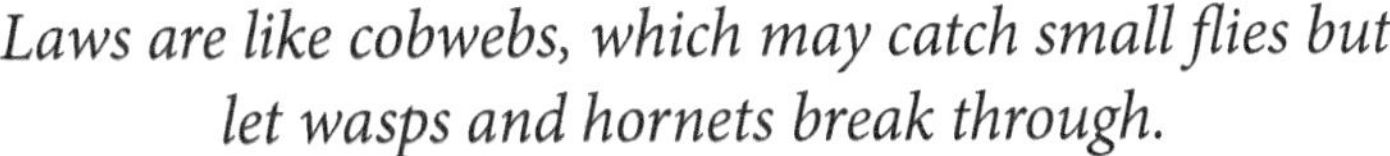

Laws are like cobwebs, which may catch small flies but let wasps and hornets break through.

– Jonathan Swift

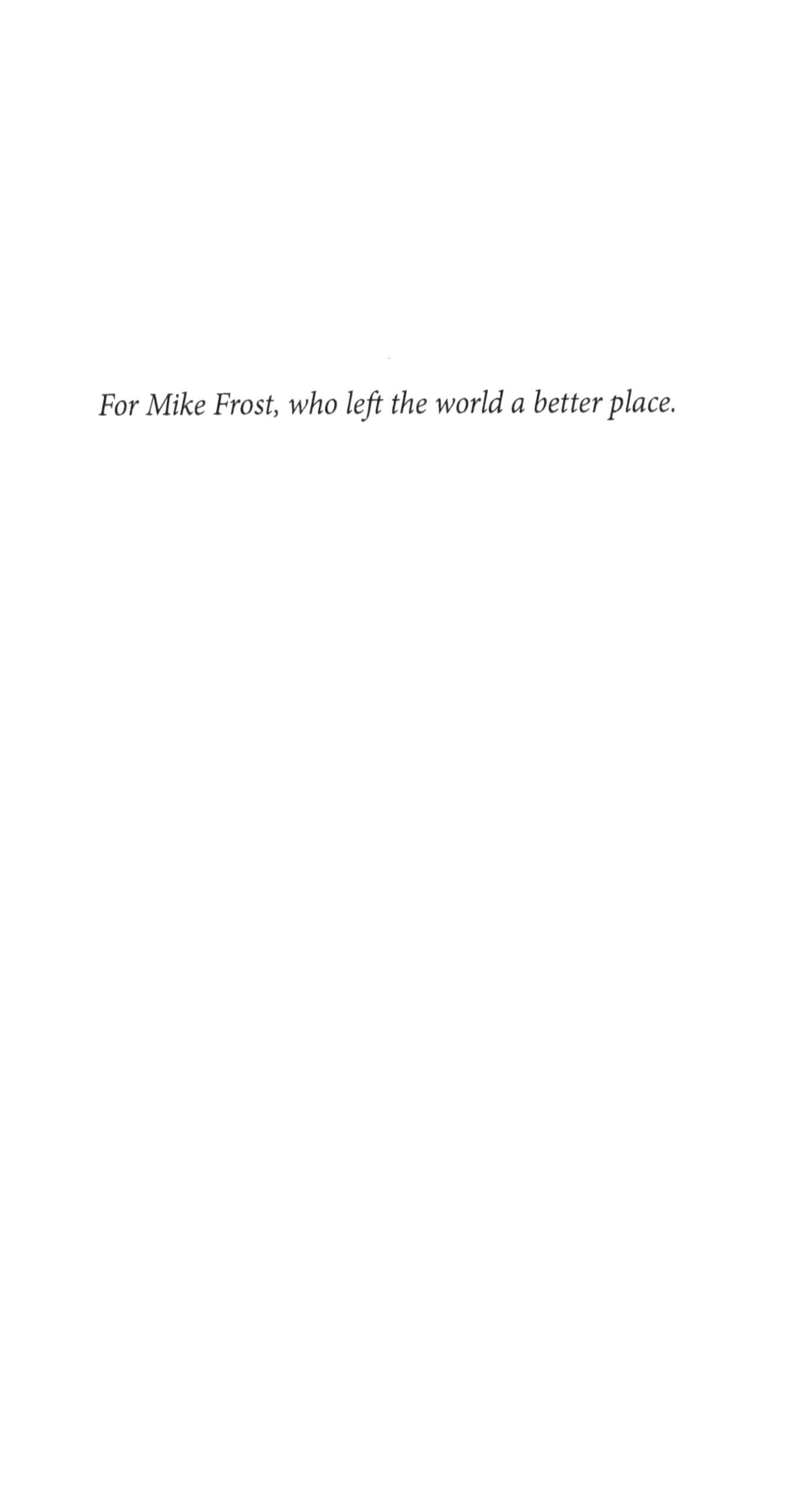

For Mike Frost, who left the world a better place.

CHAPTER 1

The man sitting next to Jack on the Qantas flight kept stealing covert glances at Jack's copy of *The Age*. 'They oughta declare martial law on the bastards.' Jack didn't blame him. Bodies were piling up in the Melbourne morgue. A violent new crime firm was butchering its way to the top of the city's gangland hierarchy and the newspapers were full of it. This time it was not just the usual 'Laura Norda' hype. The previous day, two innocent pensioners had died in the crossfire when the rival gangs opened fire.

The plane was coming in to land, so Jack dutifully fastened his seatbelt. It felt rather like donning a suit of armour for battle. He'd been seconded to the Victorian force to head up Operation Tantalus – the name dreamed up by a Greek mythology buff or spewed out at random by a computer. His friend and colleague DS Liz Flakemore would be assisting. Commander Ernie Foxcroft had been tight-lipped about why he wanted to bring in Tasmanian detectives to head up the investigation, but Jack knew better than to badger his old friend. They'd learn soon enough.

Ernie's briefing notes made appalling reading. The new firm had flooded the Melbourne streets with extra-strong 'product' – crystal meth, crack cocaine, heroin, and hashish – and there had been a spate of overdoses and death. Illegal brothels had been springing up everywhere and Ernie's team were playing whack-a-mole trying to suppress them. Anyway, the distinction between legal and illegal brothels had vanished: prostitutes would be transferred from the former to the latter, with new employees brought in to replace them before they too were shunted into the illegal knocking shops alongside women trafficked from overseas. Snouts were reporting that the new firm was muscling in on the waste storage, construction, real estate, and ready-mix concrete industries – all convenient for money laundering.

The plane banked steeply, bringing into view the parched brown paddocks beyond the suburban sprawl; the city was in the grip of an endless late autumn heatwave. They made a smooth landing on runway asphalt that looked runny as warm molasses, and the pilot taxied towards the airport arrival buildings. Jack stowed his belongings in his briefcase and watched the queue of passengers jostling for position. Funny how they'd been just as eager to get on board. Fifteen minutes later, Jack stood outside waiting for his lift. It was like standing in an oven. He wrinkled his nose at the stink of aviation fuel and shielded his eyes from the sun's glare. The towers of the distant city poked like minarets through the grey haze: the pollution not restricted to the airport. His lift was late; evidently the traffic was as bad as ever.

He skimmed a free copy of the *Herald Sun* as he waited. Both major parties were obsessed with 'stopping the boats'. Tucked away on an inside page, scientists warned about climate change. Few people seemed to notice; the country seemed asleep with its eyes open. *Sixty Minutes* claimed that wharf crane drivers were paid $90,000 a year for fourteen-hour working weeks and the English tabloids were still moaning about losing the Ashes. When the police car rolled up with a discreet toot of the horn, Jack stowed the paper inside his briefcase.

'Welcome to Melbourne, sir,' said the driver, who introduced herself as Probationary Constable Bernice King – a 'baggy-arse' as the crueller cops called new recruits; an apprentice pig to the city's criminals.

With her mass of dark curls, innocent brown eyes, and heart-shaped face, Bernice looked like she should still be in school. Jack realised he was showing his age. He stowed his bags in the boot, and they chatted inconsequentially as she drove carefully through the late afternoon traffic. She seemed pleasant enough, but Jack was preoccupied and didn't notice the covert glances she directed at him. He learned later that Bernice had grown up in Launceston, the daughter of a uniformed police sergeant he knew slightly and whose funeral he had attended some years back. For Bernice, Inspector Jack Martin was somewhere up there close to God, a famous detective whose name was often in the newspapers and who was even interviewed on TV. He was one of the best, her dad had said. Now, here he was in the flesh, sitting beside her as she drove through the thickening afternoon traffic. She studied him out of the corner of her eye. He was getting old, she decided; there were a few wrinkles but he was still not bad looking. He had bright blue eyes and had kept most of his hair. He was wearing a tweed jacket, desert boots and fawn trousers, not the awful off-the-peg bags of fruit and black dress shoes favoured by so many detectives. He was polite too; so many of the high-ranking officers were gruff and unsympathetic. He was sort of Italian-looking although she couldn't put her finger on why. She'd have to do a bit of digging into his pedigree.

The Tullamarine Freeway was busy. Melbourne was always busy; a frenzy that Jack believed was 'sound and fury, signifying nothing'. He noted the scores of cranes on the skyline and the old buildings under the wrecking ball. Concrete trucks and pumps were pouring concrete into a huge hole in the ground – the foundations of a new bridge over the Yarra. Jack's thoughts went back to Tantalus. It hadn't escaped his notice that he and Liz would make convenient scapegoats if Tantalus went belly up, but then perhaps he was just being paranoid, and besides, he and Commander Ernie Foxcroft went way back.

Jack took in the streetscape as Constable King dropped him off out the front of the Footscray police station. He recoiled at the blistering heat and sniffed the polluted air. Not much different there. Save for the expanding TAFE college, the place didn't seem to have changed much in the last few decades. Scurrying inside, Jack's nose twitched at the familiar smells of police nicks: floor polish, dust, microwaved meals, disinfectant, and something less tangible, the stink of despair from the holding cells. The air was thick, the air-conditioning straining against the heat and threatening to pack it in altogether.

Probationary Constable King had radioed ahead, and Ernie Foxcroft was waiting in the foyer. They shook hands warmly.

Ernie hadn't changed much in the five years or so since Jack had last seen him: the same wiry little terrier of a man with a direct, almost aggressive gaze from sharp blue eyes. Close to retirement now, Ernie had been a full forward for the Smelters football team in Queenstown when Jack was still in school forty years ago. He'd managed to keep his trim figure despite a well-known fondness for beer and chocolate. He had a well-deserved reputation for being fair and honest, both as a footballer and a copper. He'd shown Jack the ropes back in Hobart before transferring to the Victorian force, and they'd kept in touch sporadically ever since.

'Welcome to Western Suburbs Crime Stoppers Central,' Ernie said with a wink. 'I've met your colleague, DS Flakemore, and she's already got her nose on the grindstone. Seems like excellent value, Jack.'

He steered Jack towards his office and pulled out an easy chair. The office had a view over railway tracks towards a scruffy park with a bandstand and a sad palm tree, but it was well-appointed with leather upholstered chairs, an enormous desk, well-stocked bookshelves and a sink and cupboard. And it was blessedly cool. There were photographs of greyhounds on the walls, along with the obligatory portrait of the Queen. A young constable knocked and came in carrying a tray with tea things.

Ernie spooned sugar into his cup. 'We're relying on you and Liz to make some headway on this one Jack. Nasty business.' He slurped some tea, put his cup down and steepled his hands. 'I might as well fill you in on exactly why I've brought you both over. We were extremely impressed with the work you did last year. Against that gang I mean. But this mob …'

He passed a hand over his face as if horrified by what he was seeing. 'Tell you what, Jack, gang warfare's a bit of a pastime here in Melbourne, but this Tantalus mob are brutal!

'The old crime bosses have got rich, fat, and lazy, Jack. Into stocks and shares. Drive Beemers. Wives buy Toorak Tractors to drop their kids off at posh schools.' He drank more tea. 'The odd skirmish between gangs kept the young bucks happy. Papers too. There was a kind of corrupt balance. Bent coppers and pollies taking bribes and nothing getting too far out of control. Not saying I approve, mind you.' Ernie pushed his teacup aside. 'But this new mob Jack, the fuckers don't play by the old rules. Some of the young constables are shit-scared of them and although I can't say it outside of this room I don't blame 'em.'

'What about the Malones, that Irish mob? They were a horrible lot.'

'Old Hughie disappeared. Fitted with concrete boots, they say.'

'The Animals?' These Geordie criminals had nothing to do with Eric Burdon's R & B band and if they'd carried instrument cases they were to hide guns.

'Ha, them!' Ernie snorted. 'Legged it home after their house burned down.' He poured himself more tea and gestured with the pot. 'The Sharroufs just disappeared. Rumour has it they're in the foundations of that new bridge they're building over the river. Fat Toby Malouf's gone off the radar too but that's not unusual.'

Fat Toby was the city's biggest drug pusher. Or had been.

'What about Rocky Garafolo, the Rudolf Valentino of Lygon Street?'

Ernie snorted. 'Ha! Gone to ground like a frightened rat. All talk, that one. The bikie gangs are crapping themselves too. Body parts with club tattoos are turning up around the city. The other day a gang member's "colours" were flown at half-mast on the flagpole of the Victorian Arts Centre.' He bolted some stewed tea and winced.

'Inventive,' Jack prompted, wondering when Ernie was going to tell him what he'd only hinted at on the telephone.

Ernie puffed out his cheeks and expelled the air. 'Yeah. Someone's got a twisted imagination. So now you know what we're up against, Jack. Fact is that if we don't crack down hard it'll end up like Mexico …' He paused, clearly horrified by the prospect of gangsters threatening the state.

'Homo homini lupus,' murmured Jack. He'd been dipping into Liz's copy of Hobbes' *Leviathan* and the thought of criminals growing powerful enough to challenge the State shocked him too. 'We need a common power to keep us in awe.'

Ernie did not seem to have heard Jack's musings and probably would have confused the philosopher with the legendary English cricketer. He spread his hands. 'Look, I'll cut to the chase, Jack. I know you're wondering what the real reason is for bringing you and the lass in on this.'

Jack nodded and placed his cup down on the table. He was all ears.

'Fact is, Jack, we have lots of good detectives over here, but what I'm going to say is for your ears only. Now I'd be exaggerating if I said we're leaking like a sieve, but the fact is, we have some seriously bad apples in the fruit basket.'

'The Joke?' Jack asked, referring to the shadowy network of corrupt officers on the take. He'd heard it was petty stuff.

'Worse, mate. A few times we've swooped on this new firm, but someone's been tipping the bastards off. So I cleared it with Higher Up to bring you in. Fresh set of eyes and you're someone I know we can trust. You've vouched for the lass, too, and that's good enough for me. Now, as I say, keep it to yourself and keep your eyes peeled.'

'You can count on me, sir,' Jack said, feeling a wave of affection for his old friend and mentor. He held out a hand and Ernie shook it firmly.

CHAPTER 2

Ernie Foxcroft was bouncing on his toes when Jack entered the police station the next morning. 'EPA's got onto us,' he said, forcing himself to speak slowly. 'Toxic waste dump out at Tottenham. Huge.' He shook his head. 'Anyway, it's got organised crime written all over it, so I'll get one of the constables to run you out there.' He paused and held up a finger. 'No, tell you what, I'll get Vicky Tran to come with you. Young senior detective constable. She's excellent value, that one, and she'll be working with you on Tantalus. Got a jujitsu black belt, she has, and she's always ready for action against the criminal fraternity. She's got a puppy with her so he'll have to tag along too.'

Jack looked puzzled for a second until he twigged: 'puppy' meant a young, wet-behind-the ears constable. He raised an eyebrow. 'Where's Liz, sir?'

'Oh, yes, I forgot. She's already out on another job in Ascot Vale. Bad business. Bodies all over the place. I'll fill you in about that later.'

Jack shrugged. No point in being impatient. He'd find out

in good time and this illegal waste dump sounded intriguing. He'd read newspaper reports of the same thing happening in Italy, where the Cosa Nostra had got its claws in the waste disposal industry and were posing an existential threat to public health.

Vicky Tran came up at a hundred miles an hour with a remarkably young-looking DC trailing in her slipstream. They shook hands and she introduced the boy with her. 'This is DC Puncheon, sir. Darryl. Makes a mean cup of coffee.' Puncheon squirmed but managed to smile and looked like he'd won Tatts when DCI Martin deigned to shake his hand. Vicky Tran was a small, intense woman who wore her black hair in a ponytail. Ernie had warned she had a very sharp tongue and zero tolerance for all those she regarded as wankers. Men mostly, he said with a wink.

Vicky Tran gave Jack a critical once over. He was a man but she'd heard he was one of the better ones, and she'd find out soon enough. Now in her early thirties, she was bent on promotion after seeing off a couple of husbands who seemed to want her to stay barefoot and in the kitchen. She'd begun to wonder if she was gay. She didn't talk about her past, but Ernie Foxcroft knew that she'd arrived in Australia with her parents by boat from Vietnam when she was a small child. They'd worked hard in the new country and were disappointed that Vicky had chosen to join the police. They were delighted, however, when she enrolled part-time as a mature age Arts/Law student at the University of Melbourne.

Vicky signed out a pool car and ordered DC Puncheon to take the wheel. He drove competently and the run out from Footscray was unproblematic save for the heavy truck traffic clogging up the roads. The heat was something else and great saucers of sweat were staining the armpits of Puncheon's suit jacket. It was only nine o'clock when they neared the dump site, but the sun was remorseless, with a hot northerly wind whipping up willy-willies and a haze shimmering over the flat landscape. The distant city towers appeared to tremble in the heat and children's voices floated over from a kindergarten in the middle distance that might have been a mirage. Everything was still vaguely familiar to Jack from 'another (miserable) life' when he had worked as an industrial electrician in the western suburbs and his young soul was going through its darkest hour over a failed romance.

'Jesus Christ,' Jack gasped, winding up his window. The stink from the tip was appalling even at a distance; a mix of rotting meat and household garbage overlain with chemical fumes grabbed the throat and left the eyes watering.

'Yep,' said Vicky. 'You could cut the pong with a knife.' Puncheon's face had gone green. The dump occupied a clutter of derelict factory buildings and an old bluestone quarry and was ringed by a rusted chain link fence hung with faded *Keep Out: Private Property* signs. It sat in a kind of no-man's land of scrappy open ground wedged between a railway embankment and a housing estate. A creek flowed past the end of the cul-de-sac and meandered round past the factory. Another sign said 'No Fishing'. Vicky snorted. 'Only thing you'd catch in there is a deadly disease.'

Outside one of the nearby houses an old boy was trimming his rose bushes and having a good stickybeak. When they parked outside, he closed his pruning shears and hoisted up his truckie shorts. Mid-sixties, nuggety and tough-looking, he was clad in a faded blue singlet and had an ancient terry-towelling hat perched on his head to shield his pate from the sun. A pair of tattered sandshoes without socks completed his regalia. He squinted at his visitors through the smoke from a rollie cigarette wedged in the corner of his mouth. His eyes were dark brown and inquisitive, and he was not at all intimidated by his visitors.

'Come about that?' he drawled, jerking his head in the direction of the dump. 'Me ciggies keep the flies off. Like to give it up, but …'

'Yes, we have,' Jack replied, fanning his hand under his nose. 'Managed to stop, myself. Best thing I ever did.'

'Good on yer. Wish I could. Anyway, happy to help.' The old boy stretched out a hand for Jack to shake, then after wiping it on his shorts, extended it to Vicky too. 'Dalton's the name. Adam Dalton, but they call me Scorcher. Even the missus calls me that.' His handshake was firm and his gaze direct.

Scorcher's garden, they noticed, had been manicured to within an inch of its life and was verdant despite the blazing summer sun. There were rainwater tanks down the side. The house was shipshape, one of thousands of art deco weatherboards built across the western suburbs in the late 1930s by the William Angliss meatworks company.

'Retired?' asked Jack, anxious to start Scorcher talking.

'Yeah,' Scorcher replied, wiping sweat from his bald head with a red and white spotted handkerchief. 'I was a fitter at Harrison's. Retired early when they closed the place down. But anyway, that's not why you're here.'

'You're right, Scorcher,' said Jack, nodding to Puncheon to

produce a notebook and pencil. 'May I ask when you first noticed the smell?'

Scorcher spat over his brick fence onto the parched nature strip. 'Sorry, miss, it's this bloody dust and that stink. Anyway, it was 'bout six weeks back.'

'Did you report it?' asked Vicky, pulling a notebook from her bag and passing it to Puncheon with a frown.

'Yes love. Got on the blower to the council straightaway.'

Jack raised an eyebrow, his sky blue eyes quizzical. 'What did they say?'

'Buggers wouldn't know if you was up 'em,' scoffed Scorcher. 'Begging your pardon, miss. Got me to fill out a few forms.' He waved his shears dismissively in the direction of the distant Town Hall.

Vicky fixed Scorcher with a cool stare. 'Actually, it's Leading Senior Detective Constable Tran, but please continue.'

'Err, sorry about that, Detective. Force of habit, being polite to the ladies. Anyway, I got on to the EPA after that, dug me teeth in and wouldn't let go, but it was Trades Hall kicking up a stink that done it.'

'Trades Hall?' queried Jack.

'Yeah. I used to be a delegate from me union. Secretary's hot on the environment and that.'

'He made them act?' asked Vicky.

'Yeah. They took their time, but …' He recoiled as a whiff of foetid air was blown over from the dump. 'See what I mean? It stinks up the house and the missus is crook. Cancer.'

'I'm sorry to hear that,' said Jack. He'd warmed to the old fellow and meant it.

'Thanks mate. She's doing chemo and the doctor reckons

she'll pull through.' He went to snip at an errant flower stem, then thought better of it.

'We certainly hope so,' said Jack. 'Anyway, Scorcher, how long do you think they've been dumping there?'

'Three months, maybe a bit more? Me and the missus was away for a while visiting family in Tassie. When we got back, we noticed trucks coming and going at all hours. Nights too, under floodlights. Shiny new padlocks on the gates. Place had been deserted for oh … since way before me and the missus bought this place and that was thirty-odd years ago.'

Vicky prodded Puncheon to make a note. 'When did the smell start?'

'Mebbe six weeks ago.' Scorcher put down the shears and scratched his ear. 'Coulda been a bit more, but it got real bad about then.'

'That's right,' said a little bloke who'd come out of the house next door. 'About six weeks.' With his faded red hair and inquisitive blue eyes he reminded Jack of an elderly rosella.

'This is me mate, Herbie Wise,' said Scorcher. 'He's retired like me. A boilermaker at Harrison's back when we still made things in this country.'

Herbie's strong handshake belied his stature.

'About the stink,' said Herbie. 'We're the dumping ground for all the shit they don't want nowhere else, so you kinda get used to smells. Abattoirs, the shit farm, chemical factories, rendering plants, tips; huge trucks clogging up the streets; we've got the lot … oh, and now that bloody John Howard wants to dump a nuclear power station on us.'

'Bloke's an arse,' grunted Scorcher. 'Anyway, goin' back to this here' – he pointed at the dump with his ciggie – 'after a while it got so bad we couldn't leave the winders open.'

'Look over across the paddock,' put in Herbie, jerking his thumb towards the west. 'That's a bloody kindergarten. Makes me spew to think of the kiddies breathing this shit in.'

'No disagreements on that,' said Jack, taking in the children playing half a mile off. 'Now, these trucks you mentioned – anything about them you remember?'

'Lots didn't have no owners' names on 'em,' Scorcher replied. 'Not during the day at least. At night, it was that McArseholes Logistics mob. Buncha arseholes alright.'

Jack raised an amused eyebrow. 'McArseholes?'

'That's what we call 'em,' explained Herbie. 'Real name's McCastles. Shepparton mob. Anyway, I also seen an ambulance going in about a week ago.'

'An *ambulance*?' queried Vicky, raising an eyebrow.

'Yeah, fair dinkum love! My guess is it brung medical waste.'

'What about the McArseholes lot?' Vicky asked, suppressing a giggle.

'They was cartin' old forty-four-gallon drums in,' said Herbie. 'Me and Scorcher's had personal dealings with 'em too.'

'Personal dealings?' asked Vicky.

'Yeah. About five years back at Harrison's we went on strike. One morning a McCastle's bloke in a Batman mask drove a truck through the picket line. Reckon he was doing sixty miles an hour. They done it down at Lupton's Chemicals down at Altona too when they was on strike over blokes getting bladder cancer.'

'Did you report it?' asked Vicky.

Scorcher gave her a look. 'Report it? No offence, love, but the bloody coppers was standing there when it happened.'

Vicky shook her head and exchanged a glance with Jack. There was an uncomfortable silence, broken only by the sound of a front-end loader starting up at the tip. Puncheon was scribbling away and trying to fan the smell away at the same time.

'How about people?' asked Jack. 'Did you ever see anyone apart from the truck drivers? People working onsite?'

'Early on there was a motorbike gang around a bit. Packa thugs. Molochs Marauders. There was this puffed-up little bloke with 'em. Dodgy little prick with wraparound sunglasses wearing them truckie singlets. Haven't seen 'em for a while. After that, there was other blokes working. Dark blokes. They'd come in a minibus. But sometimes we'd see these flash cunts drive up in cars. Bling all over 'em, musta cost a fortune. Black leather jackets. White tee-shirts. Thought they was God's gift.'

'Expensive set of wheels too,' added Herbie, with a frown at Scorcher to tone down his language. 'Latest model BMW. Had a coupla sheilas with 'em. Tarts if you ask me.'

'I reckon,' said Scorcher. 'Anyway these leather jacket cu … err blokes come by a few times I saw. You'd hear 'em going crook at the blokes working on site, then they'd get in their cars and piss off.'

'Except there was always a couple of 'em would drive the bus and that,' corrected Herbie.

Scorcher nodded. 'Supervising the blokes doing the work.'

'Any number plates you'd remember?' asked Vicky, with a nod to Puncheon to make sure he wrote the answer down.

'As a matter of fact, yeah,' said Scorcher, rolling a fresh cigarette. 'The cars was always a bit far off but I got the minibus rego this morning.'

He fished around in his shorts and handed Vicky a betting slip with the registration number scrawled on it. They were on to something here.

Scorcher took a long drag on his cigarette. 'They'd bring the blokes in and lock the gates until they finished. Crazy long hours. This morning, though, the bus come barrelling back outta the place like Phar Lap on a promise.'

'Clipped one of the gates,' put in Herbie. 'If you lot had arrived just a bit earlier, you would have got 'em.'

'Make and model?'

'White Toyota HiAce. A bit old and dented,' said Herbie proudly.

'Bloke in a turban was driving,' added Scorcher. 'A bit strange because usually one of them other pricks was driving.'

'Turban?' queried Jack, his eyes open wide.

'Yeah, one of them cloth thingies. Like in India but different.'

'Light brownish bloke,' added Herbie. 'Turks or Arabs or something. And there was a couple of others in the back. Reckon they was doing a runner.'

'You've been a great help,' said Jack. 'If you see anything or think of anything, please give us a ring on this number.' He handed both men his card. 'Ring either of us any time. Footscray Police Station. Now, we'd like to send round an officer to take your statements if that's okay.'

'No worries,' said Herbie. 'We've had them pricks up to here.' He indicated a point just below his bottom chin.

Scorcher nodded his agreement, and they all shook hands.

The three detectives walked a hundred metres over the waste ground to where two beefy uniformed officers were standing guard at the gates, their faces obscured by blue face masks in a vain attempt to block the stench. One of the gates was bent and half off its hinges. The old fertiliser factory consisted of a large, steel-framed corrugated iron structure, with several smaller buildings scattered around the compound. A crow perched on top, watching them closely, a bit like Herbie Wise except for the size and colour. Everything looked in danger of collapse. A broken-down old conveyor poked skywards like a fundamentalist preacher's finger warning about the consequences of sin or pointing to the fat profits of times past. The hot wind set loose iron flapping and blew showers of asbestos from the split lagging of the old pipes. A yellow front-end loader was parked outside some big roller doors. When their eyes had adjusted to the semi-darkness inside the main building, they saw tottering stacks of forty-four-gallon drums and smaller plastic containers. Looked like hundreds, even thousands of them. There were more of them out the back, stacked over an area the size of a soccer field. A no-nonsense woman strutted over, garbed in heavy protective clothing and a full-face mask.

Vicky showed her warrant card, but the woman held up a gloved hand. 'Best you don't enter, love,' she warned. 'We've no idea of what's inside these drums, and lots of 'em are leaking.'

Indeed they were. A stream of liquid was bubbling across the cracked concrete floor. They sniffed at the ghastly medley of smells: rotten eggs, chlorine, putrid fish, and something like decaying horseradish. A whiff of nail polish too. Nothing wholesome or natural. Made the eyes water and gave you a bad taste in the mouth like you were sucking on a mouthful of two-dollar coins. Vicky was shaking her head. It was difficult to get the mind round the sheer scale of the bastardry that had been done here. Puncheon suddenly sidled off and vomited.

'Any idea of where that goes?' asked Jack, pointing at the liquid.

'Drains into the creek,' the woman replied, pointing out across the paddock. She shook her head. 'It's been going into it for a while. God knows what's happened downstream, with parks and everything. Dogs swimming in Cruickshank Park. We've had illegal dumping into the gutters for years out west, but this is in a league of its own.'

'You've no idea of the contents?'

'Nope, but my nose tells me that we are dealing with highly toxic compounds here, and the sheer volume of waste takes the biscuit. Makes me think of a huge abscess draining pus into the bay.'

She shrugged and turned away to write something on her clipboard. They thanked her and wandered round the side of the building towards the old quarry, which was buzzing with an enormous cloud of flies so thick that the surface looked alive. It was at times like this that Jack gave thanks that he was not a forensic officer or an EPA inspector. Or a lowly constable who might be impressed into combing through the muck for clues. Mounds of garbage were piled high up the sides of the quarry, spilling out at the front where the drivers must have backed their trucks. Plastic bags had burst open, and the blazing sun was accelerating the processes of decay. The detectives exchanged looks and turned on their heels. Nothing they could do here. They didn't notice the two men watching the tip through binoculars from the nearby railway embankment, but exited as quickly as they could without it being too obvious, exchanged waves with Scorcher and Herbie, and escaped along Sunshine Road towards Footscray. The sky was huge over the flat landscape, and people went about their business oblivious to the horror festering behind them. The city skyscrapers gleamed silver and black in the distance and the single stack of the Newport power station was pumping out a plume of smoke. At a safe distance they wound down the windows and sucked in great gulps of cleaner air.

'Fuck,' said Vicky, shaking her head. 'I've seen it all now. Someone's trying to poison the whole city.'

'Yeah,' Jack agreed, busy radioing in the rego number of the minibus. 'Seems like the end times. All we need is plagues: frogs and toads falling from the heavens.'

'Except frogs would die in the shit,' Puncheon said with a shudder. 'Plenty of frogs is a sign of a healthy environment.'

Jack nodded. 'You're not wrong, son.' He was wondering if the turban bloke might be a trafficked slave labourer.

The radio crackled into life as they were waiting at the Geelong Road traffic lights. 'Jack, the vehicle belongs to a male called Alwyn Terence Tudge,' said a disembodied voice. 'Goes by Terry. He's known to the police. Long list of priors.' The voice rattled off an address in St Kilda. 'The Tottenham tip property itself belongs to an Alan Badger. He's an accountant up at Shepparton.'

'Right,' Jack replied as Puncheon steered into the police station car park. He turned to Vicky. 'We'll need to get a car round to this Tudge character's house. It's a priority. We'll chase up this Badger fellow too.'

Jack was just settling down with a cup of tea in the canteen when a uniform came up and said he was wanted on the telephone. It was Scorcher Dalton, the old fitter who lived near the tip. 'Hey Jack,' he said. 'There was another bloke who was always hanging round at the dump. Big fat bloke, sorta Lebanese looking. Anyway, not long after you was out here he drove up. Saw what was goin' on and took off like he was in the Grand Prix. One of them flash Ferraris. Got his number plate.'

Jack wrote down the number and thanked the old fellow. He had closed his phone and was taking a final swig of tea when Liz Flakemore came into the cafeteria. She waved and went to the counter, so Jack called out to ask her to get him a refill. It was good to see her and he was impatient to tell her about the illegal tip; he was even more eager to hear about the case she was working on out in Ascot Vale. He frowned; she was still looking drawn. Her music teacher lover, Marg someone or other, had been awarded a scholarship to study in Vienna. After a while, her letters had stopped, then she wrote to say she'd found someone else and would not be coming home. Liz had gone into the foetal position and taken leave. But she was, he knew, a real professional and would keep her eyes firmly on the case.

CHAPTER 3

Liz leaned over and gave Jack a quick hug before sitting down at the table and taking a bite from her snack bar. Jack was impatient but let her start on her camomile tea. Her green eyes looked haunted. 'Jeez, what a morning,' she sighed, running her hands through her short blonde hair. 'We get to see some shocking things in this game, but …' She reached over for her cup, took another sip and pulled a face. 'Ernie Foxcroft just told me you've been investigating a big dump out Tottenham way. Sounds dreadful but I'm not sure it could be worse than what I've seen.' She shuddered. 'Anyway a report came in of shots being fired early this morning. Back street in Ascot Vale: middle class suburb. You'd know it.'

'Yeah, some nice places there.'

'You've heard of the bloke they call the Greengrocer?'

Jack thought for a while. 'Yeah … Italian gangster. *Capo di tutti i capi* of the Markets Mob: *Azienda dei Mercati.*' He was proud of his Italian language skills. 'What's happened?'

'Well, there was a big mob rubbernecking when we got there. We shooed them away down to the end of the street before we went in.' Liz drew a hand across her brow. 'We went round the back to the pergola and the Greengrocer was hanging on the wall. Someone had crucified him with six-inch nails then finished him off with a shotgun.' She shook her head as if to banish the appalling vision. 'Lucky for the wife that she was visiting rellies out in Dandenong. Place was a fortress: steel-plated doors, bulletproof windows, state of the art security system. Didn't help.' She took a sip of tea and pushed the cup to one side. 'They blasted their way into the house and turned everything upside down. Knew what they were doing. You wouldn't believe it, but they'd killed the two eldest sons in their beds. The doc reckoned they'd been garrotted by the look of the ligature wounds on their necks.'

'Garrotted?' Jack was dumbstruck.

'Yeah, that's what it looked like. Anyway, the young DC with me reckoned there's another son, the baby of the family. Called Dario. No sign of him so either he hasn't stopped run-ning or they've kidnapped him. Evidently the Greengrocer's second-in-command lives down the back of the garden in a fortified granny flat. Man they call "The Razor" for fairly obvious reasons. No sign of him either.'

The old desk sergeant, 'Bruiser' Macfarlane, came up to the table. A huge, overweight man nearing retirement, Bruiser was as cynical as any copper could get to be, but he had a 'thought I'd seen it all, but' look on his fleshy face. His massive lower jaw was developing a premature five o'clock shadow.

'Report's just come in that a body's been found at the Brook-lyn abattoir.'

'Dead?'

'Yeah. Dead as a doornail, sir. Anyway, I reckon you'd wanna take a squizz.'

Liz and Jack reluctantly abandoned their snack and went out into the blazing heat and commandeered the only available pool car. It was hellishly hot inside and littered with fast food boxes and stank of stale fish and chips. Someone had defied the No Smoking sign and the ashtray was full of cigarette butts. They wound their windows down simultaneously. The young constable on duty shrugged apologetically, muttering something about 'Bloody Thick and Thin' being the culprits.

'Real pigs, then?' said Jack with a wink.

'Err, yes …' said the constable uncertainly.

Liz had no idea where Brooklyn was, so Jack took the wheel, taking the precaution of wiping off the fast-food grease with his handkerchief. He made a mental note to carpet the Thick and Thin blokes, whoever they were.

A crowd of slaughtermen clad in blood-spattered white overalls were milling round the entrance to the meatworks, a collection of low-rise red brick buildings situated in a cul-de-sac off Geelong Road. Someone had spray-painted the wall with the words ANIMAL AUSCHWITZ and every so often a cow or sheep would moo or baa in terror. There was some kind of clubhouse just up the road and what looked like a brothel next door; an extension of the meat trade, Liz reckoned. A lone uniformed officer was attempting to keep the crowd of gawkers back. Liz and Jack pulled out their warrant cards, and the officer informed them that the pathologist was already inside. They went into the darkened interior, which smelled pungently of ammonia and decayed flesh, and when their eyes became accustomed to the gloom, they saw the broad backside of a man crouching down next to a bundle on the floor. There was an open bag full of medical equipment next to him. After grunted introductions and a fumbled handshake the pathologist – a large middle-aged man called Swinburne – pointed to the corpse's head.

'My guess, detectives, is that from the size of the entrance wound here, this chap has been shot with a captive bolt gun.' He pointed with his thermometer. 'There, straight between the eyes. Kapow. No ordinary gun used. We'll confirm all this at the autopsy, of course. Anyway, help me turn him over and we'll try to get a temperature reading.' His broad Yorkshire accent was as out of place here as the speech of an Eskimo. 'I doubt he felt pain, if that makes it any better.'

Liz wondered aloud. 'Why kill him here?'

'And why use a captive bolt gun, if that's what killed him?' Jack added.

'Can't help you with the workings of the criminal mind,' Swinburne replied. 'But what I can tell you is his name. Here, whoever did this to him has pinned a name tag to his shirt. Bit bloody, I'm afraid, but still legible.'

Liz and Jack bent down together. The tag read 'BEPPO SQUILLACE THE RAZOR' in thick black marker in a careful hand. They had found the Greengrocer's deputy. Jack surmised that the murderer had left him in the abattoir as a sign of utter contempt. It was a pretty safe bet that it was the work of the Tantalus gang again. The forensics team was arriving as Jack and Liz climbed back into the dirty car.

*

Meanwhile, Vicky Tran had taken Darryl Puncheon with her to St Kilda to see if she could locate the owner of the HiAce van seen leaving the illegal Tottenham tip. Terry Tudge was 'known to the police' and Vicky had flicked distastefully through his file: a summary of the sad life of a small-time burglar, drug peddler and general no hoper; a bottom feeder in the criminal ecosystem. Terry had done a bit of time but had managed to stay out of trouble since his last release from Pentridge. Didn't mean he'd gone straight; more likely the little shit had just been lucky, she reckoned. She had done a double take at his mugshot: he was the spitting image of Alfred E. Neuman of *MAD* magazine – same brachycephalic skull, same gap-toothed insouciant grin, same snub nose, freckles, and thatch of reddish hair. He was trying to look tough but failing; didn't have the face for it. She imagined how a bank teller would laugh if Terry tried a stick-up job with a dial like that. After Vicky had obtained a search warrant, they drove over the West Gate Bridge and parked in a St Kilda back street outside Tudge's apartment block. His letterbox was overflowing with bills and advertising brochures. An elderly neighbour had just puffed up the street with a bag of groceries and he confirmed that Tudge was the occupant of the flat and that yes, he did own a white van.

'Haven't seen it for quite a while,' the old fellow lisped, pushing up his ill-fitting dentures. 'Ain't seen Terry neither for oh, mussbe over a week. No, two. It was before me pension day.' He paused to get his breath back. 'Dodgy little bugger if you ask me. 'E never done a day's work in his life. His mum and dad left him the place after they passed away. Nice couple. Useless twerp could never have bought it hisself.'

The old boy seemed lonely and Vicky started feeling sorry for him. 'Any wife or girlfriend … Mr?' Half of her mind was wondering whether her ex-hubbies would end up like this. She'd have to get a grip.

'Who, 'im or me?'

Vicky smiled. 'Not you. Him: Tudge.'

'Stevens. Reggie Stevens, Miss. Me wife's dead.' He went to pick up his groceries but put them back down. 'Oh, you mean does Terry Tudge have a wife? Ha! Nobody'd want the little shit.'

'Anything else you can remember?'

Stevens scratched his bald head and pushed his teeth back up again. 'Nah … unless, yeah … These blokes started comin' round maybe a month back. Wouldn't want to cross 'em. Nasty types. Leather jackets, white tee-shirts, jewellery. Thought they was God's gift. Wouldn't say nothin' if you said g'day. Mind you, you wouldn't want nothin' to do with 'em anyway. Knew some fellas like that once back in Sydney years ago. Late fifties. Drank in a pub in Sussex Street they did; called it the Buncha Cu...'

'Thank you, Mr Stevens. Anything else you can tell us?'

'Well, they looked foreign. Like Greeks or Lebbos and that. Not Asian like you, miss. One of 'em used to sit up in the car like he was King Farook and order the others about. Oh yeah, there was an Aussie bloke too. Ugly as a hatful of arseholes he was, pardon me French.'

'Rego number?'

'Nah, carn help you with that.'

Vicky thanked him and handed him her card. He agreed to contact her if he thought of anything else or if anyone came round to Tudge's flat. The old codger shuffled off to his ground floor flat. The curtains twitched. It was probably the most excitement he'd had since Sputnik went into orbit.

Tudge's flat was up two flights of concrete steps on the second floor of the drably utilitarian 1960s yellow brick block. The sun was merciless. Vicky poked expertly at the Yale lock with a set of picks and the door swung open onto a dingy hallway. It was stuffy and oppressively hot inside. There were two small bedrooms, one with an unmade three-quarter bed and a cheap wardrobe stuffed with a depressing array of nylon shirts, trackie dacks and tops, cheap cotton hoodies and faded jocks with THE HUNTER printed on the perished waistbands. A curling photo of an elderly couple was stuck on the bedside table – the parents, presumably. Vicky felt a sudden jolt of pity. The small lounge room hid from the world behind gauze curtains: a sad man's cave with a TV, a threadbare armchair and a wobbly coffee table with an overflowing ashtray and a midden of empty beer cans. Takeaway boxes were strewn around. Looked like nobody ever visited. They took one look in the toilet/bathroom and backed off, closing the door firmly. Hygiene was not high on Terry Tudge's list of priorities. The bath was coated in a film of dust and the shower dripped in time with the remorseless ticking of the hallway clock, an heirloom by the solid look of it. Time slipped away here, frittered, wasted, like the owner's life. The bloke was a bum. The kitchen sported bowls and plates sprouting thick grey mould in the sink and a single mug half full of something disgusting on the island bench.

'What, me worry?' Vicky joked, eyeing the mess, thinking of Tudge's uncanny resemblance to Alfred E. Neuman.

'Not exactly your Mr Houseproud,' said Puncheon, sniffing the mug's contents with distaste. 'Something's not right here.'

'Spot on, Sunshine,' Vicky sighed. 'We'd best get forensics here. It doesn't look good for our Mr Tudge.'

A quick title search revealed that the flat did indeed belong to Alwyn Terence Tudge. Like Reggie Stevens had said, his deceased parents had left it to him. As for the HiAce van, the only trace was a smear of oil in Tudge's carport. Vicky very much doubted that Terry Tudge was the criminal mastermind behind the Tottenham tip, and he might well have outlived his usefulness to the criminal syndicate.

CHAPTER 4

Jack was just leaving the Footscray nick later that day after dismissing the team, when Bruiser Macfarlane called him over to report that the blue Ferrari Scorcher Dalton had reported out at the Tottenham tip was registered to a man called Malouf. 'Nasty bugger,' said Bruiser, leaning on the counter and crunching on an Anzac biscuit. 'Widely known as Fat Toby.' Crumbs spattered onto the counter. 'Kingpin in the country's biggest drug syndicate. Priors for a raft of petty crimes in his youth but appears to have kept his nose clean since.' He pushed up his horn-rimmed glasses. 'Like I say, Fat Toby *appears* to have gone clean. Bugger gets mugs to do his dirty work.'

Something else for Vicky Tran to look into. As Ernie Foxcroft had said, the young woman was a real asset. Jack trotted out to the car park to wait for his lift. When the car drew up, Jack saw that the driver was the same young probationer who had picked him up at the airport. Beatrice? Beris? No. Bernice someone or the other, a pleasant enough young woman. Seemed keen to make a go of it in the force. When she dropped him off in Yarraville, he took the steps up to the flat where he was staying two at a time. It was comfortable, unlike some of the police houses he'd stayed in over the years. There was a bit of a balcony, shaded by a huge peppercorn tree, with a view across rooftops to the Sun Theatre, the beautifully refurbished art deco cinema. Liz was in a place up in Footscray, and Jack reckoned he'd got the best deal.

Footscray also had a rich literary history. It had been the final home of the great lyric poet John Shaw Neilson, who, after a day of hard shovelling on an outback road, could write how the sun rose each day like 'red oranges in May'. Jack found it difficult to square the beauty of Neilson's words with his memory of the stench of Footscray's vast abattoirs and its dowdy streets. The meatworks were gone now, but Jack remembered them from a stay some decades before. Further pondering the place's connection with verse, Jack recalled that there were several mentions of Footscray in the 'Ern Malley' poems concocted by a pair of young scallywags to embarrass the hapless modernist editor, Max Harris.

Footscray was an edgy place. A kid had died outside the railway station as commuters had rushed past, anxious to get home and out of the heat. It would have been the same any-where, to be fair. Good Samaritans were thin on the ground. It pointed to the new gang's extra-strong or adulterated product. Yarraville, though, was on the up after decades of decay. Jack recalled it as a place of boarded-up shops and desolation. Back then, he would not have been surprised to see tumbleweed blowing down Anderson Street. Now, it was full of trendy shops and cafés. There was even a new bookshop in the Sun Cinema building. He'd get that book *Too Tough To Die*, about the fight to save the Bulldogs footy team. He must invite Liz to take in a film when they'd settled into their respective quarters. *Enemy of the State* was getting good reviews.

The long sweltering summer evening stretched ahead, and he planned to sit out on the balcony and read through the pile of documents Ernie Foxcroft had handballed to him. Get his nose in his book if he could. First though, he could murder a cold beer, so he wandered down Anderson Street to the pub. It was too hot for a run, though he could imagine Wendy's disappointed 'Dad!' if she knew he was backsliding. A beer would also wash away the taste of the Tottenham dump.

Not everything had been cleaned up in Yarraville. Five or six hoodies were lurking near the Heather Dell bakery, and they scurried into an alley like cockroaches avoiding the light when they saw him coming. Despite his casual clothes, they smelled bacon. He figured they were peddling drugs, but he was off duty and thirsty and wasn't going to give chase. Still, when one of them dropped a Ziploc bag, Jack couldn't look the other way. The bag contained brittle off-white nuggets, which he was certain weren't kids' lollies. He'd check the bag in at the station in the morning.

The Railway Hotel down on the corner was doing a brisk trade. The lounge bar was pleasantly cool, and the pint of creamy Guinness didn't touch the sides, but Jack resisted when the pretty barmaid wiggled a fresh glass next to the beer taps. It wouldn't do to spend his evenings getting pissed. He left the Railway and was keeping to the shady side of the street when his mobile phone rang. He considered ignoring it, but figured it might be Francesca or Wendy. It was neither. It was Bruiser Macfarlane ringing from the Footscray cop shop. The tough old veteran of the mean streets always seemed to be on duty.

'Jack, you're gunna have to get back out to Tottenham,' said Bruiser, his thick Strine accent exaggerated over the phone. 'They've found a stiff out there. Young Vicky Tran's driving down to Yarraville to pick you up as we speak.'

Jack thanked him and rang off. A knock on the door signalled Vicky's arrival, without her puppy this time. The traffic had eased, and they were soon driving past the enormous red brick wool stores on Sunshine Road and then turning into the cul-de-sac to the illegal dump. A couple of police cars were already there with their lights flashing, and Scorcher Dalton was fiddling with his letterbox and having another good stickybeak. The stink was as bad as ever and the heat was still tremendous.

'What's up?' Jack asked, flashing his warrant card at the uniformed constable on the gate.

'It's over in the quarry sir,' the constable replied. His face was green. 'The pathologist's already there. Forensic officers too.'

They donned protective gear and sidled cautiously up to the rubbish tip. Jack could swear it was shivering in the heat. The corpse was lying stiffly on its back next to the quarry wall and was wearing a black leather jacket and blue jeans. Doctor Swinburne, the pathologist, was crouching down next to the body and Commander Ernie Foxcroft was standing nearby with a handkerchief pressed to his nose. Seeing Jack and Vicky approaching, Ernie shook his terrier's head and growled something inaudible. A uniformed policeman was attempting to dispel the vast cloud of blowflies with a spray can of Mortein: as useless a task as King Canute trying to turn back the sea.

'We meet again, Jack,' said Dr Swinburne. He held out a gloved hand then withdrew it when he realised it was coated in blood. He pointed to the corpse's chest. 'Shot,' he said, peering over his surgical mask. 'Bullet went straight into the heart. We'll confirm that at the autopsy, of course. Anyway, it's a "he", Jack. Mid-forties, I'd say.' Swinburne's Yorkshire accent was broader than ever and he seemed completely unfazed by the corpse or the stench of their surroundings.

Jack didn't look too closely at the corpse, which was already showing signs of decay, and Vicky was looking the other way. Jack gave silent thanks that he'd remembered the Vicks VapoRub to smear under his nose – an old trick learned from his friend Simon Calvert, the Hobart pathologist. Vicky gratefully took the jar. Swinburne took a rectal temperature reading; 'Dead since early this morning,' he pronounced. 'Rigor mortis still present as you can see. Shot and buried in the rubbish. Sic transit mundus. Amen.'

A dull metallic glint in the corpse's half-open mouth caught Jack's attention and he bent down, ignoring the flies and stench, for a better view, with Vicky hovering nearby.

'I can see what you're looking at, Jack,' said Swinburne. 'The steel teeth, yeah?'

Vicky looked at Jack, but he just nodded thoughtfully. He'd seen this before on a case down in Hobart.

'Anyway, we're just about done here,' said Swinburne, signalling to his assistants to step forward to zip the corpse into a black body bag and load it onto a stretcher for transport to the city mortuary. 'Pity we haven't met in happier circumstances Jack. I'll give you a call when we're ready for the postmortem.' He paused and reached behind him to a black polythene bag. 'Ah, Jack, we also found this.' He pulled out a long grey thing with hairs.

Jack's jaw dropped. 'An arm? You're kidding me.'

'Well, obviously it's an arm,' said Swinburne with a grin. He nodded at the intact corpse and lit a cigarette. 'As you will have noticed, your man over there has two arms, so it can't be his. My first guess was that it was a hospital amputation and rogue disposal. Look closer though, and you'll see it's too sloppily done to be the work of a surgeon.' He stood aside to let Jack look. 'And this, Jack,' – he pointed to faded blue ink on the biceps – 'is a bikie gang's tattoo. The fookin Molochs Marauders no less.'

Jack nodded, feeling a bit queasy at the sight of the severed appendage. Both Wendy and Francesca were vegetarians – Liz too – and the sight almost made Jack want to join them because it looked like something beyond its use by date in a pork butcher's window. Vicky was shaking her head in appalled wonder at the sight.

Swinburne started packing up his equipment. 'Chook that in with the body,' he ordered, beckoning his assistants over and pointing to the arm.

Jack remembered Ernie Foxcroft and turned to apprise him of what he'd learned. Ernie was bearing up well for an old bloke from the uniformed branch. 'Another one,' Ernie observed, trying not to look too hard. 'They've been cropping up all over the city.'

''Fraid so,' said the pathologist, closing his bag. 'It's a bit difficult to match 'em up. Not like Lego!'

'Christ that's bad,' said Ernie when they were walking back to the car. 'Any thoughts, Jack? Vicky?'

'The teeth,' Jack replied, pausing with his hand on the door handle of the car. 'The corpse has steel teeth: it's a dead give-away of Soviet dentistry. There could be some other clues in his clothes. We'll know a bit more when Dr Swinburne gets him on the slab.'

Just then a stentorian voice yelled out 'Stop, police!' Uniformed officers were racing towards the chain link fence, on which a black-clad figure was spreadeagled rather like a hapless insect on a spider's web. An officer reached up and pulled him down by one leg and although the man struggled violently, he could not shake himself free. Soon, three officers were pinning the wriggling figure on the ground.

'Quieten down, sunshine,' ordered the first cop. He forced the man's arms behind his back and clicked handcuffs around his wrists. The man continued to struggle and was muttering in a foreign language.

'Good work, Constable … err, Zawadzki,' said Jack, reading the young policeman's name badge. 'Do you know where he came from?'

Zawadzki was busy subduing the wriggling prisoner. 'He's been hiding among the barrels, sir … Musta been there all day … Got chemicals all over him … Stinks.' He flapped a beefy hand over his nose and pinned the man down with a size 13 boot. 'Here, keep still you.'

'Good work,' Jack murmured, reaching down to pull the prisoner's head round by the hair for a clearer look. Late thirties, early forties, perhaps, he guessed. Bloodshot blue eyes. Jet black hair shot through with grey that he'd missed with the dye. Frightened but arrogant. Body bulked out from the gym or steroids or both.

'What's your name?' Jack demanded.

The man muttered inaudibly, turned his head away and spat.

'Rude bugger,' said Vicky. 'Probably never toilet trained either.'

'OK, officers,' said Jack with a grin. 'We'll get Chappie here back to the station and see if he gets more talkative.'

The man tensed upon hearing this, and Jack wondered if he feared a beating. God knows what went on in the cop shops wherever he came from. The officers dragged him to a waiting paddy wagon. He was still struggling violently and yelling in a foreign language when they shoved him inside the dogbox. They made out the word 'kurva'. It was, Jack knew, a Slavic oath. The man managed to turn his head round enough to catch sight of Vicky and he launched into a veritable tirade.

'Hey, that's enough!' shouted Constable Zawadzki, giving the man a nudge with his boot. 'I understand enough of what he's saying,' he told Jack. 'It's a bit like my family's Polish. He's calling her every racist insult he can think of. Anyway, let's get the little bastard in the paddy wagon.'

Ernie Foxcroft cadged a lift and they chatted inconsequentially as Vicky drove him to his house in Williamstown. She didn't speak but Jack could see she was still fuming about the man they now called Chappie. When the talk came back to the dump itself, Jack raised the question of the companies that availed themselves of the services of the Tottenham cowboys.

'There must be chemical companies, private garbage collection services, manufacturers, even hospitals,' he said. 'All knowingly using these crooks. Or turning a blind eye. What are we going to do about them?'

'They'll say they were acting in good faith,' Foxcroft replied, directing Vicky to turn into a leafy side street not far from the bay foreshore. 'Trouble is, they'll be believed. I'd bet London to a brick that we'd be told to drop it. Maybe some of them were genuinely unaware.'

Jack smiled sourly to himself as Vicky drove away from the boss's house. He'd got the answer to his musings. In Australia, business was as sacrosanct as sport. He'd be ordered to lay off the respectable silvertails benefiting from the illegal dump. The sunset was blazing red and yellow when Vicky dropped him off outside the Yarraville flat. He took a long shower and threw his clothes into the washing machine. Felt befouled by the tip and the ugly creature they'd arrested. And that bloody arm! He made a cup of tea and forced himself to eat a slice of toast; couldn't face the ham he'd bought earlier that day because the pink meat reminded him … Some of his colleagues could forget such horror when they went home but Jack never could. He knew that arm would turn up in one of his nightmares.

He liked the apartment, but something about it had been nagging at the back of his mind. It seemed the same as when he had left it that morning, but when he looked closer, he thought that things had been moved. He could have sworn that he'd left the newspaper on the island bench, but it was sitting on a kitchen stool. He checked the doors and windows. There was no sign of forced entry and nor was anything missing. Was he imagining things? Had he been a cop for so long that he saw the evidence of crime everywhere? But no, he was sure that someone had been in the flat while he was out. He shook his head. Not much he could do about it at the moment, so he connected his shiny new laptop computer to the phone socket, feeling like a tech whizz as he listened to the whirrs and pings. Who said he was stuck in the Steam Age or the Jurassic or whenever it was when dinosaurs roamed the earth? There was a new email from Wendy saying she had brought a big wooden trunk from Uncle Jimmy Johnstone's house at New Norfolk. Jimmy had recently died and left everything to Jack as his closest surviving relative. Jack had only a vague memory of the house: a big rundown brick place sitting in overgrown grounds. The retired Queenstown miner had spent his time in the kitchen and adjacent parlour, which had doubled as his bedroom. The other rooms had been shut up for decades, gathering dust and cobwebs. Jack had visited him years before, but Jimmy said he didn't care much for coppers, so he had never gone back.

The trunk was hidden among mountains of junk in the attic, Wendy reported. The old hoarder had never thrown anything out. There were broken rocking horses, stacks of old crockery, ancient newspapers, chipped chamber pots, old prints and paintings in heavy frames, and mice-gnawed Victorian tomes, the pages foxed with age. Even an old wind-up gramophone and a stack of 78s. 'Darktown Strutters Ball' and other curious stuff. Some of it might be worth a bit when cleaned up. There were sepia photographs of long deceased family members, and friends, maybe; exciting in a way, but then Wendy realised that nobody would possibly remember who they had been. She had manhandled the trunk down the steep stairs from the attic, lucky not to have done herself an injury. Jack would give her a stern talking to about that. She hadn't been able to open it yet but hoped the key was on the big black iron ring she'd found in Uncle Jimmy's kitchen.

CHAPTER 5

The following morning dawned hot and cloudless, promising to be yet another scorcher. Jack was already sweating when he arrived at the Footscray cop shop and draped his tweed jacket over the back of his chair. First he sent the bag of white nuggets the Yarraville hoodies had dropped – he suspected it was crack cocaine – to the lab. Then he summoned the Operation Tantalus team to an urgent briefing. Meanwhile, the nameless man they'd arrested at the dump the previous evening could sweat a bit more in his cell. The team dribbled in, listless from the heat, and when the last of them was seated, Jack bade them good morning. He had begun to hate briefings in crowded rooms because he was too vain to wear a hearing aid and as a result was starting to miss too much of what was said. The acoustics of the room didn't help: the walls were solid concrete and he could swear there were echoes.

'For those of you we haven't met,' he began, 'I'm Detective Chief Inspector Jack Martin and this is my colleague, DS Liz Flakemore. We're seconded from the Tasmania Police to head up Operation Tantalus …'

Jack heard a stage whisper down the back. A young DC was snickering behind his hand, muttering something about inbreeding and sheep shaggers. His hair was sticking up in an absurd quiff and he had a pair of huge, bat-like ears. Despite these unfortunate appendages, with his expensive suit and crocodile skin shoes the flash bastard looked like he'd stepped out of the pages of *Vogue* or *Esquire*. He was full of himself, no doubt trying to impress his mates. Jack's nostrils flared as he took in the smug face. He waited until a passing train had thundered past before fixing him with a cold blue eye. 'Care to share your pearls of wisdom, Constable?' he invited. The young man reddened and shrugged. Jack persisted. 'Name?'

'Err, DC Downer.'

Jack pounced: 'DC Downer, *sir*!'

The miscreant's neck glowed redder and although he dutifully repeated Jack's words Jack was not finished with him.

'OK. Just to get things straight, *Constable* Downer, despite what you think you know about Tasmanians, neither Sergeant Flakemore nor myself has two heads or a tail. Moreover, the average Tasmanian IQ is no lower than here.' He paused. 'Come to think of it though, certain would-be comedians may have severely depressed the Victorian average.'

Jack took a sip of water and waited for the embarrassed laughter to die down. He didn't like humiliating the boy but was aware of the old schoolteacher's adage 'start as you mean to finish.' Blokes like Nick Downer were not long out of school and sometimes behaved if they were still there. Jack vaguely wondered how he could afford such expensive clothes on a constable's salary. Daddy's money, no doubt. The bastard reeked of privilege.

'Now, on a more serious matter,' Jack said with another glare at Downer, whose metaphorical tail was drooping in craven surrender. 'The EPA asked us to raid an illegal waste dump in Tottenham. The EPA and our own forensic experts are examining the scene and will report back in due course, but I can tell you that the dump contains household and commercial rubbish and some medical waste, along with a vast number of steel barrels. The barrels contain chemicals, some of which are highly toxic. Many are rusting and are discharging liquids into the nearby creek. We also found a corpse, as yet unidentified.'

Shocked whispers buzzed round the room.

'Witnesses state that early yesterday morning they saw a Toyota HiAce smash through the premises' gates and drive away at high speed. The van has not yet been located and neither do we know who the driver or passengers were. We do know, however, that the van's owner is a man called Terry Tudge, domiciled in St Kilda. He's got a lengthy list of priors. Unfortunately, he's been missing from his flat and the neighbours haven't clocked him for weeks. We'll know some more when forensics get back.'

Jack paused and pinned a blown-up print of Tudge's face on the whiteboard. There were snorts and snickers. The American term 'loser' sprang to mind. Two watery brown eyes stared out listlessly at the camera. *MAD* magazine without the grin …

'Pathetic,' someone muttered. 'A nuisance since birth.'

Jack smiled and stuck up another mugshot. A truly mean face glowered out at the world. 'Now, this one's plug ugly too, but a hell of a lot more dangerous, I'd say. We're calling him "Chappie" for the time being because he won't tell us his name.' Jack waited until the murmurs died down. 'We found Chappie out at the dump in Tottenham yesterday evening. He was trying to escape after hiding among the chemical drums all day. We'll be continuing the interrogation later this morning. The drums were leaking, by the way. God only knows what's in them and he's been wallowing in the muck.

'Now, something for the ghouls: there was also a severed arm mixed up with the waste. It is possible that other body parts will be found, but this is speculation at this stage. The tattoo on the arm points to the arm's owner being a member of the Molochs Marauders bikie gang. The pathologist doesn't think it was surgically removed. We'll have to follow that up, because either there's a bikie running round with one arm, or his other bits or his whole corpse will turn up. What we do know is that it doesn't belong to the dead body we also found in the tip, because that is intact, save for a gunshot wound to the chest.'

Another shockwave buzzed round the room, after which it was so quiet that you could hear old Bruiser Macfarlane objurgating a junior constable in the foyer.

'The body is male,' Jack continued. 'Dr Swinburne puts his age at around forty and estimates the time of death as early yesterday morning. We'll know more once the autopsy results are in.'

Jack took another sip of water and indicated that Vicky Tran should take over. He had taken a shine to the young woman and believed she had the ability to go far up the hierarchy. There was a keen intelligence and determination in her brown eyes, and she spoke clearly and to the point.

'Thank you, sir,' Vicky began. 'Now, we have also located

a handgun near where the body was found. Preliminary examination indicates that it was fired recently. It's a Smith & Wesson but any identifying numbers have been filed off. Forensics are checking for fingerprints.

'As you will know, none of the other illegal, smaller dump-sites located before DCI Martin arrived have yielded any clues, so we are hoping for a breakthrough here. Witnesses have identified a trucking firm called McCastle Logistics as carting material to the place. You'll find the locals call the firm McArseholes.'

Jack stepped forward and held up a hand to quell the resulting merriment. 'One more thing. We have a report that Tobias Malouf, known as Fat Toby, was snooping round the tip.' A ripple of whispers spread round the room. 'Yes. That's him: the drug cartel boss. Our informant says that he drove off quickly when he saw the police and EPA people. We'll have to follow that up too.'

There was a blur of activity as officers rushed to carry out their allotted tasks.

*

Vicky rolled her eyes when she was paired up with DC Darryl Puncheon. He was very young, very green and – she considered – very annoying.

'OK, Darryl,' she said. 'We'll be questioning the Molochs Marauders. Bikie gang on Geelong Road. Bollocks Consorters, I call them, but they're nasty types. Fingers in lots of criminal pies. Now you, Darryl, will listen and learn. Let me do the talking … oh, and don't forget your notebook.'

Nasty types indeed, she thought, but she was relishing the thought of stirring them up. 'Drive,' she commanded when they got in the police car, and Puncheon meekly obeyed. She was pleased to see that he repressed his boy racer instincts and steered carefully along Buckley Street and onto Geelong Road, the traffic sewer that cuts a broad swathe through Footscray's older suburban houses. Trucks thundered past, clogging up the six lanes, but Puncheon managed a deft U-turn at Roberts Street and drew up outside the bikie clubhouse in the service road facing back to Footscray. If he had expected praise from Vicky, he was mistaken. 'OK, Darryl. Don't forget to lock the car and follow me. Remember: let me do the talking.'

The sun's rays were merciless, and the windless air reeked of traffic exhaust, with a slight overlay from the Werribee sewage farm. The Molochs' lair squatted between an abandoned ice cream factory and the Dungeon of Delights massage parlour, which, surprisingly given the heat, was doing a brisk trade if the cars pulled up outside were any indication. Vicky wondered how the Molochs had got planning permission for their monstrous clubhouse. It vaguely resembled the Alamo; a log-built structure with the modern touch of a big steel door. There were bars on the tiny windows, which looked like they could double as loopholes for riflemen. A pirate skull and crossbones flag hung limp as a dirty dishrag on a rooftop pole and the fort sprawled over a double suburban block, surrounded by a chain link fence topped with razor wire. The front yard had been concreted over to form a kind of defensive glacis and there was not a patch of green save for some sickly weeds around the fence. Three or four overweight bearded blokes were stripped to the waist fiddling with their Harley hogs in a kind of hutch. They leered at Vicky and sneered at Puncheon. A rooftop sentry spoke into a walkie-talkie when the officers drew up. His nostrils quivered, fine-tuned to detect pork, Vicky knew.

Vicky held up her warrant card when an enormous bikie lumbered up to the gate scratching his balls and eating a meat pie. He gave the two cops a ferocious glare and bolted half the pie like a snake devouring its prey.

'Well, well, well,' Vicky observed. 'If it isn't young Godzilla.'

Gordon Pritchard, aka Godzilla, the gang's so-called Sergeant-at-Arms, grunted. His little eyes flitted this way and that, slitted against the sunlight. Godzilla was wide as a Sumo wrestler and at least six feet six in his malodorous socks. His Methuselah's beard had bits of meat and gravy in it. Tran muttered to Puncheon that Godzilla's IQ was at least seventy-five on a good day, sixty if he'd been on the booze, which was often.

'Whaddya want, Viet Cong?' Godzilla growled, spitting out of the side of his mouth, revealing the stumps of carious brown teeth. He was sweating profusely in the broiling heat and was distinctly whiffy.

'I'm Leading Senior Detective Constable Tran,' said Vicky, ignoring the insult and wrinkling her nose at the BO wafting through the gate. 'But then you know full well who I am. This, by the way, is DC Puncheon. He's a tiger at the martial arts so don't get stroppy. We'd like to speak to Bobby Mudford.'

Godzilla read their warrant cards carefully, his lips moving, before unlocking the gate and jerking his massive head towards the clubhouse door. Vicky had had dealings with him before, but he appeared to have forgotten her. Memory shot; drugs, she considered. He didn't speak, either because he didn't like the Filth or because the intellectual effort was too great. Or both.

'Nice tats Gordon,' she said, deadpan, pointing at the stylised letters MM tattooed on his massive biceps. 'Better make sure you don't lose 'em.'

Godzilla grunted something unintelligible in reply and barged through the steel door leaving a trail of body odour in his wake. He didn't hold the door open.

'And they call us pigs,' Vicky muttered as the door swung back in her face.

It was dark inside and an assortment of smells assailed their nostrils. *Essence du gang de motards*: stale beer and cigarettes, rancid sweat, unwashed clothes, dirty toilets, and burnt motor oil. No Estée Lauder Rose de Grasse Rouge here, not even Ralph Lauren Polo. Vicky almost laughed aloud at the thought. Menace hung heavy in the stifling air and although his colleagues joked about Puncheon by name and punch-on by nature, she saw that the rookie stayed close by her side. When her eyes had grown accustomed to the murk, she saw a group of bikies standing around a pool table, their eyes sharp as magpies sizing up booty.

A bar ran down one side of the room, the barman polishing glasses with a dirty rag. He spat on the floor at the sight of the unwelcome visitors. The bikies' 'Old Ladies' were drinking beer by the window. Noelene 'Big Mama' Hanson and Maxine 'Cougar' Lloyd were known to the police. The other women looked like wannabes. Vicky had booked the big redhead and the blowsy bottle blonde several times. Close up, she wrinkled her nose at an alarming smell: she could have sworn they'd doused themselves with Air Wick freshener in lieu of antiperspirant! Her eyes took in the den's other features. Photos ripped out of *Hustler* and *Playboy* served as artwork and a couple of fruit machines were winking in the corner, occasionally emitting electronic noises. Big Mama put a coin in the jukebox, and it blasted out AC/DC's 'Highway to Hell.' Very appropriate. Mama started dancing, with what Vicky realised were swastika earrings jiggling in time to the music.

Bobby 'Texas' Mudford, the Marauders' president, was a surprisingly small, neat man, with a pencil moustache, neat goatee and granny glasses – more like a hippy CEO than a bikie boss. No Air Wick for him; he was well acquainted with soap and water, aftershave even. Vicky figured he drove the late-model Beemer parked out the front. He was perched behind an old desk with a calculator, totting up the proceeds of something doubtless nefarious. His long blond hair looked clean, and he looked up with shrewd grey eyes when the detectives entered his office. He was chomping on a fat cigar. Godzilla was leaning against the back wall, still scratching his balls. He'd definitely caught something nasty. There was a huge Confederate flag tacked up on the wall behind and a banner with the Molochs Marauders' logo – an entwined *M & M* in what looked suspiciously like a hairy scrotum. Vicky shuddered at the thought of Godzilla's psoriasis-stricken bollocks. She wondered how Mudford put up with his smell but figured he wouldn't notice given the smoke from his cheroot thing. He didn't offer them a chair, but she sat anyway on a wooden chair and motioned for DC Puncheon to take the other. For Christ's sake, she thought, casting a sidelong glance at her offsider, the boy looks like he's a pupil summoned to the principal's office for a caning.

'Yeah?' rasped Texas. He glanced at his watch, his head wreathed in smoke like a buddha in a joss house.

'Bloke missing an arm,' said Vicky, deadpan.

He shrugged and said nothing.

'The thing is, Bobby, we've been out at Tottenham and found an arm. A human arm.' Texas's eyes opened slightly. 'Yes, Bobby, an arm: A-R-M. Spells "arm." *Cành tay* in my language. *Bras* in French. Said arm has your club tattoo on it, and we'd like to know where the rest of him is.'

'Dunno what you're talking about ossifer,' grunted the bikie, stubbing out his cheroot and fishing out another from the box. The nervous glance he exchanged with Godzilla did not escape Vicky's notice.

'Come on, Bobby old cheese,' she wheedled. 'Who else would have your symbol tattooed on their arm?'

'Copycats and wannabes?'

Vicky gave him a level stare. 'Now now, Mr Mudford. We know your boys were driving trucks out at an illegal tip in Tottenham and we've heard about the problems you've been having.'

'No problems, copper.'

'In that case, you won't mind if we fingerprint your members.'

'Get a warrant,' said Texas.

'Yeah, we'll do that, but it so happens that we've got the prints of most of your crew already. The ladies too. Anyway, Bobbikins, believe it or not, we're trying to help you here. Can't be very pleasant having someone running round chopping off your members' bits. Ouch.' She winced theatrically. 'This wasn't the first one, was it, this arm?'

Texas shrugged again and stared back at Vicky, his grey eyes unwinking. 'All sorted,' he grunted.

'Mind you keep 'em, Bobby,' said Vicky leaning forward and pointing at the tats on his folded arms. 'Your boy lost his.'

Texas lit another cheroot and jerked his head to the door. Interview terminated.

A dozen pairs of hostile eyes followed the detectives as they walked back through the clubroom. Back out in the sun's blinding glare, Godzilla saw them off the premises. The goons out front with the hogs were running round tipping buckets of water on each other like kids, forgetting they were hard men.

'Cleanest they've been in weeks,' muttered Vicky, adding more loudly: 'Free tip, Godzilla. Rexona Men's Body Spray. You'll be a hit with the girls.'

'Get fucked, ya slope bitch,' snarled Godzilla, slamming the gate viciously.

'Temper, temper!' Vicky chided. She was smirking as she walked across the yellow grass of the nature strip.

While they were buckling up their seat belts, DC Puncheon asked her what she thought the bikie boss had meant when he said, 'All sorted.'

'Dunno,' she replied, indicating that he should pull out into the traffic. 'My guess is that Mr Mudford has tried to do a deal with this new Tantalus mob. He wouldn't tell us anything anyway. They're running scared, though.'

CHAPTER 6

Meanwhile, Terry Tudge's HiAce van had been found in North Road, Newport, the suburb sandwiched between Spotswood and Williamstown under the power station smoke-stack. The van's front was bashed in, it was missing a headlight, and the paint had been gouged all along one side. There was no sign of occupants, turbaned or otherwise, and passers-by said they knew nothing about it. Similarly, Fat Toby Malouf was not to be found at his house or in any of his known haunts. Shown a photo, Scorcher Dalton had confirmed that it was Malouf who had hurriedly driven away from the tip in a blue Ferrari. Then, entirely unexpectedly, Malouf had turned up at the Footscray police station with his lawyer in tow.

Fat Toby was sweating copiously as he sat facing Jack Martin and Liz Flakemore in the interview room. The two detectives exchanged knowing glances: so this slug was the mighty Drug Lord they'd heard so much about. Perched on the edge of his hard chair, he looked more like the proprietor of a suburban fish and chip shop than a criminal mastermind who had made millions of dollars from importing heroin, cocaine, hashish, and the newer synthetic drugs. He had small brown eyes set too close together, receding dark hair, and at least three wobbling chins, which were already sprouting a thick five o'clock shadow. He looked like an overweight weasel, but the detectives realised it would be foolish to underestimate him. He was, after all, the self-made CEO of an extraordinarily successful enterprise.

Toby had done time in Pentridge, but that was decades ago, and since then he had avoided arrest despite building up a formidable criminal empire. Now, quite unexpectedly, he had thrown himself on the mercy of the Victoria Police. He had arrived with his lawyer, Sam Birdwhistle, an unctuous little fellow with Uriah Heep mannerisms who was known to the police as 'Slippery Sam'. Sam looked harmless but he was devious. He specialised in looking after the interests of some of the most dangerous types in the country. He wasn't as smooth as some of the criminal lawyers Jack and Liz had encountered, but he was just as effective.

Toby was old school male chauvinist, so Liz took the lead after Jack had fiddled with the tape recorder. 'Now, Toby, we know you talked with the duty sergeant, but you'll have to run it all past us again.'

Toby looked from Jack to Liz and back as if asking why he didn't put this sheila in her place, but Jack merely smiled.

Toby was flustered. 'Yeah, well, I err wanna make a deal.'

Slippery Sam took over. 'My client is proposing that you grant him immunity from prosecution and provide him with a new identity. In return, he will tell you all he knows about the illegal narcotics trade, including details of the new how shall I put it … the new firm that is taking control from the older networks.'

'Including details of your client's business?'

'Yes, that is the deal we propose.' He sat back and wrung his hands as if trying to squeeze water from them.

Liz looked at her colleague and raised her eyebrows. They hadn't expected this, but then they hadn't really known what to expect since Malouf and his lawyer had turned up shortly before.

'Now that all sounds very promising,' said Liz, 'but we will have to relay this to our superior officers for …'

Slippery Sam cut in. 'With respect, Inspector, we realise that, so in the meantime my client would like police protection. His life has been threatened and we must take the threats seriously.'

Fat Toby's eyes were flitting between Jack and Liz. Hiding a grin, Liz signalled to Jack to take over.

'OK, Mr Malouf, we can do that, but we can't promise anything else at this stage. We will put you up in a safe house and resume once we get word whether immunity is an option.'

*

The police safe house to which Fat Toby was delivered in an unmarked car was a nondescript white painted one-storey weatherboard in a cul-de-sac off the Esplanade in the bayside suburb of Altona. It had a view of sorts of the tops of the Norfolk Island pines along the waterfront and there was a tiny patch of grass out the back much frequented by magpies.

'Dreary as a Sunday arvo in Wodonga,' Toby muttered,

surveying the op-shop furniture and the Sacred Heart on the wall. A tap dripped relentlessly and there was no air-conditioning. There was a flight of ducks on the wall, one missing its head. Jeez, he'd been a man to reckon with and now he was hiding in this shithole like a loser. He pulled out his mobile phone and tapped in a number. The call rang out and he swore viciously before re-dialling. Eventually his wife, Gloria, answered. 'Where the fuck ya been?' he demanded. She said something placatory and he calmed down a bit.

'Now, big boy,' she cooed. 'Tell Glo-Glo what it's all about.'

'Carn tell ya where I am,' he blurted, 'but it's a fuckin' hole.'

'Eh?'

'I'm in the shit, Glo. Now, I'd like ya to book a room in that city place … You know, where we had our wedding reception.'

'But why, dear?'

'Carn tell ya that … oh, fact is, some cunt sent me a dum-dum bullet. By courier … Oh Glo, everythin's gone pear-shaped.' He was frantically running his rosary beads through his palms.

'Oh luvvy. Don't cry. It'll be fine, I'm sure …'

'You reckon? Jeez Glo, I drove out to me shed to check supplies but there was coppers swarmin' all over the fuckin' place …'

'Oh dear.'

'Yeah. Chances are that new firm'll reckon I shopped 'em to the coppers. They don't muck about … Anyway, Glo, Slippery Sam said the best thing was for me to get police protection and spill me guts. Don't fancy concrete boots like they done them Micks.'

His phone was wet with sweat.

CHAPTER 7

Big Dixie Trumble's jaw had dropped, and his silver tabby cat was stretched up to the windowsill on her hind legs with her tail swishing, at the impertinence of the strange men who had waltzed into the front garden and were eating his tomatoes and snow peas. 'Wolfin' em down!' Dixie told Mrs Burns over the back fence later that day. The retired wharfie's vegetable garden was lovingly tended and fertilised with seaweed he carted from down the bay in his old Holden ute. He already had a bumper crop, but the intruders were going through it like a plague of locusts. Dixie had rolled up the worn sleeves of his work shirt, ready to see off the intruders. He was 78 years old, but a lifetime under the hook loading and unloading ships had left him lean and rangy. He'd never backed off from a blue though he'd never started any. Except with the stevedoring bosses.

'I was real wild at first,' he told Mrs Burns, 'but Jeez, people like us know hunger when they see it. The poor bastards was starvin.'

Dixie had grown up during the Great Depression when his

wharfie father had lined up at the dock gates of a morning, anxious to get the foreman's nod for a day's work. They'd called the Sydney waterfront the 'Hungry Mile' and it had been the same on the Melbourne wharves. Dixie recalled his dad's shame when they had to accept charity or starve.

The men looked startled when he came out bearing a tray of lemonade. 'Here you are fellas,' he said, taking in their shabby clothes and frightened eyes. They seemed to have difficulty accepting that the refreshments were for them and that he wasn't angry. The sun was pitiless. Nobody had been kind to them since they arrived in this strange country. They slurped their drinks gratefully and stood wide-eyed, taking in the big man. Dixie noticed an old bomb of a minibus outside, parked at an angle to the kerb with the doors sprung wide open like wings.

'Yours?' Dixie jerked his thumb towards the vehicle.

'We drove it here,' said one of the men, 'but it ran out of gas.' He was wearing a turban and spoke heavily accented English.

There were four of them. 'A bit like Arabs I thought. But they was Kurds,' Dixie told Mrs Burns. 'Different mob. They was shit-scared and tired. Anyway, I invited them in and cooked 'em up a feed. Toast, bacon an' eggs, fried tomatoes, baked beans. Coffee. Most of 'em wouldn't come at the bacon but they gobbled the rest. I figured they was Moslems.' He paused. 'There was a funny smell coming off them. Chemicals, like when your Bert and me would unload the ships at the Yarraville wharves. Poor buggers didn't have a clue where they was.

'I twigged they was escaped asylum seekers, so I put me thinking cap on while they got stuck into more tucker.

Buggered if I was gunna hand 'em over to the wallopers. They deport people like that soon as look at 'em.'

Mrs Burns shook her head. 'Be careful, Dixie. They'd be asylum seekers.' She wasn't wearing her hearing aid again. 'That Hanson woman is screaming about "illegals" and the Guvmint talks about nothin' else. You can get into big trouble for helping them.'

Dixie shrugged. 'You don't have to do nothing wrong to get into trouble in this country, Mrs B. Anyway, you'd remember Sister Susan Lawless? Tiny little thing. She come to the union barbecue down at Willy a little while back.'

'Tiny little thing,' said Mrs Burns. 'I met her at that union barbecue down at Williamstown.'

Dixie smiled. He was a retired member of a militant left-wing union and hard as nails. Susan was a diminutive Catholic nun. She was quiet and gentle but always prepared to stand up for the underdog. He reckoned she was tougher than him. He'd known her since the Vietnam Moratorium days and he figured if anyone would know how to help it would be her.

When the men had finished eating, Dixie let them clean up in his bathroom before piling them into his jalopy. He'd assured the turban bloke that he wasn't going to turn them over to the police. Those in the tray, he hid under the tatty old tonneau cover, apologising for the bits of seaweed and empty plastic bags. It was only five minutes' drive to the nuns' house in Williamstown: a rambling, red brick, two-storey structure across the road from the Botanic Gardens. It stood in spacious grounds and was surmounted with a large stone Celtic cross.

Sister Susan understood the situation before Dixie opened his mouth. She herded the men inside and bustled round welcoming them with tea and scones while quizzing Dixie about them. Nuns like Sister Susan Lawless were a puzzle to Dixie. The Church had always meant B.A. Santamaria and the DLP. He'd lost his faith when Franco's fascist myrmidons were crushing the Spanish Republic and the Church was cheering them on. But this diminutive nun was a gentle militant for causes that put her at loggerheads with the establishment and much of the Church hierarchy. Especially that bloody Archbishop Pell. When she'd settled the men down in the shabby-comfortable parlour, she went to ring around to find a Kurdish interpreter. Dixie took his leave and the young one they called Sister Monica waved goodbye at the front door. Dixie recalled the nuns in his long-gone, half-forgotten schooldays. Some were kind but too many were quick to wield the strap, and they had given him no sympathy when his mum died. Jeez, if they'd had nuns like Sisters Susan and Monica at school, he might still be wearing out the knees of his strides at Mass. Pigs might fly.

There was a police car parked outside Dixie's house when he got back home, and two constables were peering inside the minibus. 'Afternoon sir,' said the smaller of the two, a young woman. Looked too young to be a copper Dixie reckoned. 'You don't happen to know anything about this vehicle?'

'Nah,' fibbed Dixie. 'I seen it parked there earlier. Abandoned is it?'

'You haven't seen who was driving?' asked the other constable, a young fellow trying for the hard-boiled look he'd seen in older coppers. Or on TV.

'Can't say I have.'

'Well if you do remember anything could you give the Footscray Police a bell?' The young woman handed him her card. 'Someone will be round in a bit to tow it away.'

'Yeah, sure thing,' said Dixie, pocketing the card and opening his front gate. 'Probably kids joyriding.'

CHAPTER 8

Liz and Jack were already waiting and DC Downer ('Flash Nick', they'd learned his colleagues called him) had the recording apparatus ready to go when 'Smiler' O'Reilly, the sexagenarian custodian of the cells, frogmarched 'Chappie' into the interview room. Vicky Tran should have been in on the interview, but she was out on another job.

O'Reilly glared at the prisoner as he pushed him down onto a hard chair. 'Dirty bastard,' he said, looking as if he wanted to wipe his hands. 'Pisses all over the toilet seat. Doesn't flush it or wash his hands. Refused to talk when we booked him in last night. Anyway, he's all yours.'

'Give cigarette,' Chappie demanded. When there was no response, he tapped the table with a hairy finger. 'I say give cigarette.'

Liz leaned forward to get a closer look at him and recoiled at the chemical smell. 'You can't smoke in here,' she said. 'Stunt your growth anyway.'

'Eh?'

An ugly red rash had spread over Chappie's face and hands.

No doubt it was elsewhere under the jumpsuit. As if on cue, he began to scratch the backs of his hands, then his arms and then his sides. He needed medical assistance, so Jack paused the interview while Liz went out to contact the duty doctor. When she returned, they began recording and went through the preliminaries. Chappie was silent but they persisted, demanding to know his name.

'No? Well, it doesn't matter,' said Jack. 'You're going nowhere. Anyway, you are entitled to legal representation. We can call the duty solicitor if you wish.'

Chappie shrugged and mimed smoking a cigarette until he started to scratch again.

'Nasty rash, Chappie,' said Liz. 'Those chemicals are nasty things, and you were covered in the stuff.'

His left eyelid twitched.

'Doctor's coming,' said Jack, 'so how about you stop mucking us about?'

There was a knock and a young constable stuck her head round the door. 'Excuse me sir,' she said, 'but there's a lawyer out in the lobby. Says he's come to represent Chappie here.'

They suspended the interview and left the suspect demanding cigarettes, watched over by Flash Nick, who wasn't too pleased with his close proximity to the stinker. The boss met them in the corridor and took them into his office.

'I'll not keep you long,' Foxcroft said. 'Just give you the heads up on Chappie's solicitor. His name's Cornelius Bentley. Bent by name and bent by nature, this one. There's any number of scumbags walking round free in this city because of him. Smooth but sharp, and well-connected. He's dreaming up all kinds of complaints, so you'd best not keep him waiting.'

Bentley was sitting bolt upright in the foyer, with a well-dressed young woman by his side. Bruiser Macfarlane was making a show of ignoring them, focusing on opening a packet of Anzac biscuits. Bentley peered at his gold watch when Liz and Jack entered the vestibule. They took him in immediately: sixtyish, thousand-dollar suit, silver hair coiffured at a hundred dollars a pop, elegant Italian shoes, perfectly creased linen handkerchief in his breast pocket, brilliant white teeth c/o some exclusive city clinic, expensive Eau de Cologne competing with the young woman's perfume. She sat unsmiling, taking in her surroundings with an expression on her thin lips as if she eaten a lemon.

'He reminds me of Dorian Grey,' Liz muttered. It was possible there was a horrible portrait in the bloke's Toorak attic.

'Mr Bentley,' said Jack, professionally civil. 'I'm DCI Martin and this is Detective Sergeant Flakemore. We're sorry to keep you waiting.'

Bentley gave a condescending smile. 'I haven't had the pleasure. I assume you're new here?'

'Yes. May we ask your business?'

'I'm here to represent my client, Darko Percović, whom I believe you have in custody.' Liz and Jack exchanged a glance. Aha! Chappie had a name at last. 'Oh, and I should say, this is Miss Erica Betts, she's new to our chambers and is learning the ropes.'

Taking in Miss Betts's prim features and conservative clothing, Liz wondered if there was a female equivalent of 'young fogey'. The young lawyer's dark brown hair was cut short and neatly permed, and her tweed suit and pearl necklace were redolent of times long past in the English

Home Counties. A pair of sensible brown brogues completed her attire.

'We do have a male in custody,' said Liz, 'but he's been refusing to talk except to demand cigarettes. I assume that this is the person you mean, but may I ask how you know he's here and who engaged you to represent him?'

'Oh come, come, Inspector,' Bentley chided. 'You can't expect us to tell you that, but yes, I assume we are talking about the same person. Now, we would like to talk with our client before you interrogate him.'

They walked Bentley and Betts through to the interview room and left them with the suspect, who was still loudly demanding a smoke. He was out of luck, because neither Bentley nor Betts smoked, even if they'd been allowed to smoke in the station.

Jack looked at his watch. Lunch time. 'Time for a stroll and a bite to eat?'

Liz readily agreed and they left the station and strolled round to the Footscray mall, trying vainly to find pockets of shade on the way. There was a sizeable crowd halfway along the mall, milling around outside the electorate office of the local State Labor MP. The office looked firmly shut, although a tweaking of the venetian blinds suggested that the incumbent or some staffers were lurking inside.

A tall, bespectacled, dark-haired man was haranguing the crowd through a megaphone. 'If they want our votes, they can't take us for granted,' he declaimed, and the crowd muttered its approval. A round, grandmotherly woman was standing by his side, dishing out leaflets to passers-by. Youths were sloping in and out of the 'Gobble 'n' Go' greasy spoon, oblivious to the rally, and some boozers had come out of the pub to see what the fuss what about. The two old blokes Jack had met out at the Tottenham tip, Herbie Wise and Scorcher Dalton, were holding up a professionally made banner, which declaimed NO MORE TOXIC WASTE NEAR OUR HOMES AND SCHOOLS! and sported a drawing of a bulldog wearing a gas mask. Two uniformed constables were standing by, one of them fat and the other thin. Jack had seen them round the station but didn't know their names. They bore a striking similarity to Laurel and Hardy.

'What's up?' Jack asked the pair, discreetly flashing his warrant card.

'It's the DETOX mob again sir,' replied Thick.

'Protesting about chemicals and that,' added Thin.

'The one with the megaphone's Dr Abrams,' chimed in Thick. 'He's a professor up the road at the university.'

'Bit of a commo if you ask me,' said Thin. 'The old sheila's Doreen Cartland and she ain't much better.'

'Blokes holding the banner are union red raggers.'

'Notorious,' Thin added.

Given what he'd seen out at Tottenham, Jack could see why the DETOX crowd were protesting. It also dawned on him that Thick and Thin were responsible for leaving the squad car in a disgusting condition.

He was considering drawing them aside when a man came up and thrust a microphone at him. 'I'm the Bagman, reporting for Radio 3CR,' he said. 'I wonder if you've any comments about the protest?' Jack waved him politely away and he turned to an old chap who was standing by with a sour look on his chops. 'I don't protest!' the fellow said, and waddled off to observe from a safer distance, mumbling to himself in German. 'Bloody well should do,' muttered the Bagman, glaring at the codger. 'Bastards are poisoning us.'

Jack laughed and he and Liz went into a Turkish café and ordered falafel sandwiches and coffee. The TV was on. A panel of talking heads were denouncing Victoria University as 'Footscray's Kremlin,' a hotbed of leftist academics leading the nation's youth astray and trying to subvert the local community like a mob of long-haired Narodniks. The man with the megaphone, Dr Abrams, came in for some heavy verbal stick. Liz was shaking her head. It wasn't so long ago that Hobart police had donned rubber gloves to arrest gay rights demonstrators.

'Can't say I blame Dr Abrams and his friends,' she muttered. Jack nodded. He'd liked old Herbie and Scorcher and hoped they and their DETOX friends were successful.

The harassed-looking proprietor handed over their food and they went outside to find somewhere out of the sun to eat. A booming voice was echoing off the shopfronts down near the demonstrators. As they approached, they saw a squat, red-haired police officer haranguing the demonstrators through a loud hailer. The pips on his epaulettes and braid on his cap testified to his high rank. A phalanx of baton-wielding paramilitary officers was drawn up behind him, booted and spurred, eyeing the protest with undisguised malice.

'You've made your point, men,' boomed the redhead. 'This is an illegal gathering. You must disperse immediately. You're interfering with people going about their lawful activities.' He passed the loud hailer to an underling, thrust his hand to his breast, and turned to inspect his troops like Napoleon viewing the Grand Armée before the Battle of Austerlitz.

'What's going on?' Liz asked Thick and Thin.

'Assistant Commissioner Lennox.'

'Telling them their fortunes.'

'They'll get what for.'

'He's got the Squad with him.'

'Force Response Unit.'

'Means business!'

'I'll not warn you again,' said Paul Lennox, grabbing back the megaphone. A flock of birds startled into flight.

'Bloody fascists!' shouted the Bagman, fiddling with his tape recorder. 'You should be ashamed of yourselves!' Blasted thing was stuck.

The Squad had drawn their long batons and were preparing to move forward to clear the mall of protesters. The old bloke who was proud not to protest looked on approvingly, telling anyone close by that the Red Rabble needed a taste of the baton. The protest organisers were arguing among themselves: one faction wanted to stand their ground, but other voices were urging Scorcher and Herbie to pack away the DETOX banner. The venetian blinds twitched in the local MP's window just as the Squad started to move forward chanting MOVE! MOVE! MOVE! The front row thrust their batons before them like bayonets, the row behind prepared to swing theirs down. The banner was ripped in two and old Herbie was shoved into the side of the building, squawking like an outraged parrot. 'Fucking Stormtroopers!' yelled the Bagman just before a baton thumped the side of his head. Dr Abrams was urging everyone to leave but that didn't stop an eager *squadrista* from giving him a solid whack about the shoulders and another one in the stomach for good measure.

It was over within minutes. The mall was cleared. Law and order was restored. It was business as usual. The old German fellow went off smirking. The demonstrators limped away, leaving behind the wreckage of their banner. Discarded leaflets fluttered in the hot wind and someone sobbed. Lennox was standing jut-jawed, like Mussolini watching socialists being force fed castor oil, Jack thought. Wendy would have something to say about the fracas, for sure. He exchanged a glance with Liz and they made their way slowly back round to the police station, feeling vaguely shell-shocked. They learned later that the Squad had been seen practising their moves the day before down near the docks.

*

Darko Percović was still closeted with his lawyers when Jack and Liz returned from lunch. Finally, Miss Betts poked her neat head round the door and indicated that they were ready for the interview to begin. She sounded like a female Dalek. When the detectives entered, Bentley was fussing with a sheaf of papers, writing something with his fat white fountain pen. Or pretending to. Betts had taken a back seat, keen to absorb the Great Man's wisdom. Bentley looked up over his half-moon spectacles and started to speak, extending a proprietorial hand towards Percović, who was slouching his chair, breathing heavily through his mouth.

'All in good time, sir,' said Jack as Flash Nick finished fiddling with the recording apparatus and Liz went through the preliminaries. Jack already loathed the lawyer and had to try hard to hide it. Bentley went to say something else but closed his mouth when a dull roar from somewhere outside set the windows rattling. It temporarily drowned out the voice booming in the station carpark. Lennox had lined up his victorious troops for inspection and Liz wondered if he were pinning campaign medals on them.

'Mr Percović,' Jack began, determined not to be distracted by the noise and to forget what had happened in the mall. He tried to avoid looking at the lawyer's annoying face. 'You were apprehended late yesterday attempting to flee from a crime scene. The crime scene, to wit, is a Tottenham premises used for the illegal storage of chemicals and the dumping of other waste—'

Bentley interrupted. 'Our client wishes to state that he is totally innocent of any wrongdoing.'

'Noted,' said Jack. 'Now Mr Percović, we would like you to explain what you were doing at the premises.'

'Give cigarette,' Percović growled. The rash was very visible now and he'd torn the skin on the backs of his hands from scratching.

'Enough of that, sir,' said Liz levelly. 'Just answer the question.'

Percović shrugged. 'No remember.'

'Our client suffered a head injury when he was arrested,' put in Bentley, injecting both concern and accusation into his voice. 'He may have a mild case of amnesia. He is, however, convinced that he has done nothing wrong.'

Bruiser Macfarlane knocked, entered, whispered in Liz's ear, and left with a look of contempt at the suspect and his lawyer.

After conferring with Jack in a whisper, Liz looked the lawyer full in the face. 'If you care to look through the window behind you,' she suggested, 'you will see there's a big black cloud of smoke over the rooftops.'

Bentley twisted his head around and raised his well-groomed eyebrows. The cloudless blue sky over the rooftops was turning black with smoke. Liz and Jack conferred in a whisper. Miss Betts peered out the window and turned back with a look of alarm on her face.

'If you don't mind, Mr Bentley,' said Liz, 'we'll suspend this interview here. The doctor's arrived to examine your client so we'll resume tomorrow. That rash needs urgent medical attention.' Bentley started to huff and puff but she cut him off. 'Oh, in case you're wondering, the Tottenham dump has just exploded and it's raining god knows what over the western suburbs.'

The interview room had gone dark; the smoke cloud had blotted out the sun and was swirling up into the sky and drifting south before the hot northerly wind. When Jack and Liz stepped outside, the smoke pall was so thick that the temperature had dropped two degrees or so, and a caliginous gloom had settled over the street. Even Assistant Commissioner Lennox was silent. The blare of fire engine sirens filled the air as Liz and Jack drove out of the carpark, headed for Tottenham. Their radio crackled: nobody had been hurt in what they learned had been a massive blast. The police and EPA people out there were lucky. Fire engines were converging from across the metropolitan area and the order had been given for residents to evacuate from within a two-kilometre radius of the fire.

As they neared the site, they passed two buses full of children from the kindergarten Herbie Wise had pointed out. They parked at a distance but close enough to see flames and thick black smoke boiling up hundreds of feet into the air. Every so often, there was the thump of something exploding and a plume of orange or red fire would leap fifty metres or more into the sky. The roof had been blown off and the corrugated iron sides had been vaporised by the intense heat, which was buckling and even melting the steel frame. An unnatural stench caught the backs of their throats.

A ring of fire engines had partly encircled the site, and they were starting to play water at the seat of the fire. Firefighters were walking around in what looked like organised chaos, thick white hoses snaking this way and that in apparent confusion, but Jack knew they were acting methodically. The heat from the inferno was immense and the smoke thick and choking. An evil black sludge was flowing slowly from the ruins, smoking like lava, towards the chain link fence and the creek. If anything, the jets of water from the firefighters' hoses only seemed to make the fire seethe more angrily.

Jack and Liz found themselves speaking with the senior fire officer, Michaela Schiebal, a fit, fiftyish woman who was watching the jets of water playing onto the fire with a worried look on her face. She sighed. 'Bloody water's not working. We're going to have to use chemical foam to try to smother it.' She looked back at the flames again. 'We've still got no idea of what the chemicals are or where they came from. Some of the paler-skinned firies are already getting sunburn from the glare of the flames, they're so hot.'

It was a disaster, but there was nothing the two detectives could do to help. It was unlikely that Darko Percović would be able to help even if he'd wanted to. His rash had worsened, he had developed a rasping cough with bloody sputum, and the doctor had insisted on his immediate transfer to the Western General Hospital. An ambo told Jack later that he had demanded cigarettes all the way to A & E, where he proceeded to badger the nurses for a smoke and had to be physically refrained from assaulting the staff when they attempted to bathe him and treat his wounds.

CHAPTER 9

Denise Sugden, the McCastle Logistics receptionist, was a hard-faced bottle blonde with a sharp nose for pork. She immediately clocked the young beanpole and the Asian woman crunching across the gravelled freight yard as plain-clothes coppers. Streetwise Denise wore her dyed blonde hair piled atop her head and was tough as a roadhouse steak. She'd once played bass guitar in an all-girl country & western band and had been runner-up in the Miss Bikie's Moll beauty pageant in Broadford back in the day. She fitted the ambience of the Shepparton trucking depot with its barbed wire fences and expanses of gravel. All it needed was guard towers and men in black to turn it into the film set for a Nazi concentration camp and Denise bore an unsettling resemblance to the infamous death camp guard Irma Grese.

McCastles obviously thought that including the word 'Logistics' in their name made them sound trendy, but the feel of the place was distinctly seedy. A Confederate flag fluttered lazily in the wind. Six large rigs were parked inside the compound and two bored Alsatians had flopped down next to their lengths of wire, panting in the heat. The cops had merited a perfunctory growl; the dogs picked them as coppers as easily as Denise. There were half a dozen Harley Davidson hogs round the back along with a big red American pickup truck, which sported a yellow sticker announcing, 'WE'RE AUSSIES WE DRINK BEER WE EAT MEAT WE SPEAK FUCKUN ENGLISH.'

Quicker than a bikie on speed, Denise alerted her boss that detectives were about the enter the building: 'Pigs are coming, Brendan,' she hissed. So they were; Vicky Tran was looking forward to the confrontation with the McCastle's boss. It might have been nudging 40 degrees Celsius, but she hadn't raised a sweat. Darryl Puncheon, in contrast, was perspiring copiously and his Target suit was a sodden mass of wrinkles. Denise hated the police and she was a dinky-di racist, but she kept her sneers to herself. When they came through the door, she was sitting behind her melamine desk trying to look innocent. A stunted pot plant sat on the windowsill behind her, regretting that it had left Bunnings. The Rolling Stones 'Jumpin' Jack Flash' was thumping behind an internal door.

Denise put on a plastic smile. 'Can I help youse?' She sounded as sincere as a politician's promise.

Vicky didn't stand on ceremony. She flashed her warrant card. 'Police,' she growled. 'We'd like to speak with Mr Brian McCastle.'

'I'm afraid Mr *Brendan* McCastle is in a meeting,' Denise simpered, leaning over to show some cleavage for Puncheon's benefit. Her boss was not in any meeting and she knew they knew it; it was a game, and she had kept enough of her looks for most men to play along. Puncheon ogled her for a bit but desisted when Vicky gave him a sharp 'Down Boy!' look.

'Funny meeting where they play old Stones numbers,' Vicky Tran snapped, shoving up the hinge-mounted counter and letting it back down with a bang. 'Come on, Darryl: man to interview, crimes to fight.'

Brendan McCastle was scowling over his desk when the two detectives strode into his office after a token knock. The record player was now playing 'Get Off My Cloud.' A large, fleshy man with a thick salt and pepper mullet low on his brow, he watched his visitors through little blue eyes set a trifle too close together. His walls were decorated with posters of the Rolling Stones and there was a framed photograph of him with Denise Sugden and friends taken years before at what the caption said was his 'Thirty-Three-and-a-Third' birthday party.

'I'm Detective Tran and this is DC Puncheon,' Vicky announced, flashing her warrant card in McCastle's beefy face and glowering at the record player. 'Turn that off would you.' She shuffled a chair round the side of McCastle's desk so that the sun wasn't in her eyes and sat daintily, but with purpose. Puncheon slouched against the wall, notebook at the ready, trying for the hard-boiled look of bored contempt he'd observed in his senior colleagues.

McCastle reluctantly turned off the record player. 'What brings youse here?' His fat pink fists were parked on the desk like a pair of pig's trotters on a butcher's slab and Tran noted the faded tattoos on the knuckles – 'LOVE' on one and 'HATE' on the other – a dead giveaway that the man had done time.

'Don't come the innocent, Brian,' Vicky said evenly. 'I'll give you three guesses.'

'It's Brendan, officer,' McCastle protested. 'Has one of me

drivers had an accident?' He had a slight Kiwi accent.

'Now don't play silly buggers, Brian,' warned Vicky, wagging a slim finger in his face. 'We're CIB, not your country plod.'

'Beats me, ossifer,' said McCastle, folding his arms.

'Give the man a clue, DC Puncheon.'

'Little matter of transporting very dangerous chemicals to Tottenham, Brian.'

'Yeah?' sneered McCastle. 'Well, it's all legit. Bloke rang up and offered the job. We accepted. We did the job. We got paid. End of story. Anyway, fuck youse, the name's Brendan as you well know.'

'Ah, but it isn't the end of the story, is it?' Vicky retorted. 'The place you took the stuff to is an illegal dump site.'

'Heard the news? We just heard it blew up, didn't it,' added Puncheon, warming to the play.

'Not my problem,' shot back McCastle. 'As long as me paper-work's in order I'm in the clear.'

'We'll want to look at that,' put in Puncheon. 'Got the warrant here.' He fished around inside his suit jacket, unfolded the paper, and slid it over McCastle's desk.

McCastle inspected it and grinned. 'Nothing to find son,' he said. 'Search away.'

'Whaddya know about Molochs Marauders?' Vicky suddenly demanded.

'Err, nothin'.' McCastle shrugged, paused, and added, 'Sacked 'em, didn't I?'

'Oh, and why was that?'

'They was lazy as Poms on holiday. I had to let 'em go and got a new mob in.'

Vicky gave him a hard stare and changed the subject again.

'Didn't it cross your mind to bloody well ask about the place?'

McCastle just shrugged. 'Sad about the fire, but we only delivered legit stuff. Denise'll show you the paperwork.'

'We'll look at that,' said Vicky coldly. 'But you're dirty, Mr McCastle, and we'll get you sooner or later and put you back inside where you belong.'

'Hey! I've gone straight for years, detective,' McCastle protested. 'You can't harass me because I made mistakes when I was a young fella just over from Enzed.'

Vicky blew a raspberry, somehow managing to make it sound ladylike.

The invoices and receipts indicated that McCastle Logistics had been carting 'Chemicals, Miscellaneous' for an outfit calling itself 'Dynamic Achievers,' with the same address as the illegal dump in Tottenham. Only four deliveries spread out over three months. Picked up from various places around Melbourne's northern and western suburbs. Payment for these was in cash. There must have been more deliveries that were unrecorded and cash-in-hand, Vicky believed. They'd think of some charges for McCastle, but there was nothing in the reams of bumph that would lead them to the Dynamic Achievers crowd given that their address was at the dump and the signatures were illegible.

Vicky knew that the trucking boss had done time in Pentridge for fraud and assault years back but had a clean sheet for the past ten years – hadn't been caught, anyway. Brendan McCastle had been a bikie when he could still get his leg over a hog. His drivers wore bikie colours and they doubled as debt collectors and strike-breakers. Operated meth labs and brothels too. Denise on the front desk was married to the 'Sergeant-at-Arms' of the Sons of Odin bikie gang. She'd been arrested years back for soliciting and affray but like her boss she had kept her pointed nose clean for many years.

'Don't make plans to leave the country, Brian,' said Vicky as they were leaving. 'You can expect a visit from our corporate crime colleagues.' She turned back and inquired sweetly, 'Oh, Brian, I was wondering if you know what the locals call you?'

'Wot?'

'McArseholes. Apt isn't it? You've poisoned half of the city with shit.'

'Arrgoangefucked.' It was all one word.

Brendan McCastle lifted the phone as soon as he saw the detectives leave the building. He spoke quietly but urgently as he watched them drive out onto the Goulburn Highway. Then he turned the record over to play 'Honky Tonk Woman.' He 'loved that fuckin' song,' Denise reckoned, got her to dance to it on his desk. Striptease. High times in old Shepparton. Trust the pigs to spoil things.

The two detectives said nothing as they drove into town, stomachs rumbling, in search of lunch. There was a burger joint on Wyndham Street that would do the job. Puncheon was insistent. They 'dined in' and he shovelled in his 'fries' and wolfed his burgers with relish. Vicky marvelled that the boy enjoyed the stuff and could eat so much of it. Fair dinkum, the youth of today!

Puncheon turned and spoke with his mouth full of some fish and bacon thing: 'Reckon we've got enough to charge 'em, Vicky?'

Vicky shrugged. She'd pushed her 'meal' aside and was

anxious to get out of this depressing place with its cardboard food and the model of a clown out in the yard to terrify the kids. Not just kids either; she had a touch of coulrophobia herself ever since a man in a clown mask had tried to rape her when she was fifteen. Clowns might be the only things that scared her. Sinister things.

'We've still got another visit to make, so you'd best finish that,' she ordered, eyeing Puncheon's third burger with distaste. The thing looked like a cane toad squeezed between slabs of cardboard. The coffee had been foul.

Their destination was a small office block close to the river on Welsford Street. There were Harley Davidson motorcycles round the back and a couple of late model cars at the front. A couple of bikies were lounging about wool-gathering on a bench under a gum tree; they were spaced out on something, Vicky reckoned. One of them had baleful yellow eyes and was the spitting image of Joe Stalin. They exchanged glances as the cops walked past and made grunting noises.

'Second nature,' Vicky told the idlers.

'Eh?'

'The grunting,' she explained. 'For porkers like you, it's natural.'

'You're the fuckun pigs darlin',' the Stalin lookalike shot back.

'No second prizes Joe.'

'Eh?'

A directory board informed visitors that ALAN JOHN BADGER, CHARTERED ACCOUNTANT, was in Suite 8 on the first floor. 'Our man,' Tran informed her offsider. 'Let's go.'

'Word with the boss,' said Vicky, flashing her warrant card at the pretty platinum blonde secretary, who squawked ineffectually as they swept past. Unlike Denise Sugden, she was prim and proper. Probably had been a boarder at MLC.

Her boss was melting into his chair like a profane buddha fashioned from candlewax. He had a poker face, but they could tell he'd been tipped off that they were coming.

'Mr Alan Badger,' said Vicky, spinning out the syllables as if they were distasteful. 'Sorry to barge in on you like this.' She was nothing of the sort. Her nostrils twitched: the man even smelled dishonest. 'Now, it will come as no surprise to you that the premises you own in Tottenham have gone up in smoke. The boss just told us. The scene of a massive chemical fire as we speak.'

Badger spread his meaty hands wide. He was a corpulent middle-aged man with silver hair and small eyes set deep inside puffy cheeks, like ball bearings hiding from the light. With his bullfrog's multiple pouched chins, he could pass as Senator Mitch McConnell's Antipodean double. Business must have been good because his Armani suit left Puncheon's wrinkled old bag of fruit for dead and the gold Rolex on his wrist was a steal at $10,000, Vicky reckoned. There were framed testamurs on the walls together with photos of Badger mingling with local MPs and footballers. Vicky looked closely: there was one of him with the Cheshire Cat at a Liberal Party function. Another was a snap of Badger rubbing shoulders with the Silver Bodgie, his saturnine deputy glowering beside him like a surly Dublin pork butcher. Badger trimmed his sails to the prevailing political wind.

'Sorry,' Badger said. 'I had no idea.' The lie flowed easily off his oily chops.

Vicky grabbed a chair and sat facing Badger demurely, but

with a steely look in her eyes. 'Mr Badger,' she hissed. 'You own the Tottie dump so don't come the raw prawn with us.'

DC Puncheon was leaning up against the doorpost, practising a sneer, picking his teeth with a match. There must have been bits of burger in there. Nevertheless, Vicky was impressed. The boy was shaping up nicely. With a bit of practice, he might even look menacing.

'Oh, yes, *that* place. I'm with you now,' nodded Badger, setting his chins wobbling like jellies. 'I bought it as an investment some time ago, but apart from the once I've never set foot there. The idea was to let it accrue in value and sell it for a profit. Ripe for development, I thought.'

'So you've no idea what it's used for?'

'I honestly didn't. When it failed to sell, I leased it.'

'Life's hard,' muttered Puncheon.

'Leased to whom?' Vicky demanded.

'Fellow who lives at Mt Derrimut. I have his details on file if you would care to wait.'

'Just tell us,' Vicky Tran said evenly. 'Wouldn't be mixed up with a mob called Dynamic Achievers?'

'Oh yes, err, his name's Garth Dickins. Businessman. Straight shooter.'

Puncheon blew a raspberry. Not as good a one as his boss, but passable. The boy was getting there.

Badger made a play of looking offended. 'I don't know what you're implying, detective, but I run an honest business.' He had inflated himself like an outraged toad. Vicky wondered, if you stuck a pin in him, would he deflate and bounce off the walls before subsiding in a rubbery heap.

'Come on, Mr Badger,' she said, raising a languidly sceptical eyebrow. 'We know you're in with the Sons of Odin gang. In fact, their bikes are out the back with the bloke who looks like Stalin.'

'A starling? I don't get what you mean, sorry. But yes, I am doing the boys' taxes. Nothing illegal there.'

'Better not be.' Vicky scowled. 'Now, if your secretary can show us the lease deeds and give us Mr Dickins's details, we'll leave you to whatever it is you do.'

She stood up and moved towards the door. 'After you, DC Puncheon,' she said courteously before spinning round on her heel. She caught Badger with his hand on the phone looking like a boy caught raiding the lolly jar. 'Ah yes, one more thing,' she said, raising a forefinger. 'McCastle Logistics, what do you know about them? Sometimes called McArseholes.'

'Mc … McWhat?' stammered the accountant, his eyes sliding to the side.

Vicky stood with her arms crossed, smiling with a simulacrum of sweetness.

'Yes, yes, McCastles,' blustered Badger. 'I do seem to recall doing their tax a little while back.'

'I'll bet you did,' noted Vicky. 'Memory improving all the time.' She stared him down and added. 'Don't make any plans for a cruise, Mr Badger. We'll want another little talk before too long.'

The visit hadn't been entirely unproductive.

CHAPTER 10

Late that same day, people were coming and going through a nondescript door in a Carlton lane. Aloysius O'Donoghue's Bar was tucked away off Lygon Street in Carlton. Most of the folk who flocked to the street's Italian cafés and restaurants were unaware of its existence. Aloysius – 'Legs' to his customers – didn't advertise. There was only a small sign on the door, and he employed a couple of neckless goons to vet prospective customers. If the odd drunk or busybody found himself at the door, the minders saw him off quick smart. Five foot nothing when he left Dublin in a hurry years before, Legs stood on a raised platform behind the bar and kept a loaded pistol under the cash register 'just to be shure'. With his long oval eyes, button nose and the pronounced philtrum on his upper lip, he bore an uncanny resemblance to a rhesus monkey and spoke like one might too, in a coughing sort of voice with a thick Dublin accent.

Legs had his regulars. Alphonse 'Rocky' Gangitano, the self-styled 'Robert De Niro of Lygon Street' was a fixture and Graham 'The Munster' Kinniburgh dropped in for a snort from time to time. Legs's was strictly neutral turf: rival gangsters used to meet here to resolve differences amicably and the bouncers frisked everyone they didn't know as a condition of entry. Now, business was slack, with many of the regulars gone to ground or interstate since the irruption of the new crime firm. There was Carlton beer on tap – none of your poncy microbrewery piss here! – and hot pies and toasted ham and cheese sandwiches if you were peckish. Came up a treat in the microwave. Rocky the sophisticate had insisted on wine, so Legs catered for that with bottles of fourpenny dark that fell off the backs of trucks on the way to Jimmy Watson's wine bar further up Lygon Street. There was no political correctness here. Legs had admitted an Aboriginal gangster (now deceased) but equal opportunity for women stopped at the mouth of the lane. Old Ma Malone, Legs's reputed mistress, was the only woman ever to cross the threshold and she didn't make a habit of it. Now she'd cleared off to Sydney, taking her gorilla sons with her.

Legs was the soul of discretion; he spoke no evil, anything he overheard or saw stayed in the bar, and he was neutral in underworld disputes. If pushed, he muttered that the new firm would mellow and things would get back to normal, so they would. Strangely, this expat son of Republican Ireland had mounted a portrait of the Queen in pride of place above the bar, perhaps because his patrons, like many on the wrong side of the law, were Empire patriots and Liberal voters. Legs didn't give a rat's arse either way. He had no firm opinions about anything except money.

Two men were hunkered down in one of the high-backed booths with half-drunk pots of beer in front of them on this stuffy autumn evening. Their faces were obscured; Legs kept the lights down low, and the windows had not been washed since before the Melbourne Demons had won an AFL premiership. They were wearing hoodies, which made it even more difficult to discern their features, and you didn't look too closely or strain to listen if you knew what was good for you.

'Why you no warn us of raid?' Hoodie Number 1 hissed, leaning forward, and sloshing the remains of his beer around his glass. 'We pay you good. We expect results.' His voice was a low growl of menace.

'Sorry, but a new bloke's taken over,' Hoodie Number 2 replied, his voice sliding into a supplicating whine. He sounded young and was straining to sound tough. 'It's a big knob from Tassie and a girl copper with him. I didn't know about the raid until it happened. Honest.'

'Well in future we wanna know, or …' He left the threat hanging.

'Mate, I hear you,' Hoodie Number 2 begged, 'but it's all academic now. Place went up in smoke. Besides, the wogs got away before we arrived. Can't go far.'

'Not quite right,' said the foreign hoodie. 'Wogs got away but one of my men was arrested. Not good mister policeman, because wogs killed one of mine too.'

'Jeez, you can't pin that one on me, mate. Volatile, them wogs are. Volatile. Anyway, haven't I always given you good information?'

Hoodie Number 1 spread his chunky hands, conceding the point, but had to have the last word. 'OK, that true, but in future you tell us everything what cops plan. Yes?'

'Mate, you know you can rely on me,' the younger man

insisted. Haven't I given you the heads up every other time?'

'"Heads up." What that mean?'

'Means I've given you valuable information. Anyway,' he said, lowering his voice, 'I got some real good stuff to tell you. Fuckun A.'

'Hmm, the HiAce van was left in Newport? Livestock gone?'

'Yeah. I kept me ear to the ground though. Word around the traps is that a fuckun nun is hiding 'em.'

Hoodie Number 1 nodded slowly. 'I want to know all details. Ring me on burner.' He stood up to go, but Hoodie Number 2 held up a hand. He had saved the best till last. 'Wait up, mate. One more thing. This is kosher. That fat bloke you've been looking for. I know where he is.'

The other's head spun round. His eyes glittered as he passed a thick buff envelope to his informant and stood up to leave. After a discreet interval, Hoodie Number 2 followed him out of the bar, tugging a black beanie down over his prominent ears. He looked smug. The envelope made a satisfying bulge in his inside pocket, and he was looking forward to taking one of his girlfriends down to Sorrento on the proceeds. Snort some coke too. He'd made a down payment on a luxury flat in South Yarra. Things were looking good. He scanned the sky as he exited the cobbled lane. The city's prayers had been answered and the weather had broken. Sheets of rain were pouring down, sending the crowds of restaurant goers scurrying for shelter. With visibility down, you could no longer see the great smoke cloud out west, but you knew it was there from the smell. Amoeba-like, the crowds absorbed the man into their ranks; just another punter out for an Italian feed on a Friday night. There was a place in Collingwood that catered for his taste for pubescent girls. He was looking forward to it, but he relapsed into gloom when he recalled how the Russians had taken photographs and as the saying goes made him an offer he couldn't refuse. Still, he had to look on the bright side because they paid well, and he had expensive tastes.

*

Meanwhile, across the city in Williamstown, a small woman of a certain age was pouring tea for her guests. Sister Susan Lawless wore no habit, but her faith was strong. Her grey hair was kept short. She had a gentle smile, and her clear grey eyes were keen behind silver-framed glasses. A framed poster on the wall proclaimed the mission of her order: to find harmony where there was conflict, light where there was darkness, hope when all seemed lost. She had devoted her life to peace and in her eyes every human being was worthy of love and respect. None deserved help more than the men who sat nervously on her couch and drank their cups of tea with touching gratitude. They had shaved and showered, and she had produced a stack of clean clothes that fitted from the stocks that she collected for an asylum seeker centre. She would burn their cast-offs with the ineradicable chemical smell. She was anxious to put them at ease. They had arrived the previous day and slept in comfortable beds for the first time in many months.

'Now, before I can help,' she began, 'you need to tell me where you're from and what you have been doing. Soran's English is good enough to proceed without the interpreter.' She handed round a plate of fresh-baked lamingtons and smiled encouragingly. She had to speak up over the noise of the rain, which was lashing against the bay window.

'My name is Soran Rekani,' said the man with the turban, which he had washed and re-wound on his head after drying it on the verandah when the sun was still blazing down. 'My friends and I are Kurdish.' Soran was a neat, precise man. Somehow, he had managed to hang on to his spectacles, although they were held together with sticky tape. His English was halting, but clear. He bit into one of the strange cakes and raised his eyebrows appreciatively. His mother would like the recipe; a thought that made his face fall.

'We are from Eastern Kurdistan,' he said. 'It is called Rojhelat in our language – the place where the sun rises. I don't know how much you know about the Kurdish people, but we don't have our own country.'

'Yes, I know,' said Susan, gesturing politely that he should continue.

'We crossed the border because things were bad for us there. I am a teacher in my village, but I organised the peasants into an association, a how do you say? … Yes, a cooperative. The landowners did not like it and complained to the police.

'There has been a revolution in Iran, but things are no better. Even worse under ayatollahs.' He shook his head at the memory. 'They have so-called Revolutionary Guards. Murderers. They hate Kurdish people. Hate democracy. Hate women. Hate freedom. They will kill us if we go back there.'

Susan stood and went over to a low bookshelf. She found the book she wanted: Gérard Chaliand's *A People Without A Country: The Kurds and Kurdistan*. She brought it over and placed it in Soran's hands. 'I know a little about the Kurds.

You have had a tragic history.'

'You know about our people,' Soran said gravely. 'Not many people do. It is a cliché, but we really have no friends but the mountains.'

'No, that's true,' Susan replied with a sad smile. 'But please continue.' She knew that the world's governments, including Australia's, did not care about the long calvary of the Kurds.

'Well, Sister Susan, we made it to Java, flying you know, from Iraq. The Iraqi government also hates the Kurds. They gassed our people at Halabja ten years ago, you know, so we did not want to stay there. Same with Turkey and Syria. The border guards stole our money, but we had sewn some in our clothes. In Java, we were waiting for a long time in a village near the sea. I was teaching a little English because everyone wants to know it. We were waiting for a boat to take us to Australia.'

Soran paused to take a sip of tea and gazed out of the window at the rain, which was now falling in great tropical sheets. There was a loud crack of thunder and lightning flashed across in the palm trees of the botanical gardens and the bay beyond.

'One day a man came and said that yes, he could take us,' Soran said. 'We gave all our money and at night the man took us down to the sea where there was a big fishing boat. They were pirates, I think, but we were happy because at last we were going to Australia.'

Soran smiled to himself. Australia, he thought, was a wide brown land with room for everyone, far away from the ayatollahs, Saddam Hussein, Hafez al-Assad, the Turkish authorities, and other oppressors of the Kurds. It had been an enticing vision.

'We suspected nothing because the crew of the boat gave

us food and water. There were many of us. Men, women, children too. Kurds. Arabs. Tamils. Assyrians. Mandaeans… People from all over. Most were good people, but some were not so good and they tried to steal food and money from the rest. The sea was rough, and we were seasick, but we were thinking of freedom.' Soran placed his cup and saucer on the table. 'And then, one morning we saw the coast. The coast of Australia!

'There was a place where boats tie up with rope …'

'A wharf or jetty I think you mean,' nodded Susan, proffering the teapot for refills.

'Yes, a wharf. Thank you. There were crocodiles in the water. We were packing our bags when men came with guns. They had a big bus waiting, and they made us get in. They climbed in too.'

There were tears in Soran's eyes. Susan laid a hand gently on his forearm and bade him continue.

'We were driving for a long time to a place in the desert. The men told us to get out. It was getting dark and one man tried to run away.' Soran paused and passed a hand over his forehead. 'They shot him, Sister Susan! We begged them to bury him, but they laughed at us. They said the dingoes would eat him; they are wild dogs, I think. Next, they made us get into some aeroplanes. Light aeroplanes you call them. We flew for a long time, stopping in a desert place for fuel. Our hearts were breaking.'

Soran put his head in his hands, and could not continue. He was wondering if he would ever see his Rozhin again. He still hoped they would marry one day. He shook his head at the memory.

'When we landed, the men took us to a house. They had put cloth around our eyes … yes, blindfolds so that we cannot see. Then they made us work picking fruit and vegetables. I have no idea where this place was. The men never told us. We were thinking all the time of how we could escape but they were always there with their guns.

'It was hot and sometimes one of us would collapse but the men never showed mercy. At night we slept on the floor and before it was light they forced us out again. We were very dirty, and this made them laugh. "Dirty Arabs", they called us. Ignorant men.

'One day they forced us into a bus and put on blindfolds again. They have painted the windows black. We drove many hours until we could hear that we were in a city with heavy traffic. It was Melbourne but we didn't know this at the time. They put us in a house with iron bars on the windows. There were many beds in the rooms, stacked up you know… Yes, bunks. Then they took us every day in the big car to work in that horrible place with rubbish. Sometimes we worked at night under big lights when trucks came in, they have rubbish and steel barrels. They made us dig a big hole to put these things in. I am worried that we will become ill.

'Once, the men took us to a factory and forced us to go inside some big steel tanks. It was at night. They gave us lights on electric leads so that we could see. The job was to scrape off thick black stuff from the insides of the tanks and remove it in buckets. I don't know what it was. We tried to make the factory workers notice us, but the men said they would kill us if we tried to speak to them.

'We believed them, the men in leather jackets. They shouted

at us. Hit us. Two of us tried to escape from the waste dump place but these men saw and shot them. We were shocked and angry but what could we do?'

Soran's nostrils quivered, but Susan said it was alright. They were safe now. The other men were listening and although they could understand only snatches of the words, they too were angry.

'Then the other day I got behind one of the men. He pulled out a gun and we struggled. The gun went off and he collapsed. The bullet had entered his heart. Forgive me, but we threw him in the rubbish. We looked for the other one, but he was hiding. We got in the bus and I drove until it ran out of fuel. We had no food and money. Then the kind man found us, Dixie.'

Susan was quiet and Soran knew she was praying. He wondered how it was that some people were so kind, and others were so cruel. He had wrestled with his conscience about shooting the goon. Was it an accident? Would he have killed the other one if he hadn't hidden? But then those men had kidnapped them and forced them to work. Perhaps Sister Susan could explain? Soran desperately wanted to smoke but didn't know if it was allowed here. Daryan was speaking in Kurdish. He wanted Soran to ask if there was a mosque nearby, so Soran said he would ask. He wasn't religious himself; indeed, the ayatollahs' theocratic rule had made him hostile to religion, but he respected Daryan's rights, and even more, he respected this gentle nun. Susan said that there was a Sunni mosque not so far away in Newport and that she would contact the imam. She hoped it was the right denomination and Soran said yes, most Kurds in Rojhelat were Sunni, whereas most Iranians were Shia. He did not care for sectarian feuds. When

Soran looked out through the big bay window he could see thick black smuts settling on the garden path. They must have come down from the smoke cloud in the rain. This place was a permanent puzzle to him. Sometimes these people were so clean, but in other ways their city was filthy. One thing he was sure of was that the kidnappers would be looking for them and he would rather die than let them capture him.

*

Jack Martin arrived back at the Yarraville flat just before seven o'clock that evening. He chucked his car keys into the fruit bowl, turned on the kettle for the cup of tea he'd been dying for, and flexed his tired shoulder muscles. Then he paused. Jack was a man of reason but as a seasoned copper, he knew the value of instinct, and instinct was telling him that someone was watching him. The hairs on the back of his neck had stood up as if with static electricity. He stood, went across to the window, and pushed the curtain aside. Across the back yard and over the back fence there was an ugly block of flats, built of yellow brick in the 1960s, now streaked with rain. The windows stared back blankly but the feeling of unease would not go away. He disliked lace curtains and had pulled them aside, but he closed them before he went through for a shower.

When he emerged drying his hair, he noticed that the landline phone set was blinking. His daughter had left a breathless message: 'Hey Dad, I just wanted to let you know that I've opened Uncle Jimmy's trunk. One of the old iron keys fitted. Had to put CRC on it. The trunk's chock-a-block with old stuff. Old legal documents. Newspaper clippings. Last wills and testaments. Bank stuff. Maybe a lot of it's rubbish but there's a diary too. It's like, *really* old, Dad, and I worry about damaging the paper. I haven't had a chance to sit down and go through it all carefully. Anyway, from what I can see, the bloke who wrote it was called Sandy Johnstone. Dunno exactly what the relationship with us is, but he has to be an ancestor: a great-great something or the other. I'll keep you informed. Give me a call when you can. Love you.'

Jack rang back, but the call went to voicemail. He'd try again later. He was surprised how much he missed her. She'd been a stroppy teenage girl – given him more than his share of grey hairs and heartburn – but since she'd returned from an overseas backpacking adventure, they'd grown close. She'd divested herself of an obnoxious American boyfriend – well, Jack thought he was obnoxious – and was now doing her honours year in history, much to Jack's approval. He was intensely curious about Uncle Jimmy's trunk, but he'd just have to be patient.

Jack turned on the television. The fare was often disappointing, and tonight was no different. There was a silly quiz show on one channel and car racing on another. Jack was about to give up when he saw that a current affairs program was about to start on the ABC. Plenty about the Tottenham fire, so he made another cup of tea and settled down on the couch to watch. It was a mistake. The report on the fire ended, and the prime minister's peevish features appeared on the screen. Jack snorted. Why did the bloke always look hard done by? Maybe he was constipated? Jack flicked the switch. He would read his book in bed. *The Spanish Civil War*. It was very long – 750 pages – but he was determined to stick at it. Part of his mind was still trying to process what he and Liz had witnessed in the Footscray mall. He was also wondering about the HiAce van, and the more he thought about it the more it seemed certain that the bloke in the turban was the victim of people trafficking … forced labour … refugees … He dropped off into a deep sleep.

CHAPTER 11

Dawn broke hot and steamy in Footscray. A large party of officers were milling round in the Footscray police station car park, their capes glistening with rain. The Tottenham blaze was still burning out of control – more than a match for any deluge – and greasy smuts were falling from the dark sky. The officers shuffled impatiently, anxious to get started and get out of the rain. Apart from some shift workers walking to or from the nearby station with hoisted umbrellas, the streets were empty of people, although trucks were already growling up Hyde Street like packs of enormous wild beasts on heat. A resident had reported that an illegal knocking shop was operating in a row of terraced two-storey red brick houses in Buckley Street up from the TAFE college, and discreet surveillance had confirmed it. The girls never left the premises and there were bars on the windows, which suggested that they were held against their will. Snouts had reported that brothels were springing up everywhere across the western suburbs, with hard-faced men in black leather jackets running things; the Tantalus firm in other words. The police raid was planned with military precision. Officers swarmed from a minibus, two of them carrying battering ram 'enforcers', and crashed simultaneously through the front and back entrances of the two adjoining houses at the end of the terrace. Jack went in the front and Liz through the back behind armed officers, but they knew as soon as they entered that they were too late. There were plenty of signs of recent occupation: armchairs in the front parlour, which had doubled as a reception room; beds replete with soiled sheets and blankets; grotty kitchens with cheap takeaway containers and dirty crockery; buckets of used condoms in the bedrooms. A doorway had been cut through the wall between the two houses and next to it someone had freshly spray-painted a stylised rendition of an enormous cock and balls. The gang was giving them the finger. The whole place stank of stale cigarette smoke, cheap takeaways and – if Jack didn't imagine it – sweat and semen. In one of the upstairs bedrooms, tiers of bunks were jammed together, sleeping bags still on some of them. The fittings on the window bars were new.

'How the hell did they know?' Jack fumed.

'They had a tip-off, Jack,' said Liz. 'We've got a leak.'

The gang was at least a couple of steps ahead.

*

Later that morning, detectives Vicky Tran and Darryl Puncheon returned to the McCastle Logistics trucking depot at Shepparton, but found it closed without sign of life apart from the Alsatians, which a vet had to tranquillise so that they could search the place. Nor were the proprietor, Brendan McCastle, and his receptionist, Denise Sugden, in their nearby homes. Sugden's 'old man,' the so-called Sergeant-at-Arms of the Sons of Odin motorbike gang, shouted that he had no idea where she was and that they should fuck off. The only living thing at McCastle's house was an elderly Labrador, which Detective Tran took home. Colleagues joked that she was a burnt marshmallow: hard on the outside and soft inside. An alert had been put out to all airports, but the pair had vanished. There was no sign of any drivers either and McCastle had taken anything of value to the investigation. Nor had any trace of Terry Tudge been found. The bloke with the turban and his mates had vanished too.

It being Sunday, Jack invited Liz to have lunch with him at a Yarraville café. An old bloke with a Golden Retriever was there drinking coffee and reading the paper. This reminded Jack of his plan to get a dog when he returned to Hobart. He'd settled on the breed, too. But dogs were not the only thing on Jack's mind, nor on Liz's, although she thought getting a pooch was an excellent idea.

'Jack,' she said, pushing her coffee cup to one side. 'I just can't get what we saw happen in the mall out of my mind, but I don't know what to do about it.'

Jack nodded, and she continued.

'We should be commending the DETOX people, not bashing them up. Jeez, those old blokes holding the banner …'

'Yeah,' Jack said. 'What intrigues me is why Paul Lennox was directing the operation. What was so important that such a high-ranking officer was involved? Call me paranoid, but you just have to wonder who was pulling the strings for whom. I've tried discussing it with Ernie Foxcroft but he's like the Three Wise Monkeys: he sees no evil, hears no evil, and speaks no evil. He's a decent bloke but as far as he's concerned the whole thing was ordered by people above his pay grade and that's that. He's concerned about rats in the ranks, but not the ones with braid all over their uniforms.'

Afterwards, they went their separate ways, Liz to meet an old friend in the city and Jack to retire to the flat to catch up on some long overdue paperwork and read his book.

CHAPTER 12

The following morning, Liz braced herself to attend the autopsy of the man found dead at the Tottenham dump. Jack had offered to do it, but Liz insisted. Jack knew better than to try to shield his colleague because she was female, so she drove to the mortuary in South Melbourne, taking DC Nick Downer with her. So strong was Flash Nick's aftershave that she had to wind down her window. They had not gone very far before he started to get just a bit fresh for her liking, leaning over and purring in her ear and making eyes.

And then the creature had put his hand on her thigh! 'Keep your hands to yourself!' she ordered, batting his hand aside and correcting the steering wheel to stop the car drifting into the oncoming lane. 'And don't dare call me Liz again. It's DS Flakemore to you. Any more out of you and I'll report you and you'll be out on your ear.'

'Arrgh, don't be like that. I was only—'

'Shut up, Downer.' She concentrated on steering past a huge truck. 'And I'll be watching you, Constable.'

Flash Nick spent the rest of the journey thinking up ways

he could get back at her. Who did she think she was? One of them feminists, the stuck-up Tasmanian bitch?

It was the usual depressing ceremony at the mortuary, with the whine of the circular saw cutting through the skull, the Y-shaped incision of the abdomen, the boltcutters snipping the ribs and the careful weighing and sorting of the innards like in an old butcher's shop. Liz had to admit that Flash Nick took the grisly business – his first post mortem – well. Some first timers fainted and she herself had rushed out of her first experience to be sick. Maybe, just maybe, they could make a decent copper out of him yet.

Vernon Swinburne, the pathologist, confirmed the cause of death: a single gunshot to the heart; death would have been instantaneous. Liz had done a unit of political philosophy in her degree, and looking at the violated husk of a man on the slab, she recalled Thomas Hobbes' gloomy words in his *Leviathan*: 'No arts; no letters; no society; and which is worst of all, continual fear, and danger of violent death; and the life of man, solitary, poor, nasty, brutish, and short.' She tried to be sympathetic but chances were this man had been brutish in life. He had been in his late thirties, was well-nourished – his last meal rare steak and chips washed down with beer – and had a powerful short frame bulked out by working out in gyms by the look of him. Black hair. Blue eyes. Designer stubble. A gold pendant round the neck. Gold rings on the fingers; even the thumbs. Steel teeth, interspersed up with a few of his own and some gold ones too. The man had been a walking jeweller's shop; must have jangled when he walked. Liz wondered why a certain type of criminal felt the need to drape themselves in bling. There could be a PhD in it, and she was thinking about chucking the job in and pursuing an academic career; the job had provided her with ample subject matter for a thesis. Jack reckoned she'd be good at it and his was an opinion that she valued. She'd decide when the Melbourne secondment was over, and she was back home in Hobart.

She shook the thought aside and concentrated on the gruesome spectacle unfolding before her, taking care like Jack had taught her to let her eyes kind of glaze over at the worst bits. Flash Nick observed the procedure with interest, his aftershave competing with the chemical smells of the corpse. An inspection of the gangster's black leather jacket yielded no clues, except that it was expensive, of local manufacture. There was a roll of twenties in the pocket, along with cigarettes and gold lighter, and a couple of condoms. The underpants had skid marks, and Cyrillic script on the elastic waistband. They'd have to get that checked by an expert. The sight of the corpse laid out on the slab depressed her terribly. This man had had a mother who loved him and yet he finished up like this. Theft didn't seem to have been a motive for the killing. Nothing to identify him in his wallet. What was really interesting were the tattoos. These covered every square inch of the man's body that was normally covered with clothing. Even his buttocks and penis were inked. The torso was covered in a bewildering mass of squiggles, drawings of guns and knives, snakes, naked ladies, crocodiles, and god knows what else, but what caught Liz's attention was his chest, which was tattooed with a cross on a shield with back-to-front letter Cs between the wings of a double-headed eagle. The man wasn't Russian as she had initially surmised. He was Serbian unless someone had held him down and tattooed the heraldic symbol on him against his will.

'Your man anticipated his fate by dying first,' Dr Swinburne told Liz as an assistant moved forward with needle and black twine to begin sewing up the corpse.

'Eh?'

'Sorry, Liz, a bit cryptic, like,' said Swinburne, removing his gloves and motioning for her to wait in his office. Five minutes later, after he had climbed out of his protective gear and washed up, Swinburne trotted into the office like a little Dales Pony. He cut to the chase. 'Fact is, Liz, your man didn't have much longer to live anyway. Lung cancer. Advanced emphysema too. It would have got him within the year. My guess is he was a heavy smoker for many years.' He looked at the cigarette smoking in his hand and sighed. 'Yes, I know. I'm trying to stop.'

Flash Nick looked smug. 'Never started,' he said. Swinburne gave him a look as if to say 'who asked you.' He hadn't taken to the young man. Liz silently gave thanks that she had never smoked, and that Jack had given it up after she and Wendy had badgered him mercilessly to quit. There had been a time when the silly man had smoked Camels and even those French Gitanes when he could get his hands on them. Guaranteed to kill you before your time; the corpse's ravaged lungs were proof of that. Someone had just sped things up: his yesterdays ran out and lighted this fool the way to dusty death. After a bit of make-up had been skilfully applied to the corpse's face, it looked almost alive. Ugly and brutish, but alive. The attendants dressed his torso in a clean shirt and propped him up against a wall. A police photographer took several shots and Liz soon had a mugshot to distribute around police stations and copies along with a press release appealing for information. It just might yield something of use.

Later, when she had returned to the office from the mortuary in South Melbourne, a doctor rang from the Western General with the news that the other leather jacket man, Darko Percović, had died. There could be little mystery about what killed Percović or whatever his mother had called him. They knew that he had been marinated in a cocktail of liquid toxins. He had died of acute poisoning.

Liz shrugged. 'We wouldn't have got anything out of him anyway,' she said. 'Your turn for the autopsy, Jack.'

Jack groaned at the thought. He considered delegating Vicky Tran – she impressed him as a keen and intelligent officer – but dismissed the thought of skiving out of the job as unworthy. They needed a breakthrough soon. The whereabouts of the men in the minibus was still unknown. It was probable that the bloke in the turban or his mates – whoever and wherever they were – had killed the man in the leather coat and made their getaway. Jack had a hunch about their identity but kept it to himself at this stage. Meanwhile, he was still angry about the botched brothel raid and would run a few ideas past Liz about what they could do to flush out the plant. Commander Foxcroft might have some ideas too.

*

Out at Tottenham, the firefighters were exhausted to breaking point from working double shifts in the rain, fire, and smoke. They were falling sick too. Several suffered from painful sunburn from the intense glare, and all complained of sudden nosebleeds and a persistent metallic taste in the mouth. Now, days later, they were only just poised to finally extinguish the blaze that had sent thousands of tons of toxic particles and gases into the sky and into the waterways. The plume had extended above a wedge of residential areas right down to the bay as far as Geelong and the Bellarine Peninsula. The chances were that the poisons would get into the food chain from people's veggie patches, the Werribee market gardens and the like. Fish and shellfish from the bay. The fire brigade was still none the wiser about exactly what they were dealing with. Thousands of houses had been evacuated. Jack wondered how long it would be before it was safe for the residents to return, and he fretted for the well-being of the firefighters. Heroes. It was a grossly misused term. Bloody press rabbited on about 'sporting heroes' but they only kicked balls or pranced about. There was always something about one of them treating women badly. Not that he was anti-sport. He'd been not half bad at cricket and football in his time, but you had to keep a sense of proportion. Then there were the celebrity actors! Wasn't so long ago that actors had been beyond the pale of respectability. The firefighters, on the other hand, were authentic heroes and Jack hoped they were given their due, and that their health didn't suffer from what they'd been dealing with. Many of those poor buggers who'd attended the Chernobyl nuclear disaster had died or been crippled for life – he prayed that the Melbourne firies would not suffer the same fate.

Cornelius Bentley, Darko Percović's lawyer, rang just then, pompously indignant. His client had died because of police negligence, he claimed. He should have received medical treatment far sooner. Jack listened for a while, shaking his head. 'Tell that to the firefighters,' he snarled and slammed the phone down. To Jack's mind, Bentley's clients were human flies laying their eggs in the city's ripe flesh and the lawyer was helping to incubate the maggots. No doubt Bentley would make a complaint, but Jack didn't really care and he was damned if he would be apologising to the jerk.

Jack had wondered about leaving a little earlier to cook himself a decent meal, but his plans were soon knocked awry. Bruiser Macfarlane came huffing and puffing into his office. 'The phones … are … running hot,' he gasped. 'There's been a shootout … at the bikie place in Brooklyn.' He mopped his brow and leaned heavily on the doorpost. 'Never rains but it pours, sir. Un-be-fucking-lievable.'

In fact, it was raining. Literally. The great dome of humid air that had travelled down from the Gulf of Carpentaria to meet the cooler prevailing westerlies was still dumping its load over the city. Ten minutes later, Jack and the rest of the team were standing round under umbrellas on the nature strip outside the Molochs Marauders' clubhouse in Geelong Road. Armed officers swarmed over the property like black insects, their protective clothing slicked with rain, and uniformed officers were keeping a crowd of rubberneckers at a safe distance. Jack let Liz make the running. Quietly, efficiently, she set about organising door to door inquiries and seeing if they could get any sense out of the gawkers. Constables Thick and Thin, looking more than ever like Laurel and Hardy, had closed off the service road and were directing traffic, and very competently too, Jack had to admit. Maybe the bollocking he had given them over the misuse of the police car had sobered them up. An ambulance was standing by; its crew waiting for the all-clear to enter the premises. The rookie Bernice King had also appeared and was hanging round looking busy at something.

The front gates had been smashed in and the walls of the clubhouse were blackened with smoke. When the armed officer in charge signalled that it was safe to enter the grounds, Jack moved forward, flanked by Vicky Tran and her puppy, with the ambos coming up behind. The front wall was a splintered ruin, still smouldering despite the increasing downpour. Several Harley hogs were lying on their sides out the front, looking damaged beyond repair. Then again, perhaps the bikies had been repairing them before the attack. The steel door was intact, but whoever had attacked had simply gone round it through the walls. The roof looked precarious, but they peeked inside. It was a shambles. Bodies lay in a heap round a ruined pool table and as far as they could tell nobody was left alive. It stank of rain, smoke, and cordite. Jack ordered everyone back. They'd let the firefighters go in first.

Grey-haired Fire Chief Michaela Schiebal looked exhausted. She'd come straight from the Tottenham fire, and she'd scarcely slept for days. 'Bastards couldn't wait to create mischief,' she muttered, taking in the ruined building. She donned a hard hat and gloves and climbed over the wall to inspect the inside, keeping a wary eye on the roof. Meanwhile, a police forensic team had arrived and joined the growing throng milling about outside. Schiebal poked around for fifteen minutes before giving the all-clear for the ambulance officers to enter. They came out shortly afterwards carrying a large form out on a stretcher. Whoever it was, was groaning and had most of their clothes burned off.

'Jesus,' exclaimed Vicky, taking in the red hair and swastika earrings. 'That's Big Mama Hanson.'

Jack raised his eyebrows, then turned to the Fire Chief. 'What can you tell us, Michaela?'

Michaela shook her tired head as if nothing could surprise her. 'Looks like a siege to me and the attackers blasted their way into the building. Forensics'll give us a clearer picture, but I'd say they used a cannon or grenades. I doubt that our ambo friends will find anyone else alive.'

Kissing any chance of an early night goodbye, Jack summoned an emergency meeting of the Operation Tantalus squad and briefed them on the Brooklyn outrage. Vicky Tran reported on her earlier visit to the Molochs Marauders' clubhouse. The bikies had had every reason to seem uptight. Preliminary reports from the SOCOs indicated that there were twelve dead bodies inside the clubhouse. The bodies had been taken to the city mortuary, prompting Tran to observe that Dr Swinburne's team would be burning the midnight oil. Jack checked his watch. The watery sunset was long since gone, but officers began to go from door to door making enquiries. At least the rain had eased off a bit. First thing in the morning, Vicky Tran could interview Big Mama Hanson at the Western General to find out what she knew.

*

When he got back to the flat, Jack knew he hadn't been imagining things. The first thing he noticed was a glass draining on the sink. He had made a careful mental note of where everything was that morning. There was no sign of forced entry, but someone had most definitely been in the flat: he had left nothing on the draining board. Instinct told him that the intruder lived in the yellow brick flats over the back, but that did not constitute proof. The flats had taken on a sinister air, the walls darkened by rain, a suggestion of figures lurking behind the dark windows. He'd call forensics in the morning to check for fingerprints and hope that his colleagues didn't dismiss his concerns as those of an ageing bloke going ga-ga. He managed to get through on the phone to both Francesca and Wendy. Wendy was on her way out to the pub with friends, but she promised to ring back the next evening. A new boyfriend? he pried, but she just laughed and hung up after calling him a stickybeak.

Francesca, Jack's girlfriend, sounded thoughtful. She had been in two minds about moving into his house in South Hobart. Jack had bought the house over twenty years earlier and he and his ex-wife Helen had raised Wendy there. Helen was living up in Launceston with her new bloke, the Weaver Beaver bloke, but Francesca worried that the house was still steeped in her presence. Sure, Helen had taken all her things except, quite inexplicably, an expensive Wedgewood dinner set. Physically, she was gone, but Francesca worried that her predecessor's ghost would haunt the place. In her opinion, Jack needed to make a clean break.

She began tentatively. 'How would you feel,' she said, 'about us selling both our places and buying a new house together? With your uncle's money you could buy Helen out and we'd still be able to pay my ex off.' Francesca's ex had made a big fortune – something to do with computers, Jack knew – but the tight bastard wasn't about to give Fran a break even though he'd run off with his 19-year-old secretary. Jack was intensely fond of his Darcy Street place. He had laboured long and hard in the garden, renovated the house, and put the rambling extension he called the Scout Hall on the back, but he could see the wisdom of her suggestion. Fran was pushing on an open door. Well, half open. After a bit of hemming and hawing, he'd agreed and felt much better for it.

'We'll get somewhere big enough for my two kids and for Wendy,' Fran said. 'I've always wanted a place with a big garden running down to the water.'

And so it was decided. When Jack got back to Hobart, he would put Darcy Street and Uncle Jimmy's place on the market, Fran would put her house up for sale and they would start looking for somewhere else. Fran fancied the idea of a place in Sandy Bay. Even after paying out their ex-partners, they would have enough for somewhere swish. There was a place in Mitah Court near the Riverview Inn with stunning views over the Derwent estuary … It was expensive, but selling Uncle Jimmy's place would allow them to do it and still have money in the bank. Jack went to bed exhausted but happy and was soon fast asleep. For once, he didn't dream, or at least he would have no recollection of dreaming. He didn't see the face peering through the bedroom window, the hair soaked dark with rain and the eyes glinting yellow in the flashes of light from the big electric sign on top of the Sun Theatre.

CHAPTER 13

Early next morning, a toad-faced man was skulking in the Botanic Gardens down in Williamstown, his black leather jacket glistening with rain. If the downpour caused him discomfort, it didn't show. The boss had entrusted him with this mission, and he intended to succeed: had to succeed because the consequences of failure would be dire. (He shuddered at the memory of what they'd done to that Dusan fellow for putting his hand in the till.) The ground was littered with his cigarette butts, and he'd taken a dump in the bushes. His car was parked on the street ready for a fast getaway and he had a pair of binoculars trained on the nuns' parlour window. They'd trailed the old man yesterday when he'd driven down from Newport. '*Svi su tamo s časnim sestrama*,' he muttered: They're all there with the nuns. He grinned mirthlessly, savouring the moment, and fingered his Zastava M88 pistol; the one with notches cut in the butt. Magazine full and the safety catch off, he put the binoculars back in their pouch and moved forward at a crouch, zigzagging from tree to tree.

Inside the house, Soran and his friends were relaxing in the big parlour while Sister Susan, through Soran, explained the situation to them. They could give themselves up to the police and apply for asylum, which was their right under the United Nations Refugee Convention. The core principle of customary international law, she explained, is non-refoulement, which asserts that a refugee should not be returned to a country where they face serious threats to their life and freedom.

Soran translated and his friends smiled happily, but Susan's heart sank. She held up a cautionary hand. 'In practice,' she went on, 'the Australian government does not obey the law. The police would hand you over to the immigration authorities who would lock you up in a detention centre while your cases are processed.'

She hated to say this. 'You could be there for years, and there is no guarantee that you will not be deported.'

'So, we could be sent back to Iran?' said Soran, shaking his head in disbelief. 'But how can they do this to us? The ayatollahs' police would kill us, they believe we are Kurdish infidels and communists. Sometimes CIA agents.'

He translated the grim message, and his friends sat back with downcast eyes. They had no wish to be sent back to the Islamic Republic's torturers. Soran had tried to organise a tenant farmers' union against the big landowners who were prominent supporters of the 'revolutionary' government. He was Kurdish and the government hated Kurds as infidels, especially those who were politically active. There was no justice in a land governed by medievalist bigots.

'What can we do, Sister Susan?' Soran sighed.

Susan shook her head. The situation was indeed grim, but a germ of an idea had occurred to her. 'We'll see what we can do,' she said. 'In the meantime, you can stay here until we decide.'

She stood up and smoothed down her jeans. The telephone was along the hallway. She had some calls to make. The men helped themselves to coffee, and Soran decided to go out into the garden for a smoke. There was a gazebo where he could shelter from the rain and think. Sit down and rack his brains. Dream of Rozhin and the life they might still have together. She'd been a teacher like him; educated and forthright; a believer in universal human rights and social justice; and passionate supporter of Kurdish cultural and political rights. A neighbour had told him the goons were coming up the winding road to arrest him, so he'd grabbed what he could and fled out the back way over the mountain. He hadn't had the chance to say goodbye and had heard nothing of her since leaving. Nothing of his mother, father, brothers and sisters either, and he prayed that the Revolutionary Guards hadn't taken it out on them. Soran hoped that one day they would all be reunited in some free place.

*

Meanwhile, seven kilometres away in Yarraville, Jack Martin was sitting outside under the awning of the Java Café next to the Sun Theatre. Cars swished by occasionally on the rain-soaked street, but it was windless and warm, so he had removed his jacket. There was still a smell of smoke in the air. Apart from some old men playing dominoes, he was the only customer at the outside tables. A snatch of bouzouki music drifted from up near the Greek Orthodox Church. He stirred his cappuccino and checked his watch. Liz would be along soon. They had agreed to meet away from flapping ears back at the cop shop.

The old bloke came in with his Golden Retriever, sat down, and unfurled his *Age* newspaper. 'May I?' said Jack, reaching over to pat the dog, whose fur was glistening with rain. 'Sure,' said the bloke, proud of his pet, whose tail was wagging vigorously. 'He's a bit wet, though.' The pooch was beautiful, with soft golden hair, big brown eyes, a regal ruff, and a feathered tail. Jack promised himself that he really would get one. His old bitser, Rosie, had died a couple of years ago and he needed a dog in his life. Like the Portuguese proverb said, 'a house without a dog or a cat is the house of a scoundrel.' The bloke ticked off the breed's finer points on his fingers. 'They do shed fur,' he admitted, 'but they've got everything going for them. They're intelligent, beautiful, loyal, and good with kids and other pets. Not the least bit aggressive. They're the best.'

Liz rushed in, rolling up her umbrella, and Jack left the bloke to his newspaper. She ordered a coffee and fussed over the dog. 'OK,' she said, glancing to make sure the dog's owner couldn't overhear. 'Anything on the bikie siege yet?'

Jack went to answer but his phone rang, and he held up an apologetic hand. He listened carefully, thanked the caller, and closed his phone. 'That was the lab,' he said. 'That bag of stuff I handed in was crack cocaine. Not only that, but it was also much purer than the usual stuff that's been around. It explains why there have been overdoses.'

'Yeah. That kid died in Footscray just the other day. It's got the new firm written all over it.'

Jack nodded. 'Anyway, nothing yet about the Brooklyn

shootout business, but the door-to-door's still underway and we should get something from the SOCOs soon.'

'There's a war on, Jack,' said Liz. 'We just might learn something from the survivors. Witnesses could have seen something.'

'Anyway,' Jack said with a shrug. 'One of Vicky Tran's snouts tells her that a new brothel has just been set up down in Williamstown. The drum is that the girls aren't there by choice. We know that someone's been tipping the pimps off, so we'll have to draw them out.'

'So you're thinking that we set up the leaker?'

'Yep,' Jack finished his coffee. 'We call in the detectives who've been working on Tantalus. I'm quite sure that Vicky's kosher. Too early to say with that DC she's got working with her.'

'You mean Darryl Puncheon? Yeah, he's a possibility. He's privy to most of what we're doing.'

'Then there's that other young DC, Nick Downer. Flash Nick.' Liz looked around to make sure nobody was listening. 'Thinks he's God's gift to women.'

'He's a lair alright. Dunno how he can afford those suits he wears … Well, there are a few suspects, but let's spread the rumour that we're targeting somewhere else but arrange to be overheard talking about the real target when that pair are around.'

'Devious, Jack.' Liz chuckled. 'I like it.'

They ordered two more coffees and mulled over what they knew about the prime suspects. Puncheon was a callow young man. Seemed easily led, and they could imagine him being bullied into giving information away. As for Flash Nick Downer, he was an arrogant little prick who seemed to think he was too good for anyone in the Footscray nick. Perhaps they were being a bit hard. The kid must have something going for him. But there was no doubt that he'd been within earshot when they were planning the raid on the Footscray brothel. Liz had taken an instant dislike to him. His dirty eyes had slid up and down her body, mentally undressing her and he didn't care that it was obvious. Then there'd been the hand on her thigh in the police car. His family was well-connected. She'd heard his daddy had friends high up in the force; that Nick had joined expecting fast-track promotion but persistent rumours that he had been extracting sexual favours from women suspects had held him back. He was always flashing his money about but was greedy for more. He drove a fast BMW coupé, and she'd overheard him boasting about a shopping expedition for 'your average $400 sweater'.

Jack abruptly changed the subject. 'Liz, do you think I still have my marbles?' he asked, looking down at the table and fiddling with a teaspoon.

Liz looked puzzled, then grinned broadly. 'Ha! You're not doing too badly for an old codger. Why?'

'Oh, I dunno, Liz. Maybe the job's getting to me, making me paranoid?'

But when he explained about the intruder, Liz looked worried. 'Jack, for all we know, this is someone from the Tantalus mob making threats. We'll need to keep a watch on your place.'

'Trouble is, we're stretched already. The best we can do is to have a patrol car come past every so often.'

They finished their coffees and walked round to where Liz had parked on the cobblestones behind the railway station. They drove off and as they were waiting at the Somerville

Road lights, they discussed how they were going to hang out the bait for the leaker. If they were right about him, the raiding party would find the Nelson Place brothel closed. Back at Footscray, they briefed the team and clued up Vicky Tran to begin spreading the false rumour about the address of the intended raid, which was scheduled for early the following morning.

Vicky also brought the team up to speed on the Molochs Marauders' siege. 'We've got a pretty clear picture of what happened. Witnesses reported a series of explosions and what sounded like automatic gunfire. There are nine dead and three wounded, two of them seriously. We're tracking down relatives to identify the bodies and should be able to report back on that shortly. One eyewitness was watering her lawn. She reports seeing two large black vans draw up just before the attack. Sorry sir, but she didn't get the rego numbers. Eyesight not what it was. She says men piled out of the vans but can't give us details as they were wearing ski masks.' She checked her watch. 'I'm going round to the hospital shortly. The doctors say that Big Mama Hanson is fit enough to be questioned.'

Someone asked about forensics and Vicky replied that she was expecting a preliminary report later that afternoon. Word also came through from the EPA that another toxic dump had been discovered near Camperdown, out in the country past Geelong and Colac. A preliminary report of the Tottenham fire was expected soon, and Vicky volunteered to attend the autopsy on Darko Percović in South Melbourne. There would be plenty more to come, she told Darryl Puncheon, so he might as well get used to it.

Just before they wound up, Liz mentioned that an intruder had been in Jack's apartment. There would be a forensic examination of the premises and regular patrols past the flat would be scheduled. As if on cue, Ernie Foxcroft came in and said that Jack would be taking his service pistol home with him. They couldn't rule out that the Tantalus gang were responsible for entering the flat while he was out.

CHAPTER 14

Sister Susan hung up the phone when she heard the gun-shot. She had worked with a medical NGO in Bosnia during the recent Yugoslav wars, so she doubted it was a car backfiring. More shots followed, and it sounded like they were being fired right outside in her garden. It had to be those gangsters – the ones who had kidnapped Soran and his friends. She ran down the corridor from the kitchen to the lounge. She would have to get the men together and try to get them out to safety. Should she ring the police? Maybe not and anyway, she'd lost precious time dithering. Two of her guests turned towards her as she entered the parlour. Their eyes were huge, their mouths open with shock. They'd been so sure they were safe.

Out for another smoke under the pergola in the garden, Soran Rekani had caught sight of the man crouching in the big rhododendron bush; an ugly brute with a pistol in his hand, inching forward towards the house, his black leather jacket slick with rain. He hadn't seen Soran. '*Kurê fahişe*,' Soran muttered, quietly pulling out the Zastava pistol he'd taken from the goon at the dump. As the intruder wriggled closer, Soran recognised him as one of the guards from the dump; a man with a wide mouth like a frog, who liked to beat people. A cold rage descended over him. By what right did these men make slaves of others? Well, they weren't going to get away with it again. '*Hûn ê bimirin*,' Soran thought. You will die. He was so angry that his hands shook, and he accidentally dropped his cigarette lighter on the flagstones. The thug heard it and his head spun round, black eyes glittering like a snake's. Soran pointed the pistol and fired. He was a terrible shot. The bullet went wide, but it surprised the goon who backed off quickly into the rhododendrons. Soran fired again, and the man yelped and began to limp away, firing wildly in Soran's general direction. Soran raised the pistol again. He was going to kill this horrible man.

Susan, however, had come quietly out of the house. She pushed his hand down. 'Please,' she said. 'Let him go. We are in enough trouble as it is.'

A powerful red car grumbled into life and fishtailed off down the street, doing wheelies at the Giffard Street roundabout. Susan saw a faint blood trail from the rhododendrons to the edge of the lawn, but it was melting away in the rain. Soran must have shot the brute. Susan did a quick survey of the street. There was nobody around and no more suspicious-looking vehicles. Nobody had come out of the neighbouring houses to investigate, and she knew that many of them would be at work. Still, there was every chance that someone was inside calling the police. She'd ring Dixie Trumble; he was resourceful. Soran looked guilty, but Susan shook her head when he began to apologise. She didn't approve of guns, but she realised that if Soran hadn't been armed the thug would have kidnapped or even killed them all. They went back inside out of the rain and gratefully accepted tea from Sister Monica.

*

Mrs David Edwards had been in high dudgeon all morning. The neighbourhood had been going steadily downhill since Mr Menzies' day. Especially since they'd ditched the White Australia Policy. If they kept it up with the floods of reffos and whatnot they'd end up with a coffee-coloured community. She was stationed in the upstairs front window, keeping an eye out for shady types in the Botanic Gardens, when she saw a man in a turban standing in the bushes outside the Catholic place up the street. A turban, mind you! She'd had her doubts about the nuns, and this proved her suspicions were correct. That man would be one of them asylum seekers. She went off to make a cup of tea and was just figuring out what her David would have done when she heard gunshots! She got straight on the phone and dialled 000. Five minutes later, a police car cruised slowly along the street. It didn't stop, but it did a three-point turn up near Forster Street and drove past again.

By this time, Susan had phoned Dixie and he was on his way, warned to keep an eye open for the police and for any sign of the gangsters returning. The old wharfie turned up shortly afterwards, this time driving a beautifully polished Holden Kingswood sedan, not his battered ute.

'Borrowed it from Mrs B next door,' he explained. 'Didn't want the boys to get wet in the back of me old bomb in this weather.'

Susan smiled affectionately at her friend. 'Have you thought about a safe place, Dixie?'

'Yeah,' he replied, trying to light a rollie cigarette before he remembered that the nuns had banned it inside. 'My place ain't safe because the cops found the minibus there, but don't worry. I've got a few mates who'll look after them and I've got a plan to keep 'em safe.'

Susan said a prayer as Dixie drove away with the Kurdish men. Even if he was a self-professed atheist, she believed that God was working through him and she prayed he would manage to keep their Kurdish friends safe from both gangsters and the State. He would tell her later where he'd taken the refugees. Meanwhile, Dixie was doing his best to reassure his passengers. They trusted him and let him know that they were happy with whatever he had planned. First, he pulled up just past the roundabout at the start of The Strand, the wide street that ran along the Williamstown river foreshore towards the Newport power station. The rain had eased to a fine drizzle, but mist still partially obscured the city skyscrapers visible beyond the Webb Dock container cranes. The rain was greasy with smuts from the Tottenham fire and clumps of evil-looking scum were floating past on the water. Dixie could swear he heard it fizzing. He stuffed the pistol Sister Lawless had given him inside his jacket and strode off towards the Ferguson Street pier near the Cenotaph, keeping a close eye open for stickybeaks and police. A lone cyclist powered past on the bike path, head down against the rain, but took no notice of him. The rigging of yachts clinked in the wind and the jetty's boards were slippery underfoot, so he walked carefully. Dixie reached the end of the jetty safely and after checking there was nobody around on any of the boats, he hurled the pistol far out into the dark waters of Hobson's Bay. Just to be on the safe side, he'd carefully wiped it to remove any fingerprints, not that anyone was ever likely to find it under fifteen feet of mud and water. It made hardly a splash and sank without a trace. Satisfied, Dixie walked back quickly and started the car. Susan, he knew, was going to search her garden for spent bullet casings. Only fools underestimated the police and their forensics experts. Neither of them had given much thought to the fact that they were committing, aiding, and abetting crimes, and they both made a distinction between the law and what was right: sometimes they intersected, sometimes not. Keeping strictly to the speed limit – a sensible law, Dixie thought – he headed past the Scienceworks Museum in Spotswood, up Hudson's Road and onto the West Gate Freeway and Bridge. His passengers were chattering excitedly in Kurdish, pointing out the grey waters of Port Phillip Bay and the skyscrapers towering into the clouds above the city. Dixie turned off the freeway at the Todd Road exit and drove under the bridge towards Port Melbourne. He was pretty sure they weren't being followed but took a tortuous route through the backstreets to make sure. He pulled up outside an old Victorian-era pub and shepherded his charges inside through the residents' door. 'I know you Mohammedans don't touch grog, but don't worry. You don't have to drink the stuff and you don't have to go to the bar. An old mate runs the pub and he and his missus will look after you.'

Soran translated and they looked relieved. He told Dixie later that not all Muslims eschewed alcohol. His own family had cultivated shiraz grapes and made fine wines until the Ayatollah Khomeini's zealots arrived and uprooted the vineyard. In fact, he explained, the Kurds had been making wine for more than eight thousand years and while they had to be circumspect with the religious fanatics prowling the countryside, they continued to make it in secret. Dixie admitted that he was a beer man and didn't know much about wine, or plonk as he called it, but he thought it was a damned good idea when Soran wondered if it might be possible for him to set up as a winemaker in Australia.

Meanwhile, ten kilometres away, Jack Martin was sitting in his office gazing through the rain-beaded window at the Footscray Town Hall. A cup of tea had gone cold on his desk and Liz was on the phone at the other desk. Bruiser Macfarlane had told him about the report of gunshots down in Williamstown. A man in a turban around there too. The local uniforms had not seen anything unusual, but the woman who rang up had been insistent and had specified that the shooting had occurred in Osborne Street near the Botanic Gardens. Jack was wondering about a connection with the men who had abandoned the Tottenham minibus in Newport, just up the road from Williamstown. Was it coincidence that the illegal brothel they were going to raid was also in Williamstown? Jack didn't think so. He pushed two more red pins into the map on the wall, one into North Road, Newport and another into the Williamstown Botanic Garden, and linked them with a length of black string.

Vicky Tran and Darryl Puncheon had just taken the lift to a third-floor ward at the Western General Hospital in Gordon Street. They flashed their warrant cards to the constable who was sitting outside the door looking bored out of his mind. He jerked his head for them to enter. It was times like this that he resented the plain-clothes mob. Jeez, he couldn't even go outside for a smoke, but they were swanning about like the Queen of Sheba and Lord Muck. Inside the ward, a large form was sprawled out like a beached whale on one of the iron beds. Her coarse red hair protruded like broken bed springs from the bandage wound tightly around her head, and her swastika earrings shone dully in the weak light from the frosted window. Her grey eyes were swollen from weeping.

'G'day, Noelene,' said Vicky. 'Or should we call you Big Mama?'

The woman shrugged then winced with pain from the movement. 'Don't make no difference,' she muttered.

Vicky didn't like her, but she could sympathise: the woman had stared death in the face. Puncheon was shifting from leg to leg plainly wanting to be out of this place that stank of illness and death, and he was eyeing Big Mama's earrings with horrified fascination.

'OK, Noelene,' Vicky replied, pulling a chair to the bedside, and nodding to Puncheon to stand back. 'We're sorry about what happened, but if you're up to it, we'd like to ask you a few questions about yesterday afternoon.'

Big Mama nodded. It was the most cooperative she'd ever been. She sat up in bed wringing her hands together like a downmarket Lady Macbeth and seemed to be on the verge of tears. She explained that she'd arrived as usual round one o'clock with her mate, 'Cougar' Lloyd, and started making lunch for the boys. It had started as a day like any other.

'The boys was tinkering with their hogs or drinking beer

and playing pool,' she said. 'Texas was thinking about a run out past Bacchus Marsh at the weekend.'

'All completely normal, then?'

'Nah,' said Big Mama, shaking her head. 'It wasn't, was it?' The words came out in a rush. 'We all had the jitters cos a few of the boys had disappeared. There was that arm thing … Jeez, Stiffy Williams' colours had been put on the flagpole at that Arts place in the city. Mebbe it was his arm?' She stopped to pat the side of her head. 'Hurts like buggery. Anyway, we was real spooked.'

'That's understandable,' nodded Vicky, now a model of diplomacy. 'You didn't happen to see the faces of the men who attacked the clubhouse?'

'Nah. Carn 'elp ya. Cunts was wearin' them balaclava things, weren't they.'

'So, how many of them, would you say?'

'Mebbe half a dozen.'

'Anything else you recall?'

'They was foreign, wasn't they. Heard a couple speakin' but it coulda been double Dutch for all I know.'

Noelene wanted to help, but the raid had been so sudden, and it hadn't taken the attackers long to achieve their aim. Vicky changed tack. 'Now, Noelene, I'm wondering if you know anything about the big fire out at Tottenham. You see we had a tip-off that bikies were seen out there.'

Big Mama sighed and asked Vicky to pour her a glass of water. 'Jeez, I'd kill for a smoke,' she sighed, 'but the nurses don't allow it.' She glared at a passing nurse and gulped down the water. 'Yeah, detective. The boys was driving trucks for that McCastles mob that has a depot out at Shepparton. Some fella from Dynamo something or the fuckin' other had seen Texas about it.'

'What bloke? Any name?'

'Nah, I dunno no name but he was a tough little bastard who always gets round in a blue singlet. Looked a bit like a chook, but vicious, like. Never smiled or nothing. Yeah, anyway, this bloke come back and seen Texas again and said he didn't need us no more. Wouldn't say why but Godzilla reckoned the bloke was shit-scared of some new mob. He saw 'em when he went out for a stickybeak.'

'Did you see this new mob, Noelene?'

'Nah, and I didn't want to neither, did I? They was the pricks who shot up the club if ya ask me. Godzilla said they was wogs and was always wearing black leather jackets. Texas reckoned they was muscling in on the drugs trade. Cut the Molochs right out. Into prozzies too, you name it. They brung in them Sons of Odin wankers too to replace our boys on the trucks.'

'Thank you, Noelene,' said Vicky, pleasantly surprised by her cooperation. Big Mama had always hated cops. Ran in the family. Her father had been an expert safe cracker.

'Yeah, well just keep me name out of it, right? Anyway, straight after lunch yesterday – little boys with tomato sauce, dim sims, Chiko rolls, a real treat to cheer the guys up – the first thing we knew there was this fuckin' great bang and the front wall had sorta exploded. Then there was another great fuckin' bang and you could see out into the front yard where they was chasing some of the Molochs and shooting 'em down. Like dogs, they was.'

Noelene started sobbing at this point and Vicky had to pass

her the box of tissues and pat her good shoulder before she could continue.

'Anyway, I managed to dive under the pool table just when four or five blokes burst in wearing them balaclavas and started shootin' the place up. Automatic rifles, I reckon, because there was long bursts of firing. The line of top shelf stuff behind the bar just sorta exploded. People was screaming and that, but I kept me head down while they was going round just executin' everyone. Fair dinkum. Just like that in cold blood. Then the cunts went into the back and there was more shots, so I reckon they done Texas in there. Me shoulder was giving me merry 'ell, but I kept me mouth shut. The doctor reckoned I copped a ricochet. Part of the roof come down on me head, too, when I poked it out from under the pool table for a look-see.

'The shooting suddenly stopped, but I stayed doggo for a long time in case them cunts come back. It went all quiet but then I heard groaning. It was me mate Cougar. There was nothing I could do. She made a rattling noise in her throat, and I just knew she was dead, the poor cow.' Big Mama choked up at the memory of what she had seen next. 'Jeez, detective, Godzilla was lying next to the bar with half his fuckin' head missing.'

She broke down at this point and the ward sister came in and instructed the detectives to leave. Vicky couldn't resist a parting shot. 'Thanks for telling us all this,' she said, 'and I really hope you get better. But Noelene, a word of advice. I'd get rid of the earrings if I were you.'

'Eh?' Big Mama demanded; slack jawed with bewilderment. 'What's wrong wiv 'em? Godzilla givvum to me.'

'Small matter of the Holocaust,' Vicky prompted. 'There's Jewish nurses here and they don't like Nazi stuff.'

'Eh?'

The detectives turned to leave but just as they got to the door Big Mama called out to them, her voice firmer now. 'Now Detective Tran, there's no way that I'll testify in court. Don't forget that. I've told you too much already and from now on I'm keeping me gob shut. Comprenny vooz?'

Vicky wondered if there was some way of making her give evidence. Or if it would be worth it. The gunmen had been wearing ski masks so Big Mama couldn't identify anyone even if she was willing to testify.

The forensics report came in shortly after the two detectives got back to the station. The attackers had cut through the locks on the clubhouse gates with boltcutters, then blasted in the front of the building with rocket propelled grenades. There were hundreds of empty bullet cases, most fired from Armalite-style automatic rifles. They must have known the layout of the place because they knew where club president Bobby Mudford's office was located, although it was a warren. They'd shot him between the eyes at point blank range, and there was nothing much left of his head. Two badly injured survivors were not expected to live, which would take the death toll to eleven, but Big Mama would live to find some other gang to latch onto. It had been a military-style operation and was over within five minutes. SOCOs were still combing the premises for clues but were pessimistic of a quick break-through about the attackers' identity. Having said that, there wasn't much chance that the new firm weren't the perpetrators of the outrage. The fearsome Molochs Marauders had ceased to exist. Snouts were reporting that most of the other bikie gangs had packed up and left town, heading interstate or home to mum and dad. Patrol cars sent to investigate reported that many of the gangs' clubhouses were indeed shuttered up and silent, including those of Lucifers Avengers in Werribee, Mammons Monsters in St Albans, and Satans Sinners in Deer Park. (Apostrophes were an alien concept for these knights of the road.) The only mob still going was the one associated with the McCastles firm, the Sons of Odin – which raised the question why they had been spared.

Jack got back to the flat that evening to find that the forensics team had left everything shipshape apart from traces of talc in the bathroom. There was no indication that the intruder had been back. He found himself wondering if it had all been in his imagination. When he had eaten a frugal repast, he went down the road to the pub, drank one pint of Guinness and came back for an early night with his book.

CHAPTER 15

The rain had stopped before the police convoy arrived in Nelson Place, the broad waterfront street between the Strand roundabout and the naval dockyard in Williamstown. The blank windows stared down from the long line of double-storey Victorian buildings and the sun was a giant orange ball in the dawn sky. The sunlight had bejewelled the wet green leaves of the trees in the Commonwealth Reserve and was sparkling on the water by the jetty where the old corvette, the HMAS *Castlemaine*, was permanently berthed. Jack looked at her grey bulk. *Red sky at night, sailor's delight; red sky in the morning, sailor's warning.* There would be more rain that day and he hoped it would purify the air, which was still tainted by the great fire still raging out at Tottenham. Maybe even extinguish the blaze.

The target of the police operation was an illicit knocking shop situated on the first floor of one of the Victorian buildings. It sat above a fish and chip shop, which was closed. Liz, her slim form bulked out by a Kevlar vest, followed part of the team down a laneway to the back of the premises, and

Jack stayed out the front by a nondescript brown door next to an ice cream parlour, which was not open for the day. He had the keys from the agent, who had informed them that a woman who called herself Rhonda Nicholls had taken out a short-term lease. She had given an address in Braybrook and had 'seemed perfectly legit. Nice clothes. Expensive perfume. Sorta professional, like.' They would follow this up later but expected a dead end, despite the estate agent saying the woman's papers appeared to be in order. The street was empty, save for a mechanical sweeper whirring along the gutter further down towards the dockyard. A squad of armed police were lined up parallel to the shopfront, ready for Jack to give the signal for them to go into action. He was taking no chances.

The first officers to burst through the door and pound up the front staircase and the rear fire escape were armed with assault rifles. It turned out to be massive overkill. They found one startled young woman coming out of the lavatory and another cowering on a bunk bed at the back of the flat. Both were wearing skimpy nightdresses. With their huge eyes smudged with mascara they reminded Jack of the sad figures in the Pierrot clown posters. One of them had a nasty purple bruise on her face, but her blue eyes had lit up with relief and gratitude. She spoke rapidly in a foreign language, smiling sadly and gesticulating. Jack was no expert, but it sounded Slavic: Russian, Ukrainian, or Polish maybe. She was pointing at the other girl, who had stayed curled up on the bunk. '*Ona ochen' bol'na, gospodin*,' she repeated over and over, clutching Liz's hand desperately. After searching her memory, she added in heavily accented English, 'I am Svetlana. This one Natasha. She is very sick.' Jack looked closely and could see needle marks on Natasha's arms, one of which was badly swollen. He dialled for an ambulance, fearing that she had blood poisoning.

The brothel occupied a large Victorian-era flat, with dark rooms on both sides of a gloomy central corridor. Bunk beds occupied one room and there were more in a sleep-out at the back, which was separated from the rest of the apartment by a locked wooden door. In an attempt to humanise their surroundings, someone had tacked a print of an English fox-hunting scene on the wall of the main bedroom. The business end of the brothel occupied four bedrooms out the front. 'Reckon this is where the pimps hung out,' observed Liz, standing in the parlour overlooking Nelson Place. All the windows had been nailed shut – recently it seemed from the brightness of the nails and the freshly damaged wood – and the external doors had been deadlocked. Liz shuddered. 'Hate to think what would have happened if there was a fire.' She gestured at the brimming ashtrays left by the pimps. 'Lots of DNA, anyway.'

The ambulance officers came pounding up the stairs, took a quick look at Natasha and bore her away on a stretcher. Svetlana was able to walk to the ambulance, clutching a blanket around herself. When they had gone, Jack ordered the place sealed up and festooned with crime scene tape. Forensics would be along shortly to see what they could find, and burly constables stood guard to ensure Joe Public kept its distance. The empty street had filled up. Dog walkers and joggers had diverted from the park and were milling about with several elderly rubberneckers on the opposite footpath, and somehow the press was already on the scene. Jack irritably waved the newshounds aside, assuring them that he would be making a statement later that day.

'Hey Liz,' Jack said, as she started the car. 'Did you notice that there were only two girls, but the bunks would accommodate eight or nine?'

Liz nodded. 'Yeah. It looked like all the bunks had been slept in recently. We'll have to ask the Svetlana girl if she knows what happened to the other girls.' She paused. 'You know, Jack, I feel positively homicidal when I think of what's been done to these young women.'

Jack nodded. He knew precisely how she felt. 'But we've narrowed down our list of suspects for the leaker. Now, I dunno about you, Liz, but I haven't had breakfast. What do you say that we try the Alfa Bakehouse in Yarraville on the way back?'

'Done. I'm famished.'

They were soon tucking into big plates of poached eggs on sourdough toast – Jack's with bacon to Liz's disapproval – and reviewing the progress of Operation Tantalus. A quick call to the hospital yielded the news that Svetlana was well and could be brought to the police station. Natasha had been pumped full of antibiotics and fluids but was still very ill. A patrol car had called at the Braybrook address that 'Rhonda Nicholls' had given the real estate people, but the bewildered old woman who answered the door had never heard of her. The estate agent agreed to provide a description for an identikit mugshot, but the chances were that the so-called Rhonda Nicholls was wearing disguise. A wig and glasses could go a long way to altering a person's appearance. The agent did remember that the woman had a slight foreign accent, which had seemed just a bit strange given the Anglo name she'd given now that she thought about it. Her ID had seemed in order, though.

When they got back to the station, Liz and Jack summoned the old desk sergeant, Bruiser Macfarlane, for a conference. Ernie Foxcroft reckoned there wasn't much about the western suburbs that Bruiser didn't know. He arrived with a takeaway coffee and a big box of Anzac biscuits, which he offered round. He was plainly delighted to get away from the front desk. Liz got down to business. 'Any reason, err … Bartholomew, why anyone would be shooting near the Botanical Gardens in Williamstown?' she asked. 'Any major criminals down that way?' She was wondering how he had come by such an unusual given name. He did nothing to enlighten her on the latter score. He rubbed his Desperate Dan chin and stared out the window. 'Prefer Bruiser. Even the missus calls me that. Anyway, in answer to your question, there's crims down that way of course but they're further over towards the main drag. But let me think …' He snapped his beefy fingers. 'Put two and two together and you get … the answer!'

'Spit it out, Bruiser!' demanded Jack, but he was smiling.

'Well, my guess is that them blokes who shot through from the dump and left the bus in Newport was illegal immigrants. Makes sense?'

Jack nodded. 'And?'

'There's this nun, see. Sister someone … Anyway, she's big on refugees and other stuff like that. You know. East Timor. Aboriginal Land Rights. More like a red ragger than a nun I reckon. Anyway, she lives in Osborne Street. Opposite the gardens.' He clicked his fingers. 'Susan Lawless. Both by name and nature, I reckon. Fact is that the reports point straight at her. There was a bloke in a turban there too.'

Liz almost looked like she could kiss him. He had wandered over to the window, so she turned quickly to Jack. 'Let's give the old boy an airing,' she whispered. 'He's due to retire any-time soon and I reckon he'd jump at the chance.'

So he did. He got a colleague to fill in for him at the front desk and accompanied them out through the rain to the car. 'Change's as good as a holiday,' he chirped. 'Always wanted to be in CIB but got stuck behind that desk. Years went by and that was that. Woke up one day and I was 64.' He fed himself another Anzac biscuit.

They had wondered about the Bruiser nickname. Back in the day the police had been more liberal with good hidings than today. Jack took the wheel and Liz sat next to him with Bruiser in the back happily snacking on his box of biscuits. Liz had gone quiet, and Jack had a fair idea what she was thinking. He wasn't sure if he wanted to find the bloke with the turban and his mates either. Nevertheless, he reasoned, if they found them, they would be just that bit closer to tracking down the bastards who'd poisoned half the city. And done Christ knows what besides. They would also send Vicky Tran down to Camperdown to see what the EPA had found. The chances were that the new dump was the handiwork of the same villains.

A young woman answered when they knocked on the door of the large house in Williamstown. She was wearing jeans and a tee-shirt, not a nun's habit as they'd expected. With her hair wrapped in a blue headband and her face smiling enigmatically, she reminded Jack of the young woman in a famous painting by Jan Vermeer – 'The Milkmaid', that was the one. His ex-wife had had a framed print.

'Sister Susan Lawless?' Jack asked after he had held up his warrant card.

'No, officer, I'm Sister Monica. May I ask what this is about?' Her tone was friendly but reserved. She invited them in and guided them through to the front parlour. It was plainly, but tastefully furnished, they noticed. They sat in a line on the couch and watched the raindrops drizzle down the large bay window. It was a world away from the mean streets and the crims with whom they spent so much time. The bookshelves were stuffed with classics – Shakespeare, Milton, Dickens, Thackeray – along with works of theology and philosophy. There was a large baroque crucifix above the blackwood mantelpiece, and a stylised picture of Jesus on another wall. Bruiser seemed a trifle overawed; probably was a Catholic.

The door opened and a small bespectacled woman glided in on rubber-soled shoes. She too was in mufti. 'Good afternoon,' she said, her voice soft. 'Please be seated.' She sat in an armchair and steepled her fingers. 'Now, may I offer you tea or coffee?'

Jack said he'd love a cup of tea, and Bruiser and Liz agreed, so the nun went to the door and spoke quietly to someone outside.

'Now, officers,' she said, resuming her seat and smiling at each one in turn. 'How may I help?'

Jack cut straight to the chase. 'We have reason to believe,' he said, 'that these premises have been used to harbour illegal immigrants. We have also had reports of firearms being discharged in the vicinity early this morning. Would you like to comment?'

'Well, Chief Inspector,' the nun replied. 'Shots most definitely *were* fired out in the street this morning, but I'm afraid that I have no idea by whom or indeed at whom.' She folded her hands on her lap and looked Jack straight in the eye. Jack wondered about the Ninth Commandment but repeated his question about immigrants. On the other hand, her body language didn't scream 'Liar!'

'Dear me,' the nun replied. 'I wonder who had been telling you these things. There are no immigrants illegal or otherwise in this house except for me. I was born in Ireland. You are welcome to look around the premises if you wish.'

She hadn't answered the question, but Jack had to pause when the young nun came in bearing a big tray of tea and biscuits. She fussed about pouring drinks, and Susan passed the biscuits round. Bruiser helped himself to three, then on impulse took another before looking sheepish. When they had sipped their tea and nibbled on the biscuits, Liz took up the questions, again without learning much.

'Sergeant Macfarlane here tells us that you are involved in refugee advocacy,' she said. 'Could it be that your advocacy extends to sheltering people who have entered the country illegally?'

'Please, Inspector,' sighed the nun. 'The last time I looked, Australia was still a signatory to the UN Convention on Refugees. Persons fleeing persecution are legally entitled to seek asylum. Our government has trashed it but it's still international law.'

'OK,' Liz replied. 'I'll rephrase that. Could it be that you are helping asylum seekers who have not presented themselves to the authorities, or who have not arrived via channels approved by the government?' The truth was that Liz herself was uneasy with the official government position and she found part of herself wishing that this nun did not give anything away.

'No, I am not,' said Susan, glancing at the crucifix.

'But would you tell us if you were,' Liz riposted. She felt uneasy. Her own father had jumped ship, but he was a white European from Hamburg so there was no fuss about it. She'd done a bit of research for a university essay and knew that there were thousands of visa overstayers roaming around the country at any time, but if they were white Westerners the authorities didn't care too much.

The nun merely smiled.

The conversation went round and round after that and after a decent interval Jack stood. They thanked the nun for the refreshments and trooped out the door, scurrying to the car to get out of the rain.

'Well,' sighed Jack. 'I get the feeling that she wasn't telling us everything.'

'We could get a warrant,' suggested Bruiser, pleased to be back on territory he understood.

'Nah,' said Jack. 'There's nobody there now and she offered to let us look round. I reckon our birds would have flown if they had been there. The old bloke at the house where they dumped the bus might know something though.'

'We could go and ask him,' suggested Liz.

Jack thought for a moment. 'Nah, I reckon he'd clam up.

Better to put him under surveillance and see what crops up.'

Liz agreed.

After the car had driven off, Sister Susan rang Dixie Trumble.

CHAPTER 16

Back in the Footscray police station, Liz took a young constable with her into an interview room. Svetlana, one of the girls from the Williamstown brothel, was sitting there holding a coffee cup. She was very pretty, with shoulder length strawberry blonde hair and blue eyes set in a high-cheek-boned Slavic face. Someone had found decent clothes for her and she had tried to hide the bruise on her face with make-up. She was chewing nervously on her bottom lip but was obviously still overjoyed to have escaped. The Russian interpreter, a ruddy-faced, neat little man who introduced himself as Ivan Kuzmich, smiled as the two officers sat down across the desk. He was wearing a three-piece blue suit and bow tie despite the humid heat.

'This is Svetlana Anikanova,' he said. 'She speaks a little English. She says to thank you from the bottom of her heart.'

'Please tell her that she's welcome and there is nothing to be frightened of,' Liz said with a reassuring smile. 'She hasn't done anything wrong, and we hope that she can help us find the people who have mistreated her.'

Ivan translated and Svetlana nodded. She had already got the drift of what Liz was saying. Over the course of the next hour, she related what had happened to her since she left her home in Novoshakhtinsk, a small heavy industrial town in the Rostov Oblast, hard up on the border with Ukraine. Svetlana had worked part-time as a receptionist in a clinic and worked a few hours in a local grocery shop, but she was restless with life in a declining regional city. When an advertisement appeared in the local newspaper for clerical positions abroad for young women, she had jumped at the chance. She was 19 years old and living with her parents in a decaying 1940s apartment block. Her father was incapacitated with silicosis from a lifetime of working in the anthracite mines and her mother had lost her job when the chemical factory she had worked in was privatised. Her parents were devout Communists and although they admitted that the old system had many faults, they abhorred what their country had become under Boris Yeltsin and his sinister understudy, Vladimir Putin. Svetlana had believed she would be able to send them money and who knew, maybe they could emigrate from what had become a city with no future. The woman who interviewed Svetlana seemed nice, and Svetlana had good school grades and references. She spoke a little English, and the woman had smiled and assured her that it would improve once she was in Australia. Svetlana obtained a passport, and she was thrilled when the Australian Embassy sent her a temporary work permit.

She was so excited when she boarded the long flight that would take her to Melbourne that she could hardly sit still. It was the trip of a lifetime for a naïve young girl from a decaying regional industrial city. There were six other Russian girls and two from Ukraine, and they promised that they would keep in touch after they arrived in Australia. A Russian called Cyril met them at Tullamarine airport, holding up a sign with their names on it written in neat Cyrillic script. He smiled easily and they felt they were safe as he ushered them courteously into a big black car and piled their luggage into the capacious boot. Cyril pointed out the sights as he drove along the freeway: the skyscrapers on the skyline and then a big yellow beam that poked out above the road that had won international design awards. He drove expertly over one big bridge and then over another even bigger one from which they could see a big bay, a river, and long lines of cranes at the docks. Distant Novoshakhtinsk seemed so shabby, and Svetlana felt a stab of concern and love for her family.

'Here we are, ladies,' Cyril said, flashing his brilliant smile as he turned into a cul-de-sac and coasted to a halt outside a big red brick building. 'This is your new home.'

The front foyer was bright and spacious and the Russian woman who met them smiled and asked if they had had a good flight. Cyril piled their luggage onto the floor and waved as he went back to the car and then drove off. He seemed so nice, Svetlana told Liz wistfully before her face fell.

'I am Anastasia.' The woman spoke rapid Moscow-accented Russian. 'Before I show you to your rooms, there are a few formalities. I shall have to make photocopies of your passports, and will return these to you when you have settled in.' It seemed reasonable, so they complied without hesitation, proud of their red passports embossed with the gold eagle and lettering. The young women were so excited to be starting new lives in this wonderful country. They plied her with questions, chattering happily, but she waved her hands with restrained impatience. 'All will be revealed later. Now, if you'll follow me, we can get you settled in.'

The nightmare began when they entered the windowless corridor beyond a big steel door. Svetlana cried when she spoke of what had happened next. After the woman had locked the door shut behind them they stood uncertainly, taking in the damp smell and the unpainted Besser block walls. Fluorescent lights flickered into life and five men came loping up to them from the gloom. They were big, with unshaven faces dark with stubble and their lupine smiles were not reassuring. They devoured the girls with their eyes and one actually licked his lips, winked at his mates and fingered his bulging crotch. They spoke in a language Svetlana strained to understand, but she got the gist of it. 'They said, "pretty girls come with us" and laughed.'

'Would you recognise these men?' Liz asked through Ivan, the interpreter.

Svetlana nodded. Liz pushed two photographs across the table and the girl burst into a tirade of angry Russian.

'She says she would recognise them anywhere.'

'*Mudak!*' Svetlana hissed, pointing her finger at the mugshot of Darko Percović.

'And this one?' Liz asked, pointing to the photo of the body from the Tottenham dump.

'*Chudoviwe!*' shouted Svetlana, with tears spurting into her eyes.

'She is saying that these men are monsters,' said Ivan. 'They first beat and raped the girls. They called it "seasoning." Then they gave them "hot shots" of drugs. This went on until the girls stopped fighting. After that, they locked them in dormitories with many other women and forced them to have sex with men. Many men. Drunks. Men who would … She doesn't want to say any more about it.'

Svetlana was sobbing hopelessly now. Their captors had done so many vile things to them. There were others. Horrible creatures with dead eyes. One night, a big man had come to the brothel with the woman, Anastasia, from the office. The other men – Serbians, they were – were frightened of him. He was big, with silver hair and colourless eyes. He walked around looking the girls up and down until he stood in front of Svetlana. The other men always spoke Serbian, but this man spoke good Russian. Moscow again, she thought, but with a trace of something else. He was gloating, mocking her as a little idiot who had been too ignorant to know what was going to happen to her.

'I fuck this one,' he said.

Svetlana spat in his face, so he punched her in the head and the others took turns hitting her until she passed out. When she woke, she was lying on her bunk and Natasha – the girl who had been sick – was bathing her face. She wanted to die right then, but Natasha spoke soothingly and said she was not to give in to them. Svetlana swore that she would get them. She had taken a knife from the kitchen and began to sharpen it on the brick windowsill at night and hide it in her mattress. When the time came, she planned to kill one of the monsters and make her escape. But then the police had raided the brothel and saved her.

The thugs had left in a hurry the night before, taking several girls with them and deadlocking the doors as they left, including the one dividing off the front of the flat. They'd left Natasha behind because she was seriously ill, and Svetlana had hidden in a big cupboard, fearing that because she was the prettiest they'd take her with them too. After they'd gone, Svetlana had tried banging on the sleep-out window to attract attention, but nobody had heard. It was raining hard, and in any case they were at the back of the building, which was obscured with trees and undergrowth. There was a man digging in his garden but he seemed to be deaf even when his dog noticed them and started to bark.

'But how is Natasha?' Svetlana asked, angry with herself for forgetting her friend.

She smiled sadly when Liz told her that Natasha was being treated for septicaemia in hospital. It had been touch and go and if she had not received medical help she would have died. Svetlana had begged the men to bring a doctor for her, but they had just laughed. 'We get others,' they shrugged. 'Plenty girls.' It was a crime to treat horses like that, let alone human beings.

'I want to go home,' Svetlana said. 'I will join the police, and I will stop these people doing to other girls what they did to me.' She shoved the mugshots back over the table and declared that her big regret was that she hadn't managed to kill one of them.

Liz was not going to give Svetlana a sermon about turning the other cheek. 'I understand. If it's any consolation, we will find the rest of these men and punish them.' She wondered, though, if any punishment could make up for what these men had done. They'd be gaoled and then deported, with zero chance of rehabilitation; then back on the streets of some European city to prey on women and girls.

Svetlana was anxious to get back home to her parents but agreed to remain in Australia so that she could testify against the gang, and she was eager to help in any way to trace them. She agreed to work with the police artist to produce iden-tikit pictures of the men and the woman. Although their captors had blindfolded them, Svetlana calculated that her first place of imprisonment was a ten-minute drive from the Williamstown brothel. There were trains going past at intervals, and at night what sounded like pistol shots as they went by. Railway detonators, Liz reckoned, which narrowed things down a bit. She would instruct officers on patrol to keep an eye open for likely places and suspicious activity. It was also useful to know that many of the foot soldiers in the gang appeared to be Serbian and that they had deferred to a silver-haired Russian man and to a Russian woman who had called herself Anastasia.

'Anything else you can think of?' Liz asked.

Svetlana thought for a while before replying, her English quite fluent now. 'Yes. One Australian man sometimes come to the *bordel*. For the girls, you know. He was... oh I cannot say. The gang members, they treat him like, like … he was a boss…'

'They would obey him?'

'Yes, that is word. I think he was a very powerful man.'

'Did you hear a name for this man?' Liz was scribbling furiously in her notebook.

'No name, but they called him "Uncle". She went on to describe a stocky, red-haired, angry man. 'His face … I think he will have a heart attack … *Fu*, I hope he dies!'

The identikit mugshot produced with Svetlana's help portrayed an extremely unpleasant, truculent-looking man with the complexion of a boiled lobster, but there were no matches in any of the police files. Liz was sure she'd seen him before but couldn't remember where. It would come to her – probably in the middle of the night.

CHAPTER 17

Terry Tudge was exhausted, broke, hungry, and shit-scared. The little Alfred E. Neuman lookalike had been sleeping rough except when it got too wet, then he'd gone to a Salvos' shelter. He didn't like those places. They were the point of no return, full of tired old blokes, and smelled of death and wasted lives. He had a vision of his own life passing by, out of control, and him ending up like them wondering what the hell was the point of it all. He was fuckin' desperate. Jeez he'd have to pull his finger out, like that magistrate had warned the last time he was in court. His Dad, too, had gone on at him. He should have listened.

Now here he was, stony broke with only some fluff and an old tram ticket in his pockets. He'd picked a bloke's pocket at Spencer Street Station, but it had all gone wrong when he'd tried it on again at Flinders Street the fucker had chased him out into Swanston Street screaming blue murder. He'd only just managed to jump onto a tram to get away. The crim who'd coached him in Pentridge had stressed that successful pickpockets looked prosperous: nobody expected them to do it. Trouble was, Tudge looked like a bum, in fact he *was* a bum and was fast getting to look like the deros in the men's shelters. He hadn't had a shave and was starting to smell.

He'd scarpered from the flat when it dawned on him that the hard-faced men were going to do him in just like they'd stiffed his best mate Bazza because they reckoned Bazza was a snitch. Cut his throat, they had and buried him in a back-yard somewhere out Maidstone way. It wasn't fair. Like Bazza, Terry was an honest crook. He'd had done fuckin' everything for them. Let them use the flat. Let them use the bus. Driven it out to that dump for them a couple of times. Ferried them wogs about. Not that he could have refused. He was feeling bloody sorry for himself. He started to cry. Everything had gone pear-shaped after that tart Kimberley had left him and his big sister had disowned him.

Truth was, though, it was his own fault. He couldn't deny it. His parents had left him the flat and he'd got a position as an apprentice jockey. Should have been set up for life, but he'd taken a bribe to fix a race at Caulfield and was out on his arse. Blacklisted for life. So much for that. He sobbed out loud; wished he'd never met them wog cunts in leather jackets. He'd tried to sleep in the toilets at the Footscray TAFE last night but the security men had kicked him out with a warning not to come back. Give him a belt around the ear and it hurt like buggery. After that he'd tried to shelter from the rain under the abutments of the Bunbury Street railway bridge, but a pair of tough old guys had driven him off. Reckoned it was their patch and they said they didn't want things looking like something out of *MAD* magazine hanging about lowering the tone. Why the fuck did people go on about that magazine? He'd never heard of it. Never read nothin'.

When the sun came up, Terry was sleeping the sleep of exhaustion under a palm tree in Footscray Park, damp and aching like he was an old man. He was awakened sometime later when the rain started again. Christ, it couldn't go in like this, he sighed. He really was going to turn himself in. No bloody choice. Soon as he was able, Mabel. Gawd, he was a poet! Soon he was limping through the Nicholson Street mall. His legs hurt from sleeping on the wet ground. He'd stolen some funny Asian buns with paste in 'em and a carton of milk from outside a Vietnamese grocery and was guzzling them as he walked. The shopkeeper yelled he was gunna kill him, but Terry had run off like a doped-up Sandown Park greyhound. His eyes swivelled this way and that, ever alert lest the leather coat men or the wallopers materialised. There was safety in crowds, he reckoned, so he turned sharp left at Irving Street and joined the commuters hurrying towards the train station. The leather coats weren't likely to use public transport. Use the old loaf, like an old Cockney master burglar used to say when he was coaching him in Pentridge. Think. Plan. Don't act on impulse. He was a D-Grade student in that academy of crime, but he remembered that much.

He dawdled over the railway overpass, reconsidering whether he should turn himself in to the coppers, but when he thought of the wet and hungry alternative, he hurried down Hyde Street on his funny little legs. He knew the cop shop well. Been nicked often enough; it would be a home away from home! They'd put him in witness protection, he reckoned. He was busting for a piss. Couldn't help it. Done it against a tree in the street and didn't give a fuck when a woman said he was disgusting. He'd like to see what she'd do if she was bustin' and didn't have no dunny. Bitch.

The man was coming down the entrance steps when Tudge got to the Footscray police station. He could smell the bloke was a Big D; youngish, but hard-faced like some of them got; a fella with spiky brown hair and big ears. He might have nicked him once. The copper's eyes widened when he saw him. Terry went to walk past him, but the cop grabbed his arm, and his grip was like Tarzan's, fingers went right round his biceps. The D flashed his warrant card real quick and said 'Well, well, well. If it ain't little Terry Tudge. I'm Sergeant Flakemore. You've led us a merry dance.' With that, the Flakemore copper turned Tudge round and steered him back up the street and into the police car park, where he unlocked his car and shoved Terry inside. Flash Beemer, it was. Wasn't no cop car, Terry knew. Clean inside for starters. Terry didn't protest. He reckoned the copper knew what he was doing; that he was taking him to a safe house. Hoped he was, anyway and he was hopin' for a feed. There was another D watching from a window. Young fella. Terry hadn't seen him before. Looked like he should be in school.

The copper drove out of the carpark and when he stopped at the lights by the Belgravia pub, he dialled someone on his mobile phone. 'Twenty minutes,' he muttered, and hung up. Terry didn't like the look on his face, but the cop winked and said something he didn't catch. The Flakemore dude drove real slow, not saying nothing and by the time they turned into Little Boundary Road, Terry had a bad feeling in his gut. There wasn't no houses round here; just warehouses and factories and that. When they got to the turn-off to the Western Ring Road, Terry was certain the copper meant to do him harm. The copper had to stop at a red light so Terry used the old loaf, leapt out of the car, and hopped it faster than Kevan Gosper down the bicycle path back towards Footscray. The pig had come out of the Beemer and was yelling at him to stop but Terry didn't take no notice of him.

He stopped when he figured it was safe, and walked slowly, and thought about his next move. He knew that the bike path crossed over Little Boundary Road and was worried that the copper would be waiting for him there. Bound to be. It had started raining again and he was desperate. Was gunna catch his death if he didn't get dry. Anyway, if the cunt was waiting Terry reckoned he'd scoot across the six-lane West Gate Freeway to get away. He'd seen a bloke do it in a movie. Piece of piss. Cars going every which way in Los Angeles or somewhere like that, but the hero got across and got the girl. Turned out Terry didn't need to.

A bit further along the path, next to a reedy lagoon with old supermarket trollies and a solitary duck on it, he saw an expensive-looking bicycle propped up on its kickstand. The cyclist was pissing in the bushes, so Terry jumped up quick smart on the saddle and wobbled off furiously back in the direction from which he'd come. The cyclist cunt chased him on foot, roaring about what he was going to do when he got hold of him but gave up after a while, and Terry relaxed his pace and managed a big grin. Shit, he was bowling along like Lance Armstrong or that Opperman cunt. Things was lookin' up. He approached the intersection with the road cautiously, but there was no sign of the cop and he was able to cross at the lights and cycle along in a northerly direction past a stinking rendering plant that near made him throw up because he was breathing so hard. Still stunk of smoke from that big fire too. After a couple of kilometres the bike path looped round a service station and a McDonald's fast food joint. The rain became torrential, so he propped the bicycle up against the wall of the Maccas and went inside. He didn't have no money, so he sat on his wet arse in a booth and watched the raindrops trickling down the window. He was hungry and the burgers smelled good. The staff started to eye him suspiciously, but he didn't like the idea of going back out into the rain, so he sat quietly trying to avoid eye contact with them.

He must have dozed off, for a hand was shaking him roughly. 'Hey, you can't sleep in here,' said the man, who had MANAGER on his badge and an angry mouth under a Hitler moustache. Musta been German but Terry didn't catch the name on his badge.

'Please mate just let me stay until the rain stops,' Terry wheedled. 'I'll sell you me bike if you like or swap it for some food. I'm fuckin' starving, man.'

The manager snorted and went off shaking his head, saying something about Terry having to leave in five minutes. Terry dozed off again and when he awoke the rain had stopped, so he shook himself and went outside. The bike was gone, some tea leaf must have half-inched it, he reckoned. He shrugged and went to walk off when a uniformed cop came up with a nasty look on his dial. Terry turned round to flee but the cop's partner blocked his escape.

'Now, sunshine,' said the first cop, a big dark Lebanese-looking fella, 'we've had a complaint that you stole a bloke's expensive pushbike, so why don't you just empty your pockets so that we can see who you are.'

Terry protested feebly. 'I never done nothing, and if I did, where's me pushbike?'

'It's not yours, but it's just here,' said the Lebanese-looking walloper, taking Terry by the arm and steering him round the corner. Grip on him like Arnold Schwarzenegger latching onto that Cindy sheila in *Commando*. Shit, Terry had no hope. His shoulders slumped and a look of despair spread over his freckled face. The bike was there and the bloke he'd nicked it from was there too and was giving him a dirty look. Still had his poncy Lycra and that on. What if these coppers was in cahoots with that big Flakemore D?

'That's him,' said the Lycra bloke. 'I raced up to my car parked near the rendering plant after he pinched my bike, and figured I might head him off at Maccas. Too right I want to press charges. Bastard. Lucky you got him first otherwise I'd have punched him out. Hey, don't he look like …'

'Yeah, don't he,' laughed the big cop, motioning to Terry to turn out his pockets.

There was slim pickings in Terry's strides; apart from the used tram ticket and his empty wallet, not even a brass razoo. Them leather jacket cunts had taken all his ID: driver's licence, Medicare card, library card from when he was breaking into lockers in that book place in the city. The second cop – a younger man with amused eyes – frisked him and they took him out to the police car.

'No ID on 'im,' said the younger cop.

'What's yer name?' the Lebbo copper asked.

'Not tellin' ya nothin' till I get me brief.'

'OK, gerrin, Alfred,' said the Lebanese-looking one, pushing Terry's head down so that he didn't bang it on the roof.

Alfred? Why was everyone calling him that? 'Not me name,' he protested, but the coppers just laughed like he'd told a funny joke so he laughed too. They slammed the door and jumped in themselves. Terry knew that the back doors would be locked closed, so he slumped down, resigned to whatever happened to him. If these cops were in with that bent detective, Flakemore, he was rooted. They didn't say nothing as they drove up Geelong Road to Footscray, where they marched him inside the cop shop and charged him with the theft of the pushbike. The fat old sergeant on the counter gave him a long look and Terry could almost see the cogs whirling inside his grey head.

Bruiser Macfarlane put down his biscuit and picked up the phone. 'Liz,' he said. 'We've just arrested Terry Tudge. We've got the little shit here if you want him.'

*

Five minutes later, Vicky Tran and Liz marched into the interview room and found Terry Tudge sitting with his head in his hands. He was filthy and was smelling up the room.

'You look ratshit, son,' said Vicky. 'I'm Detective Tran and this is Detective Sergeant Flakemore.'

'Eh?' said Terry. His mouth was hanging open and his eyes flitted from one to the other. 'Is there two of youse?'

'Yeah,' said Vicky drily. 'There's me and there's Sergeant Flakemore here.'

'Nah,' said Terry. 'Is there two Sergeant Flakemores is what I mean.'

'Not the last time I counted,' said Liz, half-smiling and scrutinising the little man's face. No doubt at all about the resemblance, she thought.

'But that copper who nicked me earlier said he was Sergeant Flakemore,' Terry whined. 'He was gunna kill me. Feller with sticking out ears. Smelled like 'e'd tipped a bottle of aftershave over hisself.'

Liz produced her warrant card and that shut him up after he taken a close look with his mouth working as he read the print. She turned to Vicky and raised her eyebrows. It figured.

'Now Terry,' said Liz. 'You've been arrested for stealing a bicycle. We'd like to speak with you about some other matters and maybe we can go easy on you about the bike if you cooperate. First, though, tell us about this person who claimed to be DS Flakemore.'

'You said it was a man,' Vicky added.

Terry was eager to help. 'Yeah. I'm not bullshitting youse. This Big D grabbed me arm when I was coming into the cop-shop this morning. Said he was Sergeant Flakemore. Made me get in his flash car.'

'What did he look like, Terry?'

'Young sort of a bloke. Spiky brown hair. Expensive looking clothes. Like his wheels, a Beemer. Only one thing was his ears, they was big, like this.' He mimed two great protuberances flapping on the side of his head.

'Tell us about the car.'

'I know me cars.' (True. He'd nicked enough of them.)

'Expensive. One of them coupé things. Blue. A Beemer, you know, a BMW.'

'Registration number?'

'I didn't have no chance to see it, did I? When I jumped out down near the Ring Road, I was too scared to think.'

'Scared?' prompted Liz. 'Why were you scared?'

'I didn't like the way he was looking at me and I wondered where he was takin' me. Them gangsters was after me and I twigged he was with 'em. Either that or he was a poof and had designs on me.'

After that, Terry told them everything. They gave him a cup of instant coffee and some Tim Tam biscuits and a constable took him back to the cells. They'd figure out what to do with him when they had dealt with some other business. Vicky rang up to get a Chinese takeaway for him because he whimpered so much about being hungry. Liz relayed what they found out to Jack and Ernie Foxcroft. After that, she sat quietly, thinking about Vicky Tran.

*

Dixie Trumble arrived at the Port Melbourne pub where he'd taken the asylum seekers for safety.

'Time for your mate to go,' he told Soran. 'If things go well, I'll be back in a day or so to take you. Others are safe, mate. They're out of the country and will be able to apply for asylum, Sister Susan says.'

Soran and Daryan embraced. They'd been through a lot together and had grown close. They hadn't known each other back in Iran but had met in a Javanese village close to the sea and had travelled together across the ocean in a fishing boat they feared would sink in the huge waves. They'd worked together under the hot sun picking fruit and then had worked at that stinking dump under the guns of those cruel men. In the factory tanks, too. Now Daryan was leaving, but Dixie assured them that they would see each other again soon in a safe place. They trusted the big man, who had only ever been kind to them. Dixie took Daryan out to his old ute and drove carefully towards the docks.

Dixie's best mate was a retired seafarer called Ronnie Flanagan. They'd been best men at each other's weddings, had walked endless miles of picket line together, and had propped up a few bars together too. Ronnie's son Mick had followed him onto the ships. Dixie had dandled Mick on his knee and Mick still called him Uncle Dixie though they weren't blood relations. The sailor was waiting for them behind a big concrete warehouse next to a wharf crane on the Yarra docks, with his collar turned up against the insistent rain. His ship was moored at the wharf, and he was nervous about port security and the ship's officers. Dixie shook hands with Daryan, wished him well, and walked back to his car. Mick bustled Daryan up the gangplank and down a companionway to his cabin.

'Now, whatever you do, stay here,' Mick ordered. 'I'll bring you some food later. There's two bunks. Mine's the bottom one. We'll be in Auckland in six days.'

Daryan spoke little English, but Soran had translated what Dixie had said, so he knew that he had been stowed away aboard a freighter bound for New Zealand. Once he got there, he could immediately apply for asylum and unlike in Australia he would be released into the community while his case was assessed. New Zealand, again unlike Australia, respected the non-refoulement clauses of the UN Charter and did not treat 'boat people' as criminals.

CHAPTER 18

It was sunny and clear the next day when the police team assembled, milling around on the roadside at Mount Derrimut. The operation had been kept under wraps, with the two officers suspected of leaking kept in the dark. A place of scrappy paddocks and stunted gum trees, Mount Derrimut was right out beyond the rim of Melbourne's sprawl, which was just humming into life to the east. The chances were that the amoebic sprawl of the suburbs would soon engulf it and clamour for more. You could see the big plume of smoke at Tottenham, but the westerly wind was keeping it away.

Last-minute cigarettes were stubbed out and coffee dregs tipped out on the roadside. A kookaburra that had been observing the officers broke out into a chattering commentary on the intrusion. Thick and Thin were doing their double act but no one was interested. It was too early and everyone was keyed up. All the interlopers were wearing bulletproof vests because the man they were about to visit was believed to be armed and dangerous, psychotic even. Garth Leslie Dickins, the CEO of Dynamic Achievers, was said to hate police even more than he did his ex-wives. He had priors stretching back to his misspent youth when he had first ridden with bikie gangs. If he were the 'straight shooter' his accountant Alan Badger claimed, this referred to his suspected collection of firearms rather than his character.

When Jack gave the signal, Thick and Thin sprang forward with boltcutters and snapped the chain on Dickins's steel gates, then stood back as if waiting for applause. When as expected two snarling Italian mastiffs loped up, intent on ripping out throats, the government veterinary officers took charge. Keeping the animals at bay with long poles, they shot tranquilliser darts into their flanks and the beasts ran about a bit before flopping down, comatose. After that, the force response team led the way in a running crouch like so many dark insects, their body armour creaking and their military boots clattering. Some of them looked familiar, Jack thought, from the recent fracas in the Footscray mall when the DETOX people were violently dispersed.

The single-storey house was a veritable fortress of reinforced concrete, with embrasure-like windows protected by steel bars. It was impossible to see whether anyone was lurking inside, and the massive front door looked like it would resist the 'big red key' that Thick and Thin were lugging towards it with expectant grins on their faces. The harsh light revealed that Mr Dickins was no gardener: the compound was partly gravelled, partly concreted, and partly covered with sickly brown grass, with a few stunted trees begging for water. A blue ute was parked out the front, sporting an orange sticker screaming 'FUCK OFF WE'RE FULL' inside an outline map of Australia.

Several officers peeled off and went round the back.

Jack took the megaphone. 'Good morning, Mr Dickins,' he said, his amplified voice echoing off the concrete walls. 'This is the police. We have a warrant to search these premises. We'd like you to open the door for us.'

A minute passed. The armed officers anxiously scanned the windows for any sign of a protruding weapon. Another minute passed without a peep from the house, so Jack picked up the megaphone and repeated his request. The massive door swung open and a nuggety little fellow came out in a loose-kneed crouch, swaying from side to side like a prize-fighter. He had the look of an outraged Black Orpington and was wearing wraparound sunglasses that hid his eyes. He spread his hands wide to indicate that he was not armed and stepped forward on the concrete patio.

Thick and Thin looked disappointed. They hadn't got to use the enforcer on the door.

'Put your hands on your head,' Jack ordered, waving officers forward to grab him. 'Thank you, Mr Dickins. Here is the warrant … Now we'd like a tour of your 'umble abode if you please.'

Dickins scowled. He was struggling to shrug off the grip of the officers at his sides. He had a thin, mean face covered in designer stubble and now that he'd taken off his sunglasses, his humourless black eyes stared unwinkingly. He shrugged. 'You got the warrant, copper, so there's fuck all I can do to stop ya … Hey, what have you done with me dogs?'

'Dogs are having a little sleep,' said Jack. 'Let's get on with it.'

The entrance hallway was a dark cave, with black and purple painted walls and framed posters of sports cars, American muscle cars, horror film posters, combat troops, motor bikes and military vehicles.

'Tacky,' said Liz, nodding at the 'artwork.' 'The bloke's loaded, but he chooses to put boy racer rubbish on his walls.'

'Beam me up Scotty,' said Jack. 'There's no intelligent life round here.'

Dickins farted.

'Now, now,' remonstrated Jack, slipping on latex gloves. 'Manners, Mr Orpington. Let's see what we can find.'

'That's not me name,' snarled Dickins, his mean little face screwed up with hatred.

'Looks like one,' Liz observed, sotto voce.

The hallway's décor was repeated throughout the warren of rooms. Kitsch chandeliers hung from the ceilings and an assortment of clocks ticked away madly like in a demented watchmaker's shop. Cheap veneer cabinets contained a dazzling array of top shelf booze, brightly coloured liqueurs, and cheap glasses. Misses June, July, and August pouted, posed, and preened on framed calendars. The whole joint stank of stale beer and cigarettes but was clean enough. Jack couldn't imagine Dickins doing his own housework so he must have got someone in. The wives had shot through years ago, he knew. There wasn't a book on the premises, only piles of motoring magazines, porno mags, *Soldier of Fortune*, and the like.

'Dear me,' Jack said with a sly look. 'What would your namesake think of your library?'

'What?' grunted Dickins.

'You know; the famous English writer. Wrote *Bleak House.*'

'*Oliver Twist*,' suggested Liz. '*David Copperfield.*'

'Star of English literature,' explained Jack.

Dickins lifted his lip. 'What the fuck are youse talkin' about?"

Liz and Jack laughed and indicated that Dickins should lead the way further into his domain.

'Your bedchamber, squire?' asked Jack as they entered another room through a padded door. Inside, hundreds of videotapes and CDs were stacked in an open-fronted cupboard. Most were porn or recordings of car races. The bed was a vast white and gold plush upholstered thing, with a purple bedspread printed with a stylised drawing of a racing car. A large mirror was positioned overhead, and spotlights were trained on the bed.

'Bit of a Don Juan, are we, Mr Dickins?' Liz taunted.

'A real hit with the ladies,' Jack sneered.

Dickins farted again.

'Now, now, manners Garth,' Jack tutted, wagging a finger. He suddenly became serious. 'What we'd like to know, is where you've hidden the guns.'

Dickins's face was expressionless, but the eye twitch gave him away as he told Jack to fuck off.

Liz donned latex gloves, pulled out bedside drawers, and held up two pistols, a Sig Sauer and a Beretta. 'Aha,' she said. 'I assume you have licences for these?'

Dickins just sneered.

Other drawers contained boxes of ammunition and gun-cleaning tools and oil, various sex toys and some very hardcore porn.

'What's under the bed, I wonder?' Liz said, crouching down beside the enormous monstrosity. 'Aha!' she chirped, reaching underneath and pulling out a semi-automatic rifle. She checked the magazine. 'Loaded too. Naughty.'

'You're nicked, Garth,' said Jack, signalling to Thick and Thin to come forward and click handcuffs on the miscreant's wrists. After a formal caution, Dickins was led away, muttering curses. The firearms charges would be enough to keep him in the cells while their enquiries into the illegal dump proceeded.

Liz came back into the room and beckoned Jack over to the ensuite. 'I've been looking at his bathroom. Come and have a look.'

If it were at all possible, the bathroom was in even worse taste than the boudoir. It sported purple and green tiles and a black frieze. Jack caught sight of a snake – yes a snake! – and jumped back in alarm. There were others too; great slithering things thicker than a Sumo wrestler's leg. 'Jesus,' he exclaimed, his fear allayed by the fact that the serpents were in a large glass cage. They were alive, alright. A big one was uncoiling itself and reaching up the glass: a Chappell Island tiger snake if he wasn't wrong.

'Nasty things,' said Liz, 'but there's something else not right about this room.'

Jack steeled himself for a closer look. 'Only snakes from what I can see.'

Liz shook her head. 'Nah, the size of the room's wrong.'

They paced out the corridor outside the room and then repeated it inside.

Jack laughed. 'Figjam again!'

It was a private joke between them; something Liz had said once when she had made a breakthrough on a case back in Hobart. It meant 'Fuck I'm Good Just Ask Me.'

'Yeah,' she said with a little bow. 'Mr Dickins is hiding some-thing behind the snakes.'

'Let's get the herpetologist in first and continue having a look round.'

A young, dark-haired probationary constable rushed in breathlessly. Bernice King, Jack recalled – the one who'd picked him up at the airport. 'Sir, you'd better come round the back. You won't believe this.' She led them out through a back door to a 'Colorbond' shed half hidden behind a clump of acacias. A medium sized Volvo truck was sitting on the concrete floor. She pointed out that Dickins had been in the process of turning it into an armoured car. Behind it was a Humvee painted in camouflage colours. It looked like he was planning on starting a war.

Liz noticed that another young constable was frowning. She asked what the matter was.

The young woman's reply was hesitant. 'I don't want to sound petty, Inspector,' she sighed, 'but that baggy-arse Bernice King is always rushing off to claim the credit for things.'

Jack laughed at the cop talk for a probationer. 'Maybe she's just keen?'

'I think it's more than that, especially when the Detective Chief Inspector is involved.'

Jack was nonplussed. Liz nodded. 'I'll get Sergeant Macfarlane to have a word with her.'

Fresh horrors were in store. In a room just off the kitchen, a large jacuzzi had been converted to a crocodile pool. The inhabitant was large, too, thought Jack as he hurriedly slammed the door. It was Dickins's Reptilian House of Horrors.

They were lucky to get a snake catcher on short notice. 'Well fuck me,' he said, peering into the snake cage. 'You wouldn't want that glass to break. These babies are dangerous.'

He refused to remove the saurian from the jacuzzi and shrugged when they asked who might do it. 'Dunno.' He shrugged. 'Steve Irwin?'

The detectives stayed at a safe distance until he had removed the serpents, then enlisted Thick and Thin to shift the snake cage. After much huffing and puffing, they discovered that there was a switch to do the job and the cage slid away to reveal a door flush with the walls. They all looked at each other, fearful of what might be behind it. After a brief hesitation, Jack stepped forward and jerked it open. Fluorescent lights flickered automatically into life, and he was relieved that there were no more reptiles. The secret room did, however, contain a bewildering arsenal of weaponry: a loaded machine gun; assault rifles such as the those banned after the Port Arthur massacre; bandoliers and boxes of ammunition; tripods and laser sights; night vision goggles; flak jackets; tasers and stun guns; captive bolt guns; mace; tear gas; and a variety of clubs, whips, blackjacks, and knuckledusters. There were also some adaptors designed to turn semi-automatic weapons into fully automatic military rifles. Along the back wall stood a work-bench and some machine tools for armouring.

Liz arranged for a man from the zoo to take the crocodile away. It had been quite a morning, but more was to come. DC Darryl Puncheon was waiting in the station vestibule when they got back. He asked for a word, and she suggested that they retire to the cafeteria.

'Well?' she said, motioning for him to sit. He looked eager, but kept glancing round and she figured he was terrified that Jack might come in.

'Thought I should let you know,' he said, hesitantly. 'I was in the front office yesterday and I happened to look out the window. Well, you know that crim called Terry Tudge?'

Liz nodded. 'The one who looks like …'

'The kid on *MAD* magazine. Yeah, well when I looked out I saw him coming across the carpark. Looked like he was coming into the station, then that DC, Nick Downer, Flash Nick, he come out and he grabbed Tudge by the arm and took him away.'

'Took him away?'

'Yeah. Across the carpark and into that flash car of his.'

Liz tapped a finger on her front teeth. 'Well thank you, Constable. You've been very helpful.' She watched him thoughtfully as he left the room.

*

When Jack got back to the office, he riffled through his growing pile of internal correspondence. After he had scanned a couple of memos his eyes glazed over. A cup of tea was in order. He stood up to go, but then his attention was caught by a stamped envelope addressed to him care of the cop shop. Whatever it was, it should prove to be more interesting than the pile of other rubbish. It was. Inside were two Polaroid photographs: one of him retrieving his briefcase from his car, and the other of him unlocking the front door of his apartment. He swore under his breath. This was getting serious.

CHAPTER 19

Bruiser Macfarlane was scowling when he marched up to Nick Downer in the staff canteen. 'You're to come with me,' he growled.

'What's this?' Flash Nick protested. 'I'm having me afternoon tea.'

'Leave it,' ordered Bruiser. 'You heard me.'

Nick reluctantly left his tea, grabbed his coat, and followed the big sergeant out of the canteen and upstairs. His face had gone white. Bruiser knocked on Commander Foxcroft's door, opened it on command, and ushered Downer inside by the elbow. Foxcroft was sitting behind his desk, flanked by Jack Martin and Liz Flakemore. It looked so much like a court martial that thoughts of a firing squad passed through Downer's worried brain.

'Stand there,' Foxcroft pointed to a place three paces back. 'You may not sit.'

Flash Nick's knees had gone to water but he managed to obey. The sunlight glaring through the window was half-blinding him and he was sweating profusely. 'You wanted to see me sir,' he croaked, suddenly very thirsty.

'You will speak when we allow you to do so, Mr Downer,' barked Foxcroft. 'Place your warrant card on the desk.'

The use of the civilian title was ominous; the confiscation of the card worse. Flash Nick made a show of looking dumbfounded, but he complied with shaking hands. Foxcroft's face was cold, his eyes hooded.

'You are suspended from duty, Constable,' he said. 'You will be escorted home by our officers and your car will be impounded. You will not attempt to leave the country – or indeed the city – and you will hand in your passport and driver's licence. Is that clear?'

Downer nodded and licked his lips. Foxcroft was looking at him with open contempt.

'What have I done, sir?' Downer was hoping desperately that he could talk his way out of the situation, but as yet, like a victim of the Inquisition, he had not been told the nature of his offence.

'You will be the subject of an inquiry by internal investigations.' Foxcroft took a sip of water and pressed a buzzer on his desk. 'We have evidence that you are in league with organised crime and that you have leaked information about police operations.' Nick opened his mouth to say something, but Ernie cut him off. 'I don't want to hear your lies. Just get out of my sight.'

Two unsmiling officers entered the room and jerked their heads for him to accompany them. Nick had never seen them before; they looked hard. When he had shuffled from the room, Foxcroft visibly relaxed and held up his coffee pot.

Liz and Jack accepted and followed him to a low table near the window.

'Well, that's that with that rat,' said Foxcroft, dusting his hands. 'Now, how are you getting on with the rest of your inquiries? What about this Dickins bloke?'

They filled him in on the raid on the Dynamic Achievers' boss.

'What else?'

'Results of the autopsy on Chappie just came in, sir,' said Jack. 'As we'd worked out, he was poisoned by the chemicals at that dump. Toxicology reports all kind of things I'd never heard of. You have the report, Liz. Buggered if I can pronounce the names of half of it.'

Liz pulled the report from her bag. 'Well, here goes. Some of the stuff is reasonably well known.' She read from a list: 'There's phenol, benzene, ethanol, ethylene. A stack of polyaromatic hydrocarbons. PCBs. Stuff you don't want on your cornflakes … Then there's xylene and err, perfluorooctane-sulphonic acid …' She stumbled over the syllables. 'There's dichlorophenoxyacetic acid … Jesus, who makes the names up? Methylene chloride, quite a lot of benzene-based compounds. Various styrene compounds. The list goes on and on. Reams of it. Then there's medical and domestic waste.'

'We get the picture.' Foxcroft sighed and slurped some coffee. 'And this stuff is still being blown up into the air and draining into Stony Creek and the Yarra?'

'Yes sir, but at least the firefighters are now confident they'll be able put out the blaze,' Liz added.

'Well,' said Jack, draining his cup and standing up. 'We'd better get out and find Dickins's mates.'

'Before you go, Jack,' said Foxcroft, holding up a hand, 'I must insist that you take your service pistol home with you. This snooper business has got me worried.'

Jack had ignored previous instructions. He didn't care much for guns, but he agreed. Foxcroft sat quietly after they left. His face was set and angry. The western suburbs had seen numerous spills, explosions, and fires over the years – including a massive blaze at Coode Island – but they were dwarfed by the Tottenham conflagration. He hoped that the law would be sufficient to ensure that the culprits were put away for an extraordinarily long time. And now it seemed highly likely that they were attempting to warn Jack off. He sighed and turned his attention to the pile of documents clogging up his in-tray.

Meanwhile, the two burly officers were turning into Somerville Road in Yarraville, with Downer hunched over like a spiky question mark in the back seat of the unmarked police car. They ignored his feeble attempt at conversation and only spoke when they ordered him to get out at his Severn Street apartment block. They escorted him up to his flat, demanded his passport, driver's licence and mobile phone and left without a further word.

Downer went inside and sat at his kitchen bench with his face in his hands. He'd been worried that they might beat him up. When he peered out of the lounge room window half an hour later their car was gone, but he noticed a patrol car parked a little further down the street. It was that Zawadzki prick and yes, that little bitch of a policewoman was with him. Bastards were angling to get into CIB. Take his job quick as look at him, they would. And the way that tart had knocked him back when he came onto her a while back … didn't know how lucky she was. The car was still there at nightfall. He sat on his sofa and took deep breaths, telling himself it would all work out okay. He had connections, powerful connections, but a little voice at the back of his mind told him the game was up. They wouldn't jeopardise themselves to save his bacon. At the very least he would be kicked out of the force; at worst he would also be facing gaol time. Nah. He was rooted. If only that little bugger Terry Tudge hadn't managed to get away, he would have been sweet. The wogs would've taken care of him. It must have been the little fucker spilling his guts to those Tasmanian pigs. He knew, too, that forensics would crawl all over his car and find the Russian pistol in the secret compartment under the Beemer's wheel arch. He'd have to do a runner. He resisted the urge to use his landline. *They* would not be happy, and they'd told him only to use the burner phone in an emergency. Well, this was an emergency. He rummaged around under the loose floorboard in his laundry and pulled the hidden phone out.

'Hey, it's me,' he said. 'We've gotta meet. My cover's been blown, and I won't be able to talk my way out of it.'

The reply was an angry tirade. He held the buzzing phone away from his ear.

'Look, mate,' he whined when it died down. 'You gotta help me.' He nodded at the reply; another burst of disembodied rage. 'Sure,' he said. 'I know the place.' There was more angry buzzing. 'Yeah, I'll be there.' He closed his phone and went into his kitchen to make some coffee. They'd come through, sure they would. They'd promised him that if push came to shove they'd see him right. Find him something overseas. Well the shit had hit the fan. Might have to learn to speak

Wog: worse things than that! Suddenly things didn't seem too bad. His uncle would be able to fix things at this end. He poured the coffee down the sink: a whisky and coke would go down a treat. Two or three, dark and strong like he liked his women. Fuck. No time for jokes Nick.

The surveillance team reported later that Flash Nick appeared to have watched television until late, when the lights went out and he went to bed. In fact, he was busily stuffing things into a couple of holdalls by torchlight. He planned to travel light. He retrieved his stash of banknotes and credit cards from behind the fridge and sat impatiently waiting for the agreed time, playing with his forged passport. Looked kosher. Name of Anthony Naughton. Finally, he judged it was safe to go. The night was moonless with a thick cloud cover and a hint of rain as he crept down the fire escape on rubber-soled shoes and slunk through the garden and over the back fence. Didn't seem that the pair of dumb plods out the front had noticed. He flitted in the shadows between the streetlights and sidled into Cruickshank Park, the ribbon of green along Stony Creek.

In his dark clothing, he fancied himself as a ninja setting out on a great adventure. What was that saying? The longest journey starts with a single step. Easy does it, he muttered as a nocturnal dog walker made his way along the concrete path calling out 'Tobias, coom 'ere!' in a strong English accent. When man and spaniel had disappeared, Downer stationed himself under a tree next to the creek as instructed. The creek was in full spate from all the rain, and steaming and stinking with effluent from the Great Fire. He shuddered: wouldn't pay to fall in. He loved his life too much. He was waiting impatiently, peering at the luminous dial of his watch when a faint wind sprang up and pulled the veil of clouds aside. In the silvery moonlight, Downer could see the man limping up, his toad's face split in a wide grin.

CHAPTER 20

Jack's phone had jangled shortly after 5:30 am. A jogger had discovered a body as she ran across the Drew Street footbridge in Yarraville's Cruickshank Park. The creek stank of chemicals from the Tottenham fire and was discoloured and covered in oily scum. Thick and Thin were blocking off the entrance to the bridge and Dr Swinburne was looking at the corpse, which was bobbing up and down behind a large rock in the filthy stream. The rain had held off, but the grass was saturated and muddy by the creek bank.

'Nasty,' warned Thin as Jack came up.

'Put you off your breakfast,' echoed Thick.

Still half asleep, Jack slid down the slope to join the doctor, steadying himself on the hastily erected sign warning people to keep away from the polluted water.

'Careful, Jack,' warned Swinburne. 'Fall in there and you'll be as dead as this bloke.'

They'd have to run a rope down for people to steady them-selves with.

'What do we have, Vernon?' Jack asked, peering at the body.

There was something familiar about the corpse's shape, even though it was face down, and there was a huge exit wound in the back of the head.

'We'll have to pull him out, Jack,' said the doctor, gesturing to Thick and Thin to come down and grab hold of the body. They obeyed, donning rubber gloves before pulling the body from the water to stretch it out on the grass. It came out stiffly, cascading water. One handmade Italian shoe was missing.

'Now, men,' warned Dr Swinburne, 'whatever you do, don't get any of that water in your mouth and try not to breathe next to it. Now, if you'll roll him over …'

Liz Flakemore arrived just as they turned him face-up. 'Christ,' she exclaimed. 'It's … it's …'

'Yep, it's Nick,' said Thick.

'Downer!' added Thin.

'Flash Nick,' Thick responded.

Jack nodded, taking in the large ears and spiky hair. It was the disgraced detective.

'Well,' said Swinburne, standing up. 'I can tell you that he's quite dead. As you can see, someone has shot him in the forehead. Not much brain left, I'd say.'

'Never was much,' muttered Thick.

'No Mastermind,' agreed Thin.

'How long?' asked Jack, putting up a hand to silence the two comedians and waving them back up onto the footbridge.

'Well,' the doctor pondered, going to stroke his chin with his gloved hand but thinking better of it. 'Rigor mortis is setting in … perhaps three hours ago.'

The forensics team had arrived and were ordering everyone away from the scene. Jack shrugged. 'We'll find out all in good time.' He made his way cautiously up the bank and walked onto the bridge to speak with the two uniformed officers.

'Who found him?' he asked.

Thick or Thin pointed to a dark-haired young woman at the far end of the bridge. She looked familiar. She was dressed in full Lycra running gear and was crouching down on her haunches with her head in her hands. Hmm, Jack thought, walking up to her with his hand outstretched; it wasn't likely to be her, but then you never know. He recognised her as he drew close.

'Erica Betts,' she said, shaking Jack's hand. 'We are already acquainted, I believe.' She was the rookie lawyer from Cornelius Bentley's chambers. She was still white-faced with shock but managed to give a coherent account of her discovery and agreed to come up to the Footscray police station for a formal interview later that day. Jack wondered if maybe the grisly sight would make her reluctant to follow in Bentley's footsteps. Then again, he did agree that the mongrels who committed such awful crimes were entitled to competent legal defence, even if Cornelius Bentley was an unmitigated scoundrel and a pain in the arse.

Meanwhile, the forensics team had strung up blue and white crime scene tape and were scurrying busily around the locus in quo. Liz was quietly drafting officers to go door to door to find if any of the nearby residents knew anything. A crowd was milling about upstream, jostling each other to get a better look. One of them lost his footing and slid into the creek. Thick and Thin were yelling at them to stand back from the water as Liz and Jack headed back out of the park. Liz wondered at the ghoulish mentality that saw scenes like this as entertainment. Thick and Thin sounded exasperated and with good reason. Only a fool would go near the water. There were signs in five or six languages warning the public to keep their distance from the poor abused creek that was draining the toxic filth from the fire upstream.

'What do you make of it?' Jack asked as Liz reversed out of the car park.

'Bad business.' Liz was sombre. 'He was one of us even if he'd gone bad.'

There were kids and mums and the odd dad everywhere, attempting to get to school, so Liz drove out carefully onto Severn Street.

'Looks like an execution to make sure Downer didn't blab,' Jack said. 'They must have been onto him because of the raid. Chances are that he was doing a runner.'

'Yeah. Probably he'd asked for the gang's assistance after we got him for abducting that Tudge fellow.'

'Yeah, I reckon you're right, Liz,' agreed Jack. 'He'd become a liability and they had no qualms about killing him.'

The killing had all the hallmarks of the Tantalus gang.

'Too late now, but maybe we should have charged him and kept him in custody.'

'It was Ernie's call,' said Jack, shaking his head. 'Pity we won't get to interrogate him.'

Liz parked outside the cop shop, and they went straight to the cafeteria for breakfast. It wasn't a patch on their Yarraville regular, but it would have to do. Her veggie pastie was soggy and the tea was awful. Some el cheapo muck. Terry Tudge was waiting for them in an interview room. He looked better after a good night's sleep; the cell must have seemed like the

Ritz after nights spent living rough. He smiled his gap-toothed smile and said not to worry when they said he had a right to legal representation. He still smelled, so they drew their chairs back a foot or so,

'I don't want no lawyer,' he said. 'I'll tell youse everything but youse'll have to help me. I can't go back to me flat because them bastards 'ud kill me. Put me somewhere safe and I'll tell you everything I know.'

Jack agreed and offered to put it in writing. They'd keep him in protective custody until they could arrange for a safe house. The owner of the pushbike had reluctantly agreed not to press charges when Ernie Foxcroft himself spoke with him. Tudge hadn't damaged the bike so there was no real harm done. Terry nodded gratefully and told them his story. One afternoon like most afternoons he'd been drinking in the 'snakepit' of The Prince in Fitzroy Street, St Kilda. People he admired drank in there – heavies from the apex of Melbourne's criminal society – and he reckoned some of their qualities might rub off on him: blokes like the legendary Tasmanian hard men 'Chopper' Read and Dougie Sproule. After being around them, Terry had sauntered about with his tail in the air, feeling tough enough to take on Muhammed Ali and Mike Tyson simultaneously. Anyway, this bloke had come up and asked if he'd come through to the lounge. The bloke was hard looking so Terry couldn't refuse because he was a sook, really. He'd taken his beer with him and sat quietly to listen to what the bloke had to say. An Australian bloke he was. Sorta nuggety. Thin and middle aged but tougher than a shearer's boot. Said his name was Lance. Didn't give no sur-name. Told Terry the Old Firm was kaput, and he was lucky he was giving him a chance at – ha ha! – gainful employment. He'd noticed that Terry had wheels, so he wanted him to pick stuff up and take it round. When he got a call, someone would tell him where to go to get it and where to drop it off. Well, Terry agreed. Didn't have no choice, did he, like in that film with Marlon Brando in it. Couldn't refuse and anyway, he needed the money.

Jack helped him out: 'The Godfather.'

Yeah, like that, Terry agreed. Sure, he could identify the bloke. Recognise him anywhere. Anyway, he done the drugs run quite a few times and sold stuff himself round the pubs and schools. Didn't want to do no schools but the bloke told him he would do what he was told if he knew what was good for him. Next thing, the Lance bloke said he had another job for him. There was these wogs that they wanted running about. Them and, there'd be one or two hard foreign blokes in black leather jackets. Tooled up; cunts even had submachine guns would ya believe! Didn't have no choice again so he done what he was told. Picked up these other foreign blokes from an old factory in Sunshine and took 'em out Tottenham way. Took 'em down to Altona a coupla times too and picked them up afterwards. The leather jacket blokes made 'em clean inside tanks in one of them big chemical factories. Poor bastards had this horrible stuff all over 'em. Didn't givvum no protective gear or nothing. Still, wogs don't have feelings like Aussies, this foreman fella reckoned, so it was alright. There was always at least one bloke in a leather jacket with a gun. No, he never saw his face because he had one of them balaclavas with holes for the eyes. Eyes 'ud give ya the willies. Sorta hard with no life in 'em like that mummy in the film. Saw it once at the Astor. Scared the crap out of Terry. Terry figured they wanted him to drive because he knew his way about from when he drove a delivery van for a living: last honest job he'd had but he swore on his mother's sacred memory that he'd go back to earning an honest dollar when this was over. Fair dinkum, Mr Martin, Miss, he said. Anyway, he done the run a few times. The place stunk and he didn't mind all that much when Lance told him they didn't need him to drive no more because them leather jacket blokes had got to know their way around. That's when things got real bad for Terry. He didn't like the way Lance was looking at him, sorta smiling but like a shark, so he legged it. Didn't go back to his flat but just wandered about sleeping rough. He reckoned Jack knew the rest. He willingly agreed to take part in an identity parade to catch the Lance bloke.

'Ten to one, this Lance fellow is Garth Dickins,' said Liz when they left the room.

'We'll know shortly.'

As they spoke, uniformed officers had brought in men who had agreed to take part in the line-up. Garth Leslie Dickins – number 5 – was glowering down one end like an angry Beagle Boy when Terry came in and stood in front of the one-way mirror.

'Take your time,' counselled Liz.

Terry scrutinised the men carefully but shook his head. 'Nah,' he said. 'Number 5 looks a bit like the Lance bloke, but it's not him. Lance was bigger for a start. Older too. Something about number 5 that I can't put me finger on, but.'

'You've done fine, Terry,' Jack assured him. 'Now, Sergeant Macfarlane here will take you off for lunch and after that we'll take you for a little drive out to the place in Sunshine you told us about.'

'Interesting,' said Liz once Terry was gone. 'Our Alfred Doppelgänger almost picked Dickins.'

'Yeah,' nodded Jack. 'I'm thinking that Lance is a relative of our Mr Dickins. Brother, maybe.'

'I'll get one of the uniforms onto it,' said Liz.

After Terry had gorged on some sausage rolls and Fanta in the canteen, PC Robbie Zawadzki and a young female uniform called Sally Wilson took him out to Sunshine, driving carefully through heavy traffic along Ballarat Road, chuffed that they had been seconded to CIB. A van crammed with heavily armed officers followed. Terry guided them to the site of the famous Harvester Works, which had once sprawled across 75 acres of the flat western suburbs basalt plains. Much of it was now a blighted zone, with thistles blowing across the yellow grass and patches of bare earth. Part of the factory had been incorporated in a new shopping centre and new roads and kerbs anticipated further commercial development, looking like roads to nowhere on a science fiction set. Sunshine had once been touted as 'the Birmingham of Australia' but since the de-industrialisation lauded by the Silver Bodgie and his aggressive deputy, more and more stuff was manufactured overseas by sweated labour.

'Sad,' said Sally, shaking her head at the desolate scene.

'It is what it is.' Robbie shrugged, pulling in at the side of the road with the van close behind.

'My, we are profound today,' Sally scoffed.

Robbie looked chuffed. Didn't get irony, Sally thought, grinning.

Terry was pointing to a two-storey red brick building on the edge of the vast open space. The windows were boarded up and youths had covered the walls in tag graffiti; no more inkling in their heads of the historic importance of the place than if they were dogs pissing on it. Sally Wilson went over and spoke to the armed officers. They went off at the double to scout out the place. After ten minutes or so, they returned and gave the all-clear for Tudge and his minders to enter the building.

'Stay here,' Sally ordered Terry, checking that she had her service pistol. 'On second thoughts, I'll just slip this cuff on and clip the other end on this ring here. Wouldn't want you doing a runner, would we?'

Terry whined but didn't make a fuss. No way he'd scarper now that he had a bed and three square meals a day. And that big Tasmanian D had arranged for the bike theft charges to be dropped.

Sally Wilson went around the back while Robbie Zawadzki marched up to the front door and nodded to the armed officer standing by. The sun beat down mercilessly. Robbie pushed open the door and stepped inside, holding his pistol. The building was deserted, but it certainly had been occupied. There was a pile of dirty sleeping bags and mattresses in one corner, and it looked as though someone had been cooking in a nearby kitchen. A shower dripped ceaselessly in a filthy bathroom next to the squalid toilets, which didn't appear to work. Most of the building had been offices, and these still contained piles of mouldy paper, broken-down typewriters and other outmoded office paraphernalia. Someone had defecated in one of the rooms. Sally hastily closed the door.

'Nothing here, Robbie,' she shouted. The electricity was still on, and it was pretty clear that the place had been occupied until very recently. There would have to be a thorough forensic examination.

*

Meanwhile, Garth Dickins was sitting facing Liz and Jack over the table in an upstairs interview room. The lawyer Cornelius Bentley was seated next to him, fiddling with his expensive fountain pen and preening at his reflection in the window glass. His understudy, Miss Betts, was absent this time. The interview proved to be a complete waste of time. Apart from confirming his identity, Dickins's reply to every question was a snarled 'no comment.' When Liz demanded to know if he was frightened of something, she noticed a faint flicker of something in the man's eyes. After that, his thin face remained expressionless. In the end, irritated by his attitude, Jack had shouted at him, causing Bentley to remonstrate. Ignoring him, Jack had shown Dickins an identikit picture of the man who had recruited Terry Tudge to the new firm. Jack noticed something in the man's eyes, but the reply, as always, was 'no comment.' After another fruitless half hour they terminated the interview, and Dickins was led off back to the cells after letting fly a signature fart. He would be taken to the Melbourne Remand Centre in Spencer Street in the morning. Jack would have loved to wipe the smirk off Bentley's face, but he smiled thinly and bade the man goodbye as he left the premises.

It was frustrating, but they were piecing together the various parts of the case. They also now had identikit pictures of several of the criminals, and they believed Garth Dickins had a brother or cousin who was involved in the gang. Jack tasked Detective Vicky Tran with tracking him down, confident in her abilities. He hoped he wasn't overloading her with work, but she seemed to thrive on it. Svetlana had also provided an identikit sketch of the Russian woman in the reception at the gang headquarters. Anastasia, she'd said was her name. There was something about the face in the sketch that Jack couldn't quite put his finger on. He racked his brains but, in the end, knew that it would be best to let it lie. Whatever it was would eventually work itself into his conscious mind.

Late that afternoon, Bruiser Macfarlane came puffing up the stairs to inform Jack that there had been 'a development'. Fat Toby Malouf was missing. Cursing fluently, Jack grabbed his coat and he and Liz were soon driving down Miller's Road to Altona. They arrived to find the young constable charged with protecting Malouf in a state of utter dejection. He'd gone out to buy fresh milk and when he got back, Malouf had gone. No, there was no note, but there were signs of a scuffle: a broken table lamp and a smashed coffee cup on the floor. It was highly unlikely that Malouf would have left of his own accord. The man was terrified. They'd get forensics in to check for evidence but the chances were that Malouf was dead. There'd be all hell to pay with the lawyer, Slippery Sam, but that was someone else's worry. Chances were he'd sue on behalf of Toby's widow but that would be a can of legal worms as Jack seriously doubted any remains would be found.

CHAPTER 21

Camperdown is a pretty town of well-maintained Victorian buildings sitting on the vast basalt plains west of Geelong, a region of salt lakes, sheep, and extinct calderas. Its main street is divided by a wide grassy strip planted with fine old English elm trees. A tall clock tower keeps accurate time – though in truth a one-handed clock would suffice in this sleepy place – and the inactive volcanic cone of Mount Leura stands sentinel at the town's eastern approaches like it had done for thousands of years before Europeans arrived in the district. Like many Australian towns and cities it has a dark history, but on this cloudless autumn day it turned a smiling face on the world.

Close by was something new and dark: another illegal dump.

The sun was hot, but the elms gave welcome shade as Vicky Tran and Darryl Puncheon drove in and pulled up outside a café for lunch. There was no way that Vicky was going to eat the stuff her offsider consumed, so she ate her freshly made wholemeal tuna and salad sandwich with relish while Darryl sulked because they hadn't gone to the Maccas up the road. It was pleasant in the café, so she took her time drinking her tea, and when she wiped her mouth with a serviette and nodded, Darryl shot up.

'Calm down, Darryl,' said Vicky, 'you're jumping about like Spring-heeled Jack.'

'Eh? Wozzat?'

'Never mind. Let's get round to the local nick and see what we can find out.'

The Camperdown cop shop was a pleasant two-storey building in leafy Fergusson Street. Senior Sergeant 'Big Phil' Lucas met them in the foyer and suggested that he bring them up to speed while he drove them out to the dump site in his Land Cruiser. He was a walking encyclopedia of local knowledge. Now, just a few years from retirement, he was a local boy who had returned after spending most of his working life in Melbourne. He was greying, solid, and garrulous. He was also good-hearted and painfully honest. There was a dark tinge to his complexion but that wasn't unusual out here on the sunburned plains. By the time they had driven past the Botanic Gardens on the southern edge of the town, he had filled them in about the history of the district, whose first white settler was Fred Taylor, the architect of the Murdering Gully Massacre that had virtually wiped out the Tarnbeere Gundidj clan.

'So,' said Phil, as he turned into a dirt road by the Lake Bullen Merri reserve. 'We've had our share of scumbags in the past and now we've got 'em again.' He continued his disquisition on the mass murderer, lamenting the fact that Taylor had fled to India to avoid punishment for his crimes. One of the constables later told Vicky that Phil was descended from the Aboriginal people who had owned the land. A few years ago, in more openly racist times, the chances were he'd have claimed southern Italian or Maltese ancestry and there were still those who referred to him behind his back as 'that big boong sergeant'.

'Here we are,' said Phil as he pulled in at a large steel gate by the roadside. A farmer was leaning against his ute, which was parked just up the road a bit with a lone sheep in the back. With his wire-framed glasses perched in the bunches of curly black hair above his ears, the farmer looked like Aunty Jack, the faux fearsome 1970s TV cross-dresser: same pencil moustache, but no skirt, just a scruffy tracksuit with holes in the knees. No motorbike or boxing glove either. He strolled down towards them as they got out of the police car.

'G'day, Harry,' said Phil Lucas, adjusting the peak of his police hat against the fierce glare of the sun. 'Vicky, this is Harry Witz.'

'Reckon you'll find 'em?' Harry asked Phil, nodding towards the paddock and ignoring Vicky.

'We're like the Mounties, mate,' replied the sergeant. 'Relentless.'

'No real 'arm done if you ask me,' opined the farmer, peering slyly through his granny glasses. He was trying for the shrewd look, but just looked shifty.

'And how do you know that?' demanded Vicky, her lip curling. 'Scientist, are you?'

'Nah, just a farmer with a bitta nous,' Harry replied shortly. 'We only use the groundwater for sheep and that. Nobody drinks the water, so like I say no harm done.'

The man was an idiot, but Vicky couldn't be bothered arguing with him. 'Shall we crack on, Phil?' she said to Sergeant Lucas, turning her back on the farmer.

Phil Lucas opened the heavy gate. Someone had gone to a lot of trouble to keep people out. The fences were new and topped with barbed wire. There were heavy wheel ruts leading up the gentle slope from the gate, the ground still wet from all the rain.

'Harry's alright when you get to know him,' said Phil when they were out of earshot. 'Conservative like a lot of country folk. Prefers to ignore things if possible.'

'Head in the sand or up his arse,' grumbled Darryl Puncheon as they came to the top of the paddock, which was shielded from prying eyes by a windbreak of mature pine trees.

'Crop duster pilot told us about it,' said Phil Lucas, appearing not to have heard Darryl's interjection. 'He noticed trucks coming and going and excavators digging up the place. He was pretty insistent, so I got a warrant, and we searched the place.'

'Good job he was,' said Vicky as they came to the edge of a newly excavated pit.

It was a shocking sight: hundreds upon hundreds, maybe thousands, of rusting 44-gallon drums resting in a broad, shallow trench. There was an unholy chemical smell hanging over them. A bulldozer and front-end loader were parked on the far side of the pit. The two Melbourne detectives were gobsmacked by the size of the site.

'Some of the barrels is rusted through,' said the big sergeant. 'My worry is the stuff will seep into the groundwater to Lake Bullen Merri. The lake's brackish, but the local kids swim there, and families have picnics and that. Oh, and watch where you put your feet. There's syringes stickin' up all over the place.'

'Gunna be a bastard digging this lot up,' Vicky sighed. 'Now, any joy on who's been doing this?'

The barrels were swelling up in the heat. It was no place to linger. Walking back down to the road, Phil told them what he knew, wheezing from the exertion of trudging about in the heat. He was worried that the whole lot might explode and they'd be faced with a similar situation to what had happened in Melbourne.

'A bloke called Taylor owns the place. Christian Taylor. Businessman over in Portland. Dodgy as, but the Portland force never managed to pin nothing on him. Claims to have leased the place out to some mob called Acropolis Holdings in Sydney. They reckon they've sublet. We haven't turned up anything yet.'

'Local trucking company?'

'Dunno, love. It was all done late at night. Trucks come and go through Camperdown at all hours. Nobody gave it a thought.'

Vicky had a fair idea of who the culprits were. It had Garth Dickins stamped all over it. Him and the black leather blokes who'd tried to poison half of Melbourne. Ten to one McCastles were involved too.

'Reckon that farmer, Harry, might know something?'

'You know, it never crossed my mind to ask, but now that you mention it, maybe we should pay him a visit.'

Harry Witz's place was within half a mile of the dump. He met them at the door of his neat 1950s brick house and stood there scratching the woolly clumps above his ears. He didn't look as if he'd rip their bloody arms off like Aunty Jack had threatened, but there was something suspicious about him, Vicky thought.

'Meanin' to ask, Harry,' said Phil, fanning himself with his hat. 'Why didn't you report what was happening?'

'None of my business,' Harry shrugged, picking at something in his teeth.

'Seen anyone coming and going?' Vicky asked.

'Nah. Heard 'em at night but I go to bed early. Nothin' much else to do since the missus left.'

'Know who leases the place?'

'Nah,' he said, but his shifty sideways look told Vicky that he was lying.

They took no notice of the Ford that drove slowly past.

Back at the station, Vicky insisted that Harry Witz knew more than he was letting on. Her nose told her that the farmer was dodgy. Phil Lucas shook his head. As far as he was concerned Witz was a bit doolally but harmless. Only talked with his sheep, mostly. He'd become reclusive after his wife had taken off to America with a Mormon missionary. Vicky was not convinced, so she phoned Jack Martin to ask for his advice. Jack thought they should bring him in for an interview and when Vicky handed the phone to the big sergeant, he agreed.

Harry Witz blustered at first. He had better things to do than waste his fuckin' time on this he snapped, but his little eyes looked furtive. Vicky repeated their earlier questions but then suddenly attacked.

'You lease the place, don't you?'

'I dunno how you could think that,' Witz retorted, but he looked flustered.

'Oh come on, Harry,' Vicky retorted, her voice full of mock

weariness. 'We'll get to the bottom of this eventually, but it'll be better for you if you help us.'

After hemming and hawing, Witz caved in. He admitted that he'd agreed to lease the place 'from a mob in Sydney' when a bloke had come to see him. He 'didn't have nothing to do with the dumping and that,' he insisted. It was a straight business proposition. He paid for the lease and made a dollar by acting as a front man. He just had to keep schtum if anyone asked. Vicky halted the interview and when she returned, she was bearing faxed copies of Garth Dickins's mugshot and profile. Harry Witz readily agreed that it was the same man who had approached him to take out the lease on the dumping ground.

'What'll happen to me?' he asked.

'At this stage, it's up to the Crown Prosecutor to determine whether you've broken any laws,' said Vicky. 'In the meantime, don't go far from home without permission from Sergeant Lucas.'

'I reckon I need a lawyer,' said a crestfallen Witz.

'Good idea,' she agreed, terminating the interview.

'Never would have guessed,' said Phil Lucas as he shook hands with the detectives when they left to begin the long drive back to Melbourne.

'Too trusting, our Sergeant Lucas,' said Vicky as she buckled on her seatbelt. 'Still, we're getting there.'

And so they were. Piece by piece, the Tantalus jigsaw was revealing its patterns. Back in the Footscray nick, Ernie Fox-croft had called Jack into his office shortly after the mail had been delivered.

'Call me old fashioned,' he said, sliding a buff envelope across the desk, 'but I didn't want Liz to see this.'

Jack opened the envelope and took out a sheaf of high-res-olution colour photos. He blanched when he realised what he was looking at. In each one, the now deceased former DC Nick Downer was engaged in sexual acts with what were clearly underage girls. Jack looked closely and there was no mistake about the identity of the abuser. There was no note, but there didn't have to be. Nick Downer had been blackmailed into providing information and once his cover was blown, he was of no further use to those who had sent the photos. The blackmailers were flaunting their power and laughing at the police.

'My guess is that these were taken in a brothel,' said Jack. 'We can have forensics go over them with a fine-tooth comb, but I doubt we'll learn anything. Nothing to identify who the girls are or where the things were taken. I suppose Svetlana might be able to help but my guess is it was a specialist place catering for tastes like Downer's.'

'You're right, Jack,' Ernie replied. 'Bad thing is that this mob has no compunction about using kids in their brothels.'

Jack shook his head and looked thoughtful. 'You know, Ernie. it's pretty bloody obvious when you think about it, but I reckon this new firm has ties with the gangsters we closed down a few years back in Hobart. There's the Russian angle for a start.'

'Oh, something else too, Jack,' said Ernie. 'Word's just come in about another big toxic dump out north of Highway 8 near the South Australian border. It's probably the daddy of them all and that's saying something. Chances are it could poison the groundwater for the whole district.'

'Or go up in smoke,' Jack replied.

Meanwhile, elsewhere in the Footscray nick, Darryl Puncheon sidled up to Vicky Tran's desk. He licked his lips nervously, but his tail wagged tentatively, and his expression was eager.

'Garth D-Dickins's b-brother,' he stammered, his tongue in a twist at the sight of Vicky's sceptical smile. 'I've found out where he lives.'

'Go on, Darryl.'

'His name's Walter Raymond Dickins. Goes by Wally Ling, but.'

Vicky smiled encouragingly though she was irritated by the misplaced conjunction imported from across the Tasman.

'He spent years in Sydney and Newcastle after things got too hot for him down here. Come back, but.'

'Now let me see,' said Vicky, pursing her lips. 'He's got form?'

'Sure has,' the boy replied, confident now. 'List as long as your arm. You name it, he's done it. Started with burgs when he was a kid. Then strong-arm stuff. Suspected of murder but never proved. Been in and out of Long Bay and Goulburn prisons.'

He rattled off an address in St Albans and his tail thumped the carpet when she congratulated him for doing an excellent job. 'Let's go, Darryl,' she ordered, grabbing her sunglasses, handbag, service pistol and handcuffs. She felt like giving him a pat and a biscuit. She'd make a detective of the boy yet.

CHAPTER 22

The late afternoon sun was streaming down the long canyon of Collins Street in the Melbourne CBD when two friends entered the James Munro Club. Motes of dust hung in the air and trams thundered by, heavier than elephants, but the crowds of homeward bound office workers had thinned out. The sun's heat was still oppressive and was radiating from the bricks and asphalt, but it was cooler under the thick foliage of the venerable elm trees. This was the snooty 'Paris End' of the street, a mile or so from the raffish Spencer Street intersection at the far end where people were still streaming into the railway station or pouring ale down their throats after another long day shuffling paper or crouching in front of flickering green screens.

Inside the exclusive club on the northern side of the thoroughfare the air was dark and cool, shaded by the thick green foliage of the trees lining the street outside. The voices were hushed, and the discreet clink of glasses collected by the stewards scarcely disturbed the unruffled calm. It was 1998, but it could have been 1958, 1928, or even 1888; a timeless scene of establishment male privilege, for the 'weaker sex' never set foot here and the stiff fees kept out the great unwashed. The sentiment that the proverbial Jack was as good as his master would raise languidly amused eyebrows here. It took generations to breed a gentleman worthy of the club, they agreed, but let the plebs have their democratic illusions! We gave 'em the right to vote and that frightened some but there was nothing to worry about. In any case, the Aussie pleb, bogan or whatever, knew his place. Even under Labor, with the Silver Bodgie and his saturnine successor in control of the unions and the Labor Party the status quo had been respected. Nay, reinforced.

Two well-coiffed sexagenarians, Cornelius Bentley and Ambrose Threlfall, were deep in conversation in a quiet alcove of the club. There appeared to be tension between the two men, so the stewards had left a decanter of sherry and glasses on the low coffee table among the scattered leaves of the day's newspapers and made themselves scarce. Their fat Christmas bonuses depended on their ability to anticipate the clubmen's needs.

'Dammit, Cornelius,' Threlfall hissed, looking round to make sure they were not overheard; not that there was any chance of that. With filaments of grey and white hair above a pair of round eyes, flared nostrils, and a curious V-shaped mouth, Threlfall bore an uncanny resemblance to an ostrich. An unhappy one at present. 'Your clients are getting thoroughly out of hand. Are we living in Melbourne or Al Capone's Chicago?'

Cornelius coloured. 'Well, Amby, my old mate, you can hardly blame me.'

'Well, you represent 'em,' Ambrose retorted, taking a decent slug of sherry. 'You know more about 'em than the police do. Anyway, mate, Boofhead's getting toey. There's an election coming on. The Major Events wallah's been on the blower too about his car race. Lots of money hangin', believe me.'

He slid the more lowbrow of the city's dailies over the coffee table. The headline screamed SHOOTOUT IN FOOTSCRAY! BIKIE BUTCHERY! The editorial was in thick blazing red type and shouted CLEAN UP OUR CITY! The rag's photographers had used telescopic lenses to obtain footage of the Geelong Road massacre scene and Godzilla Pritchard's face glowered out at the world from page 3. There was a smaller photo of Big Mama Hanson replete with swastika earrings on the following page.

'I hear you Amby,' purred Cornelius, holding up his hands in surrender. 'Trust me, I know it's got to stop. Mate, we go way back.'

Indeed they did, these old boys of St Paschal Baylon College had been brought up in the same leafy Toorak street and spent long summers together at Portsea or skiing at Aspen across the Pacific. Ambrose was perched at a rarefied level of the state prosecution service and Cornelius was a senior partner in the city's most prestigious legal chambers, Campion, Wallace, Bentley, Mugabe, and Robertson, where the money moved on cushioned feet and didn't smell. Threlfall had the ear of the great and good in Spring Street, and his mate Cornelius was a well-connected fixer. They'd done lucrative deals together. Discreetly. Their latest rort was a corker. Advance notice to Old Boy developer cronies about the impending rezoning of land in Port Melbourne from light industrial to residential had netted them and a Spring Street mate a small fortune in secret commissions. Their mutual friend Paulie – an Old Boy too – kept them on top of police operations.

Threlfall was speaking again, his round eyes earnest. 'It's all about equilibrium, mate. City's always been crooked. Goes back earlier than Tommy Bent and the land boomers, John Wren, you name it. We know too that these crime firms are part of the warp and woof of the city. Always have been. Always will be. The young bucks go off half-cocked from time to time. We've gotta expect that, but wiser heads prevail. Things settle down. It's a matter of scratching backs. Yeah, the odd backhander. The cleverer of the boys in blue know that. Good friends among them, as you know.' He paused to scan the evening's menu and finish his sherry.

'I understand,' nodded Cornelius, tipping the last of his drink down his gullet and reaching for a quick refill. 'Money makes the world go round, but we gotta be discreet.'

'Glad you know that,' said Ambrose drily. 'Anyway, call 'em off, mate. This new firm's gotta be housetrained.'

Cornelius spread his hands wide. 'No brainer, mate.'

'Now, my learned friend,' whispered Threlfall, leaning forward and tapping the side of his beak. 'Word's come down from our mutual friend that the Chief Commissioner's gone apeshit and is about to pull out all the stops. Operation Tantalus is going to be beefed up and there will be a massive crackdown. The Opposition's screaming blue murder, so he means business.'

The dinner gong sounded. Cornelius patted his paunch and they stood up to go through to the dining rooms, sniffing the air appreciatively like dogs on the scent of a juicy bone. The serious business discussed, they spoke of the upcoming St Paschal Old Boys' Ball and the old friends and acquaintances who were expected to attend. It would be a prime opportunity for networking. Ambrose enquired about his niece, young Erica Betts. He was proud of her. A rising star in the Young Conservatives, he had high hopes that she was bound for great things and he was already sniffing round for a safe parliamentary seat to parachute her into when the time came. Toss up whether it would be state or federal. Cornelius concurred, although to tell the truth he was frightened of her basilisk stare and barely concealed ambition. They'd mulled over the matter of admitting women to the club but were leaning towards the status quo, regardless of Erica's talents.

'I could eat a horse,' said Threlfall, tucking a napkin round his thin neck and ogling the menu. His friend nodded agreement, and they settled down to a feed of gazpacho, tender pork loin with truffle sauce and a medley of seasonal vegetables, followed by a refreshing lemon sorbet. All washed down with a couple of bottles of *très agréable* South Australian chardonnay, and with a bottle of St Hallett's vintage port after the dessert to finish. Life was good. After finishing his pudding, Bentley belched, excused himself and waddled off to the loo, where he pulled out his mobile phone.

'Listen up,' he muttered with a slight slur. 'The shit's really hit the fan. Mate, you've gotta cool it …' There was an angry buzzing from the receiver. 'Yeah, well don't blame me … Yeah, the Premier's pissed off and wants blood … Anyway mate, you fix it.' He closed the phone and stood staring at his reflection in the gilt-framed mirrors before turning on his heel and wobbling back to the dining room. He realised he was half-cut. Room for a spot more pudding. Didn't feel like a visit to the Alhambra Pleasure Palace this evening. Samantha didn't really love him anyway. He'd snort another line of cocaine before bed if wifey was already asleep.

*

It was a Tale of Two Cities. As the two bent old goats were walking into the James Munro Club, Vicky Tran and Darryl Puncheon were driving through the Woop Woop near the Ginifer train station. They had Wally Dickins or Ling as he called himself handcuffed in the back seat. Vicky scowled at the flat, sunburned landscape. Christ, she muttered, gazing out at the thistles, which were stirring in a skittish wind; ex-hubby Number 2 still lived nearby in the yellow brick bungalow they'd rented. He was probably drunk again or skirt-chasing. She recalled how he always wanted to sit facing the door when they were in restaurants: she'd twigged after a while it was because he wanted to check for husbands coming in. Men. She'd had 'em up to the eyeballs. A mental picture of that Tassie detective, Liz, flashed before her eyes. She repressed the memory and looked at Wally Dickins in the rear-view mirror. He was sporting a black eye from where she'd clocked him, and the other malevolent orb was boring into the back of her skull.

They'd found Wally at his place in McKechnie Street near the Victoria University St Albans campus. His house sat on a double block with a motor repair workshop alongside, which is where they found him fiddling with the innards of a Holden

Commodore. It was a grim place in a grim neighbourhood sandwiched between the main road and the railway line. Nothing grew here except thistles and straggly yellow grass, and maybe washing and babies like in Dylan Thomas's *Under Milkwood*. Hubby Number 1 had wanted babies. He wasn't bad like Hubby Number 2, but babies weren't her thing and so he'd found someone else, and good luck to him.

'Wally Dickins, or is it Ling?' Puncheon had asked, walking towards him with his warrant card on display. 'We'd like to …'

Wally burst out the back door of the workshop like an overweight greyhound from a trap. There was a scream and a great crashing sound. Vicky Tran had stuck out her foot and Wally had fallen headlong into some empty oil drums. She bent down quickly, handcuffed him, and dragged him to his feet, triggering a volley of foul oaths. When he tried to head butt her, she jabbed him smartly in the left eye. Ha! Any more nonsense and she'd really put her jujitsu skills to good use. He'd calmed down after that and they'd put him in the back of the car, handcuffed him to a bar above the door and turned on the central locking.

Liz and Jack sat in when they got him into an interview room, but they let Vicky take the lead. 'You've been a *very, very* naughty boy, Wally,' she said, shaking her head in mock sorrow. 'We've got enough to put you away for a long time.' She ticked off the charges on her fingers. 'First, we have a witness who will testify that you oversaw a large-scale operation peddling Class A drugs. Second, you've been involved with the illegal tip at Tottenham. Third, you've been mixed up in human trafficking.' She paused and raised an interrogative eyebrow, but Wally remained silent and stared down at the desk. His eye was developing into a real shiner, she was delighted to see.

Liz put an oar in. 'Look, Wally, things are looking bad, but perhaps my colleague can help if you come clean …'

'I'm not telling you nothing,' Wally snarled. He turned to Jack and Liz. 'This bitch assaulted me and I'm not sayin' nothing until I get a lawyer.'

'Right-o, Wally,' Vicky sighed. 'Have it your way.'

Smiler O'Reilly came in and took Wally off to a cell, not without a brief ruckus as the prisoner shook the policeman's hand off his arm. They'd resume the interview the next day when Wally's brief arrived, and you wouldn't need to have the brains of Einstein to know who it would be.

*

Jack was flabbergasted. You wouldn't read about it! Three pairs of his underpants were missing when he got back that evening. The crusties were almost new – expensive silk ones Francesca had bought for his birthday – and he'd washed them that morning. He double checked the wardrobe and chest of drawers. There was no doubt that they were gone. It made him swear a bit, but Wendy rang shortly afterwards and that put him in a better mood. Wendy was ecstatic and brushed aside his indignant story of the underpants. She had started to skim through Sandy Johnstone's papers, and she was going to see her supervisor about incorporating them in her honours thesis. Sandy – Alexander to be formal – had been transported from London to Van Diemen's Land in 1831. She would let Jack know more when she had set aside time to sit down and read the documents properly.

Jack sat for a while sipping a cup of tea after Wendy hung up. He smiled. Who would have known it? Detective Inspector Jack Martin of the Tasmania Police had a transported felon perching in his family tree! Influential Tasmanian families had gone to great lengths to deny any association with what was once called The Stain, and it was likely that half the Tasmanian-born population had at least one convict ancestor. He was very much looking forward to hearing the details of Sandy's life and forgot about the stalker. He poured himself a small Scotch and sat to listen to the tape he'd bought a few days ago: a selection of bel canto including Handel's marvellous 'Ombra mai fú'. You couldn't get much better than that. He'd read a bit more of *The Spanish Civil War* too after he'd made himself a salad, he thought, patting his tummy.

Francesca rang just as the music was finishing. She had some good news. The kids had shamed their father – her ex – into foregoing his share of the potential proceeds of the sale of the former family home. The bloke was loaded and could afford it. Trouble was, everything with him was transactional, so he'd demand something in return; but it was good news for all that. They chatted happily after she'd relayed the news. The place in Mitah Court, down the river at the southern end of Lower Sandy Bay was still for sale, so they agreed that she would go into the agent's the following day to put in a bid.

CHAPTER 23

'The shit is about to hit the fan,' warned Ernie Foxcroft. He had been lurking next to Bruiser Macfarlane's desk, waiting for Jack to arrive at the cop shop after breakfast. 'Best come to my office, Jack.' They sat and Ernie poured them both some coffee. Jack raised an appreciative eyebrow; it was a good brew, nothing like the liquid horror his old Tasmanian boss had served up. 'I've just had the Deputy Commissioner himself on the blower,' said Ernie. 'He's spitting chips about the bikie massacre. It's all over the papers today and the Premier wants to know what we are doing about it. Anyway, we're wanted at 637 Flinders Street on the dot at eleven o'clock this morning. Prepare yourself, because Alex McBain has a short fuse.'

Jack had heard a bit about Alex McBain, or Squeaker as they called him behind his back because of his habit of delivering high-pitched harangues and rambling soliloquies. He must have just squeaked over the height requirement for new recruits, too, for he was a real shortarse and had a good dose of small man syndrome. His office was on the sixth floor of the Victoria Police headquarters building, with a view over the

Yarra River docks and the West Gate Bridge. Jack and Ernie were five minutes early and Squeaker kept them waiting until dead on time. He reminded Jack of a hamster, except that his eyes were a startlingly bright blue in his whiskery face. He bade them sit but didn't offer tea or coffee. A bad sign. McBain was the son of a cow cocky from near Ballarat and he spoke Strine in clipped, telegraphic sentences. His thick accent belied a sharp mind, and he was known for what some called plain speaking and others considered downright rudeness.

'What the fuck's happening?' he squeaked, his little blue eyes swivelling from one to the other. Jack almost expected him to start washing his whiskers with his little paws. He constantly nibbled on little mints, which Jack fantasised were sunflower seeds. He popped a couple in his mouth and watched his visitors carefully. He didn't offer them any.

Ernie Foxcroft cleared his throat. 'It's the new organised crime gang, sir,' he said. 'They're staking out their turf and getting rid of any opposition.'

'I fucking-well know that Ernie,' McBain snorted, crunching his lolly, and rummaging for another. 'Point is what the fuck are you doing about it?'

Jack coughed. 'Sir, we do have several leads …'

'Like what?' McBain's lips were curled back from his sharp little teeth. Unlike his burrowing brethren he was not herbivorous. He wanted raw meat.

Jack explained that they now had several witnesses who had been able to provide them with details of some of the gang members. They also had three suspects in custody, one of whom was cooperating. In addition, a suspected informant – a bent copper – was no longer in any position to feed information to the gang. There was also forensic evidence.

'Whaddya mean, "no longer in any position"?'

'He's dead, sir,' said Ernie.

'Not more fuckin' stiffs,' McBain moaned. 'And the gangster fella, Muldoon, any news?'

'It's Malouf sir, and no, we've heard nothing. Nor, if I'm honest, do we expect to.'

'Well, in one way that's no loss, but it doesn't look good when someone we are supposed to be protecting is missing, presumed dead. Lawyers will be all over it like Poms fighting for a feed of Spam.' Squeaker stared out of the window before resuming, banging the desk for emphasis and unwrapping a fresh packet of mints. 'Whole building's in an uproar. Arses are being kicked all the way down the line to the fuckin' tea ladies. Premier wants to know why we haven't caught these bastards. Press is having a field day at police expense. We need to go on the offensive. I'm drafting in extra bodies to Tantalus. All the overtime you need. Raids on every known criminal den across the city. Shake the tree to see what bad apples fall out. No fuckin' do-gooder kid gloves. You suspect something dodgy is going down, then hit hard in the cojones.' He clearly relished the prospect, for he repeated it slowly: 'In – the – fucking – cojones!' He finished with a loud crunch on his mint.

'Sir, the civil liberties crowd will scream from the rooftops,' said Ernie.

'Well let 'em,' McBain grunted, tossing his empty lolly box to one side. 'Be careful, but I want this new firm off the streets. Officers are being drafted from other nicks to Footscray as we speak. Hop to it.'

McBain held up a hand as Jack and Ernie stood up to leave. 'Don't let me down, Jack,' he pleaded, friendlier now. 'We've brought you and the lass over on Ernie's recommendation and we want results. My arse is on the line here. The Government and Opposition's going apeshit. You'd better convene a press conference after the raids to reassure Joe Public about progress.'

They drove back to Footscray in silence with Squeaker's voice echoing in their ears.

The Footscray cop shop was too small to accommodate the expanded Tantalus team, but this didn't faze Ernie Foxcroft. He got on the phone and arranged to move the augmented crew into the Bluestone Church community centre out the back of the Romanesque Town Hall. After much organised chaos, it was up and running, and Jack assembled the team and brought them up to speed. A big map had been mounted on the rear wall of the main hall, with little flags marking the suspect premises they needed to raid. Working with cool efficiency, Liz organised the assembled officers into teams, and soon patrol cars with armed officers were fanning out over the western, central, and southern districts of the city. Jack was pleased he could leave her to it. His hearing was definitely getting worse, particularly in crowded rooms.

The operation was a bit like scallop dredging, as Jack knew it would be. It brought all kinds of strange creatures gasping and wriggling into the harsh glare of the sun. Legs O'Donoghue's bar, for example, yielded a brace of standover men and a couple of ferrety individuals wanted for burglaries. Normally, they would have netted more of these types but since the new firm arrived many of them had gone to ground. Raids on illegal knocking shops had uncovered men both common and exalted, married and unmarried, with their pants down, and officers had closed a dog fighting ring, which staged its ghastly contests on flat-top trucks around the western suburbs: gentle family pooches were stolen and matched with pit bulls for the enjoyment of bloodthirsty perverts. Dozens of drug peddlers were also caught in the net, but most of what was caught was by-catch: the big ones had got away. As always, noted the station cynics, and Jack couldn't disagree.

One interesting catch, however, was the 'Black Leatherjacket' arrested as he attempted to escape over the back fence of the Alhambra Pleasure Palace. The male was more amphibian than fish, however, and resembled a giant toad. Snouts had tipped off the task force that this legal brothel was used as a 'feeder' for illegal bordellos. New 'girls' would be brought in to replace those transferred into the illegal wing of Mr Dennis Ho's businesses. The Leatherjacket's mate had got away, but this one had a gammy leg and couldn't make it out through the same high window. Jack wanted to bring Dennis Ho in for questioning, but there was pressure from above to desist. Ho, they claimed, was legit, paid his taxes and was a generous political donor. Indeed, the Attorney-General – twin sets, pearls, hair carefully rinsed and curled – had been quoted in *The Age* as praising the sex industry as 'a highly regulated, profitable, professional and incredibly well-patronised industry … that pays taxes.'

Yeah, right, thought Jack.

After the raids, the Melbourne Remand Centre was overflowing with lowlifes, no hopers, and quite a few sad unfortunates in urgent need of psychiatric help. Jack was unimpressed.

The operation was a public relations exercise designed to keep the Three Pees happy; that is Press, Public, and Premier. True, they had the black-leather-jacketed male in custody – the apparel and place suggested a link to the Tantalus gang – but most of the haul were petty offenders who could have been arrested without fanfare. The brothel raid had also rekindled his disquiet over legalised pimping, introduced as a supposedly 'progressive reform' by the Cain State Labor Government some years back. Jack did not wish to see the women themselves criminalised, but he was appalled by the normalisation of brothels and the legitimisation of the seedy creatures who owned them. The interface between organised crime and brothel keeping was also plain.

There were bawdy houses all over the place in city and suburban streets. Children walked past them every day on their way to school. Parents took their kids to the toy shop that shared a back fence with Dennis Ho's knocking shop. One brothel keeper had done time for trafficking girls as young as ten and was out again and preying on kids. It irked Jack that these people paraded as pillars of the community, flaunting their Rotary memberships and being touted as role models in 'respectable' newspapers, with politicians singing their praises. Brothels were even listed on the Stock Exchange. Any distinction between legal and illegal establishments was tenuous and many trafficked women were in the former. Liz reminded Jack of a recent case in Germany in which a state employment bureau had attempted to force unemployed women into sex work on pain of losing their benefits if they refused.

Bruiser Macfarlane looked harassed when Jack walked over to the police station from the temporary command centre.

'Jeez, Jack,' he sighed. 'Please stop 'em bringing 'em in. I'm run off me feet, and all we do with most of 'em is charge, bail, and release on their own recognisance. There's no crime lords among 'em for gorsake!'

Jack agreed with the old sergeant, but he shrugged. 'Out of my hands, Bruiser. Orders from the top.' He was on his way with Liz to interview the leather-jacketed goon from the Alhambra. Svetlana Anikanova had already confirmed that he was one of the men who had imprisoned her in the Williamstown brothel. As they had expected, the lawyer Cornelius Bentley was seated next to his client, uncapping his Mont Blanc fountain pen like unsheathing a sword, ready to do battle. After going through the preliminaries, Jack sat back and scrutinised the unshaven specimen in the leather jacket. Two hostile brown eyes glared back. Their owner had given his name as 'Mark Spencer', which made Jack retort 'and I'm David Jones', which caused some huffing and puffing on the solicitor's part.

'Where my rings and neck chain?' 'Spencer' demanded. He had a thick accent, Slavic if Jack was any judge, the words sliding from a wide, thin-lipped mouth. With this, plus his lumpy skin, he really did resemble a toad. Smiler O'Reilly had put the man's bling in the safe. He reckoned it represented at least a week's production of the Kalgoorlie mines.

'It's in a safe place, Mr *Spencer*.' Jack put air quotes around the name. 'What's the matter with your leg?'

'Where is this going?' drawled Bentley.

'Fair question, I'd say,' Jack retorted.

Bentley nodded to his client.

'Old war hurting,' said Spencer.

'Doctor says it's a recent bullet wound,' said Liz. 'I wasn't aware that we're at war. Care to comment?'

Bentley whispered something and Spencer declined to comment.

'We'll put that aside for now,' said Jack. 'Now what concerns us is that dependable witnesses have identified you as being involved in supplying trafficked women to brothels, including the place owned by Dennis Ho where we apprehended you.'

'No comment.'

'Further,' added Liz, 'we know that you were one of the men holding several women against their will in an illegal brothel in Nelson Place, Williamstown.'

'No comment.'

'Funny thing is that we had recent reports of shooting near the Botanic Gardens in Williamstown. Anything to do with you, Mr Spencer?'

'Never been Williamstown.'

Bentley gave him a look, and he repeated the 'no comment' mantra.

Jack raised his eyebrows. 'Hmm, soon as we have some samples from you, Mr Spencer, we'll be able to cross check them with things we've found down there.'

'Such as cigarette butts,' Liz added. 'And there was the pile of poo someone left under the rhododendrons in the nunnery garden. Lots of DNA there!'

'That someone was you, wasn't it, Mr Spencer?' Jack chuckled. 'Caught short, eh?'

'Now, now,' Bentley objected. 'You're jumping to conclusions here.'

'I don't think so,' Jack countered. 'Fact is, we think your

Mr Spencer was shot over at Williamstown. And we'll prove it.'

Spencer was ruffled, but he kept his mouth shut.

'Well, Mr Spencer,' Liz sighed. 'We know that you're just a bottom feeder. You are going to prison, but if you cooperate, we can recommend leniency.'

Liz looked to Jack for confirmation, and he nodded, but Spencer scowled and refused to say anything more. It looked like a dead end, so they gave up and Smiler took the gangster back to the lock up. They'd see if they could make the lab get a wriggle on with the various samples and compare them with samples taken from the man. Bentley trotted off, smooth and smug as ever, an ageing show pony.

It was late evening when Jack got back to the Yarraville flat and he didn't feel like cooking, so after a quick shower he tossed a frozen Indian meal into the microwave, scoffed it standing up by the window, and headed down to the local pub. It was a warm night, with crowds going in and out of the cinema and spilling out from the cafés. A band had been playing and the lounge bar was crammed, but he managed to find a seat at a table occupied by a friendly young couple who introduced themselves as George and Anthea. The band was having a 15-minute break, so they were able to chat about inconsequential matters before the pair reverted to a private conversation.

'Bloody coppers,' said George to Anthea. 'Anyway, we'll see how Mum is when we pick her up in the morning.'

Jack's ears pricked up. 'Sorry, I couldn't help overhearing …'

'My mum works at the shoe factory in Footscray,' said George, shaking his head. 'They went on strike and the boss tried to bring in scabs, so they set up a picket line. We were dead worried. Proud, too, but worried. Mum's due to retire in a couple of years. Most of her workmates are middle aged women, Maltese, Turks, Greeks, Kurds, Lebanese. We're Greek like a lot of people round Yarraville.'

George stopped and took a swig of his beer. Anthea put her hand on his arm. 'The police attacked them,' she explained. 'They came on horses, swinging batons. George's mum got hit on the neck and shoulder and she's in hospital. We hope she'll be out in the morning.'

'A sixty-three-year-old woman,' said George. 'She's never done anyone any harm in her life. Come out from Greece with Dad and worked for everything. Put me through university. Proud as punch when I graduated.'

'George's a teacher,' said Anthea. 'Me too. His dad got hurt at work and had to retire. We tried to get George's mum to retire too but she said they'd always paid their way.'

'They came out here when the colonels took over in Greece,' said George. 'Refugees, really. They never thought they'd see the day when something like this could happen here.'

The band had trooped back onto the stage and were fiddling with their instruments. Jack's beer suddenly tasted flat and stale. It was time to go. The band had begun to play a cover of Van Morrison's 'Brown Eyed Girl' as he took the opportunity to bid the couple a quick goodbye. He was debating with himself as he walked back up Anderson Street in the gathering dark. The women must have been breaking the law. Yet he could almost hear Wendy's scornful snort, and his leftist friend the Hobart pathologist, Simon Calvert, would be ready with a pertinent quote. Back in the flat, Jack made a pot of tea. He suddenly remembered the theft of his underwear, but a quick search revealed that the snowdropper hadn't been back. He settled back in an armchair to read a long report on the sex trafficking industry. It made dismal reading.

There were up to two million trafficked women in the world. The United Nations reported that it was the world's fastest growing 'industry' and was making a yearly profit of $6 billion for the traffickers. One of the most notorious local traffickers had imported over one hundred Thai women through his pub at Kew Junction. He kept them behind bars and forced them to turn up to five hundred 'tricks' without payment before they were deemed to have paid off the cost of their airfares. When one unfortunate woman begged to be released so that she could marry a man she had met, he told her she would have to pay $17,000 to get out of the 'contract'. The bum was waltzing free around Melbourne. Another pimp was back in business after serving a gaol term for prostituting underage girls. Another man did a lucrative business from a South Melbourne brothel, supplying girls for high rollers coming into the country on private jets. He and other seedy individuals were also involved in money laundering and organised crime gangs. Jack snorted when he recalled the Attorney-General's glowing endorsement of the sex industry racket.

CHAPTER 24

What the Camperdown Sergeant Phil Lucas had to report to Vicky Tran in his early morning phone call was bizarre. Jack couldn't help laughing when she told him, but he did realise that the matter was serious. Harry Witz, the Aunty Jack lookalike farmer whom Vicky had interviewed about an illegal waste dump near the town, was now in protective custody at the Camperdown nick. Phil had to get the doctor in to treat Witz's mangled feet and administer a sedative. The farmer had babbled incoherently but Big Phil had eventually calmed him down enough to get the details.

*

Harry had been rudely awoken in the dead of night by loud knocking on his front door. Lucky he always locked it last thing, for what Harry saw through the curtains could have induced a heart attack in a less robust person. Two big, nasty types standing on his porch under the security light. Something to do with that bloody dump, Harry realised. Same buggers in black leather jackets, dials on 'em like hatchets. One of them was checking the magazine on his big handgun. Christ on a Massey Ferguson, they were going to do him in! He had no time to waste. They were thumping on the door again when he snuck out the back way and legged it up the yard that had gone to seed since his missus pissed off with that Mormon bastard. He was considering hiding behind the woodshed when he heard them kick the front door down. Lights went on and they were crashing about calling his name and breaking things. Chances were they'd come out and search the garden, so Harry hared off over the back fence – well as near to a hare as an overweight cow cocky could be – and it was lucky he knew the back paddock well because there was no moon.

Lucky, too, that he'd thought to put on his granny glasses, be blind as a bat without them. He was scampering along when it dawned on him: he was stark bollock naked! Harry never slept in pyjamas; reckoned he had to let his skin and orifices breathe naturally, but now he was regretting it as he lolloped across the paddock. At least it wasn't cold, but what was he going to do? For all he knew, the bastards had torches and as soon as they'd searched the house, they'd be looking for him outside. He had to keep going. Make it to town across country so that they wouldn't find him on the road.

Fuck; he stubbed his toe on a rock and almost burst into tears. The initial adrenaline rush had dissipated, and he was dog tired, but he kept up his desperate pace, lolloping along with his tummy and bits bouncing. Think, Harry, he counselled himself. Take it easy otherwise you'll run out of puff, and you'll be rooted. Them gangsters would put a bullet in his brain quick as they'd eat breakfast. They must have seen him talking to the cops.

He'd lumbered a couple of hundred yards further when the full moon came out from behind the clouds. He glanced back fearfully but there was no sign of pursuit. He jumped a couple more fences, nearly tearing his bare arse on the barbed wire, and reckoned it was safe to take a rest. No cigarettes; he could have murdered one. He sat heavily with his head in his hands, naked in the silvery moonlight. The thick bunches of hair behind his ears quivered as he broke into heaving sobs. He sat for some time like this, until the coarse grass started to chafe his bum. He had no idea of the time but he heard someone's rooster crow in the distance. Up he got and stumbled towards town. Nearly shat himself when he heard a car close by and saw its headlights sweeping the road to the lake. It had to be them bastards unless they were lying in wait for him at the house. Yeah no, it'd be them. He hunkered down behind a bush until they'd gone past and continued through the paddocks. Something moved then; something long and … shit it was a snake and thick as his arm! Must be out at night because the weather was so hot. A brown snake … deadly poisonous buggers. He stood stock still and it slithered off. Any more of this and Harry was gunna have a heart attack, fair dinkum, but he had to keep going.

The bulk of Mount Leura rose black against the thickening eastern light, so he knew he was getting close to town. More cocks were heralding the dawn and he could hear traffic humming on the distant highway; big milk trucks coming and going from the butter factory. He hadn't dared hope that he'd escape the men, but his spirits rose slightly now he was getting closer to Camperdown. He trudged on doggedly, ignoring his painful feet, and to his relief he saw an old weatherboard house close ahead. He'd ask for help and they could phone big Sergeant Lucas to come and get him. There was a light on, so he went down the front path intending to knock on the front door. He'd just lifted the doorknocker when a great big dog ran out barking and snarling. It was one of them Rottweiler things with huge teeth glistening in the dawn light. Holy Mary! Harry fled just as the front door flew open and an angry bloke came out with a shotgun. The bloke didn't ask questions but loosed off both barrels in Harry's direction, yelling 'pervert!' so he took off down the dirt road thanking his lucky stars the bastard was such a bad shot. Better luck next time, he thought bitterly, but there were no Christians in these parts if the Rottweiler bloke was anything to go by. He staggered along for few hundred yards, until he was close enough to see the streetlights of the town.

He approached another house cautiously and banged on the door. There were some scuffling noises inside, so he cleared his throat and knocked again.

'Who's there?' It was an old woman's tremulous voice and she sounded frightened.

'Me name's Witz, Harry Witz,' Harry replied, hiding his willy with his hand. 'I need help, missus.'

There was a click, and the door opened a fraction on a security chain. Harry started to speak but the woman screamed and slammed the door. Jesus, she'd think he was a flasher prowling the neighbourhood. He'd have to scoot real quick. Old Agnes Campbell got straight on the phone. The Camperdown police station was still closed so the call went through to the officer on call, Constable Lew Amos, at his home on the other side of town.

'Yairs,' croaked Amos, groggy with sleep.

There was a frantic sobbing sound on the other end.

'Miss Campbell,' he sighed. Not the silly old bat again. She'd been quiet for a while since the Sarge read the riot act to her but now she was at it again. The way she told it, she was besieged by prowlers and perverts. Burglars too, only it always turned out that she'd misplaced whatever it was she thought was stolen.

'OK love,' he said, striving to remain polite. 'We'll get someone round there as soon as possible.' He hung up and went back to bed.

Meanwhile, Harry Witz was limping into town, shaken by his experiences, attempting vainly to hide the family jewels. By the time he reached the wide main street with the big brick clock tower on the median strip it was broad daylight. Some cars flashed past, the drivers' heads spinning round as they caught sight of him, and a big silver milk truck went by honking its horn like an outraged duck. The newsagent caught sight of him as she was bringing in the papers so she ran back inside and locked the door. By this time, Constable Amos's phone was running hot with reports of a naked prowler, so he rang Big Phil Lucas.

'Hey Sarge,' he said. 'You won't believe this but there's reports coming in of a streaker in the main street. Yeah. Some naked feller. Seems old Agnes wasn't making it up.'

'Well go and investigate, man,' snapped the sergeant through a mouthful of sausage and egg. 'Ring me back when you've got him.'

Harry Witz sobbed with relief when Lew Amos drove up in the patrol car and ordered him to get in. The constable had had the presence of mind to bring a blanket, which Harry draped gratefully around his pudgy nakedness. Amos couldn't get anything intelligible from him when they got back to the station, so he gave up trying. He was considering what he could book him for when Sergeant Lucas came in.

'Well fuck me,' said the astonished sergeant. 'We always knew you was a bit peculiar, Harry, but we never picked you as a flasher!'

CHAPTER 25

The man they called Boris was worried. Anastasia was angry, and despite them being lovers it wasn't safe to be around her when she was in a bad mood. Her metaphorical tail was swishing ominously. The diminutive blonde was a martial arts black belt and dangerous even to a tough Spetsnaz veteran like Boris. Women didn't count for much in Russian gangland so she had had to be utterly ruthless. Some of the things she'd done back in Russia and Germany made even Boris blanch. They were speaking in Russian in Anastasia's office overlooking the West Gate Bridge and the waste ground out to the mangroves at the mouth of Stony Creek.

'You are supposed to be a security expert,' she hissed, sitting back in her swivel office chair, and examining her long, blood-red fingernails. 'Some security. Ha! Brothels have been raided and we have lost girls. Lost some workers, and on top of that, my friend, police have arrested several of our men. Some are dead too.' It looked as if she might hurl her coffee mug at the wall. 'And that useful idiot policeman. He is dead, yes?'

Boris ran his hands through his close-cropped grey hair,

and his hands shook a little as he lit a Russian 'Golden Bear' cigarette. 'The policeman is no loss, my *koshechka*,' he wheedled, puffing away with the smoke curling into his cold eyes. 'He was no longer of any use to us.'

'Don't you "koshechka" me,' snorted Anastasia. She took one of his cigarettes and waved at Boris to light it for her. 'What are we going to tell Moscow?'

Boris thought that it wasn't fair to blame him for the cops finding out that Nick Downer was bent, but he maintained a level tone. 'Look, Anastasia,' he replied, ticking the points off on his fingers.

'Firstly, we've destroyed the competition. We fucking annihilated those bikies and the spaghetti munchers have made themselves scarce after what we did to the Greengrocer. The Micks too. Don't forget Fat Toby Malouf's under a hundred tonnes of concrete in the foundations of that bridge. Few others there too. We'll have a monopoly on the drugs once we neutralise a couple of his associates.' He took a puff on his cigarette.

'Secondly, we've still got the other brothels, right? Girls are coming in all the time. Thirdly, we've got more consignments of men coming in to work.' He paused and stubbed out his cigarette, worried by her narrowed feline eyes.

'Fourthly, we've also got a steady income stream from the shopkeepers we've put the frighteners on, and this will only grow.

'Fifthly, I think it is, we're just about to open the luxury car showrooms in what do they call it, yes, South Yarra.'

He'd forgotten the numbers of his points but ploughed on. 'The real estate deal on the rezoned land is in the bag too, so we can invest our earnings with no questions asked. Last, Anastasia, we have the racecourse specialists in place too. Nothing can stop us. We have destroyed the old firms, Anastasia.'

She nodded and he continued. 'I save the best to last, *krasotka*. Soon, I think we'll have another policeman – a really big fish – and you know that already we have civil servants on the payroll. VIPs.'

Anastasia took a long drag on her cigarette and nodded her blonde head thoughtfully. 'OK, my Zolotse, but we can't afford to fuck this up. You know Mr Kozlov takes no prisoners. Ivan fucked up, don't forget, and the whole operation in Tasmania went pear-shaped. Kozlov won't forget and I don't want to end up feeding the fish in the Volga.'

Boris shrugged. 'Yes, I know, Anastasia, but haven't we always delivered the goods for him? Germany? New York?' He brightened. 'Hey, that new policeman from Tasmania, let's see if we can make him jump.'

Anastasia's catlike face split into a malicious grin at the thought. 'OK, Boris, you fuck the girls now if you want. I will pay our friend in Doncaster a little visit.'

Boris felt a churning mixture of admiration, fear, and affection flood his brain as she slunk silently from the room. Anastasia and Boris were products of the disintegration of the Soviet Union. Like many Afghanistan vets, Boris had drifted when he returned from the war. There seemed to be nothing to believe in anymore. The corrupt drunkard Boris Yeltsin had seized hold of the reins of power and imposed what his Western advisers called 'shock therapy' on the country. He privatised the former state-owned enterprises and a handful of oligarchs seized the vast bulk of the country's wealth and property, often paying nothing for what they grabbed. It was the largest theft in history. At the same time, living standards and life expectancy plummeted for the people, and the country's health and welfare services were hacked to pieces. The massive increase in inequality was matched by the growth of corruption on a colossal scale. Billions of dollars in overseas and IMF loans simply disappeared into the pockets of Yeltsin's cronies. The country was falling apart and was mired in a depression deeper than the one that had afflicted the world in the 1930s.

Bewildered, the ex-soldier Boris had joined one of the new Pentecostal churches and then, disillusioned yet again with the mindless gobbledegook, he had sought solace in vodka. One day, at a low ebb, he had met Anastasia; or more accurately Anastasia had engineered it to meet him. She was attractive if hard faced, with a slim body honed by vigorous exercise, and Boris fell hard for her. She was working for the Kozlov crime syndicate, the country's biggest, and she had an eye open to recruit unmoored army veterans like Boris. Gradually she sucked him into the mob's activities. Men such as Boris made efficient enforcers and because of his intelligence service and military police experience he was an even more valuable asset.

Their first overseas venture together on behalf of the *Krasniy Mafiya* took them to New York, where they cultivated a corrupt tycoon they unimaginatively called Mr Big. They supplied him with pretty girls and ready-mix concrete for his projects, taking care to receive full payment up front because of his reputation for 'stiffing' suppliers. They provided enforcers, too, if little subcontractors got stroppy and demanded Mr Big pay what they were owed. When most banks refused to loan the tycoon any more money following a series of disastrous business ventures and dark rumours of corruption, Boris and Anastasia stepped in with loans, laundering money from the Mafiya's nefarious activities. Their boss back in Moscow was so pleased with them that he entrusted them with delicate missions to Germany and the former Yugoslavia and then sent them to continue his stalled plans for an expansion into Australasia. Failure was not an option this time.

CHAPTER 26

Liz and Jack flanked Commander Foxcroft at a hastily convened press conference in an upstairs chamber of the Footscray Town Hall. Detectives Tran and Puncheon sat to one side. Long-forgotten mayors looked down indifferently from the walls, and honour rolls of war dead looked depressingly similar to the adjacent lists of captains of darts and cricket teams. On paper, the results of the police dragnet looked impressive, but Jack and his colleagues felt the bosses of the Tantalus crime syndicate would be laughing. None of the small fry in custody would speak, either because they knew nothing or because they were too frightened. Terry Tudge was cooperative, but as Ernie said, he was as much use as flyscreens on a submarine. Likewise, Harry Witz, the Camperdown farmer, told all he knew, which wasn't much. The poor bastard was traumatised after his nocturnal ordeal and receiving counselling. He was now in a safe house, worrying about his neglected farm. The self-styled 'Mr Spencer' continued to answer all questions with 'no comment'. Neither Garth Dickins nor his brother Wally would say anything although, like 'Spencer', they could expect lengthy prison sentences.

Still, the newshounds had pounced on the morsels they'd been thrown, and the officers retraced their steps to the police station.

'What've we got?' asked Jack, poised in front of the white board in his office, marker pen in hand. An adjoining board sported an unimpressive rogues' gallery of mugshots of the dragnet catch – heads on 'em like mice according to Bruiser Macfarlane – but few if any of them had connections to the Tantalus mob.

'Well, Jack,' said Liz. 'Everything we know points to the new firm behind all the rackets. Drugs, prostitution, illegal dumping.'

'My guess is human trafficking too,' added Vicky Tran, looking thoughtful. 'That Williamstown nun knows more than she's letting on.'

'Surely she's not in on the racket?' Liz objected.

'Nah, but she's up to something dodgy,' Vicky replied, tapping the side of her nose, unaware of the antisemitic connotations of the gesture.

'Well, what about the surveillance on the nun?' Jack asked. 'Anything yet?'

Vicky didn't respond. She was staring out the window but not appearing to see anything. Jack cleared his throat and gave her a searching look. Finally, she emerged from whatever mental hiding place she'd been in. 'Err, nothing, sir,' she replied. 'She's been out a few times but only to the shops or to the place they store food and stuff for asylum seekers. That's down near the Albright & Wilson factory in Yarraville.'

'Well, it's early days on that,' said Jack. 'We'll keep up the watch on her house and my hunch is that she'll eventually lead us somewhere.' He paused, and added, 'Not that I think she's a crim either. Anyway, what else?'

Vicky was back on the ball. 'Let's not forget the attack on the Molochs Marauders. Big Mama Hanson wouldn't say much, but she did recall seeing some blokes in black leather jackets coming to the clubhouse in Brooklyn a few days before the attack. There was shouting going on in the club president's office.'

'All the evidence points to the new gang,' said Liz, smiling at the young detective. 'Whoever they are, they're from overseas. Jack picked up quickly that the gangsters from the tip were Serbian, and Svetlana – the young woman we rescued from the Williamstown brothel – is certain that some Russians are the big wheels. We have an identikit picture of a woman who called herself Anastasia, and a silver-haired character called Boris. There was a Russian driver, too, who told Svetlana his name was Cyril. Smiles all the time, but he's vicious. The other end of the trafficking ring is in Russia. How these Serbs got mixed up in it is anyone's guess. Interpol might have some ideas.'

'Pound to a penny the Sons of Odin are in it up to their necks,' said Vicky. 'All the other bikie gangs have vanished, but the Odin clubhouses are still going full bore and we know they are mixed up with that dodgy accountant from out at Shepparton. Him and McCastles.'

'Alan Badger,' said Liz. 'And that leads straight to our Mr Dickins too.'

'We'll put surveillance on Badger and on the Sons of Onan

or whatever they call themselves,' Jack said. By now, the whiteboard was a mass of black and red squiggles. 'We'll probably never be able to prove it,' he added, 'but that lawyer, Cornelius Bentley, is dirty. He's a conduit to some very powerful people and he's hand in glove with this new firm.'

They were winding up the meeting when a uniform knocked and came in with a stamped envelope addressed to Jack. This time Jack put on latex gloves before opening it. There were more Polaroid photos inside, this time of a woman's breasts and vulva. From the angles, they were selfies. Jack shook his head and shoved the stuff into a desk drawer and picked up the phone to ring Ernie Foxcroft.

'Yes, Jack?' said Ernie.

'As you know, sir, we've managed to catch a whole shoal of fish, but the big sharks weren't in danger.' Jack paused before continuing. 'Anyway, it's all a bit like the sound of one hand clapping.'

'How do you mean?' Foxcroft immediately sounded defensive.

'Well, I've mentioned it before, sir. We go after people like Garth Dickins, but what about the people who hire him for his filthy trade?'

The Commander was silent for a few moments. 'Look Jack,' he finally replied. 'Don't think that I haven't considered this, but my superiors believe it is not in the public interest to pursue such a line of inquiry.'

'Is that your opinion too, sir?'

'It doesn't matter what I think,' said Foxcroft testily. 'In the chain of command, I'm small fry.'

'I see,' said Jack, biting his tongue. 'In that case I'll leave you to it.'

Foxcroft started to say something else, but Jack had already hung up. Meanwhile, Vicky Tran and Liz Flakemore were standing to one side in the corridor, deep in muted conversation.

CHAPTER 27

The faces came to Jack in the middle of the night: the hard features of a petite woman and the brutal mug of a gangster he had investigated a couple of years earlier in Hobart. The images were of two identikit reconstructions; the first based on Svetlana Anikanova's description of the woman who had met her when she had arrived in Melbourne from Russia, and the second of a Russian mobster who had been killed a couple of years back in Hobart: Ivan Smirnov. Svetlana had said the woman's name was Anastasia. Jack leapt out of bed and rummaged around in his briefcase. The woman had her hair in a blonde bob. Shorten it and accentuate the hard planes of the face and the resemblance to Ivan Smirnov, aka Sokolov, was plain. He'd get Hobart CIB to fax a copy of Smirnov's identikit picture in the morning, along with a reconstruction of the face of the corpse demolition workers had unearthed in a shallow grave in a disused Derwent Park factory yard.

Ivan Smirnov was a former Russian Spetsnaz soldier, an Afghanistan veteran who had turned to crime after his discharge from the army. He had entered Australia either on a forged or stolen passport, to head up the operations of a Russia-based crime gang. Jack's Tasmanian investigation had led to a wave of arrests, but he was under no illusions. The gangs, he realised, were like cancer. As with nature, crime abhorred a vacuum. The roots of their operations lay deep in the kleptocracy that was the Russian state, which was run by and for ruthless oligarchs. The oligarchs had plundered state property after the fall of Communism and their taste for crime was insatiable. Many bloated *biznismeni* were former Soviet apparatchiks who had jettisoned whatever principles they might have had in the frenzy to enrich themselves.

Jack was up and into his office at dawn, drinking coffee and puzzling over the connections they'd drawn on the whiteboard the previous afternoon. When Liz arrived, the faxes of Ivan Smirnov's mugshot had just come through and he waved them triumphantly. Jack felt sure that Ivan Smirnov and the cat-faced Anastasia woman were brother and sister. He immediately contacted Interpol with a request for information.

The phone rang. It was Bruiser Macfarlane telling them that a young woman was in the foyer and was asking to speak with them. Liz went downstairs and found a tiny Asian woman waiting. She was slim, dark-haired, and very attractive, with a slightly wary expression. She also looked very tired. Liz took her into an interview room and offered tea or coffee, which she eagerly accepted. Jack joined them and sat unobtrusively at the back. The woman spoke good English, albeit haltingly. Her name, it transpired, was Tiraya Lueangsuwan. She was upfront about her profession: she had come to Australia three months ago to work in a legal brothel. She came from a poor rural family and her aim was to save enough money to be able to set up a shop or some other small business back in Thailand. The recruiter back home had not been honest. She had said nothing about Tiraya having to work off the cost of her airfare and accommodation, and at prices grossly exaggerated by the brothel keeper. The man had taken her passport 'for safekeeping' and she had slept in a dormitory in the attic of the Alhambra Pleasure Palace in Spencer Street. Months after her arrival, Tiraya was still paying off the bogus debt and she'd been forced to borrow money from the pimp at exorbitant rates of interest. There was no end in sight.

Liz's ears pricked up. 'The Alhambra; the place owned by Dennis Ho?'

'Yes,' Tiraya replied, curling her lip at mention of the name.

'So, Tiraya, what would you like to tell us?'

'Yesterday, some men come with Dennis Ho. They tell me to get my things and come with them in a car.' Tiraya took a sip of her coffee before continuing. 'They put cloth round my eyes and drive away. Half an hour later, they stop and take me into another place. There are bars on windows and the girls are frightened.'

'Could you describe these men?'

'Big. Three of them in black leather jackets.' She shuddered. 'Nasty, nasty men.'

The men had taken Tiraya to an illegal brothel. There were several other girls there and they told her that the men kept them prisoner and forced them to have sex with the customers. There was no pay. Some were, like Tiraya, paying off their 'debts' to the pimps. Others had been tricked into prostitution, believing that they had been recruited back home in Thailand or Russia for cleaning or clerical work. Several of the women, like Tiraya, had initially worked in Ho's legal brothels. Many of them had become addicted to heroin after the men had given them 'hot shots' against their will. Tiraya had managed to run out the door when the goons guarding the place were distracted by a delivery of laundry. She had always been a fast runner. She hid in some bushes next to a railway line and as soon as it was light, she had ventured out and asked a passing woman for directions to the nearest police station. Sensing her distress, the kind stranger had walked Tiraya to the Footscray police station.

Twenty minutes after Liz's interview, Vicky Tran and Darryl Puncheon were sitting with Tiraya in an unmarked police car near an abandoned bakery in a cul-de-sac in Seddon, a small suburb that sits between Footscray and Yarraville. Tiraya was certain that it was the brothel. They took her back to the police station and went back to keep the premises under discreet observation. Meanwhile, Liz and Jack set off across the city to pay an unannounced visit to Dennis Ho, the Alhambra *souteneur*.

Ho's premises occupied an uninspiring brick box on Whitehorse Road. His name and businesses were emblazoned in English script and Chinese characters on the front windows. Ho had his fingers in many pies besides the sex trade. He was a chartered accountant and the CEO of Celestial Employment Services, a labour hire company, and ran a profitable sideline as an immigration agent. The pretty Anglo receptionist smiled a welcome and asked them to wait while she finished what she was doing. Some clients were sitting in a line along one wall and they looked up resentfully when the two detectives went through to Ho's office, figuring they were trying to jump the queue. Dennis Ho looked up warily when they entered his office, his eyes magnified by the thick lenses in his black-rimmed glasses. He was sitting behind an enormous faux-mahogany desk, hunched like a giant frog over some spreadsheets, doubtless counting his loot. His face was impassive, but they could detect a trace of fear in his hooded black eyes.

'Can I help you?' he snapped in clipped Singapore English. It didn't sound like he wanted to.

'Matter of fact you can, Mr Ho,' replied Jack, holding out his warrant card and identifying himself and Liz.

Ho licked his thick lips and started cleaning his glasses, his eyes blinking, looking suddenly vulnerable. Jack pounced. 'Mr Ho. We have reason to believe that you have been using your legal business, the Alhambra brothel, as a front for illegal knocking shops, which use trafficked women.'

'I am a legitimate businessman,' Ho sputtered.

'Come, come, Dennis,' Liz chided. 'Don't treat us like fools.'

Ho's mouth contorted, but he bit back a sarcastic retort. He was used to getting his way but realised that he couldn't afford to annoy the detectives.

'So, Mr Ho,' said Jack. 'Come clean or we will haul you down to the police station and finish this interview there.'

Ho's eyes darted this way and that. They let the silence hang. Finally, when he realised that they were waiting for him to speak, Ho sighed. 'I am frightened,' he muttered. 'If I tell you what has happened, I want protection.'

He caved in and told them everything.

Just as he had finished his sordid confession, Jack's mobile phone rang. It was Vicky Tran. Jack went outside in the street to listen. She reported that two men in black leather jackets had just driven up to the Seddon brothel. A few johns had also entered the premises, looking furtive, and left with shit-eating grins on their faces. Jack tossed up whether to raid the place immediately but ordered Vicky to wait until the goons left and to follow them.

Jack and Liz left Ho's premises shortly afterwards. They had warned him that if he made any attempt to contact the Mafia gang, they would arrest him. He promised meekly to obey, the balloon of arrogance punctured. Just to make sure, they rang Ernie Foxcroft and asked him to obtain a warrant to tap Ho's phones. They found it impossible to sympathise with him. He was the owner of two other brothels besides the Alhambra and part-owner of another. The man was a human flesh merchant. One day, several months ago, said Ho, two hard men, foreigners not Aussies, had come to his house and offered to buy into his bordello business, making it clear that refusal was not an option. He had squawked about the terms of sale but agreed when they showed him blown-up photographs of his wife and daughters outside his house and the girls' exclusive private school. Yes, he knew that the legal brothels now served as conduits for human trafficking but what could he do, he whined. He nodded when they showed him the identikit drawing of the Russian woman and the photos of the dead thugs from the Tottenham tip.

They were making real progress.

Jack checked his watch. Shit, he'd forgotten about his audiology appointment! Liz had been on at him about it, and he couldn't deny that his hearing was becoming a problem, especially in crowded rooms. He'd make it if he hurried so he scurried out of the cop shop. A dumpy old bloke was just leaving the Paisley Street hearing clinic when Jack came puffing up.

'They're no good in there,' the codger grumbled, jerking a thumb at the door. 'They wouldn't syringe my ears!' He waxed indignant: 'There's two receptionists just sitting around at them computer things. What use are they?'

'Go to your GP,' Jack laughed, without stopping. Jack couldn't quite place the silly old bugger.

An hour later, after listening to a variety of beeps and buzzes through headphones, Jack had agreed he needed hearing aids. The audiologist assured him that they were scarcely noticeable; the ugly big bone-coloured plastic monstrosities were outdated, not to mention ear trumpets, she joked. Jack smiled wanly, suddenly feeling old. Back at the station, he recalled that the old bloke outside the clinic was the same fellow who had sneered at the DETOX protesters. At this rate, Jack thought, he'd soon be a silly old bugger himself; and who was he to talk about never protesting injustice?

CHAPTER 28

Sister Susan Lawless did not own a car. Never had. Walking or cycling or public transport were good enough for her, although her detractors gibed that she flew about on a broomstick. Now, she was cycling north up Melbourne Road, with an unmarked police car keeping a discreet distance behind and pulling over from time to time to keep from getting too close. The sky was a sullen grey and there was a stiff south-westerly breeze, so Susan was fairly flying along with the wind behind her. The good news for the day was that the Tottenham fire had finally been extinguished and the exhausted firies could go home.

Susan turned right at the roundabout before the Newport railway flyover, narrowly avoiding a collision with what looked like a drunk driver. Much as they wanted to book the inebriated idiot, the constables kept going after the nun. Halfway along North Road, the nun pulled into the kerb and dismounted. She pushed open the gate of a well-maintained old weatherboard house and knocked on the door. There was a battered old Holden ute parked in the driveway. An old bloke opened the door, and the nun went inside.

'Well bugger me,' said PC Zawadzki, reaching for the car radio microphone. 'It's the same place we found that minibus. We'll get the detectives down here.' With that, he did a U-turn and drove off to attend a 'domestic' in North Altona.

Jack and Liz got the message as they were driving back along Footscray Road after interviewing Dennis Ho. Five minutes later, they had cruised under the West Gate Bridge and were turning into North Road and pulling in where the police car had been. They didn't have long to wait before the front door opened, and the nun came out with the old bloke, Dixie Trumble. They climbed into the ute, reversed out, and drove off sedately up the street. Liz did a U-turn and followed at a discreet distance. Five minutes later, the two vehicles were crossing the West Gate Bridge in the Port Melbourne direction. Susan and Dixie didn't notice they were being followed. They turned off the freeway and drove through Port Melbourne, finally pulling up outside Dixie's mate's pub. Dixie was excited because his mate Ronnie Flanagan had persuaded another sailor to smuggle Soran Rekani aboard ship and take him to safety in New Zealand. Soran was now the last of the men Dixie had befriended, and Susan was anxious to say goodbye to the Kurdish refugee. The others had been smuggled to safety.

When they were settled in the back parlour, Mrs Harrison brought in a tray with tea and her specialty moist coconut cake, an old family recipe. She was a motherly old thing and she'd spoiled Soran rotten. Her kids were long gone to raise their own families. She'd been reluctant to take the men in at first, but when she'd spoken with Soran and learned about the conditions of his people she had treated him like a son. He was such a nice young man; always willing to help. He was just helping her to hand round cups and plates when the door burst rudely open.

It was a tableau that neither Jack nor Liz ever forgot. The little group were sitting round with shocked looks frozen on their faces. Soran stood and eyed the window as if planning to open it and escape, but Jack ordered him to stay where he was.

'Well,' Jack sighed, fixing Soran with an inquisitive but sympathetic eye. 'We've been looking for you for some time, and you, Sister Susan, you've known all along where he's been. Naughty.'

'The thing is,' Liz put in, 'where are the others?'

'Stiff cheese coppers,' declared Dixie, his cup still halfway to his mouth. 'You'll never find 'em.'

'And you are?'

'Dixie Trumble,' he replied with a snappy military salute. 'Retired wharfie and old digger.'

He looked set for a rant, but Susan motioned for him to calm down. 'You do know what is likely to happen to our friend here?' she asked quietly. 'It will be a death sentence.'

Jack shrugged. 'Not our problem, Sister.' He saw that Liz was looking uncomfortable but ploughed on. 'We just enforce the law. Now, if our friend here has any papers that prove he has a right to be in this country, now is the time to produce them.'

'If you enforce the law, Chief Inspector, then you'll know that in *international* law, Soran here has every right to stay here and apply for asylum.'

'Yes, and so he can,' Jack replied.

'But the Australian government will lock him up for perhaps

years on end with no guarantee that they won't deport him regardless of the strength of his case,' retorted Susan. 'He'll be trapped. It's Hobson's choice. Either way, the chances are he'd lose.'

'What sickens me,' Dixie interjected, 'is that the bloody Immigration Minister flaunts his Amnesty International badge even as he enforces the policy of mandatory detention.'

'Labor introduced it,' Jack reminded him.

'Bastards, too,' Dixie growled.

'Well, we're not here to argue with you, Mr Trumble,' said Liz. 'And we don't make the law.' She was looking anywhere but at the Kurdish refugee, who was clearly only just holding back tears. He'd been so close to freedom.

'Now,' Jack said, looking round the room. 'You do all realise that you've been breaking the law? We'll report what's happened and the Crown Prosecution service will decide what if anything to charge you with.'

'Charge away, Inspector,' Dixie muttered, 'but whatever you do, don't call it justice.'

Jack hoped his face didn't show that it had found its mark, but he reddened. He motioned for Soran to get to his feet and Liz clicked a pair of handcuffs around his wrists. She felt like an executioner. Mrs Harrison stood at the door and wrung her hands together, watching sadly as they put Soran in the back of the car.

'Have you got family?' she demanded, looking from Jack to Liz.

They shrugged, and Liz looked like she might cry.

Mrs Harrison stood watching the back of the departing car, lost in thought. She'd seen a lot of things in her time and had long ago realised that things didn't automatically get better just because they were in the twentieth century. Then, to her surprise, the police car stopped and made a three-point turn. What on earth were those wallopers up to? The car stopped and the big male copper got out and pointed Soran to the side door of the pub. When they were back inside the parlour, the woman detective came in with Soran. She unlocked his handcuffs and told him to sit down. The poor man looked bewildered.

Jack cleared his throat. 'OK, all. Here's the deal. We are going to leave Mr Rekani in your capable hands.' He looked at his watch. 'In exactly eighteen hours from now we will contact the immigration people and tell them where they can find him.'

Mrs Harrison's jaw dropped and Soran still looked bewildered. Susan began to stutter her thanks and Big Dixie looked like he was going to cry. Liz was silent and Jack shuffled his feet uncomfortably. Finally, Susan managed to get to her feet and take Jack's hand. There was a lump in her throat and she couldn't speak as the two detectives turned on their heels and left without another word.

CHAPTER 29

'**R**at's piss!' Ernie Foxcroft's voice startled them like a pair of kids caught raiding the biscuit jar. He scowled at the cup of tea he'd plonked on the table. 'Anyway, what's next, Jack?'

Jack scrambled through his mental gears. 'Right-o, Ernie. I'm thinking that we'll have to move on the Seddon brothel soon.'

Foxcroft nodded agreement. 'Yep. We can't leave those girls there. Any news, by the way?'

'The surveillance team reports that johns have been visiting,' replied Liz, 'but the two minders haven't moved all night.'

'Right,' said Foxcroft. 'Let's get a team together and turn them over. Oh, and by the way, anything to report about those asylum seekers?'

Liz was quick. 'Oh, we've had reports they're in Port Melbourne and we hope Immigration will be detaining them soon.' She didn't think she blushed and tried hard to ensure that her eyes gave nothing away. Jack gave thanks that she'd been quick off the mark. Lying didn't come easy to either of them.

Ernie shoved the offending liquid aside and stood up. 'Right then. I'll leave you to it.'

Liz took a swig of her stewed tea and surreptitiously squeezed Jack's hand. 'I love you, mate,' she whispered. 'Like old Dixie Trumble said, law and justice aren't necessarily the same thing.'

Neither of them spoke for a while after that. They were both pondering the enormity of what they had done. It was not just a sackable offence, it was a chargeable one. Never before had either of them 'failed in their duty', even when they had been forced to do some distasteful things. But all things going well, Soran Rekani would be safe through channels they didn't want to know about.

Jack looked around to check for eavesdroppers before he spoke. There was a frog in Jack's throat. 'Yeah, Liz, but we can never mention this to anyone. It's a safe bet that the nun and her friends won't say a word, but we can never be careful enough. Now, let's go and check that the team's ready for the raid.'

The raid on the illegal Seddon brothel went smoothly. Officers burst in the front door and ordered the staff, two sullen fellows with shaven, loaf-shaped heads, to get down on the floor. One of them had been rugby-tackled by Constable Zawadzki and was nursing cuts and contusions to the head. Then the police rounded up a depressing lot of remorseful or defiant johns and half-naked girls, some of whom were doped up. The raid did produce some corroborating evidence about the gang's higher-ups, and it had freed six young women from slavery, but the new firm, Jack knew, would simply open a new brothel with fresh consignments of girls to maintain their profit stream. One bright spot was that the gang wars appeared to have stopped, at least for the moment, if only because the new mob had eliminated the opposition or forced them to flee. One of the thugs had demanded to know how they had found the brothel. They ignored him but could see the cogs whirring inside his shaven skull. If his solicitor was who they thought he would be, he would convey his suspicions back to the gang's leaders. They'd have to arrange urgent protection for Dennis Ho.

When they returned to the station and Bruiser Macfarlane was checking in the two new customers, Fire Chief Michaela Schiebal trudged wearily inside. There were dark rings round her eyes and she smelled strongly of smoke and chemicals. Her crews had been working long shifts, and she had scarcely left the Tottenham fire site for days on end. Dog-tired as she was, and relieved that the fire was finally out, she was still full of suppressed fury. Jack made her coffee and invited her to sit in his office.

'The place was a dirty bomb, Jack.' She sighed. 'Just waiting to explode. We have no idea of what it's done to the public's health, and I'm worried sick about my firies. Now we learn that there are at least five other illegal dumps around the state.'

Jack nodded sympathetically and pushed the plate of biscuits over the table to her; his private stock of macaroons. 'I can't begin to understand what you've been through,' he said. 'I only ever stood right back from the fire and the heat and stink was bad enough at that distance.'

'It makes me so angry to think that my workmates have been poisoned by that bunch of arseholes,' growled Michaela. She ticked off their alarming symptoms on her fingers: 'Breathing problems … Constant headaches … Dizziness … Vertigo …

Fainting and memory loss … Insomnia … Coughing up blood … Up to six nosebleeds a day … Infected tear ducts and sinuses … It's a bloody nightmare. We can't undo what's happened, but this Garth Dickins shithead and his mates … we've gotta lock 'em up and throw away the key.'

'What really pisses me off,' Jack added, 'is that the people who used the cowboys to dispose of toxic waste are going to get off scot-free.'

Michaela nodded agreement. 'Yeah. They're untouchable. Sometimes I think the whole state is bent.' She started to collect her things together. 'Oh yes, there's one more thing. We found a shed on the perimeter of the dump – down by the creek but inside the fence. It got a bit hot but it didn't catch fire. The forensics people have had a look and they reckon it's full of the chemicals they use in meth labs to make speed, ice, and other drugs.'

'Aha!' said Jack. 'That explains why Fat Toby Malouf was hanging round the place. Maybe he would have told us, but as you might have heard, he's vanished.'

After they had chatted for a while and she had given Jack a copy of her report, Michaela bade Jack a good day. She was going to have a very long sleep and take some well-deserved leave down at her caravan at Apollo Bay, and hope that none of the other waste dumps caught fire. She reckoned she'd be carted off to the Larundel Mental Hospital if that happened.

*

Late that afternoon, down in North Road, Newport, a muscular young man was crouching behind a garden shed in the rain, watching the back of Dixie Trumble's cottage. He was trespassing, but that didn't worry him, and neither did the rain. He had got used to being outside in all weathers when he was fighting in Bosnia. He fingered the notches on the handle of his Zastava pistol, recalling his 'kills' with leering satisfaction. Maybe this one would resist, and he'd have to add another to his tally. Maybe not. The big boss had specified that the old man had to be brought in alive so that they could make him talk. It wouldn't hurt to wound him though. He still had to do the nun, too, but that could be the last job and then he could go home. Maybe, but he feared that cat-faced Russian bitch would never let him go.

Dixie was making himself a cup of tea and mulling over Soran Rekani's good fortune when he caught a glimpse of something moving out in the rain between his raspberry canes and his garden shed. He put on his distance glasses and sure enough, someone was creeping about out there. His first thought was that it was the police. Then again, that pair of detectives had done the right thing. He was still astonished. Perhaps they had to go through the motions and they'd put him under surveillance. On second thoughts, he couldn't see cops getting out of their nice dry patrol car to squat down in the rain. He debated whether he should challenge the intruder. Maybe not. Maybe they'd just piss off and leave him in peace. Nah. The chances were whoever it was, was mixed up with the pricks Soran had escaped from. If so, he was in danger. He went through to his spare bedroom and retrieved the .303 Lee Enfield rifle he'd brought back from New Guinea fifty years before. He kept it in good nick, locked in a steel cupboard, and still had some ammo clips. Satisfied that everything was in working order, the former jungle scout slapped in a mag-azine and went out the front door. He tiptoed through Mrs Burns' back yard to a little gate that linked the properties so that Dixie could do her weeding for her when her sciatica got bad. The gate was well-oiled and opened silently. Ha! The cheeky arsehole was wriggling his way between the shed and the side fence, and he had a gun, too. Looked like he'd been in the forces. The bastard was so intent on stalking his prey he didn't hear Dixie creep up silently behind him, just as he had learned to do years ago on the Kokoda Trail.

'Drop the gun!' roared Dixie as he shoved the rifle barrel into the man's back. 'Get on your knees and put your hands up!'

The man swivelled round quickly and managed to squeeze off a round. It whistled past Dixie's ear, so Dixie brought the barrel of his rifle down hard on the man's wrist. There was a crack, the man yelped and the pistol fell from his grasp. With an agility that belied his 78 years, Dixie seized it and stuck it in his belt. He was swift as a panther. Next, he bound the man's hands tightly with sash cord and did the same to his ankles.

Mrs Burns had heard the gunshot and was peering round her back door.

'Hey, Mrs B,' Dixie called out, 'call the coppers would you, love?'

Mrs B's blue-rinse head disappeared inside as Dixie was pulling the intruder by the leg into his laundry. The man was crestfallen, his light-coloured eyes fixed on the floor, his wet hair awry. He was bedecked in bling and clad in leather jacket and white tee-shirt. He clearly fancied himself, but he'd been bested by an ancient. His wrist hurt, too, where the old man had hit him with the rifle. The codger had trussed him up like one of his grandma's geese, ready for the pot back in Vojvodina. He was feeling very sorry for himself.

'What's your name, fella?' demanded Dixie.

The gunman grunted and refused to make eye contact, which to be fair was hard given his prone position on Dixie's laundry floor. He was soaking wet and smelled strongly of sweat, slivovitz, and pungent aftershave. His mouth and nose were squashed onto Dixie's lino, and he'd been dribbling. Dixie's silver tabby cat sniffed at his bum, hissed, shook a paw, and flounced off disdainfully.

'I said, what's your name,' Dixie repeated, giving the man a poke with his boot for emphasis and smiling at the cat. The man muttered something, so he gave him another prod, harder this time. 'Listen, mister, I suggest you start cooperating. You can't waltz about trying to shoot old age pensioners. The coppers will be here soon.'

The man's custard-coloured eyes flitted this way and that, reminding Dixie of egg yolks. 'OK,' he replied, his accent thick as treacle. 'Me Ratko Branković.'

'Now you're cooking with gas,' said Dixie. 'Maybe you could tell me what you was doing with a gun in my garden.'

'Me no want prison. In prison in Zagreb one time and no like.'

While they were waiting for the police, Mrs Burns came over with some home-baked fruit cake and made them a cup of tea. Dixie felt almost sorry for the bloke until he remembered what these people had done to Soran and his friends. And how he had tried to shoot him. It had to be the same mob. He tipped the bloke's head back so that he could sip at the tea and nibble the cake. There was a knock on the front door and Constables Thick and Thin came in. They'd arrived with the paddy wagon. They very generously untied Branković so that he could finish his tea and cake and accepted some themselves. They took the precaution of slipping a handcuff onto his wrist and clicking the other around a table leg.

'I think the bloke wants to make a deal,' said Dixie. 'Wants immunity.'

'He'll have to speak with the DCI,' said Thick.

'Above our pay grade,' added Thin.

'Bloody good cake, missus,' said Thick. 'Enter it in the Country Women's competition.'

'Win hands down,' mumbled Thick with his mouth full of cake. 'Anyway, cobber, let's get you up to the nice police station.'

Dixie and Mrs Burns watched the paddy wagon disappear up the street, wondering what might happen next.

Jack and Liz had to work late that day. They settled Ratko down in an interview room and switched on the recording apparatus. A young woman called Danica Jovanović sat ready to interpret, struggling to suppress her distaste for Branković, whom she scorned as 'that Chetnik'. She told Liz later that she came from a mixed ethnic family in the Bosnian city of Tuzla and still regarded herself as a Yugoslav. 'I despise all those so-called leaders,' she sighed. 'Izetbegović, Milošević and Tuđman. They are all the same underneath; petty tyrants who tore our country apart in the name of ethnic nationalism. Please don't think there were goodies and baddies in that horrible war.'

Jack nodded. He knew enough about that war to realise that it had all been a horrible tragedy. To give him his due, Ratko Branković did not appear to sanitise his story too much when he related it to Jack and Liz. He was 29 years old, though with his hard face and hooded yellow eyes he looked older. When the Balkan war broke out, he was working as a junior bank clerk in Zrenjanin, a small city in the semi-autonomous Vojvodina region of northern Serbia. The family farm had not offered a future, although he still missed the village. Nor did the bank job hold much appeal so when the war erupted, he went south looking for adventure. Vojvodina, also known as the Banat, was an ethnically mixed area. Ratko had grown up cheek by jowl with Serbs, Croats, Hungarians, even Rumanians, and had friends among them all. As much as he had ever thought about politics, he had considered himself a loyal Yugoslav, but meeting Željko Ražnatović changed all that. Ratko spoke of that man with awe, causing Danica's lip to curl as she translated.

Dr Johnson's apophthegm that 'patriotism is the last refuge of a scoundrel' fitted Ražnatović to a T. Starting as a teenage football hooligan, Ražnatović had gone on to murder and rob his way around Europe throughout the 1970s and 1980s. Ražnatović was still wanted by Interpol for those crimes, but was hiding in plain sight in Belgrade, Danica later told Liz. When the war began, the gangster reinvented himself as 'Commander Arkan' of the 'Serbian Volunteer Guard' and strutted about with an outsize Serbian cross emblazoned on his chest, murdering, robbing, and raping with impunity. He personally supervised Ratko Branković's 'blooding', leading the boy to a ditch outside Vukovar where some prisoners were kneeling, some praying and others staring stoically ahead. Ražnatović had looked into the boy's yellow eyes and saw someone he could turn into an obedient monster. From then on, Ratko had joined in butchery across Bosnia-Herzegovina with zeal. He was crazy-brave in battle and merciless with any Croat, Bosniak, old style communist or 'disloyal' Serb unfortunate to fall into his hands. The man, Jack realised, was a war criminal.

When the war ended, Ratko was too restless to return to the bank. He skulked around Belgrade drinking and whoring before meeting one of his mates from the Arkan militia. The war was over, said the man, but there was still plenty of action to be had. Better money, too, than working in a bank. He took Ratko to a smoky basement dive that doubled as the local headquarters of an international organised crime gang run by the local branch of a Russian crime syndicate. The firm was expanding internationally, muscling in on drugs and human trafficking, and needed old soldiers like Ratko. They issued him with a doctored passport and sent him to Australia. Ratko revealed that the gang's Melbourne operations were headed by a Russian woman called Anastasia and a silver-haired man called Boris, who liked to help himself to the girls.

He nodded when Liz pushed identikit drawings over the table. 'Yes, that is them. There is other Russian man called Cyril. Him job is pick up girls at airport. He pretend to be nice. Smile all time. But he is nasty just like that.' He clicked his fingers for emphasis. 'He also beat Serbs if he annoyed.'

The most valuable information Ratko gave was that the syndicate's Australian headquarters occupied an old textile mill overlooking the Stony Creek wasteland in Morven Street, Yarraville. It was the breakthrough they'd been waiting for. If his information was good, Jack felt sure they would have broken the back of the new crime gang. The higher ups had promised him leniency: a token sentence after which he would be deported to Serbia, or perhaps he could even serve his sentence there under an assumed name. With luck, his past as a war criminal would catch up with him, although Danica Jovanović was sceptical. More likely, he would awake one night to find a hitman standing over his bed, or he would drift back into a life of crime. None of the other gang members had cooperated, so Jack was curious about Ratko's reasons for confessing. He had shrugged. He was tired, he had said. Tired of all the killing. So much blood. He'd waxed sentimental. He wished he'd never left his village, that he had stayed on as a simple farmer tending his herd and growing his crops in the flat Vojvodina fields. Even stayed on as an obscure bank clerk. Jack hoped that the man felt remorse, but whenever Ratko spoke of Arkan, his yellow eyes would light up, and an unclean gloating expression would crease his face. When Liz asked him if he felt any guilt for what he'd done, Ratko shrugged and slurped from his coffee cup. 'No like prison,' he said in English. 'I tell all.'

When he had finished, they asked him why he had been ordered to go after Dixie Trumble. He didn't know, he insisted. He was simply a foot soldier trained to obey orders without question. They believed him. They also had a very good idea why the old man had been targeted, but they had to tread warily, given their involvement in the disappearance of the Kurdish asylum seekers. Ratko's employers, they knew, were thirsting for revenge. Ernie Foxcroft would want to know everything and they'd have to obfuscate and hope that Dixie wouldn't be interrogated by some relentlessly astute detective. They'd want to get to the bottom of it: shots fired at the nunnery. A wounded gangster. Vanishing Kurdish refugees. With luck they could put it in the 'too hard' basket. Well, whatever happened, Jack was not going to try to fiddle the outcome. A one-off act of decency didn't make him a bent cop.

As Ratko was led off back to the watch house, Jack found himself pondering the old Nature versus Nurture conundrum: were such men made like that or did circumstances change or mould them? But for that horrific war, might Ratko Branković have lived out his days uneventfully, working in the bank in Zrenjanin and raising a family? Or would his nature have asserted itself in other evil behaviour? Come to think of it, what might the man do when he was released back onto the streets of his native country? Moreover, while they had done a deal to grant him leniency for crimes committed in Australia, did this mean that he should avoid punishment for war crimes? Surely not. Jack made a note before striding off to the briefing room.

CHAPTER 30

Ernie was persistent. 'What the hell's going on with this Trumble character and that nun?'

Jack shrugged, hoping he would not give too much away.

'Dodgy characters,' Ernie said. 'One a commo and the other into that liberation theology stuff. It's pretty bloody obvious they've been hiding asylum seekers. And now we have this Yugoslav hitman in custody for trying to shoot the old fellow. Good that he's singing like a canary but we need to get to the bottom of this whole thing.'

'OK,' Jack replied. 'I'm a bit flat out at the moment, so let's send Vicky Tran round to see Trumble get what she can out of him.'

Vicky wouldn't give up easily, but Jack hoped the old man would clam up. From what he'd heard, Dixie Trumble was a tough old bird who didn't have much time for the police.

Dixie was weeding his veggie patch when the unmarked police car rolled to a halt outside his house. Hmm, he thought. Two detectives, he'd pick 'em a mile off: an Asian lass and her pimply offsider. He been expecting a visit because not even that pair of wallopers they called Thick and Thin believed his claim not to understand why that bloke had targeted him. He'd have to watch out. The girl walking down his path looked shrewd even if the boy looked like he should still be behind a school desk.

'Mr Trumble,' she said, flashing her warrant card. 'I'm Detective Tran and this is DC Puncheon. Could we have a word?'

'Sure,' said Dixie. 'I suppose it's about that bloke who come to take a shot at me? Anyway, you'd better come inside.'

They sat in the front lounge he hardly used and he made them a cup of tea and offered a plate of Mrs B's apricot sponge cake. The young bloke was at it like a half-starved Labrador, but the lass just pecked at it and then she kept at him.

'Tell me again, please,' she said, staring him straight in the face. 'Why would this foreign gunman want to harm you? Surely he doesn't just go around the city trying to murder pensioners?'

'Like I keep saying,' he replied. 'I'd like to help but what can I say? Maybe it's something to do with me politics, me being left wing and all?'

'What do you know about the HiAce van that was abandoned out the front of your place?'

Dixie shrugged. He played with a straight bat, like that boring Test cricketer Bill Lawry: block, block, block, flicking the occasionally loose ball to the boundary. No, he knew nothing about the man in a turban. Gangsters? Never had nothing to do with people like that. He shrugged again and kept it up for over an hour before he said he was starting to get tired and needed a lie down. No way was he going to shop those decent coppers who'd done the right thing with those refugees. In the end, Vicky gave up and they went on their way, the boy clutching a slice of cake that Dixie had wrapped up in silver foil for him.

Back at the nick, Ernie blustered a bit, but he calmed down when Jack announced that the squad was ready to raid the gangsters' lair.

CHAPTER 31

There was no escape for the gang when the raid began. Morven Street was sealed off at both ends and heavily armed officers cut off flight through the back gardens and the Stony Creek wasteland. The doors were smashed open and the squad pounded inside, forcing everyone inside to lie on the floor. The raid netted another half dozen leather jacketed thugs and freed a group of young women who had recently arrived from Russia and Ukraine. Their minder, the man Svetlana called Cyril, was found hiding outside in a putrid dumpster. Oddly, he smiled all the time, even as the handcuffs were clicked round his wrists, and despite the horrible stink emanating from his clothes. There was no sign, however, of the man called Boris, nor of the woman who called herself Anastasia, and whose surname Jack believed to be Smirnov or more accurately Smirnova. Another puzzle was why the gang had been after Dixie Trumble. Ratko just shrugged. He obeyed orders, didn't ask why. Maybe just revenge, he suggested and, good anti-communists as they were, perhaps they wanted to punish the old Red. Smiling Cyril refused to talk, but word came through from Interpol sometime later that his name was Scriabin and that he was wanted in several European cities for gang-related crimes. His nickname was 'The Garrotte'. In the Interpol mugshot he was smiling, and Liz shuddered to think that he probably smiled as he was dispatching his victims with his wire noose. She recalled that the sons of 'The Greengrocer' of the Markets Mob had been garrotted and figured that Cyril Scriabin was the culprit. They would compare the forensic evidence from those cases and compare it with samples from the prisoner. Jack had also contacted the Russian police regarding the woman he believed to be Anastasia Smirnova, but the answer was a curt *nyet*, they had no information. Nor could they help with the man called Boris. Jack found this difficult to believe and wondered at the extent of *Mafiya* penetration of the Russian state.

Jack made himself a cup of tea and slumped down on the sofa when he got back to the flat. It had been a long day, and he was tired, but he couldn't switch off. He was looking forward to going home to Hobart; surely it wouldn't be long now. The Yarraville flat was lonely, and he was missing Francesca. Wendy too. There were piles of empty fast-food containers in the rubbish bin, and he realised that he'd put on weight. He'd been so focused on Operation Tantalus that he'd barely exercised. He had a sudden vision of himself back in what he thought of as his 'Whale Days' when dinner was a packet of potato chips, a meat pie and lashings of beer. Christ, keep this up and he'd be back on the Chiko rolls and potato cakes or wolfing down sausage rolls and beer at all hours in the back bar of the Royal Exchange Hotel. The thought so appalled him that he put on shorts, tee-shirt and runners and went for a jog through the Yarraville Gardens and up Whitehall Street. He returned feeling virtuous. After a quick shower he sat in his armchair to continue reading the report on sex trafficking. Without noticing, he dozed off and woke up dribbling. Time for bed. He slipped between the sheets and his elbow caught on something. 'Jesus Christ,' he yelled, sitting bolt upright and fishing round for the offending object. It was a bloody bra! And, bloody hell, there was a pair of frilly knickers too!

CHAPTER 32

'**B**loody hell, Liz,' Jack roared. 'I am not a cross-dresser!' Liz giggled and Ernie Foxcroft chortled. Realising that he was being teased, Jack laughed too. It was surreal, no it was worse, it was utterly creepy. First, someone had nicked his undies. They'd snooped around his flat and then sent him photos of their girl's parts in the mail. Now someone was putting female smalls in his bed! It was highly unlikely that it had anything to do with the gangsters, unless one of them had a twisted sense of humour or strange fetish. Ernie adopted a more serious tone. 'Surveillance cameras, Jack. We should have done it earlier.' He picked up his telephone, dialled a number and spoke briefly to Bruiser Macfarlane before turning back. 'It'll be done this morning. The bloke we use knows his business. They'll be well hidden and he's trustworthy. Anyway Jack, the way things are going, you'll be home soon.'

Indeed, the Tantalus gang seemed to be on the ropes. They were seeing the cautious re-emergence of the old firms that had gone into hiding since the irruption of the new mob into

Melbourne. Snouts reported that Legs O'Donoghue's bar was slowly getting back to normal. A trail bike rider found a decaying one-armed corpse in scrub near the Patterson Lakes and the pathologist, Vernon Swinburne, reunited it with the arm dumped out at Tottenham. The remnants of the Marauders refused to cooperate with the police, but DNA evidence identified the body as that of 41-year-old Barry Kemp, aka 'Snorter'. Snorter had form for assault, pimping, selling drugs, possession of unlicensed firearms, and attempted murder. On the debit side, Anastasia Smirnova and the Boris character were still on the loose, so Jack felt there was still work to do. It outraged his sense of justice to think of the 'respectable' firms who had taken advantage of Garth Dickins's knockdown rates for disposing of their waste walking off scot-free.

Vicky Tran had visited the firms named in the McCastles accounts, but they turned out to be small fry, an automotive workshop in Sunshine and the like. Brendan McCastle himself had gone missing, along with his bass-playing receptionist, Denise Sugden. Her husband Sam, aka 'Basher', the so-called 'Sergeant-at Arms' of what Jack called the Sons of Onan bikie gang, would not be happy. When Liz and Jack visited the gang's Deer Park clubhouse they found 'Basher' tight-lipped about everything. He claimed to know nothing about the new organised crime firm and when Liz asked about the whereabouts of his missus his left eye twitched dangerously. He could barely restrain himself when she suggested that Denise had run off with her boss. The shaven-headed Basher was at least six and a half feet tall and half that wide and had a long list of priors for violence so they thought it prudent to leave.

When Jack again raised the matter of Dickins's clients with

Ernie Foxcroft, the Commander informed him that Assistant Commissioner Lennox had ordered him not to follow this line of inquiry. It was not in the public interest. 'Best thing, Jack,' Foxcroft advised, 'is to forget about it. Just dot the i's and cross the t's and you'll be no doubt anxious to get back home. You and Liz will need to come back and don your Truth Suits when the cases go to trial, but except for this Anastasia tart and that Russian bloke we're done here.'

At least he looked shamefaced.

But Jack was feeling bolshy.

He invited Liz to join him for dinner at Café Terroni, an Italian joint in Yarraville. It served good, solid southern Italian food and it was his shout. He approached the matter obliquely with Liz when they were waiting for their desserts. If she'd demurred, he would have let the matter drop and pursued it alone. Liz, however, needed no persuasion.

'The higher-ups don't see this as a legal question,' she said. 'For them, it's all about politics. If we go treading on the toes of well-connected people, they will go running to their mates and we'll be warned off.'

'We'll be sent back to Hobart under a cloud,' Jack warned.

'Don't really care,' Liz replied, taking a spoonful of her Tiramisu. 'I mean, we helped Soran Rekani escape...' She stopped at a look from Jack.

'Right-o,' nodded Jack, sampling his gelato. 'First up, we should pay our beloved Garth Leslie Dickins a visit and see what we can get out of him. Maybe he won't want to carry the can for these people.'

'Yep, as they say, he'll know where the bodies are buried.'

Jack finished his wine and gave Liz a probing look. 'Hey

Liz,' he said, 'tell me to bugger off if you like, but you and Ms Tran seem to be getting on rather well …'

Liz blushed. It was time to leave.

The next morning, bright and early, they were back at the Remand Centre in Spencer Street. Dickins glowered over the table when the guards brought him from his cell. It looked like he was working out behind bars, for his thin body was still ropey with sinew under his blue singlet.

'What now?' he snarled. 'I got better things to do than listen to you wankers.'

'Garth,' Jack began, ignoring the crude insult. 'Things aren't looking good for you. Just for starters you face a long stretch for the arsenal you've assembled at your house. Looks like you wanted to start a war, and the public is spooked about the Port Arthur massacre. They'll want to put you away forever.' He paused and watched Dickins carefully.

'Then there is a raft of charges for the illegal dump,' Liz reminded him before suddenly changing tack. 'Incidentally, Garth, what was Fat Toby Malouf's interest in the place?'

They knew the answer, but the question took Dickins aback. 'Dunno nothing about him except what you hear on the TV. Anyway, I don't have to sit here and listen to this shit.'

'Well, Garth,' Liz said, leaning over the table and staring him down with her sharp green eyes. 'Just hear us out.'

'Thing is,' said Jack, 'do you think it's fair that you go down and those who paid you to take their poisonous rubbish walk free?'

Dickins looked flustered, but he shouted at them to 'go and get fucked!' He stood and called to the warders to take him back to his cell.

'At least think about it,' said Liz to his retreating back.

Maybe he would, but they doubted it. Dickins was playing by the underworld code of silence, and he was scared. Unless they could locate the McArseholes trucking boss it would be difficult to pin anything on the firms that used Dickins's services even if the higher-ups permitted it.

There was an email from Wendy waiting when Jack got back to the flat that evening. She had some news that would pin his ears back, she said. She'd met someone. Well, not just anyone. It was *Simon Calvert*. Jeez, that did pin his ears back. Dr Simon-bloody-Calvert, understudy to Professor Peregrine Rowley-Samuels, the chief pathologist back in Hobart. The Prof always referred to Calvert as his 'Communist Boy', shaking his white patrician head at the absurdity of it. An image of Calvert's sunburst of auburn hair flashed into Jack's mind. They had become friends over the years, unlikely given Jack's job, and Simon's politics, but they enjoyed each other's company and there was a real respect and camaraderie between them. But Simon and his daughter? Bloody hell! That was an entirely new dimension. He wandered down to the pub on the strength of it and downed a pint of Guinness. And yet … and yet when he thought about it, why not? Wendy was in her mid-twenties, Simon was not much more than 30 years old, and he was a good lad. It was just a bit of a shock. Jack didn't notice the Guinness slipping down his throat, but he politely waved off the barmaid's offer for a refill and made his way back up Anderson Street.

He donned the glasses he was usually too vain to wear and looked back over Wendy's email. Christ! He'd been so flummoxed by her announcement of her liaison with Simon Calvert that he'd overlooked the attachment, which was entitled 'Our Ancestor Sandy Johnstone'. Wendy would be proud of him; he'd got the hang of opening attachments now. He sat down and was soon absorbed in what she'd written. Stowed away in Uncle Jimmy's trunk was a diary-cum-autobiography written by a Scottish convict called Alexander, or Sandy Johnstone. Chances were that the document had lain undisturbed since his death in 1867. It was too long to summarise. She reckoned it would be best for him to read it himself when he returned to Hobart. The bare bones were that Sandy was a Scottish Jacobin who had run afoul of the local laird during the Lowland Clearances in Dumfriesshire. He'd fled to England, where he had organised peasant resistance to the enclosure of common land. Because of that he had been tried in the Assizes and transported in chains to Van Diemen's Land. It was getting late so Wendy said she'd continue her email later.

Jack was intrigued to discover that he had convict ancestry and looked forward to learning more about Sandy Johnstone. Just then, another email came in, this time from Simon Calvert. He was over in Melbourne for a few days and would like to catch up. Jack replied, suggesting a rendezvous in Chloe's Bar at Young & Jackson's Hotel in the city. Given recent developments, Jack was very keen to see the young man.

CHAPTER 33

Jack received a call from the Melbourne Remand Centre the next morning to say that Garth Dickins wanted to see them again. It sounded promising; Dickins had probably never willingly spoken with police in his life. Jack and Liz drove along Footscray Road through thick traffic and parked on a yellow line outside the big red brick prison where prisoners on remand were kept until sentenced. The sun was beating down mercilessly from a cloudless sky. It was already 35 degrees Celsius although it was barely nine o'clock, and the car's air-conditioning was kaput, so they were sweating when they arrived. Prisoners were shuffling around in the exercise yard, vainly trying to stay in the shade. Jack guessed there was a pecking order to decide who got to stay out of the sun. No doubt the members of the Tantalus crew on remand would be at the apex. Indeed, Cyril Scriabin and his cronies were hogging the deepest shade, squatting like malevolent toads on the thin grass.

Dickins launched straight into a harangue about the people he did business with; at least the ones whose waste he processed. 'They treat me like muck,' he muttered. 'High and mighty types who think their shit don't stink. Well, I thought about what you said and if I go down, I don't see why I shouldn't take some of 'em down with me.'

'Silvertails, you reckon?' said Liz.

Dickins ignored her, dyed-in-the-wool misogynist that he was.

After a while Jack nodded that he should continue.

'Thing is,' Dickins continued, 'What's in it for me if I put you onto them cunts?'

'Well, Garth,' Jack replied. 'You'd know that we can't promise anything, but we would put in a good word, and it'll be on the record if you cooperate.'

'You're looking at a long stretch, but why should you carry the can?' added Liz, determined not to be sidelined by this MCP. 'Best that you just tell us and if it helps us, we will be suitably grateful.'

Dickins started to sneer but thought better of it. 'OK,' he said, and he began to talk, naming several prominent firms and individuals as his clients.

'Did they know what was happening to the toxic stuff you took off their hands?' asked Liz, her eyebrows raised.

'Well, they musta known it wasn't by the book,' Dickins snorted, 'but they didn't ask no questions, did they? Knew they was on a good thing cos they was payin' under a third of the normal fuckin' rates. Jeez, we was taking so much waste that the reg'lar firms was wondering where all the shit had gone.'

'Distorted the market?' Liz asked.

'Fucking A, miss,' Dickins grunted.

Jack fixed him with his keen blue eyes. 'And what can you

tell us about your business partners, the ones you ran the Tottenham place with? What about Fat Toby Malouf too?'

Dickins held up his hands. 'Look, I'm not telling you nothing about that, alright? I'll tell youse about whose stuff we took but that's it.'

'Is that because you're frightened?' asked Liz.

Dickins sat back and folded his arms. 'Whaddya reckon?' he scoffed. 'I don't fancy a shiv in the guts. Even if I survived, them people have long memories. No way, neither, that you could arrest 'em all. Bottom line, though, is that I ain't a grass. Them rich cunts is one thing, the fuckin' hypocrites, but the others is off limits, ok?' He gave more details on links with several prominent manufacturing companies and a couple of 'legitimate' waste disposal companies.

When he had finished, he stood up to leave and added as an afterthought, 'Keep me name out of it.' He suddenly looked old and grey, and Jack almost felt sorry for him until he remembered what he had inflicted on the people of the western suburbs. A vision of old Scorcher Dalton with his sick wife flashed through his mind, the kindergarten kids too.

After the screws had taken Dickins away – screaming and shouting as arranged to bluff Scriabin and Co – the two detectives sat for a while in the reception room. Dickins had given them some valuable information and some of his customers were well-known manufacturers, and doubtless 'well-connected.' Jack's nose told him they would make the most of these connections.

'We should pay these "pillars of respectability" a visit,' said Liz.

Jack agreed. There was no time like the present and they

wouldn't give them advance warning. They signed out of the prison and scurried through the blistering heat to where they'd parked. 'Uh, oh,' sighed Liz as she caught sight of what Melbournians called a Grey Ghost sidling up to the car, pen poised to write out a parking ticket. Liz produced her warrant card, but the attendant peered at her through bottle-glass spectacles and gave her a pitying look.

'Law's the law, darlin',' he drawled. 'If ya park on a yellow line, ya has to pay the fine.' He thrust the yellow slip at her and moved on in search of other prey.

Liz jumped into the driver's seat, scowling, until Jack reminded her that they were in an unmarked police car. Victoria Police could sort it out with the Melbourne City Council.

The Grey Ghost had a point, though.

Jack looked at his watch. 'Lunchtime, Liz,' he noted. 'Let's have something in Yarraville and then head out to Altona to see some of these "pillars".'

The Java Café was doing a brisk business, but they managed to find a seat and ordered lunch. The old bloke with the Golden Retriever was eating spanakopita and reading *Green Left Weekly*. The headline caught Jack's eye: 'AUSTRALIAN DEMOCRATS: CAN THE BASTARDS SURVIVE?' Liz was more interested in the dog. Jack should get one, she advised, tickling the pooch's ears. There was a sudden gust of wind. Melbourne was renowned for its mercurial changes of weather. Bits of rubbish blew along the street, the temperature plummeted, and a greasy rain began to fall. At least the Tottenham fire was out. Jack considered returning to the topic of Vicky Tran but thought better of it. None of his business, really, but he was intrigued.

Afterwards, Liz drove carefully out along Francis Street and turned down Miller's Road towards where the smokestacks of the Altona petrochemical industry lined up against the lowering sky, some of them spurting yellow flames, others plumes of black smoke. The air was full of sickly-sweet chemical smells and fine black smuts were falling with the rain. Liz wondered how the residents dried their laundry. Presumably, they all had clothes dryers. Jack jerked his thumb at one sprawling plant on Miller's Road and told Liz that he had worked there for a little while back in the early 1970s. Maintenance electrician. She gave him a searching look; the old bugger never ceased to amaze her. He said nothing more about it, for the sight of the place brought back a flood of unhappy memories. Not long before he had worked in the plant, Lily Ferenczak, his first love, had turned her back on him, or so he had thought, and there had been a time when he'd been so low that he contemplated jumping off one of the soaring steel structures of the plant.

He dragged himself back to the present and phoned Bruiser at the nick to say where they were going. Then he busied himself flipping through the Melways street directory before directing Liz to turn right at a big roundabout to find the Lupton Bros. plastics & chemicals factory on Kororoit Creek Road. He'd managed to get them lost, but eventually they found the right way. They drew up in the parking lot out the front of the red brick administration block just as a squall of wind blasted off the flat marshlands. The front of the building boasted a portico with white pillars and an imposing flight of steps leading to huge double doors. Behind it was a tangle of gleaming metal pipes and silver tanks, with a single black chimney belching smoke into the low sky. A giant Australian flag hung limp and wet on a flagpole in the forecourt. The factory entrance itself was down the side next to a razor wire fence. If Jack remembered rightly, this was the place where old Scorcher Dalton from Tottenham said McCastle's Logistics had driven trucks at speed through a union picket line.

Just then, a Claytons cop slouched up from a kind of dog-box and gestured for Liz to wind down her window. The rain was pouring down. He had prominent buck teeth in a thin face and didn't look like he was enjoying life. Liz flashed her warrant card and he retreated, muttering to himself, his white shirt dark with rain. There were many like him these days: men who had once done skilled work but were now reduced to jobs such as security guards and customer service officers, or shop assistants selling the products Australia no longer manufactured. Jack wondered if this plastics mob would shut down and move offshore to somewhere without unions and even laxer environmental regulation. Jack waved to the guard as he and Liz jumped out of the car and sprinted past his shanty and up the steps of the office block. The man's face was mushroom-white in the gloom, and he responded eagerly, happy to be noticed.

The big wooden and glass doors swung shut behind them with a soft hiss and they stood dripping rainwater on the thick carpets of the foyer. There was no hint here of the chemical smells from the adjacent factory. Maybe they had an air filtration system, Jack thought. The place was almost silent despite the industrial racket outside. Clerks were striding around purposefully, bearing armloads of documents, and a middle-aged tea lady was pushing a trolley wearily through the deep pile of the carpet. A polished wooden counter sat at one end of the foyer. Liz hit the bell and a young receptionist sashayed up, clad in the company's red and blue livery. There was not a hair out of place on her blonde head and her smile was practised.

'How may I help you?' she asked, the Strine edges filed off her voice.

'Police,' Jack replied, holding up his warrant card. 'We'd like to see whoever is in charge here.'

'Oh,' said the receptionist, her toothy smile fixed. 'May I ask what this is in relation to? Mr Savage from HR may be able to help. Security has been outsourced, I'm afraid.'

'Nah,' said Liz. 'It's the head shebang we'd like to see. Your manager or CEO or whatever they call themselves.'

'Oh,' said the receptionist. There was a hushed edge to her voice. 'That's *Sir Barnaby Lupton*. Do you have an appointment?' She paused to let that sink in. For her, the CEO was God or at least an archangel.

'Sorry, miss … but we don't need an appointment. We are here on police business.'

She bit her glossy lip, nodded, and disappeared through the office behind the counter.

The tea lady came up and offered them a drink, which they politely declined. She sounded Irish. 'You're here to see the Suits.' It was a statement not a question. 'Give 'em a hard time for me, please. It's twenty-two years I've been here and now they're bringing a contractor with a bloody machine to replace me.'

Liz gave a sympathetic smile. Her own mother had worked

at jobs like this, with little pay or appreciation. The woman shrugged. Liz half-expected her to call out 'bring out your dead!' as she went on her melancholy way, invisible to the desk wallahs, soon for the last time.

A tall, immaculately coiffured woman swept up to the counter. 'That will be all, Maureen,' she commanded. She fixed Jack with imperious brown eyes and invited the two detectives to follow her round the end of the counter. 'I am Sir Barnaby Lupton's private secretary,' she informed them as they walked across what seemed like an acre of springy grey carpet. When they reached a polished wooden door, she knocked and a gruff voice bade them enter, after which she trotted off like a beautifully groomed mare returning to the stable. Three figures were waiting inside the room, standing with the light from the tall window behind them. It was deliberate, Jack knew. The window gave out onto a panoramic view of the sprawling plant. A gang of men in yellow wet weather jackets were manoeuvring an enormous steel cylinder into place with a big mobile crane. It took him back to his days in the industry. The crane was blowing out clouds of black smoke, but the thick plate window glass cut off all noise. Back in the room, the tall male figure on the left gestured to a ring of chairs in front of him, so both Jack and Liz angled their chairs to avoid looking into the light. The three figures also sat, perched forward, their faces intent, like the three wise monkeys.

'I am Sir Barnaby Lupton,' said the figure in the middle, a middle-aged fellow who peered at them over half-moon glasses. 'I am the CEO of the firm.' With his flying eyebrows, patrician air, and posh accent, he reminded Jack of Bob

Menzies, the former Tory prime minister who had governed Australia for 23 years. Dressed in a three-piece tweed suit and polished brown brogues, he was trying for the laird look, the factory his estate. He extended a pink hand towards the others. 'This is Dr Leah Sheridan, my deputy.' With her straight brown hair framing a long and lugubrious face, the Sheridan woman reminded Jack of an Afghan hound. She looked ready to bite.

'I believe you are acquainted with Mr Bentley, our solicitor,' said Lupton.

Bentley smirked at Jack. The bad penny was turning up everywhere. How the hell did he know they were coming? Jack exchanged a glance with Liz. Maybe they were being paranoid and the bugger had another reason to be there at that time.

Sir Barnaby cut to the chase. 'Now we assume that this is not a social call, detectives, so we would appreciate it if you told us the reason for this visit.'

There was a knock and Maureen the tea lady pushed her trolley through the door. It was laden with Italian biscuits, fine bone crockery and what looked like silver spoons and teapots. She must have parked the inferior stuff elsewhere. She gave Jack a wink before fussing about pouring tea and handing round plates of biscuits. When she had gone, Lupton extended his palm, inviting the detectives to speak.

'Garth Leslie Dickins,' said Jack, one eyebrow raised, inviting a response. He had not touched his Earl Grey, didn't care for the stuff, but he took an almond pistachio biscotto. They were too good to miss.

The CEO's eyes slid sideways. 'I'm afraid you'll have to be less cryptic, Chief Inspector.'

Liar, thought Liz, catching the involuntary gesture. 'We have reason to believe that you have done business with Mr Dickins. He trades, or rather did trade, as Dynamic Achievers.'

'Well, if we have, I have no recollection of it,' piped up Dr Sheridan, baring her sharp teeth. 'We are a very large firm, and we can't be expected to have the details of every Tom, Dick and Harry at our fingertips.' She had managed to look both impatient and indignant. Jack imagined her chewing delicately on a bone as he popped the biscotto into his mouth and resisted the urge to take another. He imagined this mob would send him an invoice for it.

Cornelius Bentley looked up from polishing his glasses and smiled urbanely. 'May I suggest,' he purred, uncapping his Mont Blanc pen, 'that you tell us the nature of this, err, relationship with this Mr Pickens?'

'Dickins,' Jack corrected, knowing that the lawyer had deliberately got the name wrong. 'As you know, Mr Dickins is currently in custody as a person of interest in relation to the recent chemical fire at Tottenham and the existence of a number of other toxic dumps around the state.'

'Yes,' said Liz. 'Your colleague Nick Campion is representing Mr Dickins and several of your clients were involved with his illegal dump at Tottenham. Or should I say "dumps", plural?'

'Now, Sir Barnaby,' said Jack brusquely. 'We have reason to believe that your firm contracted Mr Dickins's company, Dynamic Achievers, to remove and process toxic waste.'

'Surely nothing illegal there,' said Bentley. 'That is *if* my clients availed themselves of this company's services.'

'Then you would have no objection to us looking through your books,' Jack replied, looking at Lupton.

'Oh dear, oh dearie me,' chided Bentley, languidly pushing his teacup to one side with his pen. 'There is such a thing as commercial-in-confidence, you know. I'm afraid that you would need a warrant for that, and even then, there is every chance that my clients would direct me to seek a court order to restrict what you can see.'

'We also have reports that this firm used contractors to clean out tanks used to store toxic waste, and that these contractors used forced labour,' said Jack. 'That is clearly unlawful.'

'Oh, I say!' Lupton retorted, nettled. 'We had no part of any of that and I resent the insinuation. Why, I've a good mind to—'

Bentley held up a hand and took over. 'My client runs an honest business, DCI Martin. Luptons regularly contract out cleaning and maintenance and while every care is taken to ensure conformity with the law we cannot be held responsible if some of these contractors occasionally, how shall we say, cut corners.'

There was more of this malarkey before the detectives gave up and left the meeting seething at the company's obstructive behaviour but determined to press on with their enquiries. The receptionist donned her plastic smile and bade them have a nice day. The security guard peered from his humpy and gave a forlorn salute as they drove off. Jack almost felt guilty for leaving him there like a stray dog desperate for a home. They'd have to hurry to get to their next place of inquiry. They suspected that as soon as they left the premises Lupton would be on the telephone. Or had had someone ring around all the suspects.

The trip down the Princes Freeway was uneventful. The

Werribee sewage farm was as smelly as ever and the flat plains stretched out endlessly. Eventually the sharp granite peaks of the You Yangs came into view, softened by rain, and they made it to the Corio petrochemical precinct in good time. Alas, they fared no better at Scott Abbott & Sons Ethical Recycling Solutions at Corio. CEO Dr Quentin Bushby, AO, and his solicitor, Marcus Barnes, refused to reveal any details of the firm's business but stoutly denied any wrongdoing. It was still raining when they drove out onto the Princes Freeway to return to Melbourne. Both big firms and a smaller rendering outfit at Laverton were clearly guilty as sin, but Jack had a sinking feeling about the whole business. The establishment would look after its own, masters of mutual back-scratching, rorts, hypocrisy, and double standards. As the NSW Labor maverick Jack Lang once said: 'Always back the horse named self-interest, son. It'll be the only one trying.' It was doubtful that they would get warrants. Phones would ring in high places. Old Boys – and sometimes Girls – would raise draw-bridges. Plebeian detectives would be seen off. What was it that Simon Calvert had quoted in one of their interminable arguments? Something by Jonathan Swift. Yes, that was it: 'Laws are like cobwebs': they trapped petty offenders but allowed rich malefactors to get off scot-free. The bastards would probably also be on the blower to the Commissioner and Jack would get his arse kicked for upsetting the High and Mighty of the Land.

Jack cheered up when he got back to the flat and saw that there was an email from Wendy on his computer. He made himself a cup of tea and sat down to read what was a continuation of her earlier summary of the life and times of Sandy

Johnstone. She was pleased to report that Sandy's life in exile appeared to have been less brutal than was the case for many convicts. He was an artisan and his ironworking skills were in great demand. Yet he never accepted the legitimacy of what he considered to be a morally bankrupt and criminal system. When his sentence expired he was over 40 years old. He lacked the money to return home, but as he hated the Governor and 'the strutting officers and parsons' he moved to a bush property near the Great Western Tiers and became a 'staunch man'. He died aged 73 in 1890, and his sons moved to the Mt Lyell mines at Queenstown.

Jack removed his glasses and sat back quietly to digest what he had read. Like most Tasmanians he had always been aware of the dark past of his island home – and of Australia as a whole. Moreover, his ancestor's story gave it all a pressing personal dimension. Buggered if he could think of Sandy Johnstone as a criminal, though. He sighed and went to pour a glass of water. Standing at the sink, he again had the uncomfortable feeling that someone was watching him. There were lights on in most of the rooms of the big block of flats over the back, but he could not see anyone looking, but the feeling would not go away.

CHAPTER 34

At nine o'clock the next morning, rain was still pouring down over the city, with more forecast and flooding imminent along the Maribyrnong and Yarra Rivers. The great container cranes at Swanson Dock and the towers of the city were invisible in the humid murk, but the procession of trucks rumbling along Napier Street testified to business as usual. Jack was catching up on paperwork in his office. He ignored a sudden burst of shouting downstairs, figuring it was Bruiser Macfarlane upbraiding an insolent crim or hapless junior constable. There was some sort of kerfuffle in the corridor and the sound of heavy footsteps coming up the stairs. Then a squat figure exploded through his office door without knocking. Jack opened his mouth but closed it quickly. The intruder was Assistant Commissioner Paul Lennox, whom he had last seen directing the ejection of the DETOX protesters from the Footscray mall. Ernie Foxcroft hovered uncertainly behind the man, his eyes imploring Jack to sit back and take what was coming to him. Jack invited Lennox to sit, but the man just glared as if he had made an improper suggestion.

'What the fuck do you think you're doing?' Lennox snarled. He swung his head this way and that before grabbing hold of a wad of documents from Jack's in-tray. His bloodshot blue eyes blazed, and his face was the colour of raw beef. He was well on his way to a coronary.

'I, err, maybe you …' ventured Jack, watching the red points of Lennox's Spitfire pilot moustache with alarm. They were sharp enough to puncture an eyeball.

'Don't fuck with me, *Inspector*,' Lennox growled, emphasising Jack's theoretically lower Tasmanian rank. 'We brought you over to do a job with the big boys, but you went charging off like you're some sort of private dick. You were ordered to stay away …'

'If I understand what you mean, sir,' Jack interrupted, 'there was no direct order.' A low Pitbull snarl erupted from Lennox's throat and his face turned scarlet, but Jack pressed on. 'Sir, here's an analogy: do we prosecute the hitman but let those who hired him go free?'

'Don't get smart with me,' Lennox snarled, twisting up the paper in his meaty red paws. 'I've had the fucking Premier on the fucking blower fit to blow a fucking fuse! What the hell do you think you're doing annoying some of our most important citizens? Have you any idea of just how influential these people are?'

'Sir, the law is the law,' Jack began. 'We …'

Lennox held up a red paw, demanding silence. Jack had seldom seen anyone so choked up with anger. Had Lennox's square form been rubbed against the wall, Jack reckoned it would have burst into flames. He smirked at the image and his 'insolence' caused a further explosion of incoherent rage. After the assistant commissioner had worked off some of his anger by ripping up the wad of paper in his hands, he regained his voice. 'You are insubordinate, Inspector,' he hissed, punctuating the words with jabs of a thick forefinger. 'You will cease and desist from harassing Luptons and any other respectable company you have in your sights. Clear? You will apologise to Sir Barnaby Lupton and Dr Bushby. Clear? You will wind up your whole investigation and you will return to that inbred island of yours when you have finished. Is that all clear, Inspector?'

'Yes, sir,' Jack ground through gritted teeth. 'I understand *perfectly*.'

Lennox knew that Jack's words were laden with irony, but he had calmed down sufficiently to let them pass for the moment. He dropped the mauled paper on Jack's desk, muttered something unintelligible and turned on his heel. Jack watched his retreating back and sniffed the air. He could smell sulphur. Ernie Foxcroft spread his hands in a 'what can you do?' gesture and followed Lennox from the room.

Half an hour later, Foxcroft returned and sat down heavily.

'Well, that went well,' he joked, raising an eyebrow.

Jack said nothing.

'Jack, I did try to warn you off,' said Ernie. 'You don't have to dig very far in this city to uncover a web of connections. Family connections. Old school connections. Business connections. Political networks. Luptons is a generous political donor and Sir Barnaby Lupton knows everyone who's anyone in town. The whole country, come to think of it.'

'It's corrupt, sir,' said Jack. 'Lennox should be ashamed of himself.' He started to rant that Lupton should be strangled with his old school tie but thought it prudent not to continue.

Foxcroft spread his hands: a gesture of impotence. 'Lennox shouldn't have abused you like that, Jack. Just between you and me, he's been a bully ever since he stood at the intersection of Swanston and Spencer Streets directing traffic. Yes, he was a jellyback like me and he has a massive chip on his shoulder that he never made it to CIB. His weakness for good whisky doesn't help. I wouldn't normally say this, but Lennox is more into politics than policing.' Foxcroft stared out the window at the railway tracks for a minute or two. 'Now, there's another thing,' he said, desperate to change the subject. 'Those surveillance cameras we put in at your flat. Your stalker.'

Jack sat up at that.

'You can look yourself, but the stalker is one of our own,' said Ernie.

'Someone in the job, you mean?'

'Yep,' nodded Foxcroft. 'Bernice King; one of the new baggy-arses. Lives close to your place in Yarraville. Big block of flats over the back, they tell me.'

Jack thought for a while before recalling the dark-haired young probationer who had been over-eager to impress during the raid on Garth Dickins's property. He shook his head and sighed. When he looked back, he realised that she had often contrived to bump into him.

'She's out of the job, of course,' said Foxcroft. 'Up to you, though, if you want to prosecute.'

Jack mulled it over. 'Nah, I don't think so, but let's make sure she gets psychiatric help as a condition of not pressing charges.'

'OK,' agreed Foxcroft, 'but before I go, let me say that you and Liz have done a great job. That said, Lennox wants everything tied up by the end of the week, and the pair of you on a flight back to Hobart. He thinks we can track down the rest of the Tantalus mob without you, and we do have people coming back from leave soon.'

Foxcroft extended his hand, and they shook.

CHAPTER 35

When Foxcroft had gone, Jack sat gazing blankly out of the window. He did not see the raindrops coursing down the glass and nor did the trains rushing by register in his conscious mind. In Jack's opinion, those who used the illegal dumpers were just as culpable as those who took their toxic rubbish. It was a matter of out of sight and out of mind and no questions asked. No doubt the cowboys were much cheaper and that was all that mattered. More broadly, the manufacturers could keep on making or using inherently polluting products without questioning whether they were necessary or whether they could be replaced. Governments could be relied on to do their bidding. The companies gave large donations to the big parties and Jack suspected, nay knew, that more than a couple of pollies were on the take. He had a depressing vision of this great city sprawled out like a living thing on the shores of Port Phillip Bay, awash in its own toxic excrements. Crooks like Dickins and the Tantalus mob charged way below half of the rates of legitimate operators and sometimes threw in free transport. The scam had thrived in part because of lax oversight and paper-based certificates. Huge volumes of waste were simply unaccounted for; in fact, there was a large drop in the recorded amounts of processed waste in the city and state. The disaster mocked government boasts of 'current world's best practice'. Garth Dickins and his associates had created half a dozen other illegal dump sites around Victoria and Jack wondered how many more were undiscovered. Dickins certainly wouldn't tell them.

Jack had been a copper for the best part of 25 years. He had drifted into the job if he were honest. When he signed up, he'd just lost the love of his life and his soul was going through its darkest hour. He'd always had an idealistic streak and he joined the force genuinely believing he would Protect and Serve without fear or favour. He didn't have tickets on himself. He knew he was as flawed as the next person. He'd never taken bribes and he'd never doctored evidence. At most, he'd accepted the odd free cup of coffee and that more from friendship than anything else. He was painstaking and did not cut corners. There were times when he'd been sorely tempted to thump some lowlife, but he'd always counted to ten and kept his fists to himself. He'd always believed that all were equal before the law and entitled to due process. He was no utopian; he knew there were flaws in the system but believed it was fundamentally sound, or … what were those words in Voltaire's *Candide*? 'All is for the best in the best of all possible worlds.' Dammit. He was confused. He didn't believe those words and he knew Voltaire had used them ironically. And all too often there was a niggling little voice at the back of his mind. Why had so many of his colleagues been so gung-ho about arresting gay rights protesters back in

Hobart? With rubber gloves, would you believe! They were doing the bidding of reactionary politicians, one of whom wanted gay people wiped out. It was only with difficulty that Jack had been able to persuade Liz Flakemore not to resign. More recently, he could not forget the young Greek man whose ageing mother had been bashed by Victorian police on a Footscray picket line. He'd been horrified, too, by the sight of Lennox's booted *squadristi* bashing the DETOX people from the Footscray mall.

And now, why was it that he was blocked when he raised the question of investigating the companies that contracted the likes of Mr Dickins to dispose of its poisonous wastes? He tried not to think of the tyrannical Assistant Commissioner who'd bawled him out. He smiled, though, when he thought about the Kurdish fellow, Soran Rekani. By now, he should be safe across the ditch and looking forward to a new life. Just that morning, though, he'd learned that the immigration authorities had deported the Thai women he'd wanted to act as witnesses against the human traffickers. Like his friend (and now Wendy's boyfriend) Simon Calvert insisted, the establishment would protect its own, and all too often the police could be relied on to assist them. You could take the police motto of 'Uphold the Right' in more than one way, Simon said.

Jack was still mulling over all this when Liz came in through the door.

'Got a minute, sir?' she asked, the formal address indicating that she had someone with her.

Jack nodded and Liz led the young Russian woman called Svetlana Anikanova into the office. She was smiling shyly.

'Jack,' Liz began. 'Svetlana has something important to tell us.'

'Yes, Inspectors, I am here to sign some papers and when I am near the front door, I see a man who was in the Williamstown brothel.'

'A prisoner, do you mean?' asked Jack.

She shook her head vigorously. 'No, I do not think so. This one was policeman.'

Jack's eyebrows shot up. 'What was he doing there? At the brothel?'

'He was there for sex. I see him when he is leading one of the young girls into a bedroom and hear … I hear him in there.'

'Are you quite sure he was a policeman, Svetlana?'

'Yes, I am sure. Today he is wearing the blue uniform. He is important man in police because he was shouting, and the other policemen were frightened of him.'

Jack's eyes narrowed. 'Can you tell me any more about this man?'

'I do not know how he is called but I can tell you how he looked.'

'Go on.'

'He has red hair and looks like a squashed tomato. I think he will have heart attack coming.'

Paul Lennox; Assistant Commissioner Paul Lennox! It fitted. There was no reason for Svetlana to make it up and it was unlikely that she would have seen the man anywhere else. She had been unfailingly cooperative and a truthful witness. Her ambition, she had told them, was to become a police officer. With her help, they had identified key players in the crime gang. It didn't surprise Jack in the slightest that Lennox was bent.

'I'll take Svetlana home now,' said Liz. 'We can figure out what we're going to do about this.'

'OK,' Jack agreed, looking at his watch. 'Let's meet at the Java Café first thing in the morning. I'd do it sooner, but I've arranged to meet Simon Calvert in the city. Oh, and thank you, Svetlana, for all of your help.'

CHAPTER 36

Simon Calvert was ogling Melbourne's most famous nude when Jack entered Chloe's Bar upstairs in Young & Jackson's Hotel opposite the Flinders Street Station. It being a cool evening, the bartender was fussing about closing windows, abruptly cutting off the rumble of the trams lumbering over the intersection of Swanston and Flinders Streets. Jack took in Simon's starburst of red curls perched atop a set of bony shoulders with a burst of affection. He'd known Simon since he was an intern at the Royal Hobart Hospital. Once investigated him for a crime he did not commit. Now, the boy was getting ahead. Old Professor Rowley-Samuels had retired, and Simon was now the chief pathologist down in Hobart … and Wendy's new lover.

Jack grinned and came up behind him. 'Perving on our Chloe, eh?'

Simon spun round, his thin face split in a slightly embarrassed grin. 'Ah, Jack,' he drawled, recovering his composure. 'Just paying my respects to an Australian icon.'

The painting of Chloe had hung on the hotel's walls since 1909, when god botherers had had it banished from public galleries. Acquiring her had been an astute business move by the pub's proprietors, for there could be few Melbournians who did not know of her and the hotel she graced. Both men settled for pints of Guinness and exchanged news while the barman went through the ritual of pouring the rich black stout. Simon was over in Melbourne for a reunion of the Royal Park Reds, the cricket club he'd played for in his medical student days. Jack was amused by the thought of a bunch of left-wingers turned 'flannelled fools at the wicket'. The revolution would be won on the playing fields of Parkville! They took their drinks over to a vacant table and Jack broached the subject that was uppermost in his mind.

'How's my daughter?' he asked, watching Simon over the rim of his pint glass, always the copper.

Simon reddened. 'She's … err … very well,'

Jack let the silence hang until he felt bad about giving the young man a hard time. 'It's ok, Simon,' he said finally. 'Wendy's an adult. She can make her own decisions.' He took a pull on his stout and added slyly, 'Anyway, you're an improvement on some of the dickheads she's gone out with.'

'Damned with faint praise,' groaned Simon. 'Jeez, I thought you might punch me out. You're a dangerous man.'

Jack had meant it. An image of Milton Orgreave-Clothier III, an obnoxious American with whom Wendy had once gone backpacking in South America flashed into his mind. There was no doubt about it: the young man sitting nervously at the table was streets ahead of that wanker. Jack had had nightmares about his daughter bearing a new generation of

Orgreave-Clothiers and had sighed with relief when she told him she was coming home, and that the bastard had gone back to what he called 'The World'.

'Anyway, Simon,' Jack said with his blue eyes twinkling with mischief. 'If Wendy thinks you're a good catch that's good enough for me.'

A look of relief crossed Simon's face. He was normally such a self-assured young man and not slow to give Jack a piece of his mind if he deserved it. 'Another Guinness?' he suggested, and Jack said why not.

'Wendy's been telling me about your ancestors,' said Simon when they sat back down with fresh drinks. 'I must say that the stuff she's found sounds fascinating.'

Jack nodded. 'Yes, I'm looking forward to a look at it myself.'

'Not worried about the old Convict Stain, then?'

Jack laughed. 'Nah. Anyway, from what Wendy's been telling me about Sandy Johnstone, whatever he was he wasn't a criminal, no matter what you think of some of his methods! It's made me think too.' Jack took a sip of stout and put his glass down gently on a beer mat. 'To tell you the truth, Simon, I've begun to wonder whether I've been barking up the wrong tree. Maybe I should have stayed an electrician.'

'Apart from the Johnstone business, what's brought this on?' Simon was watching Jack carefully.

'Well,' Jack replied, weighing his words. 'We're always told that we're all equal before the law, but I've started to doubt that.' He took a pull on his Guinness. 'Look, Simon. They brought me over here to head up Operation Tantalus; a worthy operation indeed, given the disgusting people who've poisoned the bloody joint. They need to be put behind bars as a deterrent to any other bozos who might think they can get away with it.

'All good coppering. But it's only half of the story. I've been ordered to leave the people who use their services strictly alone. Can't go after the "respectable businessmen" who use their services. They do it knowing full well that something's dodgy, but they're off limits.'

Simon nodded and indicated Jack should continue.

'I dunno Simon. I've been an honest cop, but sometimes I think we've got it wrong. What sort of law and order was it to arrest those gay people down in Salamanca Place ten years ago, wearing rubber gloves against AIDS, I kid you not! And then just the other night I was talking with a nice young Greek chap and his girlfriend. The police had bashed up his sexagenarian mother on a union picket line. Sent in bloody horses! And if that's not bad enough, Liz and I saw the Swat squad roughing up people who were protesting about pollution in the western suburbs.'

'Yeah,' Simon put in. 'That must have been just before that dump blew up?'

'It was.' Jack searched his pockets for a cigarette until he realised he'd given up.

'I seem to recall that there was a violent attack on a Trades Hall picket line at that secondary school the other day,' said Simon, really warming to the theme. 'Developers wanted to pull the school down and erect luxury apartments on the prime riverfront site. They expected results for the donations they made to the governing party.'

Jack started to say something about Soran Rekani but thought better of it, remembering his agreement with Liz.

No doubt, though, Simon would have approved of what they'd done.

'Welcome to the class society,' said Simon when Jack ran out of steam. 'You're beginning to sound bolshy!'

Jack wiggled his glass and looked at him questioningly, but Simon declined. 'I think I'll have mineral water,' he said. Jack was not surprised. He guessed that in his professional capacity Simon had seen too many pickled livers. Didn't stop him from smoking, though he must have seen many people dead from lung cancer and emphysema. No doubt Wendy would be on his case about that.

'Doesn't surprise me that the establishment has closed ranks behind the polluters,' Simon said. 'It's the established wisdom that they are morally upright, but history says different. You just have to look at the slave trade.' He paused to take a drink of his mineral water and eat some bar nuts, ready to go into full-on lecturing mode. 'Then we can't forget the Opium Wars, which Britain fought to force the Chinese government to accept Jardine Matheson's drugs. Endorsed By Appointment to Her Majesty Queen Victoria. By the way, that firm still exists. They're into property, retailing, luxury hotels; you name it.'

'I think I heard Wendy talking about that,' Jack nodded. 'Supermarkets in Scotland.'

'You know, Jack, there's an investigative journalist called Günther Walraff who blew the whistle on "respectable" German firms who were using Turkish and Kurdish "guest workers" to clean out tanks full of toxic chemicals without protective equipment. They were even prepared to send them to their certain deaths by cleaning out radioactive wastes.

Many of these firms had also done a roaring trade under Hitler using slave labour.'

Jack suddenly wondered about the time; they'd been deep in conversation and didn't notice it passing. Now, the barman was giving hints that he was about to close. Simon saluted Chloe as they left the bar. A thin drizzle was leaking from the sky when they stood out on the footpath and shook hands before going their separate ways. The talk with Simon had clarified many things in Jack's mind. But he'd have to think about what it meant for his future. He'd let that asylum seeker, Soran, escape and how could he square that with being a copper?

Jack didn't know it, but while he was with Simon Calvert at Chloe's Bar, Liz Flakemore was only a few blocks away in the Sherlock Holmes Bar in Collins Street. She was deep in conversation with a round-faced, slightly porkerish middle-aged man who was clad in a corduroy jacket. He didn't say much for once but scribbled away in his notebook and took the odd swig from his pint of Hargreave's pale ale. He left the pub looking delighted and Liz sidled out shortly afterwards with a look of grim satisfaction on her face.

Jack took the train back to Yarraville, narrowly missing bumping into Liz at Flinders Street Station. After alighting from the train, he strolled deep in thought up Anderson Street with his coat collar turned up against the cold rain. Autumn had suddenly arrived, and he felt a stab of nostalgia for Hobart in that season – his favourite – with the leaves turning russet and yellow and a suggestion of snow in the air. Still, he'd be back home soon to see Francesca and make the most of having Wendy at home while she still wanted to be there.

There was a large buff envelope in his letterbox when he

arrived back at the flat and he threw it on the table while he made himself a cup of tea. Blow it, why not, he thought, although he knew that his middle-aged bladder would have him up in the night if he drank any more fluid. The envelope was addressed in a large, looping hand, with no sender's details on the reverse side. He hoped it wasn't another stalker as he slit it carefully open with the bread knife. Inside there were two blown-up photos, professionally done. One was of Wendy on her bicycle, looked like she was on her way to the university. The other showed Francesca sitting with a cup of tea and a book on her patio, oblivious to the watcher with the camera. A feeling of utter dread welled up inside him, followed by the strong desire to return home immediately, but he forced himself to think rationally. Despite the late hour, he telephoned his boss, Commander Derek Holmes, in Hobart. Holmes's voice was groggy with sleep, but he listened carefully, instantly aware of the gravity of the situation. Holmes was honest and efficient, and Jack would trust him with his life.

'Do you have any idea of who it might be?' Holmes asked.

It was a good question. Was Jack being paranoid to suspect the silvertails whose cages he'd been rattling? That lawyer, Cornelius Bentley, had the underworld connections. He wouldn't put it past the creature, but no, more likely it was the remnants of the Tantalus gang. The image of a hydra-headed monster jumped into his mind. Whoever it was, though, would have covered their tracks and dealt with those they had employed to make the threats at several removes. The surveillance cameras here at the flat might turn something up. There was one trained on the front door and letterbox, but Jack doubted that the person who left the envelope would be stupid enough to allow their face to be filmed.

'OK, Jack,' said Holmes before hanging up. 'I think the idea was to send you a warning to stop whatever it is that you've been doing to upset people. It's unlikely that they will do anything so soon after delivering the photos, but first thing tomorrow we'll move Wendy and Francesca to a safe location. Now, Jack, you should try to get some sleep. You're going to need a clear head.'

It was impossible, of course. Jack tossed and turned and when he drifted off, he was troubled with terrifying dreams and woke up sweating and bewildered. Dawn seemed an impossibly long way off, so Jack got up and prowled around the flat until the sun came up. Part of him wanted to leave for Hobart immediately, but then there were still things to finish here in Melbourne.

CHAPTER 37

The following evening Liz was waiting with umbrella ready at the corner of Punch Lane and Little Bourke Street in the city's Chinatown. She'd arranged to have dinner with an old friend, Georgina Triffitt, at the Golden Panda restaurant. Liz liked Chinatown, the Celestial precinct that had existed since the 1850s, with its facades festooned with lanterns and colourful red banners with the Chinese characters picked out in gold. She loved the ambience and loved the food and was hungry enough to eat a whole sheep raw, wool and all, except she was vegetarian. Melbourne's mercurial weather had changed again. It was a steamy evening after the brief cold snap. The rain had stopped but the street was glistening, and cars swished slowly past on the wet asphalt that was reflecting the shop front lights. True to form, Georgina was running late, and Liz hoped that her scatty friend hadn't forgotten. Georgina had recently moved to Melbourne to enrol in a PhD at Monash after finishing her honours degree in Hobart. No doubt her mind was on her thesis. The woman was obsessive. The Golden Panda served good vegetarian food and Liz's stomach was audibly rumbling. Crowds were swirling hungrily around the precinct and Liz swore she'd murder Georgina if they couldn't get a seat. She was checking her watch again when big Georgina barrelled up breathlessly with her orange kaftan blazing among the more soberly clad crowds.

'Sorry!' she puffed, drawing Liz into a bear hug. 'Bloody supervisor wanted—'

She got no further. Liz brusquely disengaged from her friend's embrace. 'Hey!' Liz shouted, cutting off across the narrow street with cars honking angrily at her. Georgina later recalled catching sight of a woman's head spinning round – a white blotch of fear – just as huge raindrops began to fall golden in the light from the lanterns and brightly lit windows.

Georgina was flummoxed. She tried to follow Liz across the street but there were no breaks in the traffic with its bad-tempered drivers looking for somewhere to park. Liz had disappeared, so Georgina unfurled her umbrella and settled down to wait. After five minutes she began to get worried. Liz was dependable, she knew, so when another five minutes had elapsed, she managed to cross over the street and entered the alley into which Liz had vanished. Georgina was a large woman and rather ungainly, so she trod carefully on the wet cobbles, holding her umbrella aloft against what had turned into a downpour. There were a couple of restaurants near the entrance but soon the only light came from dim streetlights and the odd naked bulb in a curtainless window. Georgina peered through the restaurant windows but could not see any sign of Liz within, and she knew Liz would never simply leave without good reason. The alley came to a dead end where a dilapidated multi-storey brick building bulked darker against the sky. A Council sign said it was slated for demolition. By now, Georgina was frightened, so she pulled her illegal container of mace spray from her handbag and brandished it before her.

'Hey, Liz,' she called tremulously. 'Are you there? Stop playing silly buggers!'

The only answer was the steady hiss of the rain and the gurgle of water in the gutters. Georgina's hand tightened on the aerosol can. I'm a big New Norfolk girl, she told herself. We breed 'em rough and tough in Tasmania. She knew she was whistling in the dark.

There was a large steel door in the building's façade, and it was very slightly ajar. Liz must have gone in there! Georgina summoned up all her courage and heaved at the door handle. The door creaked open, and a fluorescent light snapped into life as she crossed the threshold. Jesus, there was something … someone … lying at the foot of the flight of concrete stairs leading up into the interior of the building. Christ, there was a pool of something dark … Georgina fell to her knees as she made out Liz's face. Liz did not respond to her voice. Georgina had no medical knowledge, so she turned and scurried up the alley to the nearest restaurant and demanded to use the phone for an emergency call.

Ten minutes later an ambulance and a police car were standing in the alley, their lights blazing in the rain falling steadily from the dark sky. The ambos looked grim and would not say anything about Liz's condition before they drove off with lights flashing and their siren wailing. Georgina sat stiffly in the police car while one of the constables painstakingly wrote down her account of what had happened. Later, looking back, she had no recollection of how she got back to her shared flat in Carlton. The police must have taken her and they must also have rung her GP, because he arrived shortly afterwards and gave her a sedative.

Across the city in Williamstown, Jack was just ordering dinner at Café Cirino in Nelson Place. He settled for the ravioli with a green salad on the side, and a coffee to start. Gone were the days when he would have gobbled down a pie or fish and chips and washed it down with a six-pack, and he felt slightly smug about it. Sister Susan Lawless, who had been sitting at the back of the restaurant, saw him when she went to the cash register to pay. She stopped by his table.

'Good evening, Chief Inspector,' she said politely. 'You perhaps remember me …'

Jack immediately recognised the little grey-haired nun. 'Yes, of course, Sister,' he said, wiping his mouth with a napkin.

'I won't take up too much of your time,' she replied, keeping her voice low. 'As they say, first the good news and then the bad news. The good news is that a certain person is safe and sound in New Zealand.' She winked surreptitiously, then her face fell. 'The bad news is that we're being plagued by Immigration. They are most concerned about another Kurdish asylum seeker who's gone on the run. It seems there's been communication between the Australian and Iranian governments. They say this man is a member of PJAK, the left-wing Kurdish guerrillas in Iran. Actually, he's a pacifist.'

Jack mumbled something inconsequential. He hoped she wasn't going to make demands of him but dismissed the thought as unworthy of the woman.

'It's not illegal here, but it would be a death sentence in Iran. Anyway, I'll leave you in peace. As you know, there's no chance of them getting their hands on him now.'

Jack's dinner arrived shortly after she left, and he attacked it with a good appetite. He had just pushed the plate to one side when his mobile phone rang. It was Ernie Foxcroft informing him that Liz was seriously injured and was undergoing surgery at the Royal Melbourne Hospital. It seemed she had been shot, Foxcroft added, so Jack wasted no time and was soon pacing up and down in the hospital waiting room anxious for news. The hours ticked by. He drank cup after cup of foul vending machine coffee, chewed his fingernails and warded off a sudden powerful craving for a cigarette. He could not sit still, and he must have pestered the poor receptionists a dozen times asking if there were any developments. He even found himself praying to the Virgin though he'd jettisoned his Catholic faith decades before. Finally, when a faint light began to trickle through the windows, a receptionist told him that Liz was out of surgery. Was he a relative, she asked? Jack explained that he was a friend and police colleague, and that Liz had no living close relatives. He found himself talking with a severe-faced ward sister, who once again interrogated him about his relationship with Liz. The old dragon clearly wanted to refuse him entry.

'Close friend and colleague,' Jack said, showing his warrant card.

It wouldn't have surprised Jack if the Sister had smoke coming out of her nostrils, but she relented. She picked up the phone and spoke softly. Five minutes later, a doctor appeared, wiping sleep from his exhausted eyes. They shook hands and

Dr Ferris, for that was the young man's name, invited him to sit in a small waiting room. Ferris was pale with fatigue but he was a patient and humane man.

'I'm afraid that your colleague is in a bad way,' he said. 'No use in downplaying things, Chief Inspector. She was shot multiple times. The good news is that the shots missed her heart and spine. The bad news is that she has damage to the lungs and other internal organs and another bullet entered and exited the side of her head. I won't give you false hope; there is every chance that she won't make it.'

'Could I see her?' Jack managed to croak.

'Yes,' Ferris replied. 'You can even talk quietly to her. She just might be able to hear you even if she can't respond.'

'Really?'

Ferris shrugged. 'Who knows, but it can't hurt.'

It was past five o'clock in the morning, but Jack had no desire to leave. He nearly cried when he saw Liz's head lying swathed in bandages on the white pillow. She was festooned with tubes and a bewildering array of machines were clicking and beeping around her bed. Jack sat close by and took her hand in his. He began to whisper, telling her that she would be fine, that he would look after her. When the sun rose in a clear sky outside of the hospital window, a nurse found Jack asleep, still sitting holding Liz's hand. She shook him gently awake and told him they had to run some tests, so he quietly took his leave.

After a quick shower and shave, followed by a cup of tea drunk standing up at the island bench, Jack took off to Footscray. Ernie Foxcroft was already at the station when he arrived, and he invited Jack up to his office for coffee and a briefing. The clock on the wall said it was almost 11:30 am, much to Jack's surprise.

'Now, Jack,' said Foxcroft as he poured their coffees, 'Let me say for a start that what has happened to Liz is just shocking, but we'll go over that in the briefing this afternoon. Before I forget, though, Paul Lennox has been on the phone all morning, spitting chips. He's been trying to reach you.' He paused and gave Jack a long stare over his glasses.

Jack shrugged. He hadn't a clue about why the Assistant Commissioner wanted to speak with him, and he realised he was too tired and worried to care. To borrow Scorcher Dalton's description of the prime minister, 'the man was an arse'.

'I take it that you haven't seen today's papers, then?'

Jack shook his head, so Ernie slid a copy of the city's tabloid daily over his desk.

'Down the bottom of the front page,' he said, tapping the paper with his pen. 'It's continued on page 5. There's a sidebar recapping the facts of the fire, but the meat of it's in the boxed article. Syndicated.'

'Fuck,' muttered Jack, taking in the title of the article. 'Before we go any further, sir, I had nothing to do with this.' He opened the paper and began to read.

Double Standards in Policing?
Major Polluters To Walk Free After Tottenham Fire?
Exclusive by Terry Houlihan

'It's like this,' said a trusted source inside the police: 'If someone hires a hitman to bump someone off, we don't just prosecute the one who pulls the trigger. Yet when it comes to those behind the recent toxic fire that endangered the health of our city, we only go after the ones who stored the poisons, not those who paid them to get rid of it.

'We have many competent, honest officers in this city at all levels, but some powerful higher-ups are preventing them from doing their jobs. We've always had bent cops, but what was once a matter of accepting the odd bribe to look the other way has become a huge problem.'

Our source went on the say that many of the men who stored hundreds of thousands of litres of deadly poisons in illegal dumps are in police custody and are facing lengthy prison sentences.

'That is as it should be,' said the officer, who agreed to speak under condition of anonymity.

'These criminals knowingly exposed our citizens to death and disease. Hundreds of our firefighters have fallen sick and fear that their lives have been shortened. A kindergarten was just a few hundred metres from the toxic inferno.

'We should take them out of circulation for as long as the law allows.'

But the source expressed great frustration about 'double standards in policing.'

Joe Public is entitled to ask what will happen to the management of the chemical companies who contracted the cowboy operators at cut-price rates they must have known were dodgy.

Yet disgruntled police say they will walk free.

We have a list of these companies, but for legal reasons we cannot run the risk of exposing them to the opprobrium many say they richly deserve....

There was more in this vein, with broad hints to help identify the culprits, but Jack had seen enough. 'Christ,' he said.

'Lennox will be mad as a cut snake!'

Ernie nodded. 'I imagine that there will be a Spanish Inquisition and there's no second prizes about who'll be burnt at the stake. I did try to warn you, Jack.'

'Well, I can't say that I'm unhappy to see this in the papers,' – Jack put on a Cockney accent – 'but I didn't do it, guv'nor.' He didn't need to say who he suspected, nay knew, who was the leak, and Foxcroft didn't need to ask.

'Well, Paul Lennox is gunning for you, so be prepared,' advised Ernie. 'Now this is strictly entre nous as they say in Paris, but he's a disgrace to the force. Trouble is, he's part of a powerful network. I'm too old to try to change the world, but now the ball's rolling it's a huge relief.' He swilled the dregs of his coffee before clearing his throat to continue. 'Chances are, you've heard of "The Joke"?'

Jack nodded. 'Network of corrupt coppers?'

'Yeah, that's them. It's petty stuff. Backhanders. Cops looking the other way for a consideration, free leg-overs, and booze. But Lennox moves in another circle where the takings are in a very different league. The bastard went to St Paschal Baylon College, and he's kept in with his old schoolmates. There's a powerful circle of them in business, politics, and the upper levels of the public service. Conflict of interest is par for the course.

'Lennox lives in a South Yarra mansion that a little bird tells me was built for a song by one of the big builders who normally only does industrial and commercial work. He's vicious as a viper and cunning as a shithouse rat. Just watch your back, Jack.'

Jack wondered about the photographs left in his letterbox.

Maybe there was also a connection with the attack on Liz? Before he could comment, Foxcroft spoke again.

'Now, putting all that aside for the moment, our number one task is to find the bastards who tried to kill Liz. My money's on those Tantalus bastards who escaped. Briefing's after lunch. I'll see you then.'

Jack was halfway out the door when Foxcroft held up a hand. 'Oh Jack, one more thing. The surveillance tape doesn't help us with the bloke who left those photographs. Bastard was in a hoodie with a bandanna round his face. Sorry.'

Jack wandered off up to the Footscray mall in search of lunch. He ordered souvlaki and coffee from a Turkish place and as it was a beautiful fine day, he sat at the outside tables and chairs, fighting off sleep. Several other diners were enjoying the sunshine. There was a sudden disturbance as a flock of hoodies erupted into the mall, some of them on BMX push bikes, all of them in a kind of uniform of shiny 'Easy Access' tracksuit pants and plastic-looking windcheaters under their cotton hoodies. They made no eye contact with the diners, but were clearly bent on making nuisances of themselves, swearing, hawking, and spitting and even farting loudly. The people sitting at the tables pretended not to see or hear them, but Jack was having none of it.

'Hey!' he called, standing up and holding up his warrant card. 'You're disturbing these people.'

''E's a fuckin' pig,' said a boy with a thin rat face and yellow incisors. With that, the hoodies took off up through the mall, kicking over a newsagent's advertising boards and calling an old bloke a 'fuckin' cunt' when he remonstrated with them.

Jack had just finished his lunch and was walking back

through the mall when he bumped into someone. He apologised automatically then took a double take as he recognised it was the rat-faced youth from earlier.

The youth sneered. 'Fuckin look where ya goan, old cunt.'

Jack clouted him round the ears and instantly regretted it. What was wrong with him? He'd always prided himself on keeping his hands to himself even under extreme provocation yet here he was thumping this pathetic specimen. The youth cowered; his potty mouth silenced. Jack grabbed his arm and shoved him away and the boy slunk off.

Jack very much wanted to go home to Hobart, but he couldn't leave Liz. After he had returned to the police station and sat through Ernie Foxcroft's briefing on the attack on Liz, he packed his briefcase and caught the train into the city and a tram up to the hospital. Liz was still comatose. He sat by her bedside for an hour before making his way back to the Yarraville flat. To his great relief, there were no more unwelcome envelopes in the letterbox.

He rang Francesca and she was surprisingly upbeat about her enforced move from her house. 'So sorry to hear about Liz,' she said. 'Tell her we're thinking of her. Just come back soon. I miss you and I know that Wendy does too. We've got Norman the cat here and Derek Holmes has been marvellous. Love you.'

It had been a long day, but tired though he was, Jack was restless. The doctor's words went round and round in his head: 'I won't give you false hope; there is every chance that she won't make it.' Fuck it, he thought. He pulled on his coat and wandered down to the Railway Hotel where he ordered a pint of Guinness. It tasted so good that he ordered another and the world didn't seem too bad. He felt a surge of affection for Fuller and Langdale, Ernie Foxcroft and the Tran woman. Derek Holmes too. Good people. Honest coppers. Jeez, Liz would pull through, he just knew she would.

Jack felt a sudden urge to re-visit his old haunts, so he drained his glass and made his way through the back streets into Seddon. He stopped off at the Mona Castle Hotel and had several more beers. They didn't stock Guinness but the Carlton Draught was just fine. There was quite a crowd watching a re-run of a Doggies game on the big screens by the time he reached the Victoria Hotel in Footscray, where he knocked back three more pots in quick succession. Full of bonhomie, he engaged in some aimless chit chat with the TV watchers and bought a round for strangers he'd never see again. Several more beers disappeared down his gullet. He knew he should call a taxi but still more beer came between the thought and the act. He was bat-faced drunk and caution thrown aside, he added whisky chasers to his steady intake. He was too far gone to realise that he'd reached an emotional tipping point. Suppressed images came flooding unbidden into his inebriated mind: corpses, autopsies, bereaved relatives beyond comforting, battered wives and ruined lives. Soran Rekani the asylum seeker who'd narrowly escaped the Ayatollah's torture chambers and swinging from a noose from the jib of a crane. That bent bastard Paul Lennox. The children were the worst thing. He wanted to protect them but couldn't. He just fucking couldn't. And now Liz, his dear friend, was lying close to death – *Call a taxi*, urged the small voice at the back of his mind, but fuck it; what did it matter when everything was rooted? When the sour old publican called last orders,

Jack drank his umpteenth beer and staggered off into what was now a rainy night, carrying a six-pack of Victoria Bitter under his arm. He sheltered in the Victoria Street railway underpass for a while, where he opened one of his stubbies and gulped it down. It was raining harder now but he lurched up to the Buckley Street intersection, oblivious to his sodden clothes and the ferocious downpour. At the top of the incline he suddenly started to cry; weeping in the gutters of Footscray in great sobs that convulsed his body as if he were a child. A patrol car crew saw him sitting on a bench in the rain swigging another stubbie. When they realised who he was they loaded him into the back seat and delivered him to his flat in Yarraville, tender as lambs yet gobsmacked that a Great One was brought so low. His sleep was dreamless and he snored like a bulldog in need of a CPAP machine.

CHAPTER 38

Jack was up with the birds the next day despite a throbbing head, nausea, and the awful knowledge that he'd made a complete fool of himself. Snatches of the previous night surfaced in his aching brain. He cringed mentally … Christ on a broomstick … a patrol car had brought him home! He'd be the talk of the copshop. He gobbled some paracetamol and washed it down with a huge glass of water. After a night on the tiles his beloved grandfather, Pop Johnstone, would fry himself a breakfast of bacon and eggs. The thought almost made him vomit, so he forced down a bowl of Weetbix and drank half a gallon of tea. Jeez, Wendy would have him on toast and Liz … dear god, how could he forget Liz? In an attempt at atonement, he went for a run up past the TAFE college Berry Street annex, vomiting up his breakfast in the Yarraville Gardens and promising it was the last time he'd get on the turps. At least the rain had stopped, although there were big puddles on the footpaths. He rang the hospital from a callbox, but they could tell him little more about Liz's condition than the night before. He was sitting at his office desk when Ernie Foxcroft came in with an enigmatic half-smile on his face.

'Lennox wants to see you in at police HQ,' Ernie said. 'Best not to keep him waiting. Get one of the constables to drive you so that you don't have to muck around trying to find a parking space.' He paused, shook his head, and sat down at the desk. 'Jack, you've been under a lot of strain, but the crew who found you last night, well, they're good kids. There's nothing in the log book.' He patted Jack on the shoulder. 'Look, you can tell me to fuck off if you like, but if I were you I'd be looking at some counselling.' Jack was impassive, so he continued. 'No shame in it, Jack, and I'm worried for you.'

Jack was non-committal, but contrite enough to know that what Ernie was saying made sense. He'd think about it.

In at the Police HQ, Lennox's secretary bade Jack sit in a chair in the vestibule. The woman looked up from her keyboard every so often to give him a hostile stare through a truly awful pair of pearl-encrusted glasses that would do Edna Everidge proud. With her sharp nose and dyed black hair she bore a striking resemblance to a bad-tempered emu.

Lennox was in no hurry to see him. After Jack had been waiting for half an hour he stood and approached the woman's desk. 'You did let the assistant commissioner know that I'm here?' said Jack with forced politeness. He had a terrible thirst and the blasted emu woman hadn't offered him anything to drink. She looked affronted. 'Of course,' she snapped, making a great play of being too busy to be interrupted by nobodies.

'It's just that I have been waiting here for over half an hour and I'd like to know how much longer this will take.'

'The assistant commissioner is a very busy man,' said the

woman, pursing her lips and looking down her beak at Jack.

Jack sat obediently, but he was fuming inside.

After a further fifteen minutes had elapsed, he'd had enough. He hated the man and by extension this rude Cerberus. 'Tell your boss I'm here and either he finds time to see me now or he can make an appointment to see me out at Footscray.' With that, he stood with folded arms and glowered as the woman fumbled at her intercom.

She mumbled something he couldn't quite catch – his hearing was getting worse – and smiled sourly. 'The assistant commissioner will see you now, Mr Martin.' If she had had her way Jack would be waiting all day.

'Thank you,' said Jack with exaggerated politeness. 'And by the way, madam, it's *Detective Chief Inspector* to you.'

The woman sniffed and pointed the way into the assistant commissioner's lair, which Jack entered with some trepidation, for even though he despised the man, he had power. It was the cave of a petty bourgeois parvenu. There was the standard portrait of the Queen on the wall, flanked by framed family photos and certificates of appreciation from Rotary and the like. The man held the Queen's Police Medal and sundry other honours, Jack saw. How was it that they dished out this stuff to these overpaid desk jockeys while the real police made do with tokens from cornflake packets? Dozens of tacky golf trophies sat on the shelves together with a line of legal tomes. If Lennox had read them, Jack was a Rhodes scholar. The assistant commissioner was standing with his back to the tall window overlooking the docks and despite the strong light behind him, Jack could see that his face was mottled with rage. He held a newspaper in one red paw and smacked it with the other. 'What the fuck do you call this?' he shouted, waving the offending newspaper in Jack's face. Jack feared the man might burst a gasket and start leaking hot oil all over the carpet.

'Good morning, sir.' Jack was determined not to be intimidated.

'Well?'

'I don't know anything about the article.'

Lennox's face twisted. '"Double Standards in Policing?" This is your handiwork, Martin, and you are going to pay for it.'

'With all due respect, there *are* double standards here, but regardless of that, I had no part in leaking anything to the press.'

Lennox's complexion reddened to a deep beetroot colour. He hurled the newspaper onto his desk. 'I don't want to hear your lies! First you exceed your authority and disturb important people and then you go running to some bloody hack …'

'Sir, even the common burglar is entitled to the presumption of innocence …'

'Bah! I'm not prepared to listen to your smartarse ideas.'

Jack felt strangely detached. He listened with half an ear to the man's ranting. He fixed his eyes unwinkingly on Lennox's angry red face and suppressed the urge to laugh. For all his gold braid and crisply ironed uniform, the man was a puffed up nothing: 'an arse that everything except a man had sat upon' – the phrase leapt from a forgotten reach of his mind. E. E. Cummings, that was it, *The Enormous Room*. He was the width and shape of a beer barrel and Jack had a sudden intense vision of how pathetic he would be nude in the brothel

Svetlana had mentioned. He was tawdry little thing with little man syndrome, and he was dirty, there was no doubt about that. Jack couldn't help what came next.

'You've obviously never been told.' The words leapt from his mouth.

'Told? Told what?' Lennox barked.

'To shut the fuck up … *sir!*'

Lennox's little red mouth opened and closed like a sea anemone expelling salt water, but no words came out and his eyes were wide with shocked disbelief. For once, he was speechless and could only stand there as Jack plunged on: 'Now Mr Lennox, I have more important things to do than come in here and act as your punching bag. My colleague almost died the other night in the course of duty, and she is lying in a hospital bed. She's a thousand times the officer you are … *sir!*'

With that, Jack stalked out of the room and left the door wide open. The secretary tut-tutted as he strode past, her eyes venomous behind the horrible glasses. Outside, he hailed a taxi and asked the driver to take him to the Royal Melbourne. What he had done had not been a good career move, but he had a big smile on his face despite the headache pounding behind his eyes.

To Jack's delight, Liz's eyes were open. It might have been his imagination but the battery of machines surrounding her bed seemed to be more subdued. He bent and kissed her on the small patch of forehead that was not swathed in bandages. She had an oxygen mask on her face, and she looked so pale and weak that he had to suppress the tears.

'Liz,' he said. 'You had me bloody well worried there.'

She nodded acknowledgement and although she winced with pain from the movement, she managed to raise her left hand to push up the oxygen mask from her mouth. Jack had to bend down to hear what she wanted to say.

'Chased woman into an alley,' she whispered. 'Saw her in the street. She was fast … sprinted into the alley and into a derelict building. I went to follow her up some concrete stairs … Jack, it was the woman who looks like Sokolov or Smirnov. Anastasia. She must have shot me.'

She had developed a lisp, and the effort of speaking had been too great for her. She pulled the mask back down over her face and closed her eyes.

Jack thought back to Svetlana's description of the woman who had met the girls at the airport, and to the lookalike gangster, Ivan Smirnov, who had ended up in a shallow grave under a pile of girders back in Hobart. If Jack was right and they were related, Anastasia might be out for revenge.

Liz pulled down the mask again. Jack stooped to listen. 'You smell like a brewery, Jack.'

He wasn't sure if she was amused. 'Don't tell Wendy,' he begged, and she winked.

Just before he left, she tugged at his sleeve. 'One thing, Jack,' she whispered. 'Please tell Vicky Tran that I'm ok. We're …' She was interrupted by a fit of coughing.

He left her then, pleased that she was recovering faster than expected. Vicky Tran, eh? he thought. He'd wondered whether there was something going on between them. Anyway, he liked Vicky, and he'd make a point of seeking her out. No doubt she would want to see Liz.

Jack knew what was coming when he walked in through

the front doors of the Footscray cop shop. Bruiser Macfarlane put down his packet of biscuits and looked up over his half-moon glasses. 'The Commander wants to speak with you urgently,' he said. He was looking at Jack with a look of mingled admiration and sympathy. Jack winked, for his rebellious mood had not dissipated and he didn't much care about what was in store.

'Jesus,' said Ernie Foxcroft, shaking his head slowly and standing up to greet Jack as he came in through the door of his office. 'You've really dumped a load of manure on 637 Flinders Street.'

Jack spread his arms wide. 'We aim to please.'

Ernie laughed but turned serious straight away: 'Lennox wants your blood, mate, but then that won't be a surprise to you. He's too gutless to come here and tell you himself, but your services are no longer required. He wants you out of town at the earliest possible opportunity and he's gunna set the Toe-Cutters on you: the internal investigations unit.'

'Yeah, I knew that was coming, but he's just going to have to wait. I'm not going back to Hobart until Liz is out of danger.'

'You'll have to give up the flat,' Ernie pointed out, 'and give back all your keys for this place. Car keys as well.'

'No problem, sir. I'll take some leave and move into a hotel.'

'Jack, as far as I'm concerned you've done a great job over here and I will tell your boss back in Hobart the same thing. I can't hide what you said to Lennox, but my report will be positive. Anyway, let's have a cup of tea.' He rubbed his hands together and picked up the phone to order it.

There were copies of the day's newspapers on Foxcroft's desk and Jack scanned the headlines. Things were returning to what passed for normal in Melbourne. The old crime gangs were crawling out from underneath the stones and a junior cabinet member had been sprung dining with a gangster in a Sorrento steak and seafood joint, inspiring one tabloid subeditor to compose the flaming headline 'REEF & BEEF WITH MAFIA CHIEF!'

'There's just one thing, Ernie,' said Jack, dropping the papers on the table with an amused smile. 'As I'm leaving, please pull out all the stops to find that woman who tried to kill Liz. Anastasia Smirnova or whatever she calls herself, and that other crim called Boris.'

'I will,' replied the Commander. 'That's a promise.'

'It's personal, I know, but this Smirnova is the real boss of the gang.'

Jack was about to leave the office when the phone rang. Foxcroft picked up the receiver and listened carefully. 'Yes, Colonel,' he said, signalling for Jack to stay and switching to the speakerphone. 'I have the officer in charge of the investigation with me now; Detective Chief Inspector Jack Martin.'

The voice was heavily accented, but the English was fluent. 'I am Colonel Burmakin, Vladimir Burmakin. I am an officer in the Moscow *Militsiya*; if you like, our federal police. I will not speak long, and I ask that you keep this call confidential.'

'Yes, Colonel,' agreed Foxcroft.

Jack's ears pricked up at the Russian's name. 'Colonel Burmakin, Vladimir. We met at that Interpol conference …'

'Yes, Jack Martin, I remember well.' Burmakin sounded delighted. 'It was in Warsaw. We put the world to rights over that Polish Zwiec lager beer!'

'Yes, that was it,' said Jack, 'but please continue.'

'OK, my friends. I trust you and I will get straight to the point. You made inquiries about Russian gangsters, but my colleagues have been unhelpful, yes?'

Foxcroft nodded to Jack to take over. 'Yes, that is correct, Vladimir. We are interested in two people in particular; a man who calls himself Boris and a woman who calls herself Anastasia. Both Russians, we believe. We think Anastasia is the sister of the *Mafiya* man Ivan Smirnov, who was killed in Tasmania a couple of years ago. We faxed copies of the identikit pictures of these people.'

'And they are wanted for serious crimes in your country?'

'Yes, Colonel. They are the leaders of a crime syndicate that has attempted to force the established organised crime gangs out of business. They are involved in drugs, human trafficking, enslavement, and extortion. They have also infiltrated legitimate businesses and are involved in toxic waste processing.

'We believe we have smashed the gang's operations for the present time, but a couple called Boris and Smirnova are still at large. We believe Smirnova tried to murder one of our colleagues.'

Colonel Burmakin confirmed the gangsters' identities. 'Your "Boris" is of Ukrainian origin but was brought up in Moscow. His real name is Andriy Kravchenko. The Anastasia woman's surname is indeed Smirnov, or rather Smirnova, but the given name on her birth certificate is Anna.

'As you will know, Inspector, you are dealing with very ugly people. My country is now a kleptocracy, governed by thieves for thieves. These are the oligarchs who have stolen all the country's wealth since the end of Soviet Union. They control the government and state. We do not have top civil servants; we have Mafia dons and Kravchenko and Smirnova are their lieutenants.

'Our President is a corrupt drunk, and the one who he has chosen to follow him is a how do you say? mobster. Yes, that is the word. Mobster. These people have bought much of the judiciary and the reason you did not receive cooperation from my colleagues is because they have taken *Mafiya* money. I am old enough to remember Stalin. My father was sent to the Gulag, but I must tell you that in some ways what we have now is worse.

'Kravchenko and Smirnova are high up in what is the most powerful crime syndicate in Russia. It has tentacles reaching right around the world. They engage in every criminal enterprise and they have expanded into what were once legitimate businesses. They are taking over Russian banks and they do business with big foreign banks. Such takeovers are of course lucrative, but it also allows them to launder vast amounts of dark money.

'This is dangerous for me, so please, it is off-the-record. My friend, I am an old communist dinosaur. Either I will retire soon or the *Mafiya* will kill me. I no longer have influence and I am sidelined into trivial office tasks. Oh, and gentlemen, please don't think that your country or any others are immune from criminal contagion. The Russian *Mafiya* has enormous wealth and has even made big inroads into the United States and the City of London. Cut out this cancer in your country. Alert honest politicians, businesses, and officials. You may have disrupted the *Mafiya*'s activities in your country, but I must tell you that they will be back. I will fax everything I have privately but please do not mention my name.'

After the Colonel rang off, Jack and Ernie sat in silence for some time, pondering his words. Eventually, Jack bestirred himself and returned to his office to start clearing his desk. No sooner had he started than the phone rang. He hurriedly picked up the receiver: perhaps it was someone ringing from the hospital, or maybe it was Colonel Burmakin again. Instead, he heard a strangely distorted voice, grating, echoey and metallic, sounding like something out of Doctor Who.

'Listen,' ordered the voice. 'Don't hang up, Jack Martin, and you don't need to know who this is. You are listening?' They were using a voice distortion device.

'Yes,' Jack's throat was dry as a Salvo's wedding. 'What do you want?'

'We have your daughter.' The voice made a series of choking sounds; evidently the speaker was laughing. 'Mr Martin, we are reasonable people. Do as we say and your daughter – Wendy, yes? – she is free.'

It was like a gut punch and it was some time before Jack could say anything. 'W …What do you want me to do?' he managed to croak. Bruiser Macfarlane had entered the office and Jack made urgent signals to indicate that he should go back downstairs and start recording. Bruiser caught on quickly and disappeared.

'Jack, we should be friends, yes?'

'Well, I don't even know who you are.'

The horrible laughing noise came out of the receiver. Jack hoped that Bruiser was recording the conversation.

'Some friends best hidden, Jack. But look, I no beat around woods. We can make it worth your while. Comfortable life. You would like to buy nice new house, yes? You help us and you buy finest mansion in Hobart, yes?'

'And if I don't?'

The awful laughing noise erupted again. 'Then your daughter is feeding the sharks! Your Francesca next. Big white pointers off Tasmania coast.'

'Wait!' Jack shouted, but the line had gone dead. This was alarming. Someone must have tipped them off about his family, or they'd managed to tap his phone.

The telephone rang again, and Jack cautiously lifted the receiver. It was Commander Derek Holmes, his superior officer in Hobart. Derek dispensed with the usual pleasantries. 'Jack, it's not good. We took all precautions but whoever these people are they must have followed Wendy from the university. Once they knew where she was staying, they could bide their time and snatch her or Francesca when the opportunity arose. I'm so sorry.'

'But wasn't there a twenty-four-hour watch on the house?'

'Yes,' Holmes replied. 'We had officers stationed inside the house and an unmarked car in the street outside with two officers in plain clothes.'

'And?'

'Sorry, but one of the officers had to leave the car to answer the call of nature. The car's doors were locked, but while she was away, two characters arrived with and big hammer and guns. They smashed the car windows, put a cord around the officer's throat. Pulled a bag down over his face and then chloroformed him. From what we can gather, the next thing was they snatched Wendy and drove away.' Holmes sighed. 'I am so sorry, Jack, and I take full personal responsibility for this.'

Jack was bewildered and angry, but he didn't blame Holmes

and not even the two officers charged with guarding Wendy. They were up against professionals. 'Please don't beat yourself up, sir,' he replied. 'These people are former members of the Russian special forces and veterans of the Yugoslav wars. Part of the Tantalus crew. I'll be on the first flight back to Hobart.'

After Jack had bid a hasty goodbye to Ernie Foxcroft, Vicky Tran, and a few other members of the team, Constable Robbie Zawadzki drove him back to the flat in Yarraville to pack up his belongings. He refused Robbie's offer to drive him to the airport. Packing up would take him a while and he would take a taxi. He later wondered what would have happened had Robbie come up to the flat, for as he walked through the door, strong arms seized hold of him and pushed him to the floor. He caught a glimpse of two figures in ski masks. They were armed with machine pistols. He didn't get a good look, but one of them might have been female.

'Stay down,' ordered one of his assailants as the other slipped a flour bag down over Jack's head and secured his wrists and ankles with cable ties.

The voice was deep, with a strong foreign accent. Russian. 'Now, Mr Martin, sir. You would like to go to Hobart, yes?' When Jack didn't answer, one of his captors kicked him savagely in the small of the back. 'I say again. You go Hobart?'

'Yes,' Jack snarled. The pain in his kidneys was excruciating.

'You are sensible, Mr Big Policeman.' The voice was purring now. 'So you just listen, yes?'

Jack scowled and when the boot caught him again, he screamed and agreed that yes, he would listen.

'Now you daughter is on little holiday. You do as we say,

Mr Martin, and everything alright. Or, you know she is food for sharks. Yes?'

'Yes,' spat Jack, angry now, but loath to antagonise the thug.

'So, we go now. When you are in Hobart, we tell you what to do next. We no fuck with you.'

Jack tensed, expecting another blow, but to his relief he heard the door opening and the clatter of military-style boots on the concrete garden path. Meanwhile, he was trussed like a chicken for the pot. He tried calling out for help but gave up when there was no answer. His neighbours were all out at work. His assailants had done a good job of securing his wrists and ankles but with a supreme effort he was able to get up and crouch semi-upright. He began also to flex and unflex his wrists and managed to back up against the kitchen bench and begin to rub the cable tie on its edge. It didn't work; or rather it would take until next week to cut through. Shit. The drawer, Jack thought, hopping like a disabled kangaroo along the edge of the bench to where he thought the cutlery would be. His legs were aching and the pain in his kidneys was only slowly ebbing. He thought, absurdly, that at least his hangover had gone. He almost gave up trying to open the drawer with his bound wrists, but it finally slid open. Shit again. It was the wrong drawer, the one with the tea towels and whatnot. When he managed to open the right one, he grasped hold of a dinner knife and began painstakingly to saw through his bindings. After dropping several knives, he managed to cut right through and was able to pull off the hood and untie his ankles. Both relieved and enraged, he rang Ernie Foxcroft to inform him what had happened. They would have to get a forensics team round to see if they could find anything.

By the time Jack had returned to the Footscray station and made a full report of the assault to Foxcroft, it was too late to fly back to Hobart. Ernie insisted on putting him up for the night. He would only get in the way of the forensics officers anyway, and the flat didn't seem like a safe place anymore.

After a surprisingly good meal cooked by Ernie himself – Boeuf Bourguignon followed by chocolate mousse – Jack and Ernie settled down in the comfortable living room to discuss the day's events. Jack was a seething mass of nerves, but he forced himself to breathe slowly and relax.

'What I don't understand,' said Ernie, 'is why these people are doing this.'

Jack shrugged. 'Payback I guess.'

'Maybe they thought you would agree to become an informant? These people have unlimited funds, and you would be a valuable asset.'

'If so, they've got Buckley's. It's fucking insulting.' Jack patted his pockets for a smoke before he remembered he'd given up. 'Anyway, they haven't said what their terms are, and we'll have to wait until I get back home to learn what they are.'

They sipped their drinks for a while before Jack remembered what Svetlana Anikanova had told him about the copper in the brothel. It had quite slipped his mind in the turmoil, with Liz lying close to death and threats being made against his family.

'Lennox! You're pretty sure she described Paul Lennox?' Ernie tapped the top of the coffee table for emphasis.

'Yep,' Jack replied. 'Of course, he'll deny everything, so to tell you the truth I'm not sure we can do anything about it.'

'Well, you'll have to leave it with me. I'll raise the matter with the Deputy Commissioner. You've met Squeaker McBain. He's honest as the day is long.'

Later that evening, just as Foxcroft was retiring to bed, Jack inquired about his wife. 'Cancer,' he replied. 'She's been gone three years now and I think about her every day.'

CHAPTER 39

Ernie insisted on driving Jack to the airport for him to catch an early flight. They made it in good time through the light traffic on the Tullamarine Freeway. They had promised to keep in touch, and it was a promise Jack intended to keep. He jumped out of the car at the terminal, and began to take his bags from the boot, sniffing the smell of aviation fuel that hung sharp on the cool air. A parking attendant was advancing, anxious to enforce the strict 'Kiss and Fly' regulations, when Jack's attention was caught by a tall, straight-backed, silver-haired figure striding past in the direction of the international terminal zone. Never one to forget a face, even an identikit version of one, it took Jack a split-second to realise it was the Russian gangster, Andriy Kravchenko, alias Boris.

'Hey,' Jack called, dropping his bags on the road behind the car and pulling out his warrant card. 'Stop right where you are!'

Boris's head spun round, and his eyebrows shot up in alarm before he shoved his sports bag under his arm and sprinted along the footpath, bumping people out of the way like ninepins.

'Call the airport police!' Jack shouted to the parking attendant and gave chase.

Jack was fit these days, and the effects of his booze-up had faded, but Boris was a fast runner and soon disappeared into the crowds of people hurrying into the terminal. Jack didn't give up. He kept going, holding his warrant card aloft and shouting at people to get out of the way, his tummy wobbling just a little bit. A parking attendant pointed to the international terminal doors and told Jack that his quarry had entered through them. Jack paused, panting a little, and did a quick scan of the departure lounge. There was no sign of Kravchenko in any of the check-in queues, nor in any of the food outlets.

An old bloke tapped Jack on the arm. 'I seen him go into the dunnies,' he said, pointing at the nearest men's lavatories. Jack trotted over and pushed open the main toilet door. A few men were washing their hands at the sinks and several others were standing at the urinals. All the cubicle doors were closed.

Jack held up his warrant card. 'Police!' he shouted. 'Everyone out!'

There was a ripple of subdued grumbling, but everyone obeyed. Several startled-looking businessmen emerged from the stalls and joined the exodus. An old codger was shambling out of one dunny when the door next to him was flung open and Boris leapt out brandishing a knife. He went to grab the old man, but he was not quick enough. Jack bundled the old fellow out of the door and turned to face Boris, who was crouching in the middle of the floor with an evil leer on his face brandishing the knife.

'I take you, Mr Policeman,' he snarled.

Jack could either run or confront him. Jack had done unarmed combat training in the past, but he was rusty, and his youth was long behind him. These days he usually left it to the young officers to deal physically with aggressive characters, but he would never forgive himself if he fled. He automatically went into a loose-kneed stance with one foot in front of the other, bracing himself for the assault. Boris was fast. He was looking forward to dealing with this policeman regardless of the consequences. He'd been a Spetsnaz officer in Afghanistan and had lost count of the number of men he'd killed during the war and in his subsequent criminal career, sometimes with his bare hands. He intended to kill this policeman, the nuisance who had destroyed a lucrative business. He leapt forward, lithe as a cat, with his mouth twisted into a savage rictus, poised to plunge the knife into Jack's belly and twist it upwards into the heart. The toilets were due for a regular clean. Hundreds of men had used them, and the floors were slippery with soap and water from the wash basins. Just then an old man who turned out later to be profoundly deaf came out of one of the cubicles and made for the washbasins. Boris's attention was momentarily diverted, and he slipped on the wet floor and sprawled face down on the terrazzo. Jack moved swiftly to stamp on his hand to release his grip on the knife and boot it across the floor under one of the dunny doors. Boris started to get up, swearing in Russian, but Jack kicked him in the head and pounced on his back to pin him to the floor. Boris was enraged and stronger than Jack, but Jack held on doggedly until armed police burst in through the doors. They looked uncertainly at the two men, wondering who was who, but when Ernie Foxcroft appeared and set them straight, they handcuffed Boris's hands behind his back and hoisted him to his feet.

After the gangster had been taken away in a paddy wagon, Jack and Ernie wandered into an airport café and ordered coffees. Ernie was looking mightily impressed. 'Jeez, Jack,' he said with a big grin, 'you're no spring chicken but you could still teach the young whippersnappers a thing or two!'

They applied themselves to their coffees, which were more than drinkable. Jack needed a sugar hit and ate a white chocolate muffin while Ernie looked on. An airport police sergeant came up with a satisfied grin on his face. 'We found your man's luggage,' he said. 'Turns out that he intended to fly to Paris first class on a false passport in the name of Peter Mikhailovich.'

Ernie finished his coffee and stood. 'Better be off. The parking attendants will be going spare about the car, and you have a flight to catch.'

They almost gave each other a hug.

Jack caught his flight with minutes to spare. The adrenaline rush had worn off and he felt tired and vaguely nauseous. He fidgeted in his seat until he realised he was annoying the woman next to him and then dozed off. He hadn't slept much from worrying about Wendy and Liz and woke with a start when the captain came on to announce they were descending into Hobart. Jack's first thought was of Wendy. It hit him forcefully then that he was lucky to be alive. He'd protected the public from murderous gangsters, but then he hadn't been able to keep his beloved daughter safe from harm.

CHAPTER 40

After the sprawl and bustle of Melbourne, Hobart International Airport seemed Lilliputian. Jack stood impatiently, waiting for his luggage to come round on the carousel. The taxi driver wanted to make conversation as they drove to the city, but Jack had to force himself to speak, wanting only to be back in harness and looking for Wendy. The journey seemed interminable, with roadworks slowing traffic to a crawl near Tunnel Hill, but eventually the tall white arch and slim piers of the Tasman Bridge had come into view, with the mountain rising imperturbably behind. The waters of the Derwent were sullen and grey. Summer was over, but Jack felt a momentary sense of security under the sheltering mountain until he recalled his daughter's plight. He paid off the driver outside the police HQ in Liverpool Street and raced inside, semi-aware of the familiar smells and the surprised faces of colleagues as he mounted the stairs to Derek Holmes' office.

Holmes held out a hand and ushered Jack to a chair. 'Jack, good to have you back. Except for the circumstances, that is … Look, I'm afraid I can't add anything to what I told you yesterday.' He smiled wryly. 'No sightings of Wendy.'

The tea arrived and they took sips before Holmes continued. 'Look, Jack, best thing you can do is to go home and wait for some word from these kidnappers. We've already put a trace on your home phone and Jerry Fuller is going to take the first shift with you.'

'But what about Francesca?'

'She's safe, mate. I can vouch for that. Anyway, it slipped my mind but Ernie Foxcroft rang just before. They've nabbed one of the bastards who assaulted you in that Yarraville flat. Evidently it was quick work by someone called Vicky Tran. You'd know her?' Jack nodded. 'So, a male person is in custody, but his partner was still at large. Ernie was pretty confident that DNA testing will link the thug to various other crimes'

They applied themselves to their tea and Jack stood up to go.

'Oh, and Jack,' Holmes called as Jack was leaving the room. 'I'm authorising, no, *ordering* you to take your service pistol home with you. No ifs or buts …even if you are the hero of the hour!'

Jack snorted.

'Seriously, Jack, we're all bloody well proud of you, so go home and try not to worry too much. We've got teams out everywhere looking for Wendy.' He paused. 'Another thing, Jack. When we've worked through all of this, I want you to take some leave. We'll talk about it later.'

After Jack had retrieved the pistol from his office he made a brief phone call to Francesca. She, not surprisingly, was beside herself with worry about Wendy. Word of Jack's Tullamarine airport heroics had spread rapidly, and Sergeant

Jerry Fuller, tasked with driving Jack home, kept giving Jack sidelong glances as he drove them up Davey Street and finally blurted out, 'Fucking good work, mate.' A flood of memories surged up inside Jack's head as they pulled into the driveway of his Darcy Street house. The clouds had blown away, and it had turned into a beautiful late autumn day. The weeping Japanese cherry tree out the front was beginning to shed its leaves on the lawn and the grass needed cutting. He and Helen had bought the place together when Wendy was little. They'd scrimped and saved for years to pay the place off. It had been shabby when they moved in, but they'd restored it and built the big, echoing extension on the back that Jack called the 'Scout Hall'. Jack had spent much of his spare time working in the large garden, which he'd planted with fruit trees and flowers along with a veggie patch right at the back, although he had to admit that he'd also spent far too much time sucking on unfiltered Camels in his garden shed. Helen had up and left him not long after the mortgage was finally paid off. It made a mockery of those years of sacrifice.

Jack became aware that Fuller was talking to him and shook himself from his reverie. 'I was suggesting, Jack,' said the big sergeant, 'that we need to tread carefully here. You take the front and I'll take the back. We can get your luggage afterwards.'

Jack nodded. Jerry Fuller was a competent officer despite the prodigious amounts of beer he consumed with Damian Langdale in the Royal Exchange bar. An ageing, bulky man, Fuller was vain and still wore his thinning hair in an outdated Beatles style. He'd been a rower in his younger days but had long ago given up the sport. Langdale joked that he'd sink the rowing eight if he could still fit in the bloody thing. Not that he could talk, Fuller scoffed; Langdale's rugby days were a distant memory.

They found nothing untoward either inside or outside the house. Jack busied himself unpacking and drank some coffee. There was no food in the house so Fuller walked down to the corner store in Macquarie Street. Predictably, he returned with a couple of bags of hot pies – his staple – and wolfed them down slathered in tomato sauce. Jack pecked at his, too wired to eat and not needing Wendy's admonition against eating junk food. He paced the floor and was irritable with Fuller before apologising and trying to sit still next to the phone.

When it rang, shockingly loud and shrill in the deep silence of the Scout Hall, Jack almost jumped out of his chair. He lifted the receiver with dread, announced his name and waited while there were a series of clicks and buzzes at the other end. It was the same creepy voice he'd heard back in Melbourne, distorted by some kind of electronic device. It asked how he was, to which Jack snorted to get on with it and say why they were ringing. This elicited the horrible laughing noise.

'Now, Inspector,' the voice said. 'New situation. We have already your daughter. She is safe now, but we kill her unless you release Boris and give him safe passage back to Russia. You have twenty-four hours to arrange, yes?'

'You must know that I can't authorise that.'

'So tell your superior officers, yes?'

'OK, I will ask.'

'Very good. Remember you have twenty-four hours.'

The line went dead.

Jack knew the woman was not bluffing – he guessed it

was Smirnova – so he rang Derek Holmes to relay her new demand. Holmes said he would get back with an answer but he couldn't promise anything. In the meantime, he briefed Inspector Langdale on the case. They would try to trace the call. The minutes ticked by with Jack pacing up and down in his loungeroom. The minutes became hours.

The phone rang, and Jack recognised Damian Langdale's gruff tones. 'We have a lead, Jack. We've traced the call to Pillinger Drive in Fern Tree; you know, the road up to the top of the mountain. We'll be there soon and don't worry, we'll be discreet.'

Jack knew Pillinger Drive well. He wanted to drive up there, but Jerry Fuller said it was not a good idea. They should leave it in Damian Langdale's competent hands. More time passed as the afternoon shadows lengthened. The telephone was silent, and the tension was becoming unbearable. Jack found himself craving for a cigarette but managed to stave it off. The sergeant came in with a pot of tea and Jack drank a cup abstractedly. Then Langdale rang again.

'We've just interviewed a resident up in Fern Tree. A silly old woman. She rang to say that a young girl had been trying to break into her house … No, she did not let her in. Says she was too frightened to do so. We have officers with her now. She was able to give a pretty good description of the young woman and it matches your Wendy … No, she didn't see where the girl went. She said the girl jumped over the back fence into the bush.'

'OK Damian, I'm on my way.'

'No, Jack …'

'No nothing.' Jack slammed the phone down and rushed out

the front door, ignoring Jerry Fuller's half-hearted protests. He started the car and accelerated up Darcy Street, overtaking an old woman who was dithering, and was soon hurtling up Huon Road from South Hobart towards the mountain, ignoring the speed limit signs. His throat was dry and the blood was pounding in his temples. 'Out of the fucking way!' he shouted, honking furiously at slow traffic and almost clipping the side of a garbage truck that was slowing to empty a kerbside bin. Oh Jesus Christ, if those bastards hurt Wendy he would make them wish they'd never been born. When he reached Fern Tree, the suburb nestled in the bush under the mountain, a police car was blocking the entrance to Pillinger Drive. Jack waved his warrant card and was off again with a screech of tyres on the gravel.

About half a kilometre up the steep winding road, three more police cars were parked with their blue lights flashing. Jack slowed just as two burly officers came out of a driveway, shoving a handcuffed man clad in a black leather jacket before them. The man was struggling violently but had no chance of escape. Other heavily armed officers were following, and portly Inspector Langdale was bringing up the rear. He was perspiring copiously and one eye was closed up.

'Found this bird lurking in the woodshed,' Langdale growled. 'Dangerous cove. Fucker punched me out. No sign of Wendy or the Russian sheila though and this character is refusing to tell us anything.' He cuffed the prisoner round the back of the head and the man told him to fuck off in heavily accented English. They were shoving him into the back of a police car when Jack drove off again. Fifty metres further on, another police car was parked in the driveway of a green-painted weatherboard house with a few dozen garden gnomes, some concrete lions, and a big leprechaun out the front. Jack jumped out of the car and went inside without knocking. A constable was sitting on the couch in the living room talking with an elderly woman.

'Jack,' she said, standing up expectantly. 'This is Mavis.' The woman looked shocked by Jack's wild eyes and dishevelled appearance.

'Have you seen her?' Jack demanded.

'I was telling the officer here,' she replied. 'I'm sorry. I turned her away when she came knocking on the window … I thought she was …'

Jack tore back outside. He'd drive a bit further, up the road towards The Springs where the old hotel had been before the 1967 bushfires. She'd be up there somewhere. Had to be. Something was driving him on. But shit, the car park was empty and there was nobody around. Dark clouds drifted like smoke over the Organ Pipes, the fluted dolerite cliffs near the summit of the mountain, and in the gathering gloom below, the city's lights were coming on like strings of glittering jewels, but he saw nothing of this. He heard a great silence, broken only by the odd gust of wind and the sound of a distant car horn far below. He'd give anything to find Wendy safe, but maybe his instinct was wrong. Maybe … He stood uncertainly on the asphalt. No, he couldn't give way to such thoughts. His gut told him his daughter was close by. He pulled up his collar against the chill and peered into the shadows. The minutes passed and full darkness fell with the huge bulk of the mountain rearing darker against the night sky. Then he heard the unmistakable sounds of footsteps. Over there – the walking path leading down from the mountain. Jack drew out his service pistol and crouched down behind a pile of rocks, his senses straining. If the walker were Anastasia Smirnova, he would be in grave danger, if her friend Andriy Kravchenko, the so-called Boris, was anything to go by. Several times the walker seemed to stumble on the uneven ground. Whoever it was did not have a torch, which seemed like a good sign: Smirnova would surely be well-equipped. Jack could scarcely keep still. A slight female figure was stumbling along.

'Wendy!' he shouted. 'Is that you?'

'Dad!' she replied, and he felt like praying.

'O thank Christ it's you!' He hugged her tight and kissed the top of her head; wanted to keep her safe forever. Eventually, she disentangled herself from his embrace and he found the voice to ask how she was.

'I'm fine, Dad,' she replied. 'I'm very tired and I was so frightened, but they didn't hurt me.'

Jack had to pinch himself to make sure he wasn't dreaming as he drove down to the house in Darcy Street. When they drove into the driveway Sergeant Fuller came out and gave her a massive bearhug. She'd known him since she was a toddler and still called him Uncle Jerry. Jack rang Francesca and Wendy put the kettle on and started making toast. As she ate – more to please him than from hunger – Wendy related what had happened. She had no idea where the kidnappers had first kept her because they put a hood over her head when they snatched her off the street. She could hear waves and occasionally cars would pass by but what direction they had taken her she couldn't tell. Maybe it was inside the greater city, but she couldn't be sure. Then they blindfolded her and drove her to the house she knew was in Fern Tree. There'd been two of them, a big foreign man and a tough woman. They spoke between themselves in a language she did not understand and gave no names. They gave her the creeps, especially the man, who ogled her shamelessly and was only restrained from raping her by the woman. Wendy was dog-tired; so tired that she could not keep her eyes open, and she begged to be able to sleep. There was no way Jack was going to let her out of his sight. He slept in the armchair in the corner of her room with his service pistol by his side. When Wendy woke in the morning the sun was streaming in through the east facing windows and her father was fast asleep.

They had just finished breakfast when the telephone rang. It was the same weird, distorted voice. 'Inspector Martin,' it rasped, 'now you know what pain is. I too know pain and is you fault. You are responsible for my brother's death even if you did not pull trigger. You arrest my friend Boris, too. Also, Jack Martin, I did not want to shoot that little bitch in Chinatown, but she chase me, and I have no choice. Anyway, shooting bitch cause you pain and that for me is good, yes?

'So, you have you precious slut of daughter back. But remember, Inspector, we know where she is. Also, where you woman is, and where *you* are. Da? Perhaps when you are not expecting, there will be more pain. We come back.' There was a pause before the distorted voice continued. 'There is another way, Inspector. Why work you whole life for nothing? We make you good offer. You can contact Mr Kozlov in Moscow. Address in you letterbox. *Da svidania*. I go now, but you never know.'

There was a click, and the line went dead.

CHAPTER 41

A massive police search failed to find Anastasia Smirnova. Her accomplice, the man who called himself Boris, refused to cooperate. His reply to all questions was 'no comment.' He'd been charged and the evidence was watertight. He'd spend decades in prison and when his term was up, he'd be deported to Russia. Three days later, Ernie had not forgotten his promise concerning Paul Lennox. He'd met with Squeaker McBain and raised the allegation that Lennox had patronised the illegal Williamstown brothel with its trafficked women. McBain was inclined to believe it but when Lennox flatly denied it, he had had to let the matter drop for lack of corroborating evidence. All they had to go on was Svetlana Anikanova's word. Lennox swore that she must have been mistaken and his diary entries backed him up. McBain would, however, keep the allegation on file and believed that sooner or later Lennox would come unstuck. It was the best he could do.

Jack was not impressed. He was certain that Lennox was bent; that he had been in with the Tantalus crew and that he would continue his criminal behaviour when the opportunity arose. After brooding at his desk, he picked up the phone and dialled Carlo Di Lana's number. He had known the journalist for many years, and they occasionally had a drink together. A socialist in his youth, Di Lana still despised whited sepulchres in high places. The two men met in the Alabama Hotel in Liverpool Street, just along from the Hobart nick, and Jack related what he knew about Paul Lennox. Di Lana had a terrible thirst that afternoon. 'Bloody good beer,' he said, downing a ten-ounce beer in three gulps. Mindful of his Footscray binge, Jack switched to mineral water, much to Di Lana's disappointment. The journalist was sceptical of the Lennox story. 'Jeez Jack,' he said, shaking his head and proposing another round. 'Unless you have cast-iron evidence my editor won't have a bar of it. I've heard enough about our Mr Lennox over the years to know that he's dirty, but it's just rumours. It'd be an open and shut libel case if we print his name without hard evidence.'

'OK,' nodded Jack. 'I get that, but can't you write it in such a way that without naming the bastard everyone who knows anything about anything will know it's him? That might make him do something stupid.'

Di Lana slurped his ale and looked thoughtful. 'Yeah, I see what you mean. The bastard is certainly *distinctive*-looking, so people over there would know who we were writing about without naming him. Leave it with me, Jack.'

'Call him the Squashed Tomato, and they'll get the picture,' Jack suggested.

Carlo looked at his watch. 'Good idea! Look, gotta fly, mate. I promised the missus I'd be home for dinner, so I'd better go.

I'm not exactly the blue-eyed boy these days.'

Jack was relieved to see Di Lana go, although he had a soft spot for the old rogue. He was feeling virtuous because of his moderate beer intake, especially in the company of the veteran journo, a toper who could drink even Fuller and Langdale under the table.

A week went by with no word from the journalist, and Jack had more or less forgotten about the matter. One morning, Jack was waiting at his old place in Darcy Street when Jerry Fuller arrived with a sly grin on his face, brandishing a copy of the newspaper.

'Seen this Jack?' No? Well, cast your beady eye over it.' He waited expectantly while Jack read the article he had pointed out. It started on the front page and continued on page 5:

BAD APPLES IN THE VIC POLICE BARREL?
Explosive allegations against 'Squashed Tomato'
Exclusive by Carlo Di Lana

The fallout from last month's huge chemical fire in Melbourne's West continues … Numerous arrests were made as part of the Victoria Police's Operation Tantalus, which uncovered the operations of a violent crime firm … Credible sources inside the police force have revealed that several officers including one of high rank were working with the ring …We can reveal that one of the state's highest-ranking officers, a man known to colleagues as 'the Squashed Tomato,' was a client at an illegal brothel run by the Tantalus gang in bayside Williamstown and is believed to have taken backhanders from the gang … Inside sources claim that the Squashed Tomato covered up for firms that used the

Tantalus gang's illegal waste disposal services to dispose of hundreds of thousands of tonnes of highly toxic chemicals and medical waste. The Tomato, sources claim, was part of a powerful old boy network of former St Paschal Baylon College students. A police spokeswoman declined to comment on the allegations …

Jack's face broke into a broad grin. Fuller reckoned you could hear Paul Lennox screaming with rage clear across Bass Strait. No doubt the finger would be pointed at Jack for leaking the information, but he reckoned it would be worth it. Jack was half-expecting Derek Holmes to quiz him about the article, but his boss didn't mention it. Instead, he insisted that Jack go on extended sick leave and that he undergo counselling. It was not negotiable. Jack suspected Derek had been comparing notes with Ernie Foxcroft. Part of him resented it but his rational self knew it was for the best. The Superintendent and the Commander had his best interests at heart.

A day or so later, Jack's phone rang. There was a rustling sound then Deputy Commissioner Alex 'Squeaker' McBain came on the line. There was no preliminary small talk. 'Jack, we're nominating you for a National Police Bravery Award.'

There were some nibbling noises and more rustling.

'Thank you, sir, but if this is about that Boris business at the airport, the fact is I just got lucky.'

'Nonsense. You deserve it.' (Crunch: you could almost smell the mints over the line.) 'Fact is you could easily have died and you knew it. Yet you put yourself in the firing line. There's some would deny it but you're a credit to the profession.' After another crunch, the line went dead.

POSTSCRIPT

Late Winter, Roaring Beach, Far South Tasmania

'You'll soon be back rock climbing,' Jack observed as Liz scrambled down the dune. She pushed back her hair and smiled with her luminous green eyes, then suddenly pointed out into the bay excitedly. It was a pod of dolphins, their shining backs rising and falling in the water. Wendy positively squealed with delight and Kenzie, Jack's new Golden Retriever puppy, looked up inquisitively, wondering what the fuss was about until he saw the movement in the water. Liz stumbled in the loose sand and both Francesca and Wendy rushed to steady her. It had been touch and go whether she would survive the brutal shooting in Chinatown. Months of physio had helped, but she still walked with a limp, and Jack knew she was still in pain.

After his return from Melbourne, Jack had taken an extended leave of absence on medical grounds. Down here, he was able to find a measure of peace, his demons kept at bay. Liz had hinted that Vicky Tran would appear. The Melbourne detective was hoping for a transfer to Tasmanian CIB, and Jack looked forward to seeing her.

Jack spent much of his time walking with Kenzie on the beach. The cottage was comfortable, bought fully furnished from an old boy who no longer felt safe driving down the long and twisting roads from Hobart. Jack felt guilty about it, but Francesca reckoned the old fellow would at least know that they would look after it in the manner to which it was accustomed. When the winter gales howled off the ocean the stove kept the place warm. They could buy locally made bread, wine, and apples, and at times fresh fish from the fishing boats at the jetty at nearby Dover. Jack felt more at peace than he had been for many years. The extended leave and the counselling sessions had gone a long way to exorcise the horrors that had accumulated in his brain, but he still had a lot of thinking to do.

The squall came up from nowhere; this far southern coast was famous for its sudden changes of weather; clear blue skies would be followed in quick succession by slanting rain and by magnificent rainbows that gave colour to the sombre seascape. Jack had thought to wear his waterproof jacket, so he stayed on with Kenzie when the others retreated to the cottage to put the kettle on.

The waves boiled angry and grey, and sheets of rain obscured the horizon. Jack's mind went back to the cover-up of privileged malefactors back in Melbourne. Paul Lennox, aka 'the Squashed Tomato,' had resigned from the force, allegedly for health reasons. His mates were looking out for him, though, and he had received a hefty payout; an undisclosed sum that was perhaps more than a constable earned in a lifetime. Ernie Foxcroft reported that Lennox had been pre-selected for a safe upper house seat and had secured a number of 'consultancies' and places on company boards. Word had it, too, that he had left his wife and shacked up with Cornelius Bentley's understudy, the heiress Miss Erica Betts. Jack thought of Raymond Chandler's words in *The Big Sleep*: 'He didn't know the right people. That's all a police record means.' Well, the Tomato certainly knew all the right people.

Ernie also told Jack that Svetlana and the other girls were safely back in Russia and Ukraine, and that the various crims they'd collared over the fire and the gang wars and human trafficking would soon be coming to trial. DNA evidence had pointed to Cyril 'The Garrotte' Scriabin as the culprit in seven murders and Ratko Branković had fingered Andriy 'Boris' Kravchenko as one of the syndicate's leaders. Jack's faith in his calling had been dented, but he still believed that what he did was worthwhile, and he prided himself on being an honest cop.

The thought of honest cops took him back to the Russian police colonel, Vladimir Burmakin. Tucked away in the national newspapers several weeks ago was a small article reporting Burmakin's death. He had been found dead on the footpath outside of his Moscow apartment building. The journalist hinted at defenestration, and Jack recalled Burmakin's prediction that the Mafiya State would like him killed. Jack hoped that he had done nothing to draw the gangster state's attention to Burmakin and that the man's family were safe.

Alas, Ernie said, there was no trace of Anastasia Smirnova. Interpol could tell them nothing new and the Russian police were ignoring requests for assistance. Ernie promised that they would not let up the search for her, but Jack knew that as time passed the hunt for the gangster would be put at the bottom of the pile of cases. Besides, the chances were that she was out of the country. After all, Smirnova's employer, the head of Russia's most powerful crime syndicate, had purchased an entire airline to expedite his international trafficking operations. If the oligarch could do that, spiriting his operatives out of Australia would present few problems. On a brighter note, Brendan McCastle and Denise Sugden had been extradited from New Zealand, where they were co-habiting as Mr and Mrs Brian Jones.

Wendy was hard at work on her thesis, which drew heavily on Sandy Johnstone's long-lost diaries. Jack found himself sharing her indignation over the injustices heaped upon Sandy and the common folk of the British Isles. She had unearthed an eighteenth-century song called 'Stealing the Commons from the Goose' and Jack wondered how much had changed:

> *They hang the man and flog the woman*
> *who steals the goose from off the common,*
> *yet let the greater villain loose*
> *that steals the common from the goose.*
> *The law demands that we atone*
> *when we take things we do not own*
> *but leaves the lords and ladies fine*
> *who take things that are yours and mine.*
> *The poor and wretched don't escape*
> *if they conspire the law to break*
> *this must be so, but they endure*
> *those who conspire to make the law.*

There was one law for the rich and powerful and another

for the powerless and meek. Laws, as Jonathan Swift had observed, were like cobwebs.

Jack was due to return to work in a week's time. Perhaps he would toss a coin to decide what he was going to do? Was there life beyond policing? He'd put away his share of villains over the years, some of them genuinely awful types, and he felt he had carried out his promise to 'Serve and Protect' the community. But there was law and there was justice, and it would not do to confuse them. That old wharfie, Dixie Trumble, had been right about that. Jack's mind went back to the Port Melbourne pub where he and Liz had left that Kurdish man, Soran Rekani. He knew they'd done the right thing, whatever the government and the law said, and he hoped that Soran was doing well in New Zealand. Wendy's kidnapping had also rattled him, and he wondered if it were fair to keep exposing his loved ones to the criminals' violence. 'Quid agendum est?' as old Father O'Farrell might have asked of Jack's future back in Queenstown when he was a child and a young man. He would sleep on it. There was a snatch of voice on the wind – he really must get those bloody hearing aids! – and he saw Wendy waving a mug on the verandah. 'Come on, Kenzie,' he commanded, and the little pup followed, wagging his tail, as Jack walked up the path from the beach to the cottage. Lost in thought, he didn't see the figure watching him from the clump of trees in the dunes.

Author's Note

The title of this work is taken from Jonathan Swift, *A Tritical Essay upon the Faculties of the Mind* (1709).

Victoria has been the site of numerous toxic fires and spills in recent years, most of them in illegal waste dumps run by criminals. I have drawn on some of these incidents, but my account is a work of fiction. No reference to any real waste disposal company or its clients is intended. Some small details of Melbourne locations or chronology have also been changed to suit the story. Russia was indeed an autocratic kleptocracy as in the text and today can be fairly described as a fascist dictatorship. Some of the major thieves mentioned do exist, but the Russian gangsters operating in Australia in the text are figments of my imagination.

The reader may have noticed the allusion to a line in the 'Ern Malley' poem 'Petit Testament' when Jack is 'weeping in the gutters of Footscray.' Malley never existed. He and his work were an elaborate hoax cooked up by the poets James McAuley and Harold Stewart to embarrass Max Harris, the modernist editor of the *Angry Penguins* literary magazine. I'm told they later felt bad about setting him up. The two poets placed little value on Malley's work, but Harris insisted that the poems had real literary value and they are indeed now widely regarded as classics of surrealist verse.

Acknowledgements

I must thank my wife, Dorothy Bruck, for always being there with encouragement and support, which included proofreading the finished manuscript and making thoughtful suggestions on how the book might be improved. Many thanks too, to Susan Young for her meticulous attention to detail and for her suggestions on how to improve the text. She also patiently put up with my technological incompetence leading to my computer eating a version of the text. Thanks also to Stephen Young for his valuable comments.